D0050120

"Fiercely entertaining, fascinating . . . Olsen offers a unique background view into the very real world of crime . . . and that makes his novels ring true and accurate."
—*Dark Scribe*

## *A Cold Dark Place*

"A great thriller that grabs you by the throat and takes you into the dark, scary places of the heart and soul."
—**Kay Hooper**

"You'll sleep with the lights on after reading Gregg Olsen's dark, atmospheric, page-turning suspense . . . if you can sleep at all."
—**Allison Brennan**

"A stunning thriller—a brutally dark story with a compelling, intricate plot."
—**Alex Kava**

"This stunning thriller is the love child of Thomas Harris and Laura Lippman, with all the thrills and the sheer glued-to-the-page artistry of both."
—**Ken Bruen**

"Olsen keeps the tension taut and pages turning."
—*Publishers Weekly*

# A COLD DARK PLACE

A WATERMAN AND STARK THRILLER

# GREGG OLSEN

PINNACLE BOOKS
Kensington Publishing Corp.
www.kensingtonbooks.com

PINNACLE BOOKS are published by

Kensington Publishing Corp.
119 West 40th Street
New York, NY 10018

All Kensington titles, imprints, and distributed lines are available at special quantity discounts for bulk purchases for sales promotions, premiums, fund-raising, educational, or institutional use. Special book excerpts or customized printings can also be created to fit specific needs. For details, write or phone the office of the Kensington sales manager: Kensington Publishing Corp., 119 West 40th Street, New York, NY 10018, attn: Sales Department; phone 1-800-221-2647.

ISBN-13: 978-0-7860-3969-2
ISBN-10: 0-7860-3969-8

First printing: April 2008

11  10  9  8  7  6  5  4  3

Printed in the United States of America

Electronic edition: April 2008

ISBN-13: 978-0-7860-2922-8
ISBN-10: 0-7860-2922-6

*For Kathrine*

# PROLOGUE

*4 P.M., nineteen years ago*

Women with transparent vinyl purses that exposed the shredded remainders of coin wrappers stood in line. They took deep breaths as the uniformed prison matron with icy hands prepared to probe their bodies. Talc-dipped rubber gloves snapped. It was humiliating in every sense of the word. The matron, a woman with ashen skin, pencil-thin lips, and with glasses on a cheap silver chain around her neck, knew those waiting to leave the institution felt her power, her *supreme authority*, and it made her smile. The women had lined up to leave after a long day of tears and excuses in the high school cafeteria milieu of the visiting room—a cavernous space of bolted-to-the-floor tables and fixed-position chairs. The matron's husky voice intoned them to "cool their jets" and "wait your turn or I'll have something to say about it."

And so the women lingered, each feeling violated and angry. Having a husband, boyfriend, or brother inside the razor-wire-trimmed walls of Bonneville Max-

imum Security was bad enough. Being told with unfet-
tered contempt by someone to wait your turn in the
processing line was ptomaine gravy over a bad slab of
beef. And they had to eat it. *Every goddamned bite.*

"Are you going to be a problem for me?" the matron
asked, her gray eyes as sharp as awls pitched firmly at
the distressed gaze of a young woman. The younger
woman let out a measured sigh. She'd spent all day
trying to tell her wannabe-drug-lord husband that she
was thinking of moving back east to Indiana. She
wanted to be free. All of them did.

"Uh? Me?" the younger woman answered. She was
barely twenty and still wore her chestnut hair in a
ponytail, but she held a kind of weariness on her face
that indicated she'd seen it all. She faked a smile of
recognition at the matron. She knew when someone
had it in for her. It had been her life since she left
home. Ran away. Met the wrong man. Trashed her future. She could hear her mother's words echo at that
moment. *You've thrown away everything your father
and I had hoped for you. You screwed up, Donita. You
really botched it.*

"Yes, *you,* Ponytail," the matron said, nodding in
her direction. The rest of the women felt relief wash
over them. *Good, the bitch found someone else to
bother.* She motioned for her to step forward. "I need
you to spread your legs. You've done it before, I'm
sure. *Wider.*"

The young woman silently seethed, but she acquiesced. She had no choice.

"You know, if I can't get my mitts between your thighs,
either you're gonna have to go on a diet or you're gonna

have to practice your splits in the back room. I don't like you, I don't trust you, and I think you're carrying some contraband on your person. I just feel it."

The back room was a dimly lit hospital-style space where women were forced to endure indignities based on their physiology. Flat on their backs, legs apart, feet stuck in metal stirrups.

"I'll do better," she said, all the while wondering what it would be like if she'd been an actual prisoner there, not a lowly visitor?

The altercation caught the attention of a chubby-faced woman in the back of the line. Her strawberry-blond shag had matted unflatteringly to her forehead. Her pulse quickened, but she kept her affect blank. She didn't want to stand out and she didn't want a trip to the back room for any kind of exam. She carried something so precious, so vital, that its discovery would ruin everything.

*Be cool, Ponytail's taking the heat. Thank you, Jesus.*

She concealed her prize in a place she hoped no one would dare probe. *Inside. Personal. Private.* Besides she knew the matron only groped because she got off on it. No one was looking for someone to take much of anything out of here . . . they mostly watched for contraband coming in to the visiting room.

The matron fixed her eyes on the strawberry blonde with the secret. Her eyes held her with unyielding grip. She waited a beat.

"You can go," she said.

The woman with the secret acknowledged the command and started walking in the direction of the lockers in which she had stored her coat and car keys before going under the arbor of razor wire, through the gate, to the visiting room.

"Wait a minute," the matron said.

It felt like her heart stopped beating. She was going to die. Going to be caught. Adrenaline kicked her ticker back into play. *She's going to take me in the back room. She's going to ruin everything.*

"Did you hear me?"

She slowly turned.

"Are you speaking to me?"

"No, I'm talking to the man in the moon."

She stared. Her heart bounced. *Thump. Thump. Thump.*

"Get over here."

She stepped back toward the matron.

"You forgot your purse."

Her hands were sweating now, so much so, she thought the vinyl zippered purse would slip from her fingers. She reached for it and acknowledged the gesture with a quick smile.

"Oh, thanks."

Like others who had been around the matron, she faked a smile.

The woman smiled, hers strangely genuine. "No problem. And you have a nice day."

With that, the strawberry blonde hurried to the lockers. Soon she'd be home, and in time destiny would come to pass.

# BOOK ONE
# THE EYE OF THE STORM

# CHAPTER ONE

Emily Kenyon was thrashed and she looked it. She pulled herself from her gold Honda Accord, picked up her purse, and walked toward the front door. She turned to view the end of Orchard Avenue. The neighborhood of vintage homes was safe. Unscathed. Not a single fish-scale shingle from the three-story painted lady across the street had been harmed. Not so much as a splinter. Emily could even hear kids playing a couple of doors down. Everything was as it had been. The only hint that the world had turned over was the slight scent of acrid smoke that wafted through the air. It was faint, but enough of a reminder that across town homes and cars had burned.

It had been two days since the tornado pounced on a section of Briar Falls Estates two miles away. It came almost without warning and left a jagged swathe of destruction that stole the hard work of homeowners and gardeners in ten minutes' time. Roofs had been peeled off. Play sets and bicycles hurled into trees. There was no making sense of whose house had been spared and whose hadn't. Destruction reigned on the west side of Hawes Avenue, while the east side remained pristine. Across the street from a home that had been nearly ripped in two, a birdbath stood without a drop spilled over its chipped stone rim.

No one died. It was true that an elderly lady who had holed up in her bathroom was in bad shape and had been hospitalized. Emily expected that the woman, in her eighties, would survive despite her trauma. The lady was a retired junior high social studies teacher with a classroom assignment that indicated she was tougher than most. After all, if she could endure teenagers of the 1960s, she'd survive the tornado, too.

Emily stepped into the foyer. As she set down her purse on an antique walnut console table, its contents shifted. Her detective's badge holder slipped out along with a pink lipstick she wished she'd used up and could toss. But she was thrifty and, despite the fact that it didn't really work with her dark brown hair and eyes, she'd wear it until it was gone. She scooted the badge and lipstick tube back inside the pouch and called out for her daughter.

"Jenna? I'm home."

The scent of cinnamon toast and an empty glass of milk on the counter indicated Jenna was somewhere in the house. Emily didn't wait for a response.

"I'm going to take a shower. Then let's go out and get something to eat."

"Okay, Mom," a voice finally came from down the hall. "I'm on the phone. I'll talk to you when you're out. I'm hungry. Take a fast shower!"

Emily smiled. Jenna was seventeen, but still very much her little girl. It was just the two of them now. David had left for Seattle and become a somewhat shadowy figure since the divorce was final. There had been a few dates with new men—even a kind of serious affair with a local lawyer. Cary McConnell was too possessive and controlling and Emily had enough of that with her first— and *only*—marriage. Cary still called but she avoided him whenever she could. That wasn't easy. Cherry-stone, Washington, was a town of less than 15,000 people. She was in the courthouse two or three times a week. So was he.

Emily snake-hipped out of her black skirt, unbuttoned her blouse, and let it fall to the floor. She was slender, blessed with long legs and a figure that looked more twenty than forty, which she was approaching on her next birthday. She twisted the shower knob with the red *H* all the way to the left. The *C* was moved a quarter turn. The old pipes clanked and steam swirled. Emily liked hot water.

"Pietro's?" she called out before stepping inside the white-and-black tiled interior. "I'm thinking pizza."

Of course she really wasn't. She was thinking of the tornado and its aftermath. Twisters were rare occurrences in Washington state. Only a handful of damaging storms had been recorded there; the worst had been one that killed eleven people near Walla Walla in 1952. The twister that came to Cherrystone on Saturday had howled in the darkness and snatched up all in its wake. Houses and cars were shredded in a giant steel-toothed blender. A dairy near the junction of Wayne Road and U.S. 91 had been so pulverized that a magnifying glass was needed to determine what color the barn paint had been before the storm. The Cherry-stone Granary was flattened, which meant already scarce jobs instantly had become even more limited. Five trucks, carefully parked in a row after the shift change, had been tossed to their absolute ruin. Power lines snapped like frayed jute. A semi was lifted more than a hundred yards and slammed into a hillside.

Emily tilted her head backward; hot water beyond a temperature most could endure flowed over her body, sending the stress of the freak storm, and the worries of a long day, down the drain. Stepping from the shower, Emily wrapped a thick cotton towel around her body. She bent over, wrapped a second one around her head, then flipped her hair back. She called once more to Jenna.

"You never answered, honey. Is Pietro's all right?"

Again, silence.

Steam swirled and Emily flipped on the bathroom fan. A moment later, she slipped on a terry robe and padded down the hall to Jenna's room—a space that had been her own bedroom when she was a girl. A rectangle of yellowed glue on the door revealed the spot were she'd once put up a "NO BOYS ALLOWED" sign to keep her little brother, Kevin, at bay. With each step, a memory. Through a knife-slit of light in the doorway, she could see Jenna typing out a message on her silvery Apple iBook computer. Jenna was a little small for her age. Her stature didn't diminish her; it only made her stand out. Long hair like her mother's framed her delicate heart-shaped face. Her eyes were blue, the cool color of the Pacific. She tapped on the keyboard with frosted pink fingernails, chipped and ready for another mother/daughter manicure session in front of one of the *Law and Order*s on TV.

Emily pushed open the door, startling Jenna, who looked up with a frozen smile.

"Oh, Mom, I didn't hear you." She closed the chat window and swung around to face her mother.

"Are you up to no good?" Emily asked, allowing a smile to come to her lips. Deep down, the very idea of her daughter chatting with anyone was more than she could take. She'd seen the way perverts worked the keyboards of personal computers and stalked their prey—unsuspecting children in seemingly safe and cozy homes all across America.

"Just talking with Shali," she said. "And yes, we *were* up to no good. There's a nice guy who wants to meet us at the Spokane Valley Mall next weekend. He says he looks like Justin Timberlake and Jude Law. *Combined*."

Emily sat on the edge of the bed, smoothing out the sateen spread.

"He does, does he?" She knew when her daughter was pulling her leg and she started to play along. "Maybe I could meet him, too?"

Jenna shook her head. "Sorry, Mom, but you're too old for him. Shali and I are probably too old for him. He seemed to lose interest when we said we were old enough to drive."

"That's not funny."

"Sick, I know."

"You know how I worry."

"And you *know* that you don't have to worry about

*me*. I know the drill. I don't make mistakes. My mom is a cop, you know."

"So I've heard." Emily removed the towel from her head and shook out her hair. "I'm not going to dry this mess. Let's get out of here and eat. I'm beat."

Jenna grinned. "Okay. Jude Timberlake can wait."

With that, Emily returned to her bedroom, where she put on a pair of faded jeans and a cream-colored boatneck sweater. She looked in the mirror and gave herself a once-over.

"Not bad for almost forty," she said, loud enough for Jenna to hear, which, of course, she did. "Maybe this Jude Law look-alike of Jenna's would be interested in an old chick like me."

Jenna appeared in the doorway and put her hands on her hips.

"You're disgusting," she said, a smile widening on her pretty face. "Shali and I had him first."

### Monday, 7:16 P.M.

Twenty minutes later they were sitting in a maroon and black vinyl booth at Pietro's, the only place in Cherrystone that made pizza that didn't taste like it came from the frozen-food section of the Food Giant. Emily was grateful that Jenna had outgrown the "cheese-only" topping option for something a little more adventurous—pepperoni and black olives. Emily ordered a beer and Jenna nursed a soda.

"You know, you don't need to order diet cola, honey."

Jenna swirled the crushed ice with a pair of reed-thin plastic straws. "You mean I'm not fat? Yeah, I know. But I'm hedging my bets. I've seen the future. Look at Grandma Anna."

"Jenna! That's not nice." Emily tried to act indignant, but Grandma Anna was her ex-husband's mother and it was true that she had thick thighs. "Besides, your body shape is more from my side of the family."

Jenna drew on her straws and nodded. "Thank God."

The pair sat and ate their pizza, but their mood shifted when the conversation turned to the storm. "We are lucky. All of us. The tornado ravaged those homes on Hawes, but no one was killed." Emily swallowed the last of her beer, regarding the foamy residue coating the rim of the schooner. "I don't use the word lightly, you know, but it was a bit of a miracle, really."

"I know. Shali and I were talking about that," Jenna said. "Now you know that Jude Law Timberlake is not real. Nice fantasy, though."

Emily managed a faint smile. "I'll say."

Emily Kenyon was a homicide detective, not an emergency responder, but Ferry County was so small that when the storm hit she immediately reported to work to do what she could. She had to do something. *Anything.* She'd grown up in Cherrystone and it was *her* town. Always would be. The house on Orchard Avenue had been her childhood home. Her parents, who died in a tragic car accident, had left the family home to Emily and her brother. Since only one could live there, Emily bought out Kevin with savings and took a small mortgage. The house, with its bay windows and high-pitched roofline, was the reason she returned to Cherrystone. Not the *only* reason. Her divorce from David, a surgeon with a quick wit and an even faster fuse, was the other. The divorce made him mad.

Emily made him mad. The world was against him. Cherrystone was about as far away as she could go for the safety net of feeling like she belonged somewhere. Leaving a detective's position in Seattle wasn't easy, but the move was never in doubt. It had been the right thing.

Of course, in the middle of it all was Jenna. She loved both her parents, but felt her mother needed her more than her father. At sixteen, the courts allowed her to schedule her own visitation with her father. She saw him once a month, usually in nearby Spokane. And that, she was sure, was enough.

Emily asked for a pizza box to take home the remainder of the pie.

"We can have it for breakfast," she said.

"Only if it lasts that long."

Emily's cell phone rang, its dorky ring tone of Elvis Costello's "Watching the Detectives" chiming from her purse. The number on the LED was dispatch—the sheriff was calling.

"Kenyon," she said.

Her mother's hands full, Jenna picked up the flat carton and they walked toward the door. With her free hand, she fished some Italian ice peppermints from a bowl by the hostess lectern and offered one to her mother.

Emily shook her head, her ear pressed tightly to her flip phone as they walked to the car.

"I see," she said. Her tone was flat, like someone checking a list for which there was no need. "All right. Okay. Got it. I can take a drive out there tomorrow, first thing."

Emily looked irritated as she put away her phone.

"Do you know Nicholas Martin?" she asked.

"Sure. Who doesn't? He's a senior and besides, he's kind of a freak."

Emily turned the ignition and the Accord started. She put it into drive.

"Freak? In what way?"

"You know, one of those country kids who didn't get the memo that the Goth look was so last millennium."

"Black clothes? White face?"

"And eyeliner, Mom, *even* eyeliner. But what about him?"

Emily sighed, glad she didn't have a son to deal with.

"Did you see him at school today?"

"I don't know. Although, if I *did* see him, I'd probably remember. He's the memorable type. What's up, Mom?"

"Probably nothing. His aunt in Illinois has called the office a couple times. She's panicking because she hasn't been able to reach anyone from the family since the storm. The big cell tower past Canyon Ridge was knocked out in the twister. Sheriff wants me to drive out to their place tomorrow morning and have a look around."

"I think Nicholas has a brother, Donovan. He's younger. Third grade?"

"Oh, now I remember. Nice family. I'm sure they're fine."

"I could IM Nicholas when I get home. He hangs out in that Goth chat room Shali and I go to all the time."

Emily attempted to suppress a weary smile. "Uh, you're kidding, right?"

"Yeah, I'm kidding."

"No need, honey. I'll handle it."

Emily parked in front of the house. The night air was filled with the scent of white lilacs her mother had planted when she was a girl. They were enormous bushes now, nearly blocking the front windows. Emily didn't have the heart to give them a good pruning, though they desperately needed it. She only thought of the job when springtime rolled around and the tallest tips were snowcapped with blooms. The memory brought a smile to her face that fell like a heavy curtain with the ring of another call.

Sheriff Kiplinger, *again*.

She glanced at Jenna and flipped open her cellular. "Kenyon, off duty," she said, putting a reminder of her status up-front.

"Emily, you'll need to go out to the Martin place tonight. Jason will meet you there. Neighbors say they think the twister might have touched down that way."

"Jesus," Emily said, waving Jenna inside. "Can't it wait until morning? I'm about half dead right now."

"You know the answer. Once we get a call from a concerned citizen we have to act on it right away. Damned public relations. Damned lawyers."

Sheriff Brian Kiplinger had a point. An adjacent county nearly went bankrupt in the late 1990s when a woman reported that her sister was being abused by her husband. When law enforcement arrived two days later, the woman was paralyzed from a beating that happened after the sister phoned in her concerns.

"All right," Emily said. "I'm going."

"Jason's already on his way."

Emily exhaled. She was needed. She told herself that she'd be back home in bed within a couple of hours. She grabbed one of Jenna's Red Bulls from the fridge, thinking that the energy drink's sugar and caffeine could fuel her for the drive out to the Martin ranch on Canyon Ridge, about fifteen miles out of town. Once there, she knew adrenaline would kick in. So would Jason Howard's bottomless reserve of energy. Jason was only twenty-five, a sheriff's deputy with a four-year degree in criminology from Washington State University. He was single. Bright. Always up for anything. Youth and enthusiasm counted during the grindingly long hours after the storm.

She glanced at it, but ultimately ignored the red Cyclops of the answering machine light. Whoever had called could wait. She blew a kiss at Jenna, who was now in front of the TV watching some trashy dating show set on a cruise ship. Emily was too tired—and too preoccupied—to say anything about it. She clutched her purse and went for the door. The car radio was playing a B. B. King song, which was like comfort food for her soul. She loved that New Orleans sound—B.B. was her favorite.

This, too, shall pass, came to mind as she drove.

The sky had blackened like a cast-iron pan, pinning her headlights to the roadway. A tumbleweed, a holdout from the previous season, skittered in front of the Accord. The wind that had converged on Cherrystone and obliterated everything in its wake had become gentle, but was still present. Dust and litter swirled over the roadway as she drove into the darkness of a spring night. Lights off the highway revealed the neat ranch homes amid fields of hops and peppermint—the two most important cash crops of the region. Emily felt the buzz of the Red Bull's caffeine as she took a sharp left off the highway.

The mailbox announced who lived there: MARTIN. She'd been out there before, of course. She'd probably been to every place in the entire county before she got her detective's shield—despite her big-city credentials. Growing up in Cherrystone had also brought even more familiarity, though much of the place had changed. She vividly remembered the Martin place as a typical turn-of-the-century two-story, with faded red shutters and gingerbread along a porch rail that ran the length of the front of the house. The roofline featured a cupola covered with verdigris copper sheathing, topped with an elegant running horse weathervane. The house sat snugly in a verdant grade etched by meandering, year-round Three Boys Creek.

Emily pointed the Accord down the gravel drive-way. Dust kicked up and the sound of the coarse rock crunched under her wheels. She was surprised by the contrail of dust following her car. It billowed behind her, white against the night sky. She didn't think she was going fast and she didn't think that any dust could have remained in the county. She negotiated the last curve and saw Jason's county cruiser, a Ford Taurus made somewhat more legit by its black-and-white "retro police" car livery. It was parked with its blue lights stabbing into an empty darkness.

"What in the *world*?"

Emily Kenyon could barely believe her eyes—the Martin house was gone.

### Before the tornado, exact time and place unknown

Those who saw it later considered it to be a scrapbook of horror, a dark album of so much that could never be forgotten. *Why memorialize such things?* Affixed to each black paper page were the yellowed clippings of his unspeakable crimes. The most notorious among the nine he claimed were the ones for which he was convicted—Shelley Marie Smith and Lorrie Ann Warner. They were college roommates from Cascade University in Meridian, a midsize port city in the extreme northwestern corner of the state. Both girls worked at a store that specialized in hardware and garden supplies. Shelley had wanted to save the world one child at a time; elementary education was her major. Lorrie Ann had been less sure of her future than her roommate. She'd bounced from major to major, unable to decide her life's calling. She told her parents that she was still "searching for a passion."

The young women were found bound, shot in the back of the head, dumped along a sandbar along the Nooksack River late in the summer. An unlucky kayaker had found the dead young women some three months after they'd been reported missing. Their bodies were badly decomposed, but the telltale evidence of their horrific last hours had not been obliterated by the warm summer days or the icy mountain waters. They had been sexually violated and tortured. It was the most disturbing crime ever reported on the pages of the *Meridian Herald*.

Yet they were not his first victims. Certainly not his last. Even so, they held the distinction of commanding a full ten pages of *Herald* clippings in the black memory album. It might have been because there were two victims or because they were so young. But when their photos and clippings were pasted into the book, it told a story.

No one knew it, but it was a love story.

In turning the pages it was easy to see there was more to come.

# CHAPTER TWO

*Monday, 10:48 P.M.,*
*Cherrystone, Washington*

The temperature had dropped and Emily Kenyon felt the chill of a late spring breeze nip at her. The strobe of blue from the police light made her shudder and she grabbed a jacket as she got out of the car. Jason Howard, his flashlight like a light saber, raced toward her. Broken glass and splinters of wood were everywhere. It was like the heavens had opened and snowed fragments of the Martin house all around them.

"Glad you're here," Jason said, his flashlight's beam aimed at Emily's face, making her look even more tired and almost ghoulish. She blinked back the light and made a quick nod. "I think I found Mrs. Martin," he said. Emily caught the fear in his voice. She also saw it in his deep-set dark eyes, burrowed into his head under a characteristic knitted brow. *The kid is scared shitless.*

Before she could say anything calming, her eyes

followed the swift movement of the young deputy's flashlight beam.

"She's over here," he said.

Amid the darkness, the light fluttered over the ground like a moth. Emily's heart sank when a white figure popped against the darkened backdrop.

"Oh, dear, there she is," she said, her voice catching slightly.

"I'm pretty sure she's dead."

"I can see that, Deputy."

Margaret "Peg" Martin was splayed out nude; her clothes appeared ripped from her body by the fury of the storm. She was facedown in the mud. Kitchenware was scattered helter skelter. Broken dishes. *Fiestaware*, Emily thought. Shards of glass glittered around her chalky frame. Pieces of fabric and slivers of paper fluttered as the wind passed through the gully that once held the pretty home. It was as if a bomb had gone off. It was Bosnia. It was Baghdad.

It was Cherrystone, Washington.

"Jesus," Emily said, stooping next Mrs. Martin's lifeless body. "We need some help out here. We need to find Mark Martin and the kids."

Jason stood frozen, his brown eyes dilated to near black. Perspiration rolled from under his thick, wavy hair.

"I heard that one time a chicken was plucked by a twister in Arkansas," he said, a non sequitur that came from a nervous mind.

Emily knew he was rattled, so instead of saying, "What the hell are you talking about?" she shrugged, and said, "Heard the same thing." She retrieved a Maglite of her own and pointed its beam over the wreckage, noticing for the first time that the roof had been ripped from the house and planted some twenty yards away. The walls had fallen like dominos, one on top of the next. The light swept back over to the naked body. Emily leaned closer and touched Peg's neck. It was a formality, of course, but it had to be done. She was, very sadly and very completely, dead.

"Calling the sheriff, now," Jason said, now with the cruiser's radio in hand. A cat meowed, something shifted somewhere in the dark, and Emily steadied herself. She turned toward the noise. Glass crunched under her feet.

She couldn't think of the little Martin boy's name, but she called out the others.

"Mark? Nicholas? Anyone? Can you hear me? Try to move something, *say* something."

She stood still, but nothing. Again the cat yowled and Emily found herself wishing the poor thing would stop.

*Shhhh kitty, kitty,* she thought.

"Ambulance is coming," Jason announced, inching his way back toward the corpse.

Emily nodded. "The others have to be around here somewhere."

"Mr. Martin?" Jason said, his voice thick with dread. He ran his light over the debris field. "Are you here? Can you hear me?"

Emily moved her light methodically over the remains of the house. With each pass from north to south, she covered a bit more ground. And with each swipe of the light, more of what had once been was revealed. A chair. A tabletop. A child's toy. Her heart nearly stopped when the light passed over the blank-eyed stare of another woman. It was so fleeting that it took a second for it to register.

*A magazine cover.*

"I've heard of people surviving in India after an earthquake for up to ten days or more," Jason said from the other side of the remains of the house.

"I've heard the same thing. Let's hope that they are that lucky."

"Yeah, luckier than Mrs. Martin," he said.

"That goes without saying, Jason. You know, sometimes you just don't have to say the obvious."

As soon as she said the words, she regretted it. She was tired. So damned tired from the last couple of days. She had done more than double duty. She was on edge.

"Sorry, Ms. Kenyon," he said. His apology was so genuine, so much like the way he was, that Emily felt like she had kicked a puppy or something.

"No apologies needed. Been a long last few days, hasn't it?"

"Yeah. I haven't slept more than four hours since Sunday."

They continued to scour all that remained of the house, but it was useless. There was so much of it and their flashlights were too weak for the task.

"We need to cordon off the area and look at first light," Emily said.

"Okay. Will do."

Emily looked down at her watch. First light was in five hours.

"I hate to do this to you Jason, but after we transport

Mrs. Martin to the morgue, I'm out of here. I have to get home to Jenna."

Jason didn't look happy about it, but he couldn't say anything. Motherhood was more important than hanging around an accident scene. At least he figured his mother would say so—and he still lived with her.

"Fine by me," he said. "I'll manage."

Emily stood still in the dark, scanning. *Could there be anyone alive?* She called out for the Martins once more, but her voice was mocked by the sounds of ambulance sirens—a faint wail in the distance at first, moving closer and closer.

"Donovan," she said to herself first, then over to Jason.

"Huh?"

She called out louder, irritated that she had to repeat herself. "The little Martin boy's name is Donovan. Donovan, are you out there, honey? Donny? Mark? Nicholas? Are *any* of you out there?"

The ambulance swung down the driveway, moving faster than it had to, of course. Ricky Culver was at the wheel, and Ricky still thought that driving an ambulance was the next best thing to NASCAR—his real dream. He parked next to the cruiser and two paramedics, sisters Anna and Gina Marino, jumped out of the vehicle.

"Where's the vic?" Anna asked. She grabbed her bag and swung around looking into the rubble pile that had once been such a pretty house. Something caught her eye. The running horse weathervane had managed to stay put on the cupola, which had been tossed aside like baggage in the underbelly of an airplane.

"Better question," her sister, Gina, the older of the pair, a petite young blonde, mused, "is where on God's green Earth is the house?"

Her sister, who wore her curly dark hair short, almost a white woman's 'fro, answered back.

"It's this pile of junk, all over the place. God, Gina, use your head."

"Twister touched down here," Emily interrupted. She waved over the darkened terrain. "You can see the path of destruction. It must have landed here, then pulled up and touched down right at the house and plowed across the field like a sonofabitch."

"Anna, you can be such a bitch. Nobody said a damn thing about the tornado when they dispatched us. They said the victim was a woman with serious injuries. Life threatening."

"It's all right," Emily said. She liked the girls, but she was tired and their ceaseless banter grated. "I'll take you to Mrs. Martin. And she's not a vic. She's not a patient. She's a corpse."

Anna Marino bent over the body, while her sister, Emily, and Jason hovered like fireflies, their lights brushing the immediate area. With the increased illumination, Emily could see that Mrs. Martin hadn't been covered in mud after all. The dark brown coloring over much of her torso was dried blood. As Anna lifted her arm it was apparent that she'd been dead awhile; rigor had come and gone.

And there was something else.

"Gina, let's roll her on the board and get her out of here."

"Okay."

"Just a second," Emily said, bending closer, her beam trained on a darkened circle of bloody flesh.

"What's that?" Jason asked.

"She probably got poked by a wood splinter or something during the storm," Anna said. "I've heard of nails flying through the air and being embedded into a tree."

"I was telling Emily about a chicken that got plucked by a tornado."

"Say that five times real fast," Gina said. The other two laughed, letting off a little tension. No one meant to be disrespectful but it was the middle of the night, cold, creepy.

Ignoring their banter, Emily was on her knees now, pitched over the dead woman and staring intently. She was so close to Mrs. Martin's body that a nudge would have pushed her face down into the wound that had captured her interest.

"I don't think so." She looked up at Jason and indicated the circular tear in Mrs. Martin's chest. "We can't move her. The tornado didn't kill her."

"Huh?" Jason was confused. He had no idea what she was talking about.

"Jason, secure the scene. It looks like Mrs. Martin was shot."

"Shot?"

"You need me to repeat it? I'm so tired I don't think I can, but yes, *shot*. Close range, too. GSR burns around the wound here."

She pointed to the smudged edges of the injury.

"I see it," he said.

Gina looked at her sister. "Shit, we haven't had a murder in Cherrystone since we were kids."

"That was a suicide," Anna corrected, referring to the case of a local pet shop owner who had been poisoned to death.

Gina made a face. She'd had this argument before. She spoke a bit louder so Jason and Emily could hear.

"I never was so sure about that. I mean, he died of arsenic and that's a slow death. His wife said he had Parkinson's for years. Sounded a little feeble to me."

"Some things are never meant to be known," Jason said.

Emily stood up, glad she'd put on a pair of jeans. Her knees were muddy and hurt like hell.

"That won't be the case here," she said. "We will find out what happened to her and her family."

Jason went to the radio for backup. Photos would have to be taken. The debris had to be searched, piece by piece. Mrs. Martin was dead, but there were other potential victims, too.

"Tell the sheriff I've gone home. I'll be back at first light," Emily said. She looked at the illuminated face on her gold watch. It was after midnight. "See you in a few. Nobody touches anything. Where I come from this is a crime scene."

To avoid puncturing a tire, Emily thought it best to back her car out of the long driveway. She looked back at the ambulance and the cruiser as their spinning lights duked it out in the night sky. Red. Blue. Red. Blue. The lights pulsed like a heartbeat. What had happened back there? Who shot Mrs. Martin? Where was the rest of her family? A shiver ran down Emily's spine and she turned up the heat. Maybe she'd been wrong. Maybe the injury was the result of the tornado and the gunshot residue she thought she had seen was something else. Dirt. A burn. *Anything*. She was so tired her eyes blurred; the streetlights passed by like a wand of a light.

It was almost one in the morning; she'd get a couple of hours' sleep and get back to the scene. She probably wouldn't even see Jenna. All she knew was that with the light of day, answers would come. Maybe some hope, too. Hope was so very, very needed.

### *Weeks before, exact time unknown*

A cache of letters was tucked into the back of the scrapbook, a kind of secret meeting place where, whenever the need for arousal or remembering was needed, they'd be there. They were flat as if they'd been ironed under steam and pressure. Though they had once been damp from the heat of fingers, even the wetness of tears, they were stiff now. Crisp. Treasured. *Charged*.

One missive began:

If only we had a song, I'd sing it in your ear, my hot breath, moist and gentle. If only we could touch, I'd play my fingers all over your body. Only you know me. Only you know how I feel. Break down the walls. Break down the barriers. Feel me take off your clothes, one button at a time . . . lingering as they fall to the floor. Your hunger for my touch, insatiable . . . but I try. I try . . .

The memories were a torrent and the reader's breath accelerated to near gasping as the forbidden feelings of desire washed over head to toe.

. . . Naked we stand, our arms around each other, our mouths searching for the hotness and wetness of our passion. I look you in the eyes. You stare back, longing for us to become one. Your hands slip between my legs . . .

# CHAPTER THREE

***Tuesday, 1:46 A.M.,***
***Cherrystone, Washington***

**D**ead *tired.* Emily thought that would make the perfect title for a book of her life. So exhausted, but still aware. Frogs that had taken up residence in her neighbor's Home Center terracotta fountain caused a little commotion there, but everything else on Orchard Avenue was calm and benign. The air barely stirred the scent of the old white lilac bush. Jenna had left the porch light on for her mother and a swarm of gray and white moths swirled around without pausing to land. Emily bent down to keep them from her hair and inserted her key. The dead bolt slid. Inside, she dropped her overstuffed handbag on the console and when the contents spilled for the second time that day, she just left everything where it fell. Once down the hall, she peeked in on her sleeping daughter. Jenna was curled in a ball, pink-cheeked and dreaming—her mother hoped—happy dreams. *We could use some happiness wherever we can get it in this life,* Emily thought.

She shifted the Indonesian batik spread and Jenna moved. Her blue eyes were narrow slits. She half-smiled at her mother, but said nothing.

*Good, she's alive.* Emily knew the thought was absurd. But nearly every mother experiences that feeling of deep worry whenever they leave their children alone—six or sixteen—a few minutes to get the mail, or a couple of hours to check a crime scene. When they sleep in too long. When they don't come down to dinner right away. The worst always seems possible, even plausible, when love is so strong. All mothers know that.

Emily picked up a small dish and spoon, the apparent remains of a late-night snack. Chocolate ice cream, it seemed. Probably Brownie Batter, Jenna's favorite. For a second the coagulating ice cream made her mind flash to Peg Martin and the dried blood on her chest, but she swallowed hard and tried to pass it out of her memory. She crept across the room, shut the door with her hip, and walked to the kitchen. The red light on the answering machine atop the antique butcher block beckoned once more and though she could barely stand, she pushed the play button.

"I don't like being disregarded, Emily."

It was Cary McConnell. The jerk of a lawyer who made *other* lawyers seem like marriage material.

"I've called you three times since the storm," he went on. "I want to make sure you and Jenna are all right. I mean, I know you're okay, because I've seen you twice in town, but Jesus, I thought we had something going—"

She pushed the FAST FORWARD button and the tape whirled, making Cary sound like a helium inhaler.

"And if you think you can ignore me—"

*You really know how to win back a girl,* Emily thought, selecting the ERASE button. The machine clicked and shut off. The red eye blinked one final time.

"Good night, Cary. And good-bye," she said, softly to herself.

In her bedroom at the end of the hall, she adjusted her alarm clock to allow three and a half hours' sleep. She was glad she didn't have on any makeup because she'd been raised by a mother who thought going to bed with makeup still applied was akin to a mortal sin. Emily put her head on the pillow and thought of Peg Martin and the one vivid memory she could recall. It was the time she'd seen Peg at a school carnival the October before last. They had worked the bakery booth together for two or three nights. Emily brought chocolate chip cookies from Safeway and rewrapped them in home bakeware. Like a gas thief with petroleum breath caught with a gas can and a rubber hose, she confessed.

"I guess I'm not fooling anyone."

Peg, older than Emily, by ten years, was gracious. "Some people prefer when it's store-bought anyway."

"Yeah, but *yours* aren't. They look *too* good to be from any store."

Peg smiled. "I'm not a detective. I'm a homemaker. Ask me to solve a crime and I'll bring in a DVD of *CSI* and we can watch it together. That's about as close as I'd ever get."

Peg was a lovely woman, the kind who'd always show up with more than what was requested. She gave time to whatever the cause. She'd made the best macaroons outside of a bakery, tall, fluffy, and dipped in dark chocolate. And she always smiled.

"Take two," Peg had said that chilly autumn evening to a boy with a crumpled dollar bill, "They're kind of small." Then she winked the kind of exaggerated conspiratorial move kids make when they know they are being bad and want everyone else to know they know it, too.

But they weren't small, of course. They were like cocoa-covered Mount Rainier, Washington's tallest, grandest peak. Peg was just that type of woman. Now she was dead, under a pile of tornado trash, a gunshot wound in her chest, and her family strewn somewhere out in the darkness that enveloped her property. Emily willed herself to think of something positive, the carnival, the cookies, but the image of the dead bake-sale lady, probably *murdered,* kept materializing.

*I'll find out what happened to you,* she thought, drifting off to sleep.

### Tuesday, 3:10 A.M., *a rural area near Cherrystone*

The moon was slung low in the sky, dipping to the horizon that drew a hard edge from Horse Heaven Hills, a basalt rock formation about twenty miles outside of Cherrystone. An old lead mine had flourished there decades ago. The remnants of the mine camp had been used by teenage partyers proving their prowess with Budweiser since the 1960s. Maybe even earlier. Cans and bottles scattered along the roadway up the hill. Not everyone could wait to get up to the top.

But *he* did. He made it up there the night after the storm. It was dark then, with the lantern moon obscured by a ghostly cloud cover. He could barely see ten feet in any direction, but couldn't think of anyplace else to go. He'd abandoned the pickup when it ran out of gas, and started walking the rest of the way. The miners' hiring office was nothing more than the most primitive shelter. Windows were smashed out. Graffiti about who'd give who a blow job—male or female— were spray painted in an agitated script over the boarded-up old pay window. A nylon plaid couch retrieved from the court-ordered ladies' lounge area was in decent shape, considering how many teens had romped on it over the years.

None of that mattered. He was so exhausted. It was a bed right then and it was where he'd wait. Animals with tiny claws, mice, maybe squirrels, skittered in the walls. The smell of urine stung his nose. But he curled up. *Slept. Waited.* Tried to figure out just what he'd do. What had happened before his world literally turned upside down.

More important, he wondered who he really was.

*Tuesday, 5:40 A.M.,*
*Cherrystone, Washington*

Emily was furious. She held her cell phone with a death grip. She ran to the bathroom, phone clamped to her ear, rinsed her mouth with Scope, and skipped the brushing. Certainly no flossing, about which she was nearly obsessive, to the point of working the fiber between her teeth in the car as she waited in traffic back in Seattle. She looked worse than she ever had, but she had a new vigor. She was pissed off. *Royally.* She listened to Jason and spat out the icy blue liquid and rinsed the sink.

"Yes, I know I said I was beat. Everyone is. But, Jesus, Jason, why in the hell didn't you call me?"

"I did," the young deputy said. "Sorry, but I *did*."

Emily regarded the same jeans she wore the night before and pulled them from the upholstered chair that functioned more as an open-air closet than a reading place, as she'd intended. They'd do. She was nearly in a frenzy. Things were happening down at the Martin place and that was officially her territory. She didn't like it one bit that interlopers were there.

"Peg Martin is *my* case," she said. "I should be notified before the lab rats and techies come over from Spokane and work the scene. *My* scene."

"You didn't answer, Emily."

"*Detective*, call me *detective*. Why don't you start calling me *detective* for a goddamn change?" The operative word of her rant was pounded out with a hammer. Jason couldn't miss her irritation.

She looked at her phone and the blue face showed two missed calls. She scrolled the phone numbers and ranted some more. Jason had called twice—at 2:45 and 4:30.

"Maybe if you acted like I was your superior, which I am in every way, you'd know better. I'm not your cousin. Your sister. Your buddy."

"Detective," he said, correcting himself as he sunk into the mud of the Martins' ravaged yard. "We found Mr. Martin's mangled body about an hour after you left. I called the sheriff, and I guess he called Spokane for backup. They showed up at four-thirty."

Emily Kenyon felt lousy just then. The kid was flustered. He was doing what the sheriff had told him.

"Emily, err, *Detective*, there's one thing you ought

to know," he said. She was so mad at him, he could feel it. He didn't wait for her response. "I saw the same wound on Mr. Martin. I think he's been shot, too. So do the guys from Spokane."

Emily paused. She hadn't expected that. Adrenaline pulsed. "Jesus, Jason," she finally blurted, "what the hell happened out there? Are you sure? And where are the boys? Have you seen any sign of them?"

"No. Nothing. Backhoe's on its way. We're taking video and stills as soon as the light's a little better here. Then . . ." he caught himself. "When you get here and give us the go ahead we'll see if we can find them. I remember reading about a kid who survived longer than a week . . ."

She cut him off. "Yes, you told me, in Pakistan."

"It was India," Jason said, slightly glad he could trump her on something. She'd hurt his feelings and it was a tiny payback. It felt just a little bit good.

Emily Kenyon got that, even on the tiny cell phone.

"Yes, *India*," she said. "I'm on my way. Be there ASAP."

She hung up, put on a shirt, and ran a brush through her hair. A rubber band was the only remedy. The ponytail was ridiculous at her age, and Emily knew it. But there was no time for anything like washing and blow-drying, which on a good day was a fifteen-minute chore. Not when there were two bodies west of Cherrystone and two kids missing.

*Need to cut this mess,* she thought, thinking of her mother's advice that a woman should cut her hair when she reaches forty. *And, if you ask me, that's stretching it, Emily,* her mother had added.

She didn't have the heart to wake Jenna as she

passed her room. Leaving her alone again wasn't right, but Jenna had school. Besides, somebody deserved some rest around there. She wrote a note and stuck it on the refrigerator—the first place Jenna was sure to go.

*"Come home right after school. Serious case. Love, Mom"*

And Emily was out the door.

# CHAPTER FOUR

**J**enna Kenyon grabbed a Stawberry Pop-Tart and
started for the door. There was no time for the
toaster to do its thing that morning. She'd have to eat it
gummy and cold. Jenna hastily wrote, *"See you after*
*school. I love you, too, Mom,"* and added a smiley face
to the note her mother had left on the fridge.

It was after seven and Shalimar Patterson, her best
friend since she moved to Cherrystone, was *never* late.
Jenna locked the door behind her, and stood in front of
the old house on Orchard wondering just what her
mother had been up to all night and this morning. The
past few days had been anything but routine. With
school and work, routine was always a little on the
fragile side. But the storm was completely unexpected,
and her mother had thrown herself into a 24-7 schedule. What with her breakup with that jerk Cary, and her
dad's constant button pressing, Jenna knew her mother

was enduring what she called a "bad patch." It would pass. They always did.

Shali's classic VW bug—cream with a slightly tattered black ragtop—lurched into the driveway. The car radio's volume was cranked up loud enough for Jenna to make out the song lyrics from the Kenyons' front door. Not good. But that was Shalimar Patterson to the nines. In your face, but forgivably so. Jenna hurried to the car. A half-empty bag of kettle corn and a backpack occupied the passenger seat. She was also anything, but neat.

"Sorry about that." Shali revved the engine. "Oops, foot slipped."

Jenna smiled and scooted both items to the backseat. Popcorn fell on the driveway.

"Birds will eat it," Shali said.

"Yeah. Hey, something's up at Nicholas Martin's place." Jenna slid into the duct-tape-repaired bucket seat as Shali, a decidedly ordinary girl with a name that always promised so much more, grinded the gears as she found reverse.

"You mean that freak with the black eye makeup?"

Jenna fished for the seat belt, wincing as her fingertips touched an apple core stuck between the door and the seat. *Got it.* She pulled the belt across her lap. Her mom was a cop and she followed every rule. It irritated some of her friends, but that's the way it had to be.

"I had that art class with him," Jenna said. "He was kind of cool in the obviously tortured-soul-seeking-attention way."

Shali checked her makeup in the rearview mirror, permanently tilted toward her for just that purpose.

The blush on her right side was heavier than the left, so she evened it out with her palm.

"What did he do? Meth?" she asked.

Jenna shrugged, but Shali kept pushing for details. She did that even when she didn't know Cherrystone's criminals and losers, but had merely read their names in the paper and knew that Jenna's mom had the dirt on someone.

"I'll bet it was *meth*." She spat out the words. "Or pot. He comes to school baked half the time. Must have been doing a lot of it if your mom's on the case."

Shali's Volkswagen sped by kids without wheels who'd lined up to catch the bus to the high school a few miles away. A few stared hard at the car as if they could stop it and get a ride. Anything was better than the bus—even a ride with Shali Patterson behind the wheel.

"Probably. But I don't know. My mom's been out there all night."

"Yeah? Cool." Shali scrunched her long dark hair, over-gunked with a hair product she'd ordered from a TV shopping channel. She wore a hooded sweatshirt and a baby-T, cropped pants, and chunky gold ankle bracelet (also from the home shopping channel) she had put on in the car. Jenna wore her uniform—7 blue jeans and a sweater. If Shali was the ho' in the video— or at least an all-talk wannabe—Jenna was the good girl who never got any airtime.

Their friendship worked because Jenna was confident about who she was. A friend like Shalimar Patterson could be over-the-top annoying, the type that sought the spotlight whenever she could find it. Jenna wasn't like that. She just didn't feel the need to sell herself so hard. Shali did.

Jenna changed the subject. "Want to get a latte? I could use a boost."

"No kidding. Me, too. A white chocolate soy mocha sounds kind of good."

Shali pressed the pedal to the floor as they drove the short stretch of roadway to the school. They passed a place where the twister had set down. Shali scrunched her hair again and made a face as the splintered house zoomed from view.

"Never liked the color of that house anyway," Shali said. "What were they thinking?"

Jenna nodded in slight agreement, though she hadn't really felt that way. Shali could be such an idiot. The people who owned that house were without far more than good taste. They no longer had a place to live.

"You can be such a bitch," she finally said.

Shali knew that. This was almost a game between the two best friends. She smiled.

"You got a problem with that?"

"No. Not really." Jenna hesitated. "*Maybe* sometimes."

"Make up your mind."

Jenna reached for her coffee card as they pulled up to the window of Java the Hut.

"Just *sometimes*. Like after a tornado trashed someone's house. Times like that."

"I can be harsh. But that's why you love me."

Jenna looked out the window as Shali gave the kid at the drive-through their espresso orders. Her thoughts had turned back to her mother. She must be beyond frazzled. She got that way every now and then. As cool as her mom could be, she could also unravel. She did that more than once during the divorce. It might have been justified but even so it wasn't pretty. She hated seeing her mother cry or talk bad about herself and her life. It stung deeply. She wished she could run a triple tall latte to her. She'd need it. *What was going on over at the Martins'?*

*Tuesday, 7:46 A.M., Martin farm,*
*east of Cherrystone*

The morning sunlight poured itself slowly over the striated hillside like syrup, exposing the shattered ruins of the Martin house and a parking lot of Cherrystone police cars, two aid cars, and assorted sedans, including Emily Kenyon's much-maligned Honda ("an American cop ought to drive an American car," Sheriff Kiplinger had said, but didn't press it further because the officer's car allowance was less costly than leasing a new vehicle). None of the observers of the scene had ever taken in such a disturbing sight as the remains of Mark and Peg Martin's farmhouse.

And it was about to get worse. Far worse.

"Can I get the photog over here?" a call came from one of the Spokane police techies. He was about thirty-five, tall and lanky, and had arrived on the scene with a pristine lab kit and an unmistakable countenance of superiority. The look on his face just then, however, was utter horror. He stood about twenty-five yards into the debris pile on the southwest side of the property.

"Pretty ugly," he said recoiling at what he was seeing. "Looks like his arms were pulled off."

Emily Kenyon balanced herself on a large piece of

Formica countertop from what had once been a seventies-era kitchen. It annoyed her that the Spokane tech was taking over the scene. She moved closer, to claim her turf.

Mark Martin had been a handsome man, in good physical condition for someone in his early fifties—lean and muscular. He worked for the local power utility as its chief engineer and was known to bike the dozen miles to the office in the summer. His curly silvering hair was matted with mud. His blank eyes stared into nothingness.

"Let's shoot stills and video and get him with his wife," Emily said, kneeling by the body and studying every inch of its battered form.

Peg Martin's body was already ziplocked and ready for the ambulance and the ride to Spokane where she'd be processed as if she were nothing. Not the bake-sale lady. Not the woman who did everything for the community whenever anyone asked. Peg was an apparent murder victim. Emily looked at Mark Martin's battered and nearly sanded-off skin. He had on boxer shorts and a single sock. He might have had on a shirt, but it was gone with his arms.

She was sure he, too, had been the victim of a gunshot wound. A scenario played in Emily's mind. It was a familiar one. She'd worked at least three cases of similar presentation back in Seattle. She thought about the position of the wounds and whether or not they were dealing with a murder/suicide. She hadn't heard there were any problems between the Martins. She had checked. There had never been a single domestic violence call from their residence to the sheriff's office. Not a single one. They had seemed a happy couple, though they did tend to stick to themselves. Peg did her school stuff like a trooper, but Mark was a more introspective type—the typical engineer.

"The kind that snaps," Emily said to herself.

A gentle breeze blew from the north, picking up a little dust and fiber. The scene was not really the type to yield much in the way of trace forensics. A tornado had likely stripped away any scraps of evidence. The processing going on now was more about documenting that everything had been done properly when the defense got Emily on the stand. She doubted it would ever get that far, though. It seemed like the shooter was dead. The only question was where were the boys?

Emily caught the loose tendrils of her long ponytail and stuck them behind her ear. The wind blew harder. It seemed that time stood still. People were frozen in their duties, digging through the debris, ferrying a body bag to the second victim. Even the flashing lights atop the cruiser seemed to become still. Her heart stopped, too. Out of the corner of her eye, she saw something she didn't want to see.

She knew they had to be there.

*Where else could they be?*

"Please, no," she said softly as the world started to crank back into action, at first in a stop-start fashion like one of those old school filmstrips. Then faster. Then finally at normal speed. She turned her attention to a chunk of drywall with some obvious blood spatter. It was about ten feet from where she stood.

"What is it?"

The voice was Jason Howard's. The earnest deputy could see that Emily was frozen in her tracks. Stiff. Intent on something in the remains of the house.

"He's over there," she said, indicating the drywall.

Jason walked closer, but didn't see what Emily had discovered.

"Help me move this," she said. The pair bent over and lifted the chalky board. It was like turning a rock at the beach to see what might scurry out to get away from the exposure of the light of day. Yet nothing moved.

"It's Donovan, I think. Maybe Nicholas," she said. "I saw the tips of his fingers."

"Jesus, Detective," Jason said, remembering how touchy Emily had been. The boy was in jeans and a button-down shirt. Remarkably, he was intact. Even his face, which struck Emily as resembling his mother's so much that it was disconcerting, was untouched. It was almost like he was asleep.

"I know him," Jason said. "He's in my little brother's Cub Scout troop. Nice kid."

Emily waved the techies over. "Let's process this area as best as we can and get a board over here and get him out of here."

"He looks so peaceful," Jason said.

Photo flashes ricocheted off the boy's pale skin. Two coroner's employees hoisted him on to the stretcher, which they had spread with a midnight-blue body bag. Handles for easy transfer flapped in the wind.

"Wonder if he died of internal injuries related to the storm," Jason added.

Emily was wondering the same thing, but not for long. The two coroner assistants, both young men from Spokane, set the body on the bag and started zipping, working from the feet toward Donovan's angelic face, white and calm.

"What?" the younger of the two said to his partner, as his gloved fingertips slipped from the zipper.

"Your hands are covered in blood," Emily said. "Where did all that come from?"

She stared at the dead boy.

"Roll him over."

"We'll look at him in the lab," the other said.

"You'll roll him now."

"Not protocol, sorry."

"Maybe you don't hear too well up in Spokane," she said, almost amused with herself that she'd now felt more of a kinship with the tiniest of law enforcement operations.

"This is our scene, *my* scene, and you'll follow *my* orders."

"Someone's cranky." It was Sheriff Brian Kiplinger, lumbering his meaty frame across the debris field. Emily and Jason were so involved with what they were doing that neither had heard him arrive. He just appeared in the morning light.

Emily acknowledged her boss with a nod.

"Someone hasn't had a good night's sleep for I don't know how long," she answered. She shifted her weight and waited for the sheriff to blast her, but he didn't.

"Tell me about it." He fixed his steely eyes on the coroner's assistant with the bloody glove and the bad attitude. "I was speaking to *him*."

The young man sank into the mud.

"I'm trying to preserve the evidence." He was embarrassed and defensive.

"What evidence? This is a goddamn disaster zone.

If the lady . . . If my *chief* detective wants to see the backside of this kid, she's gonna."

The *chief* was a nice save from the "lady" comment. She was the *only* detective in the office.

It flashed in the young man's mind to roll his eyes, but he refrained. Instead he rolled the body to the side.

"Good enough?" He fought once more to suppress a smirk. Lucky for him, his effort worked.

"Yes, thank you."

With the sheriff, Jason, and the two interlopers from Spokane looking on, Emily lowered her gaze to the darkened backside of Donovan Martin. His shirt was stiff and shiny. It was soaked in blood.

"Can't say for sure," she said. "But it looks like we've got another homicide victim here."

"Jesus, that makes three."

"Or four?"

"Depending on where we find Nicholas's body."

Sheriff Kiplinger watched as Emily followed the dead boy to the coroner's van. The panel doors were open. A set of steel racks filled the back end. There were no seats. It was more a hearse with a lab destination than a family vacation van headed to Yellowstone, which it closely resembled. A mountain scene was painted on the spare tire cover. The Spokane County coroner approved the secondhand purchase of the van and liked the airbrushed painting. Not only did the coroner have a bad eye for artwork, he was cheap to boot.

By 10:15 A.M., it was tragically clear that there were no bodies left in the wreckage of the home. Dogs had been used in the surrounding field and back wooded area that fed off the creek. But nothing was found. No sign of anyone. No sign of Nicholas Martin.

Sheriff Kiplinger pulled his smokes from his breast pocket. "I hate to say it, Emily, but it looks like Nick Martin has some explaining to do."

An hour later, Sheriff Kiplinger and Emily Kenyon stood in front of a pair of cameras from two of the three Spokane TV stations. For the second time in a week, Cherrystone had made the news. First the tornado and now a triple homicide.

*Twenty years of nothing happening around here and now this,* Emily thought as she stood next to the sheriff and the cameras recorded the story for the evening news. The attention was unwanted for a couple of reasons. One deeply personal. The other had to do with pride. Both were rooted in an incident that had shaken the foundation of her life and sent her to Cherrystone to start over. To hide. *And if this story gets picked up by the Spokane station's sister station in Seattle they'll think I've let myself go.*

"We don't know exactly what happened or even when it happened," the sheriff said. "It appears Mark and Margaret Martin and their son Donovan are the victims of a brutal homicide."

"What about Nicholas? The oldest Martin boy?" The reporter shoved her microphone as if it were a fire poker. She wanted Kiplinger to spill some major news.

"Is he a suspect?"

Emily took that one. "No. We do, however, consider him a person of interest. If anyone knows of his whereabouts, please contact the sheriff's department."

*Tuesday, 12:25 P.M.,*
*Cherrystone, Washington*

It was the biggest mistake of a very long day and Emily knew it when she absentmindedly answered her cell phone without looking at the caller ID panel. She just flipped it open and there he was. It was Cary McConnell's husky voice. Her heart plunged.

"I thought you were avoiding me," he said.

"I've just been busy," Emily lied.

"I know. I saw you on the Spokane news." He paused. "Twice."

There was an awkward beat of silence as Emily toyed with pretending that she had a bad cell and couldn't hear him. She was more direct than that and as much as she was beginning to loathe Cary McConnell, he deserved to know the truth.

"Yeah. Brian's hooked up with Diane Sawyer and I'm stuck with Spokane TV talking to a reporter just out of communications school." She tried to inject a friendly tone in her voice, but mostly Emily just wanted the call to be over. She knew what he was after. But she was too tired to be quick with an excuse as to why she had to cut the call short.

"Are you busy tomorrow night?"

*Damn it, he asked.*

"Now isn't a good time," she said, wishing she'd been more direct and used "*never* is a good time."

"We have something, you know."

She found her footing. "No, Cary, we don't. We dated. It didn't work out. And now the best we can be is good friends."

"We're not friends. Last time I looked, friends don't mess around like we did."

Her skin crawled. Sleeping with any man who still used the term "messing around" for making love was confirmation that she had, in fact, *really* made a mistake.

"Listen, Cary, I don't want to hurt you any more than I apparently have. I didn't mean for things to go so far."

"So far?"

His voice became tight and she could imagine the veins on his neck popping like night crawlers on a rainy pavement.

"You know what I mean. I'm not ready for a relationship." Again, Emily censored herself. She didn't add the last bit that passed through her mind: "with you. Ever."

"Don't do this. Let's talk."

"We already have."

"Let's work it out. Let's have a drink tonight so we can talk."

Emily lost it. She felt like their roles had been reversed. She was operating on logic and rational thought and he was fluttering around with hurt feelings, treading water in a stormy sea of emotions.

"I can't talk," she said. "Hear me on this. I don't want to talk. I don't want to see you. It was a mistake, Cary. Let it go."

"I can't stop thinking about you," he said. "We had something and I'm not going to let it go. Why should I?"

"What do you mean? Are you forcing me to get a restraining order? Jesus, Cary. You're a goddamn lawyer. You know you can't harass me."

She pulled the phone from her ear as Cary's voice carried like a gunshot to the side of her head.

"You are a stupid bitch and you can't do this to me. You belong to me . . ."

She pressed the CALL END button.

# CHAPTER FIVE

*Tuesday, 2:00 P.M.,*
*Cherrystone, Washington*

Java the Hut loomed like a mirage and Emily pulled
in and absentmindedly ordered the special of the
day—a double-tall white chocolate mocha. She wondered about the wisdom of making a mocha with white
chocolate anyway. Was white chocolate really chocolate after all?

The young woman at the window took her order.

"Make it a triple shot," Emily said. "And no whip."

Emily stared out the window and mentally sorted the
preliminary findings phoned in from Spokane County's
coroner's office. The coroner's assistant talked with the
dispassionate voice of someone who worked with violence every day. She rattled off the findings, laundry-
list style, without taking a single breath. None of what
she said was earth-shattering, but it was good that what
Emily had seen at the crime scene matched what the
techies were finding in the dank, cramped, and acrid-
smelling basement lab. Observation and science went

hand in hand in the courtroom provided they ever got that far. It appeared that both of the parents had been shot at close range, nearly execution style. The youngest victim was shot in the back from some distance, perhaps indicating flight. Maybe Donny had come across Nicholas as he fired away at his parents? And in running to get help or save his own life, he had been blasted by Nick with the shotgun? Their dress—or lack of it—suggested evening or early morning as the time of attack. Then again it could have been the raging fury of the tornado, ripping off their clothes. Jason's plucked-chicken comment came to mind.

The barista attempted to make small talk as the espresso machine sent a cloud of steam into the interior of what had once been a Fotomat.

"Busy day?"

"Absolutely killer," Emily said without an iota of sarcasm.

The young woman smiled and shrugged as the steam forced its way through the tamped coffee.

"Tell me about it," she said. "I had to make seven drinks for a lady who was taking them to her office. My lineup of regulars was madder than you-know-what."

Emily smiled. She didn't say anything about the stupid white chocolate coffee she was going to drink. She didn't say anything about what she'd seen at the Martin place. Or who she was looking for. People would find out soon enough. Cherrystone, which had just dodged a bullet with the tornado in terms of no loss of human life, was about to be put on the map as the hometown of a gruesome and frightening family murder.

Emily paid and drove over to the school. She told

Sheriff Kiplinger that she'd talk to the principal at Cherrystone High about Nick Martin. The Spokane media was already swarming, and reporters from Seattle were also making inquiries about hotel rooms. A triple homicide was big, fat, unbelievable news. It was after lunchtime, and the usually tidy streets of Cherrystone were oddly quiet, given the coming of the second storm in a week—the media storm.

Emily sipped her mocha and nearly gagged. It was sickeningly, almost throat burning, sweet. If she hadn't considered the combination of sugar and caffeine as a necessary elixir given her past few days, she'd have tossed the paper cup out the window. Damn the city's littering ordinance.

Her cell rang. It was David.

"Emily, we have to talk," he said, without so much as a hello.

"David," she answered, her voice slightly brittle, "we don't have anything to talk about. At least not now."

"Yeah, we do. We need to talk about Jenna. I don't want her growing up in some Podunk town."

Her brow narrowed and she rolled her eyes. "Thanks. I grew up here, David."

"No offense, but I'm sure you'll agree that Jenna deserves more opportunity."

"She'll get that opportunity when she goes to college. *I* did. We all did." Given the circumstances of the last few hours, she couldn't bring up her old argument that Cherrystone was a safe haven. Seattle had a rave culture. Cherrystone was still 4-H. Certainly there were drugs in the town that David derided as "no more than a pockmark on the map," but Emily knew more

kids were concerned about showing how high their sunflowers grew than how high they got. Seattle teens got
beaten and murdered and abused everyday of the week.

And now Cherrystone had a murder times three.
The idea pounded at her cranium. Was it lack of sleep
or the realization that some kid had slaughtered his
family for no apparent reason?

"Really, David, I can't talk about this right now."

"Someone's dog loose? Cow get out of a pasture?"
David could be cutting and never missed the chance to
remind Emily that she was slumming in Cherrystone.

Her head pounded. "I'd answer that, and since
you'll probably relay everything back to Dani, I'd better use small words so she'll understand." The second
they spewed from her lips, Emily wished she hadn't
been so harsh and could pluck them from the air before
David heard them. If she hadn't been under so much
pressure because of the storm and now the Martin murders, she'd have held it together.

"Now, I remember why I couldn't stand being around
you."

His words cut to the bone. She knew they'd been
deserved, but she hated the idea of their entire life together being cast in an odious light. They did, after all,
have a few good years earlier in their marriage. Maybe
even more good years than bad. And they *did* have Jenna.

"Sorry," she said. "I do have to go. David, I'll call
you. But for now, please understand that Jenna is going
to see you this summer—for the two weeks we've
agreed upon in the parenting plan. Nothing more."

"Dani and I think she's old enough to change her
mind—"

Dani was David's girlfriend and Emily couldn't stand it that she was closer in age to Jenna than she was to David. They'd met once, not long after the divorce was final. Dani had seemed nice enough. She wasn't particularly beautiful. She wasn't even blond. And her chest? Just average for a second wife, or at least what most men tend to go for when they trade up. Emily hated the age disparity. It just seemed wrong, ugly, and predictable. David was a lot of things in their marriage, many of them annoying, but he'd never been predictable.

"I didn't call you to argue," he said, his voice icy. "I wanted to tell you that I've been talking with Jenna and she wants to live with me for the summer. The hospital PR department says she could help out on the Web site. It would be a good opportunity."

Emily was stunned, but she tried to keep cool. *Why would Jenna collude with her father? Wasn't she happy?* "She said so?" she asked, before she thought better of it, and laid the blame at David. "Or is this something you've cooked up?"

"I'm her dad. She needs her dad. Studies say that girls grow into stronger, more self-actualized women if they have close relationships with their fathers." He was superior, cool, and oddly detached; it was as if he was reading his words out of some journal that Dani probably nabbed off the Internet.

"Really? That would have been nice to know when we were all still living together, wouldn't it?"

"Okay. This call is going nowhere."

"Right." *Like our marriage*, Emily thought, though

she held it in. "Good-bye, David. I'll have my lawyer call yours."

As she moved the phone from her ear she heard him say, "When are you going to tell him? Tonight in bed—"

It was a cheap shot and Emily snapped her flip phone shut. An argument with David always ended with a calculated abruptness. Even though it was a pattern that had been repeated ad nauseum during the more difficult times of their marriage, Emily never got used to it. Her face felt hot with anger. Her pulse raced. It was true, Cary McConnell had been her divorce lawyer. She and Cary hadn't so much as shared a meal until after the divorce was final. *Stupid. Stupid. Stupid.* The phrase *out of the frying pan* came to her mind.

Emily got out of her car in the Cherrystone High School parking lot. A girl sat in her big brother's blue Nova and smoked a More cigarette. She looked over at Emily, pulled the brown stick from her mouth, and waved. It was a girl who'd visited the house a few times when they first returned to Cherrystone. Emily smiled back. The girl turned her head to exhale a steady stream of smoke. A couple of teenage boys sat on a curb in front of the totem pole that marked the school's entrance. Both wore holey jeans, wallet chains, and sweatshirts that had seen better days—or at least had been distressed enough to appear so. One was a faux vintage shirt for the band Poison. The other boy had a pair of gold earrings—thick and pretty enough that Emily thought they must have cost a bundle if they were real gold.

"You here about Nick?" the one with the Poison shirt asked.

The question caught Emily off guard. She thought for a moment before answering. It shouldn't have surprised her much. The Spokane TV news had already broadcast the discovery of the three bodies.

"Do you know him?"

"Not really. We hung out a few times. Kind of quiet. But cool, too."

The earring boy looked up; his dark hooded eyes seemed empty when he probably meant to cop a menacing affect.

"Nick Martin was screwed up. Always has been. His whole family was f'd up."

She narrowed her gaze. "That's quite an endorsement. What do you mean?"

Golden earrings shrugged, but the other boy answered.

"Kyle says everyone is screwed up."

"Yeah, I guess I do," Kyle said, nodding in a slow and exaggerated manner, before adding, "I barely knew the guy."

Emily thanked them, and handed each a card.

"Whoa," Poison said, "you've got a business card. Cool."

She didn't know if it was sarcasm or if he was truly impressed by the ivory and black sheriff's department card, but she smiled nonetheless.

"Call me if you can think of something that will be helpful, okay?"

With that, she pitched her coffee cup into a trash can by the front door and made her way to the front office. A wave of silence seemed to follow her. There would be no need for introductions. There was no need to say why she was there. The school was abuzz with the news.

"Dr. Randazzo is waiting for you," said the secretary, a cheerful lady with an apricot chignon that looked like it had been spun from sugar at the county fair. "Go right on in."

# CHAPTER SIX

*Tuesday,*
*exact time and place unknown*

It didn't add up. Anyone could see it. How could she rebuff him? Deny him? Deny *herself*? He thought about those things as he tried to fit the tiny pieces of his life together. She had been all he'd ever wanted. She had been the one who made him whole. She was all he dreamed about. When he was eating a meal, it was she he was consuming. Sweet. Tender. Juicy. When he was masturbating, it was her soft hand stroking his penis. Faster, slower, down his hard shaft. Only she knew how to touch him. When the wind blew softly over his ears, it was her voice whispering for him to try harder. She loved him. He alone understood her. As she alone understood *him*.

The memory faded. His face grew hot. He could feel his disappointment, then anger and rage well up in his throat. It tightened and burned. He wanted to scream at her for ruining everything by choosing the wrong man. *And what a stupid choice.* She could never be to the other man what she could be to him. He alone could love her. He could cherish every goddamn inch of her body.

*Stupid bitch,* he thought as he tore up one of the copies of the letters that he'd saved. It had once been so precious. But no more. Shards of paper fell like confetti, all over the floor. He looked down at the mess. It seemed so perfect in its destruction. She'd cost him everything.

He started to weep and it made him hate her more. Even then, after all that he'd done for her, after she'd unceremoniously dumped him when he told her how he felt, his feelings were conflicted. Mixed. A jumble.

# CHAPTER SEVEN

*One week before the tornado, 2:45 P.M.,*
*Des Moines, Iowa*

Miranda Collins parked her Silver BMW sedan in front of her expansive redbrick home. The house overlooked the pale green waters of Des Moines's lazy Raccoon River. That quiet Sunday, when the chill of winter had been decidedly chased away with the promise of an early spring, she doubted there was a prettier place in the world. The sun's rays wove their way through the leafy overhang of the only elms in all of Iowa to survive the Dutch Elm disaster of the 1930s. It was among the most desirable neighborhoods in the city. Droplets of light fell over the lawn and cobblestone walkway to the ten-foot leaded-glass doors that led inside the turn-of-the-century Tudor-style home that Miranda shared with her husband, Karl, and their son, Aaron. She threw her Coach bag over her shoulder and hooked her fingers into the loops of plastic grocery bags holding the ingredients for tonight's dinner—chicken, button mushrooms, shallots, and a decent bottle of Bordeaux. She knew better than to buy the cheap stuff.

"Cooking wine should never be anything less than what you'd imbibe from a Baccarat glass," Karl had said a time or two. He was only half-kidding, and Miranda had learned not to repeat the remark because it made him seem like such a snob. And a snob he could be.

*He's a proctologist, for goodness sake*, she thought. *He's a success, of course, but bottom line he's no neurosurgeon. What he knows of wine he's learned from the pages of* Wine Spectator *or what I've told him.*

An attractive woman with symmetrical features and dark brown hair that had been artfully streaked gray by nature, Miranda balanced the sacks of groceries on her hip as she reached with her key for the doorknob. Her charm bracelet with its collection of miniatures revealing a happy life dangled from her wrist. A baby carriage. A typewriter. Books. Miniature maps of Washington and California. A tiny Space Needle replica had been placed next to the Eiffel Tower and the St. Louis Arch. She considered each memento a keystone in her life.

The measly pressure of her inserting the key made the door move inward. It wasn't locked. It wasn't even shut. It only alarmed her for a second that DJ, the cocker spaniel that had been an unwelcome birthday gift from her son, might have gotten outside. If he hadn't, he'd have been at the door like a rocket to greet her. The dog saw every shadow through the glass as an opportunity for escape.

"Karl? Aaron? DJ got out!" she called from the foyer. Her heels clacked against the marble flooring as she moved from stone to carpet.

No one answered.

In turning to go down the hall toward the kitchen, Miranda noticed several reddish spots on the surface of the oriental rug that she'd purchased from a street vendor in Iran before the shah lost power. Miranda had been a correspondent for a network affiliate and the carpet, with its intricate pattern of green, cream, and pink, was the one souvenir she'd allowed herself.

"What?" she said softly. It looked like the dog had gotten into something. She set the groceries on the floor and touched the red spot with her fingertips. Wet. She rubbed the stain between her fingers.

"Karl!" she screamed. "Aaron!" She stared at her hand. The red liquid wasn't dye. It wasn't tomato sauce. She knew in an instant that it had to be blood. "Guys! Where are you?"

Miranda started for the kitchen. Her heart threatened to burst through her chest. She knew she was hyperventilating, but in her horror and worry she did not know how to stop herself. *Slow down. Get a grip.* The phrases meant to give her strength and composure only got in the way of her real thoughts. Her sense of smell picked up the odor of something that had burned. It was a wisp of a scent.

"What happened here?" she asked aloud. "Where are you?"

She turned in to the kitchen and gasped.

Then, as if a curtain had hurriedly been closed by the cruelest of unseen hands, everything went completely dark.

# CHAPTER EIGHT

The blood had dried on his hands by the time daylight came through the Krueger-like slashes in the old roof over the smelly nylon plaid couch in the abandoned mining office where he'd spent a restless night. Or had it been longer than a single night? *Maybe two?* In a second of frazzled introspection, he struggled to knit together all that had really happened. He gripped his hands tightly, and opened them to reveal his lifelines, clear, clean. He almost smiled at the irony. The blood had turned to powder. He faced his palms downward and the fine dark particles snowed to his chest. Blood had stiffened his T-shirt, the taut fabric now more brown than green. He shuddered as he shifted his weight. If he had always felt somewhat alone, somewhat alien, he felt it no more so than then. His mouth was dry. His body ached. And all he could think of was her. She alone would understand.

But how could he get to her? To find her, to *talk* to

her, would be to risk everything. He sat up. God, he hurt. His dark hooded eyes followed a rat as it skittered across the debris that blanketed the floor. It stood on its haunches and started to climb a power cord to a broken vending machine. As he watched the rodent, its scaly tail coiling around the cord like a snake, made its way to its source of food as hunger propelled him. He could feel tears push to the edge of his eyelids, but he flatly refused to allow any to fall. He knew he could be stronger. He had nothing left to lose.

*No time for crying,* he thought.

# CHAPTER NINE

"Isn't this unbelievable, Detective?"

Dr. Sal Randazzo, the Cherrystone High School principal, was a small man with dark, flinty eyes and rounded shoulders that sloped to such an unfortunate degree that he looked more like an oversized bowling pin than a man. His bald head didn't exactly assuage the visual connection. Neither did his pasty white complexion, which belied his Italian heritage. Emily had never liked him much; he seemed high strung and pompous.

She greeted him warmly and took a seat in one of two metal-framed visitors' chairs across from his desk—a desk that seemed to be nothing more than a platform for an array of time-wasting toys. There was a collection of wind-up plastic cars and a miniature Slinky. A pendulum with six steel ball bearings was still swinging to and fro and softly clacking from his last play session.

He also had a Chia Pet in the form of a man with a pate in the same hairless condition as his own. A few half-dead alfalfa sprouts bent toward the sunlight that streamed from a pair of floor-to-ceiling office windows.

Randazzo smiled sheepishly when he caught her looking at the Chia Pet. "That's me, I guess."

"I think it's sweet and a little funny," Emily said, though she really didn't. She changed the subject. "I guess you realize I'm here about Nick Martin."

"Yes, I thought so. Coffee?"

"No thanks. I had the world's worst mocha on the way over here."

Randazzo tugged at the knees of his pants as he bent down to sit. He wore a gray flannel suit, probably from JCPenney.

"We're hearing all sorts of things," he said. His eyes fixed on her. "Do you think he killed his family?"

"We really don't know what happened."

"But you can tell me what you think, can't you?"

Emily kept her eyes riveted to the principal. "You know I can't."

"Interesting how the police never want to share information with us and anytime our kids breathe on the wrong side of the road, you're here in riot gear and tasers."

"Sorry. I know it seems unfair. I'll take that coffee after all."

Randazzo frowned and buzzed his secretary and she instantly appeared, smiled thinly, and deposited a badly stained plastic mug of tar-colored coffee.

"What can I tell you?" Randazzo gripped a file folder

and drummed his fingertips lightly on it. "I probably can't tell you what you want to know. Brianna's Law, you know."

Of course, Emily knew about Brianna's law. As a mother she was fine with it, but as a cop, the whole idea that kids had some rights to privacy in the middle of a murder investigation seemed completely ludicrous.

The rules had changed after what happened to Brianna Lewis, a twelve-year-old schoolgirl from Yakima, Washington. She was picked up at school by a supposed caregiver and subsequently was raped, beaten, and left for dead. The alleged caregiver, a pedophile who'd seen her at the local mall and trailed her to the school, got her name from the bus driver. The girl's name got him into the office and more information from a helpful clerk. Before anyone caught on, Brianna had been abducted by the creep who stalked her.

Law enforcement officials theorized that the girl went with her captor because he knew so much about her, her parents, her life. He got all of that from a school district file. The laws in Washington State were hastily rewritten to squelch any possibility of any more Briannas. School information was locked up and not shared with anyone—not even parents—without a court order. Cops without kids hated it. But the law was the law.

Randazzo continued to drum his fingertips on the manila folder. Emily wasn't sure if it was a nervous habit, or if he was taunting her. She decided it was the former. Randazzo was kind of a nervous little guy.

"You probably want to know everything in this file," he said.

Emily nodded. "That would be nice."

"I can only tell you what's allowed under Brianna's Law, you know."

"Fine. But I'll be back with a subpoena in twenty-four hours. Do you really want me to go through all of that trouble, and let this kid do more damage? That would be on you, you know."

"Don't get cranky, Detective."

"You haven't seen cranky, Dr. Randazzo."

"Don't be formal. Our families have been friends for years."

*Don't remind me,* she thought, but said, "Yes, I know, Sal. We all are a part of the Cherrystone family."

Randazzo opened the file and held it to his chest, like a poker player. His eyes started to scan the documents.

"Nick's a good kid. Basically. He's been written up for smoking a couple of times, but nothing else."

"Teacher complaints? Concerns?"

Randazzo sat quietly, absorbed in the contents of the file.

"One," he said, finally. "And I'm only telling you this now to speed up the investigation. I want the subpoena here in the morning. CYA and all that stuff."

"Certainly."

"Last Thursday he was excused to go home early because of a family emergency and he didn't come to school Friday. Let's see, the family didn't call to say he was home sick. So when we called Mrs. Martin, she said he was home with the flu."

"I see." Emily knitted her brow. Sure she understood what Randazzo was saying, she just didn't get why he thought it was so confidential, or even particularly noteworthy.

"Mrs. Murphy, our attendance secretary, sent an SCM to the office on Thursday."

"SCM?"

"Student Concern Memo," he said, his tone now somewhat smug. He leaned back and folded his arms over his chest, his suit jacket riding up over his round shoulders. "Part of the big CYA we all have to do in the event some parent wants to sue us later."

"More Brianna's Law?"

"I guess so. Hard to keep up with all those hoops, rules, goddamn laws, we have to juggle when all we want to do is a good job with their kids."

His pontificating sounded phony, but Emily acknowledged his frustration with a knowing shrug. "So what did Mrs. Murphy say?"

"She said Nick went home because of a family emergency."

"What emergency?"

"I don't know and that's not the point. What I'm getting at is that the SCM follow-up indicates the call to the Martin place turned up 'sick with the flu, out again for the second day.' But he didn't have the flu on Thursday. Why would his mother send him to school, then call him out of class later if he had the flu?"

Emily thought the same thing. She also wondered something out loud. "Just what in the world *was* the family emergency?"

### Tuesday, 4:00 P.M.

Jenna Kenyon stood on her tippy toes and pushed the broad edge of butcher paper flat against the brick wall, a tape gun at her side. She and Shali Patterson were doing their best to try to create a poster proclaiming FOOD AND BLANKETS FOR THE PEOPLE OF OUR 'TWISTERED' TOWN. The block lettering shrank precipitously as it moved across the paper when the writer quickly saw that there was not enough room for the lengthy message. A gift from the custodial staff, a box that had held a new dishwasher, was positioned below it. It was empty. Jenna could barely keep focused on the task at hand. She heard from one of the girls in the attendance office that her mother was in talking with Dr. Randazzo after lunch. Hell, within the hour, everyone knew.

"I wish you hadn't volunteered us for this," Shali said from the opposite end of the sign, now drooping precariously from the middle. "I could be watching TV now or chatting online."

Jenna sighed. "Tell me about it. It seemed like a good idea at the time."

"That was yesterday when we didn't know an entire family was used for target practice."

"I wish my mom blabbed more about work, so I knew what was going on."

"Yeah, you'd be my pipeline to *Inside Edition*." Shali let out a laugh and hoisted herself up on a borrowed cafeteria table to tape the middle section of the banner. The table wobbled and she caught herself before falling.

"Like I could tell you anything. Like my mom would tell me anything. She never does. Never has. Sometimes it makes me so mad."

"Get over yourself. We already know what happened. Nick Martin wasted his family, high on meth probably. I've read about it. Those freaks do whatever. You know?"

Jenna didn't. Not really. She liked Nick. She thought he was sweet. "I don't think we should rush to judgment."

Shali made a face and put her hand on her hip in mock disgust. "Doesn't take a Fox news analyst to put two and two together to tell you who did what. I'd say the person who ran away is the one who did the shooting."

Jenna tossed Shali the tape gun and stepped down from the table. The banner looked good, but it dawned on her that someone would change TWISTERED to TWISTED before the day was done. She also knew Shali made sense, for once. Even so she knew that Nick Martin didn't have the soul of a killer. She was sure of that.

"You don't know Nick. I *do*. I sat next to him for half a year. The guy has some weird ideas. He's been through a lot. But he's basically decent."

"I'll bet Laci Peterson thought the same thing about her husband Scott."

### Tuesday, 4:45 P.M.

The City and County Safety building had once been city hall, before a bond was passed in the mid-1960s and a new government office was built. The old brown masonry building with a handsome limestone crown made the building look like a baker's nightmare with piped-on swirls of white glaze—a wedding cake run amok. It was old, dank, and reeked of Pine-Sol and urinal cakes. Sheriff Brian Kiplinger's office overlooked Main Street. Next to his was Emily Kenyon's, a smaller, but serviceable, space that indicated with its lesser dimensions who was the top dog in the office. She kept a spotless library table desk behind which she was seldom seen. She was what the staff called a "walker," a person who just can't sit behind a desk. Itchy feet. Short attention span. The truth was Emily had battled lower back pain for years. The only relief was getting up off her butt and moving around. She never mentioned it because she didn't think it was anyone's business. Besides, people hated a complainer. She knew she did.

She nodded at Kiplinger, ensconced in his over–Rotary Clubbed and -Kiwanised space. There wasn't a bit of room for another plaque touting the sheriff's relentless community involvement. A two-year-old Easter lily that Emily was sure would bloom a second time if he took care of it sat glumly on a bookcase brimming with the minutia of law enforcement—binders, binders, and more binders. Kiplinger was on the phone, but he waved her in and covered the mouthpiece.

"It's *Good Morning America*," he mouthed. A broad smile spread across his handsome face. "Guess who's going to talk to Diane Freaking Sawyer tomorrow?" He beamed.

Emily smiled back. "That would be you, I'd say."

"Be sure to watch. Got a stack of messages on your desk. You can have the next big one," he said.

Emily didn't care about the media, be it Meredith Viera or Matt Lauer. None of them. She cared about two things. Finding out where Nick Martin was and getting a good night's sleep. She returned to find a deck of pink WHILE YOU WERE OUT slips by her phone. The office secretary, Sammy Jo McGowan, had placed them in perfect chronological order: KREM TV,

KING TV, and Northwest Cable News. (Seeing that one, Emily was sure it would be one of the "biggies" that Kiplinger would leave for her to handle once his preening with one of the national TV divas was finished.) The stack went on: Cherrystone High School, Mark Martin's office, the reporters from the local and Spokane newspapers, and even a guy from a Seattle radio station. The last was a message from Cary McConnell: "Call me! We need to talk!"

Emily separated the phone message slips into three piles: Call back, give to sheriff, and toss in the trash. McConnell's note was destined for the third pile. That was easy. The media calls were designated for the sheriff, leaving Emily actual potential leads. She dialed the number for Mark Martin's office and got his administrative assistant, Maria Gomez, on the line.

"Detective Kenyon," Maria said, her fluty voice, suddenly raspy with emotion, "I knew something was wrong. Mr. Martin got a call from home and was told to get there right away. That was on Thursday. He left like a bat out of hell. Friday morning he didn't come in . . . and oh, then the storm, and well, I didn't even think about them until Monday morning."

Emily could tell from her voice that Maria had started to cry.

"It's all right," Emily said, "you had no way of knowing."

"But I *did*," she said. "I knew something was wrong. Mr. Martin has never left like that. Ever. He's never missed a day of work without calling in. I should have gone over there or something. Called the police."

This was typical of the last person to see a victim alive. Second-guessers, Emily called them. They were right up there with the neighbor who didn't have a clue what the guy next door was up to. She called them "mushroomers" because they claimed they were completely in the dark. In reality, they wanted to be in the dark. Being aware that the neighborhood's cat and dog population was being served at the church potluck was too much to take.

"Did he say anything about the call to come home? What did Peg say?"

"It wasn't Peg."

"Who was it?"

"He didn't say. He just asked to speak to Mr. Martin."

"Was it Nicholas?"

"Oh no. I know Nicky's voice. This one . . . this one I'd never heard."

Emily thanked Maria and hung up. She was mystified. *What was going on over at the Martins' on Thursday that had both Mark and Nick leaving early?*

She looked at the clock. It was time to get home to Jenna.

# CHAPTER TEN

*Tuesday, 5:40 P.M.,*
*Cherrystone, Washington*

Red spattered the countertops. A German-made butcher knife dripped crimson. A pot of water sent a cloud of steam from the stovetop toward the kitchen skylight. Emily Kenyon surveyed the kitchen. Orderliness had been replaced by chaos. Schoolbooks were scattered all over the tabletop; a navy sweatshirt was on the floor. Yet everything was still, save for the rolling boil of the six-quart Calphalon pot. A blue flame licked its blackened sides.

"Jenna?"

There was no answer and Emily's heart rate accelerated. Her eyes darted about the room.

"Jenna? Where are you?" She reached for the knob and turned down the gas. The pot slowed its boil to a simmer. "Jenna!"

Emily heard a sound and spun around.

"Hi Mom!" It was Jenna, emerging from the hallway. "Spaghetti tonight."

"So I see," Emily said, lightening, and feeling a little foolish, but not wanting to say so. "And a mess to clean up."

Jenna reached for a dishcloth. "Yeah, it did get out of hand." She picked up the knife she used to cut tomatoes for the sauce and deposited it in the sink. "But I wanted to make the sauce the way you like it and that takes work. Probably too much work. Next time, it'll be out of a jar."

Emily smiled. She opened the refrigerator and saw that Jenna had made a salad—more tomatoes, Bibb lettuce, English cucumber. She grabbed a half bottle of merlot on the counter, uncorked it, and poured herself a glass.

"Pepsi for you?" she asked.

"Sure."

Emily retrieved a second stemmed glass and filled it with Pepsi. Jenna had gone to a lot of trouble making a special meal and a fancy glass was in order.

"I had the proverbial day from hell," Emily said. She slipped off her shoes and took a seat on one of the kitchen barstools while Jenna dumped a box of pasta into the water.

"Did you salt it?" she asked.

Jenna nodded. "Yes. And I already heard about your day. Everybody at school is talking about the Martins."

The merlot in Emily's hand swirled in the crystal globe of the stemware, coating the sides and flowing back into a deep pool of garnet. The blood she'd seen at the Martin house flashed in her mind. She set down the glass.

"I'll bet. Seems like the whole world has literally turned over since the tornado." Emily swiveled the barstool to face her daughter, now stirring the pasta with a wooden spoon as it foamed, nearly boiling over. "You know Nick Martin, don't you, honey?"

Jenna shrugged slightly, her eye still on the pasta. "Well enough to know he didn't kill his family, if that's what you're asking." She set the stainless steel colander in the sink and retrieved the heavy pot of water.

The steam rushed from the sink as the water drained into the colander.

"I really don't know that much about Nick except I just can't believe he'd kill anyone. He was an artist. He looked a little creepy but his art was always sweet. Birds and nature stuff. He wasn't drawing death avengers or violent images of women being stabbed and bound like half the other guys in the class."

Emily knew exactly what she was talking about. The schools did a good job about being PC and tolerant when it came to every other group besides women. It was still all right for boys to run around with images of tied-up women on their T-shirts.

"That looks great, sweetie," said Emily as her daughter transferred the pasta to a bowl and began pouring on the sauce. "I'm getting to bed early," she said. "Sheriff's going to be on Diane Sawyer tomorrow and I don't want to miss it."

Jenna's eyes widened and she started to laugh. "Oh wow! That would be worth seeing. I'm calling Shali. The girl will think your boss is a superstar."

*Wednesday, 6:39 A.M.*

The bed held her like a coffin. Despite all that had gone on in Cherrystone, Emily slept more soundly that night than she had in a week. She'd laid her head on the pillow and the next moment the alarm clock beeped to wake her. *The merlot,* she thought. *Better than knock-out drops.* She put on the thinning white terry robe she'd taken home from the hotel in Cabo San Lucas where she and David had honeymooned. They'd been so happy. It hadn't all been fury and vitriol. The man that made her angrier than any other had also been the love of her life. She couldn't bear to toss the robe, even though it was frayed at the cuffs. Her wedding ring was buried deep in her jewelry box, never to be worn again, but not the robe.

She padded down the hall toward the kitchen. Passing her daughter's room, she knocked once. "Jenna, get up! Kiplinger's on TV in ten minutes or so. I'll make coffee."

The kitchen was still a mess, but Emily could deal with that. She turned on the burr grinder and it made its interminable racket. Fresh ground coffee never smelled so good. She imagined Kiplinger getting his big handsome face powdered by some assistant provided by the Spokane ABC affiliate, where he was going to appear via satellite.

"Jenna!" She called once more, as she filled the filter with the dark roast that smelled heavenly at that hour. Always did. She poured distilled water in the reservoir and flipped the switch. The machine rumbled.

Diane Sawyer, all sunny and blond, was on the tube, talking about Cherrystone and the twister that miraculously had killed no one, but now the town was the scene of a murder investigation.

The show broke for the local Spokane weather.

Good, it was just a tease, telling the audience what

was coming after the next commercial break. She hadn't missed the sheriff.

Emily hurried down the hall and pushed open the door. Jenna's room was empty. The bed made. She looked at her watch. It was almost seven. Shali must have come to get her early. It passed through her mind that earlier this week Jenna had mentioned something about posters and banners needing to be put up at school.

"First a devastating tornado and now a small town in Washington State is reeling with a mysterious homicide."

It was Diane Sawyer talking.

Emily, her robe flapping as she ran to the living room, fixed her eyes on the TV screen.

Brian Kiplinger stared into the camera. *Or stared at something.* Emily couldn't be sure what he was looking at. His eyes looked around nervously. He nodded like a doll with a spring neck as Diane coolly asked what was known about the Martin family.

"This is a good family. The kid was troubled. We're not sure what happened, but we think the answers will be uncovered once we find him. I have my best detective on the case."

*Nice,* Emily thought, *a shout out from the sheriff. Of course, I'm the only detective so that makes me the best by default.*

"What theories do you have about what might have happened?" Sawyer asked.

"We don't know. We don't speculate. But we do want to find Nicholas Martin." His eyes darted in search of a place to focus, and the camera mercifully cut to a high school yearbook picture of Nicholas. Unsmiling, with his dark locks and spooky blue eyes, Nichols did look troubled. "He's not a suspect, but he is a person of interest." Kiplinger's face came back into view. Sawyer thanked him and as the camera cut away, he continued to talk, thanking her for the opportunity to be on her show, but the sound was cut off.

Emily made a mental note to tell him he did a great job—and that he could have the next biggie when it came to interviews. She didn't need the grief.

Emily poured her coffee and given the state of the world, the effects of the wine from the night before, and what was facing her that day with the Martin investigation, she used the steaming brew to swallow three aspirins. No cream in the coffee that morning. She still needed the buzz.

A familiar horn beeped from the driveway. It was Shalimar Patterson's VW bug. The girls must have forgotten something. Emily wished they'd come back ten minutes sooner; they'd have seen Kiplinger's media debut.

The horn honked again and Emily went to the door. Not wanting the neighbors seeing her in her bathrobe, she stuck her head out.

"Hey Mrs. Kenyon," Shali called from the open driver's window, "tell your daughter to get her butt out here."

"What? Jenna's not home. I thought she was with you."

"Here I am. And she's not here?" She turned off the ignition and the VW coughed until the engine stopped. "Where is the weirdo?"

Emily ignored Shali and hurried down the hall. The bed was made. The desk light was on. Jenna wasn't in her bathroom. Everything there was in its place. She looked in the shower stall and it was dry. She touched a towel. *Dry*.

"Where is she?" It was Shali Patterson, who must have let herself inside.

Emily tried to stay calm.

"Did she say anything to you? Did she have a meeting at school this morning? Early?"

Shali Patterson stood frozen, searching her memory for something that she had probably screwed up. She never paid attention to anything.

"I don't know," she finally said. Shali slumped down into the cushioned desk chair in front of the pink computer. Its dark empty screen stared at her like an enormous blank eye.

"Think. *Think*, Shali. This isn't like her. You know it." Could Shali see panic starting to emerge on her face?

"I don't have a clue. She's Jenna. She probably went jogging or something." Now Shali was looking panicky.

"That's an idea," Emily said, realizing now that she was scaring the girl.

Right now, she was scared witless. It was one thing to have some kid missing from the mall, but with the Polly Klaas case had come an indelible marker in the annals of crime. Parents across America had learned that brazen lowlife creeps driven by the need to fulfill their twisted needs will go right into a little girl's bedroom to get what they want. No fear. No worries. Just a way to get what they want.

Emily was jumping to conclusions and she knew better. Facts first, feeling second. The room was in perfect order. The window was shut and latched. She looked around. Jenna's pink Juicy sweats were hung on a peg. She hadn't gone for an early morning jog. And even though all of that was apparent, she didn't let on that her heart was pounding with fear.

"This is crazy," she muttered. "This is Jenna. There must be an explanation."

Suddenly, Shali started to cry. "Right. Yes. There is. Maybe I was supposed to meet her at school." The teenager buried her face in her hands. As she did so, her elbows nudged the computer mouse. The screen sprang to life. Emily put her arms around Shali's shoulders and tried to comfort her.

"It's fine. There's nothing to worry about. We'll find her," said Emily.

"Jenna has been a little off lately."

"What do you mean?" Emily was startled.

Shali didn't answer. Her eyes were riveted to the computer screen, its ghastly blue glow casting a pall over her tear-streaked face.

"Mrs. Kenyon," she said, her voice full of fear. She pointed to the screen.

Emily's eyes followed Shali's finger. A chat window had been left open. She bent closer and read each line

Batboy88: Don't give up on me.
Jengrrl: Never.
Batboy88: I messed up.
Jengrrl: We all do sometimes.
Batboy88: Yeah. But this is big.
Jengrrl: Where RU?
Batboy88: I'll meet U.
Jengrrl: Same place?
Batboy88: Y.

Jengrrl: When can you be there?
Batboy88: Two hours.
Jengrrl: OK. R U sure U don't want me to tell mom?
Batboy88: She won't understand.
Jengrrl: K.

"Who is Batboy88?" Emily tugged at Shali's shoulder.

Shali shook her head.

"Do *you* know?"

"I don't know. She's never mentioned him to me. I never heard of Batboy. A chat friend? She didn't say anything about him last night."

"Last night?" Emily brightened. "You talked with Jenna?"

"Yeah, she said she'd tape the *Good Morning America* show so we could watch it later. I told her okay. She said she was too distracted to get up super early."

"Distracted?"

"I don't know. I'm thinking. She said you had a blowup with her dad yesterday. Does that help?"

Emily remembered. But Batboy88 surely wasn't David's handle. "Was she upset?"

Shali watched as Emily frantically moved around the room, looking for something—anything—that might indicate where Jenna had gone. Her coat was missing. Her purse was nowhere to be seen. The hamper was empty. She'd left wearing what she'd had on at dinner.

"She seemed a little off, but she didn't tell me to forget coming to pick her up this morning."

Emily processed what she was hearing and seeing. The bedroom that she had grown up in, the room that she lovingly painted pink for her daughter when they returned to the big old house in Cherrystone, made her shudder.

She dialed David's number and he picked up. Noise like an ocean growled in the background. He was on the freeway, probably headed to the hospital.

"Are you alone?" she asked.

"Do you mean is *she* with me?"

"Not *her*. Is Jenna with you?"

David adjusted the volume of the speaker phone, his fingers too big for the tiny controls. Traffic whizzed past. He leaned closer to hear.

"For a second, I thought you said Jenna," he said.

Emily let out a breath. It seemed like the first one since she dialed her ex. It was as if she was one of those apnea patients and had forgotten how to breathe.

"I *did*, David. Jenna's missing."

"Missing?"

"Did you hear from her last night?"

"No."

"Our daughter is gone."

# CHAPTER ELEVEN

*Wednesday, 9:15 A.M.,*
*Cherrystone, Washington*

It was midmorning the day after Jenna Kenyon went missing. She hadn't been seen anywhere. Not at the school. Not Java the Hut. Not the arcade on Main Street. *Nowhere.* Just a day after it all started, Emily Kenyon dug into her own life and remembered how she'd barely given another mother's worry a second thought after a similar passage of time. She had worked missing persons before in Seattle and her own words echoed in her head like a mantra that was meant to stall and placate.

"Sorry," she had once told a mother facing similar circumstances, "but your son's barely a missing person. He was only classified as missing a few hours ago."

"That's why I'm here," the mother had said. "You told me to go home yesterday."

"I realize that, but really, kids today, you know, they are different than we were."

The woman shook her head, sending a spatter of tears across Emily's desk. Emily pretended not to notice.

"But my son isn't like *that*. He's an honor student."

"He'll turn up," she said, sending the woman away.

The end of the story, Emily never forgot, was that he was a *dead* honor student. He'd been found two days later in weedy vacant lot less than a mile from their house. A week or so later, two boys were arrested for murder. The reason? A girl one of them liked had said she thought the honor student was "cute." Being cute got the honor student killed with a tree branch club and the broken end of a beer bottle.

The police, of course, jumped on Jenna's disappearance right away—something they likely would not have done if it had been a girl or boy outside the family of law enforcement. There had been endless phone calls. And the sheriff had called in a computer specialist from Spokane who was trying to figure out just who Batboy88 was, and if he could possibly be Nicholas Martin.

No media attention, though. Emily had not wanted to rally the media—not just yet. It seemed as if it would be more a distraction than a help. After all Jenna was a good girl.

*An honor student.*

Emily and Shali had driven all over Cherrystone, but no one knew a thing. The worst part of it was that the town wasn't so big that she'd be missed if she was anywhere. She thought of Elizabeth Smart and Polly Klaas—the two girls who had made the country wake up and take notice that the worst possible things can happen in the bedroom down the hall. That tucking in your daughter and kissing her good night did not guarantee that she'd be there in the morning. All the ugliest scenarios in the world came back to her like an avalanche, yet she did her best to dismiss them. One by one. As she sat in her office and saw the worried faces of those who knew her best, each with anxiety and concern etched over all their features, she prayed.

Her cell phone rang. It was her ex-husband.

"David," she said, doing her best to remain calm, "have you heard anything? Has your mom gotten a call from Jenna?"

"No. Not a word. Anything there? Should we really be alarmed?"

"You know something? I don't know why you even bothered calling. Or maybe you dialed me by mistake. FYI, your daughter is missing. You know, the cute little girl you left behind when you went off with what's her name?"

"Do you really want to go there?" David was ice. It was a practiced affect. He used to be a different kind of man, gentle, caring, even loving.

"Go where? I just want to find out where Jenna is."

"She's my daughter, too." David kept his answer curt. "And I love her."

Emily softened a little. She hated herself for badgering him. After all he didn't take her. He didn't know a thing about her whereabouts. It sputtered through her mind that he might know, but she set the idea aside as beyond cruel. Even for David. Ultimately, Emily didn't think he'd stoop so low as to conspire with Jenna to get her back to Seattle.

"I know," she said. Her teeth were clenched and her eyes hurt from crying.

Sheriff Kiplinger appeared in the doorway. He motioned to Emily that he needed to speak with her. He mouthed the words: "It's important."

"I have to go," Emily said into the phone. "Call me if you hear anything. I'll do the same." She looked up, clutching her cell phone tightly against her breast.

"What is it?" she said, almost daring the sheriff to tell her. She could barely read the man. She had no clue what was coming.

"There's someone here to see you."

It passed though her mind that Jenna was there. *Thank God! I'll read her the riot act, but thank sweet Jesus that she's all right.* But as the sheriff motioned around the corner, another young girl appeared in the doorway.

It was Shali Patterson. She'd obviously been crying. Her usually somewhat heavy-handed makeup had left a pair of mascara tributaries down her cheeks. Kiplinger ushered her into Emily's office.

Emily stood up, and then froze, reading Shali's face like a search warrant. "What's going on? What is it? Have you heard from Jenna?"

Kiplinger backed off toward the doorway, removing his hand from Shali's shoulder, now visibly shaking. The teen shook her head in an exaggerated "no" indicating that she wasn't bringing any news. She looked like a ten-year-old, not the reckless driver who terrorized the neighborhood with a too-fast VW bug.

"Mrs. Kenyon, I've been thinking a lot." Tears had already fallen, but her big eyes threatened a deluge.

"And I think I remember one thing about Nick and Jenna."

Emily moved closer. "What was it, Shali?"

"It's about Nick Martin." She hesitated.

"What about Nick?"

"I know that he'd talked a lot about like finding his real dad. That he and his adopted dad weren't that close. His dad was an engineer and he was, you know, artsy. His dad just didn't get him, you know."

"No, I didn't." Emily wondered if the scenario that had played out before the tornado held something even darker than she could imagine.

"Did his father hurt him?" she asked.

The question seemed to stun Shali. She shook her head. "No, not that I know of."

"Then what? Was it worse?"

"No. Not that. It was just that he wanted to find his real dad."

"Was he actively looking?"

The girl nodded. "He registered on one of those Web sites." She reached for a tissue box, and Emily pulled one out and passed it to her. Shali was pulling herself together. There was guilt there, of some kind, but it wasn't so sinister as Emily had imagined.

Emily prodded her. "And?"

Shali wiped her eyes. Her tissue was black. "Not that I know about, but it really wasn't my thing. Jenna was helping him because she felt bad about her dad."

"*Her* dad?" Emily had no idea where this was going, or if Shali was even paying attention to her best friend's status. "She wasn't adopted."

"I know *that*, Mrs. Kenyon. What I mean is that

Jenna was mad at her dad and didn't think she could be that close to him after what he did to you and her. You know. Like the new girlfriend, Dani."

Emily winced. It seemed like this teenager that peppered her entire speech pattern with extraneous "likes" was getting a little personal. The conversation wasn't going in *that* direction. Not even an inch.

"All right." *Better just to acknowledge what she said and move on.*

"She and Nick kind of bonded over that. I think once she got to know him, you know, once she got to see that there was a reason for him acting all sad and artistic, you know."

None of this was tracking. None of it was making sense. *What did Jenna's disappearance have to do with Nick not knowing his biological father?*

"I'm sorry. I'm afraid I don't understand, honey."

The word "honey" seemed to help. Shali found her footing.

"Well, that she could help him. Get to know him. Maybe once she got to know him, she could like him. You know, like, hook up."

It was a shot to the heart. No mother likes to hear that they've been excluded from their child's life in some small way. Emily had no idea about Nick and Jenna. No clue whatsoever that there'd even been a potential boyfriend lurking somewhere in the background. Hooking up? Never. Jenna would have told her. She and Jenna were close.

But that wasn't the worst of it. Jenna was missing and Shali had held out information. Emily knew by reading Shali's face more was about to come.

She was right.

"Mrs. Kenyon, I'm sorry. I lied to you about something else." She started crying so hard, that whatever she tried to convey, was lost in her sobs. "Sorry . . ."

"It's all right," Emily said. "Take your time. What do you know? Where is Jenna? Do you know where she is?"

"No. That's not it," she said. "I don't know where she is now."

Emily pulled back a little, looking into her eyes, her face calm. Her daughter was gone and Shali Patterson was about to actually be helpful. This was good. Unexpected. Joyful. But good.

Shali held out a wrinkled piece of copier paper folded in quarters.

"I let her use my computer before the storm. I found this a day or so later, but with the storm and everything I just didn't ask her about it. I don't know why she'd write this kind of a message. If it was for English class, I missed the assignment."

"Let me see," Emily said, her eyes still riveted on Shali. Shali pressed the paper into her outstretched palm, and she carefully unfolded it.

The detective looked down and read:

Do you think it is possible that someone could really possess another? Do you think that a love could be so powerful as to be sick? So good it could become bad? Tell me how you feel? How you want to possess me as I want to possess you. Never be lonely again. Never.

She looked up at Shali, her disbelieving eyes now full of even greater worry than she'd ever felt possible.

"I don't think she wrote this either," she said. "Who do you think did? Who do you think it came from?"

Sniffing for a second tissue, Shali nodded. She pulled her feet up to her chair and tucked them under. She looked small and scared.

"Batboy88," Emily answered for her. "Do you know who this is?"

"I think it's Nick Martin," she said. "He liked Jenna."

Emily started for the door. "Stay right here. Don't move a muscle." She hurried down the hallway, her heels clacking like gunfire on the linoleum. She held the paper like it was a telegram and she was rushing it to the recipient. But that wasn't true. Her daughter had been the *recipient*. The tone was scary. It was as if Nick Martin had a fixation on Jenna. Images of the Martins, Nick, the tornado debris ran through Emily mind. Now a twisted e-mail spoke of good and evil, of love and possessing another.

*Why, Jenna? Why were you nice to him? Didn't you see the danger? What happened to you? I want you home. Now! Jenna!*

She turned in to Kiplinger's office and planted the note on his desk.

The sheriff slid his glasses down the bridge of his nose and set down a newspaper. He'd been scanning *USA Today* for mention of Cherrystone and the Martin murders or the tornado. But the town was no longer national news. *So fast had the media dropped them from page one*. A few days before, Diane Sawyer's people were banging down the door for an interview and now nothing. *Zip*. He looked at Emily. She was wound tighter than he'd ever seen. There was good reason for it, of course. But he knew that whatever Shali Patterson had told his best—and only—detective it was going to be big. *USA Today* was merely a diversion as he waited. Emily's face was red and her eyes bulged. She panted for breath, not because of the hurried gait down the hall, but because of the heartbeat ramming inside her chest.

"A killer's got my daughter," she said.

### Wednesday morning, exact time unknown, at the abandoned mine

Morning light came through the rusty slits in the roof, the same openings that had ensured that the indoor environment was acrid and damp. Jenna lay very still on the stinky sofa, her eyes scanning the ceiling for a clue as to the size of the room that had provided shelter. It had been a moonless night when he brought her there, after hours of walking and hiding. She repositioned herself and rubbed her right knee. She remembered how she'd hurt it from crouching in a weedy ditch as a car went by. *Was it her mother?*

At that moment things could have been different. She could have called out. She could have ended everything right then and there. But she didn't. She just crouched low and waited until the headlights became two red eyes fading into oblivion.

She felt a breeze blow through the drafty building and she pulled herself together. She was a potato bug. Curled up. Protected from whatever dangers might befall her. *Was this a dream?* She started to shake. *What am I doing here?* She saw a rat and let out a scream.

"Shhhhh! It's all right. I'm not going to let anything happen to you!"

*It was him. It wasn't a dream.*

"It's a rat!"

"Big mouse," he said, trying to calm her. "Think a very, very big mouse."

# CHAPTER TWELVE

*Wednesday, 2:40 P.M.,*
*Cherrystone, Washington*

The wind kicked up and blew just enough dust across the parking lot in front of the safety building so as to make the hairs stand up on the back of Emily Kenyon's neck. Jenna had been missing for thirty-two hours. Thirty-two hours is a lifetime. Life and death. Emily had cried until no more tears were left, but she also put on the kind of brave face that only a person who'd seen the worst humans can do to others can muster. It was a mask, she knew, but somehow it held her steady.

Sheriff Kiplinger was elated when KREM TV from Spokane called saying the network honchos might want to do a story on the missing detective's daughter. Emily was oddly ambivalent about the prospect. She'd been the first to jump at the chance when the media came—*so concerned, so sincere*—to profile a missing person. *But not now*. It felt more intrusive than helpful. She tried to explain herself to Kiplinger.

"I want to *find* her," she said, "not embarrass her to death."

He didn't get it. "That's flat-out stupid, Emily."

"Tell me how you'd handle it if it was your daughter?"

"I'd call out the cavalry," he said. "You know I would."

Emily put that out of her mind. The day had become one of those evidentiary roller coasters or maybe a merry-go-round, as it seemed to go in circles with no end. She'd been on the phone with the bank card company. Nope, Jenna hadn't taken out a dime. She'd called every parent in the PTA phone book, grateful that it was still hard copy and not some goddamn on-line system. Old ways sometimes worked best. God knew if the Internet hadn't been invented, her daughter probably wouldn't be off who-knows-where with Batboy. She hoped, no she *prayed*, that Jenna had gone willingly.

Jenna wasn't Polly Klaas or Elizabeth Smart. No way. Emily hoped that there was some connection that was reckless and wrong, but ultimately less scary. She was living in a fool's paradise and deep down she knew it. Shali's printout from her computer was proof enough that something was terribly awry.

*Do you think that a love could be so powerful as to be sick?*

The words made Emily's skin crawl. She knew there was only one answer for such a question: "In your case, yes. Yes. Yes."

Jason Howard slipped into her office. He carried a pair of paper cups embedded in a cardboard tray.

"Latte?"

Emily barely nodded. "Thank you."

She pulled off the plastic lid and sipped.

"Any news?" he asked.

She shook her head, swinging her ponytail. It reminded her that she probably looked like garbage. Her hair was oily. Her makeup nonexistent. Looking good wasn't on her mind. Only Jenna.

"We'll find her," he said. "She'll be all right."

Emily stayed mute. She felt so empty, so devoid of feeling. She never knew how it felt to lose someone in the night. Others had. She always comforted them. But just as no one really knows what it is like to be a mother until she holds her first child, no one who hadn't felt the sudden loss of a child could ever even approximate the stabbing ache that came with every breath.

"I know you're not thinking about the Martin case right now," he started to say.

"Oh, but I am." Emily cut him off, summarily snapping herself out of the pity that had mired her, sucked her down, into the depths of despair.

"I know," he said, his bright eyes, now surprisingly compassionate for a young man who couldn't even begin to understand her pain. "I know . . . if we find Nick, we might find Jenna."

"We'll *find* her," she corrected. She looked down at her latte, trying hard not to cry.

Jason spoke to fill the awkward silence. "Anything more off Shalimar Patterson's computer? Jenna's Mac?"

"Not a goddamn thing. Both girls use something to avoid spyware, viruses, and all the rotten stuff out there. I can't even tell what sites she visited. She must have cleaned it just before the chat with Batboy."

"Nick. Nick Martin."

"Right, *Nick*." Jason hesitated a moment. "I know I'm just a deputy around here," he said. "But I did call the Spokane ME about the Martin case. For an update. I know it isn't my job, but you and the sheriff were so busy with Jenna stuff. Are you mad?"

Emily sighed and leaned forward. She even managed a little smile. Despite all that was going on Jason Howard was still doing his job. That was good. She regretted how she'd chewed him out at the crime scene. It was like shooting the Easter Bunny.

"That's good, Jason. Did they have anything for us?"

The young man pulled up a chair. He tried to temper his excitement, but he was bursting with the news.

"Yes, they did. They told me that the victims had probably been tied up before they were shot."

With those words, Emily found herself back at the crime scene. The bodies had been such a mess. So battered by the debris of the tornado, she doubted that outside of the gunshot wounds there'd be little in the way of forensics. But this was good. This was real information.

"Bound? Then murdered?" she asked. Her bloodshot eyes widened. She looked down at her cup, already empty. She hadn't even remembered drinking it, let alone sucking it down as she apparently had.

"Yup. That's what she said. Paperwork's on its way.

Some sick puppy really did a number on that family. They were held captive, like animals. Maybe he tortured them, too. Maybe he made them really, really suffer."

*Sick puppy. The term was not only at odds with the deed, but it lessened the truth of what the killer had done. A puppy doesn't rage. A puppy doesn't do the unthinkable. But a Batboy just might.*

Emily's thoughts swung back to Jenna. It was like Jason Howard had slammed a door in her face. He didn't mean it. But she wondered why it hadn't dawned on him that the so-called sick puppy was Nick Martin. And that the sick puppy might be holding her daughter.

*Jenna! Where are you?*

"I'm going over to the high school," she said, abruptly rising. "I need—*we* need—every bit of information we can get about Nick." She drummed her fingertips on a manila folder on her desk.

Inside was a copy of Judge Crawford's subpoena for all of Nick's school files.


*Wednesday, 3:25 P.M.*

As she walked from her car to the school's administration office, Emily Kenyon was acutely aware of the looks of concern coming at her from in every direction. Kids she didn't know, but who probably knew Jenna and why her mother the cop was there, were fixated on her. They stared, mouths slack jawed. Only one had the courage to come forward, a boy of about sixteen. He had tiny white shells strung on jute around his neck. A chain dangled from his belt loop to his pocket. He'd been fighting acne and the smell of the ointment he used was heavy.

"Sorry 'bout Jenna. She's a good girl," he said.

Emily nodded. She could have said something, but she just had no words. Her silence seemed to make the boy step back. He looked suddenly insecure and awkward.

"Everyone liked her," the boy added, looking down at the ground.

"Likes her," Emily finally said, correcting his tense. "I'll find her. She'll be home. She *is* a good girl."

"Yup. Just wanted you to know."

Emily swung from mom to detective mode. "Who are you?"

"Kev Bonners," he answered, this time, looking her in the eye.

"Do you know my daughter?"

He shifted his weight and looked down. "Not really. But she's talked to me a few times. Nice. Always nice to everyone."

"Do you know Nick Martin?"

"Hell, I mean *heck* no. The guy's a freak."

Emily stared hard at the boy. His blotchy face. His gangly arms. He was only a notch above Nick Martin on the lowest rung of the high school's social ladder. Yet in his own somewhat earnest manner, he was trying to help.

"It's been awhile since I was here, but all of us have had our turn being a freak," she said. "That's just the way high school is, or was."

"Guess so," he said.

She fake smiled before turning away and walking into the office.

"I'm back with the court order for Nick Martin's student file," Emily told the secretary. She could see the top of Sal Randazzo's beaconlike pate as he looked up from his desk. He got up and started toward her. His mouth was a straight line. His dark eyes sparked.

"Let me see that," he said.

Emily slid the subpoena across the counter. A couple of girls tabulating the day's absences pretended to be busy at work. When one looked over and caught Emily's gaze, she smiled.

*Making Randazzo squirm was fun.*

"Is Jenna going to be okay, Mrs. Kenyon?" said a pretty blonde with a mouthful of metal.

Emily recognized her from the intramural basketball team that Jenna had been on a few years ago. She was a nice girl. *God, the whole school was filled with nice boys and girls. Why this? Why did her daughter find the only bad apple in the barrel?*

"I'm sure we'll get it all sorted out," Emily said. She shifted her attention back to the principal, who by then was done reading the paperwork.

"I'll get you the files myself," he said. With an irritated look on his face, Randazzo vanished around the corner to the file room. He returned with a green folder. A very thin green folder.

"Is that it?" Emily asked.

He shrugged, and she opened it. There were no more than ten sheets inside. One was a permission slip from Peg Martin for her son's participation in a field trip to a dairy outside of the county. A few pages indicated some visits to the nurse. Finally, the basics of his life—his gender was male, he was born in Seattle, his parents' names and occupations.

Nothing more. Nothing at all.

*What did I expect?* Emily asked herself. *He was a kid. He didn't have a life yet.*

"This is it?" she repeated.

"'Fraid so," Randazzo said, impatiently. "We don't carry a lot of paper on our kids. I'm surprised that the permission slip for the trip to Clover Dale Farms is in there. That should have been purged long ago."

Emily looked up from the minidossier on a troubled high school kid. She held her tongue. The pretty blonde looked over. A beat of silence. It wasn't Randazzo's fault that he was a complete nincompoop. He probably was born that way.

"Judge says I can take these." She turned for the door. In doing so she caught the eyes of the girls working at the attendance office one last time and smiled in their direction. It was an invitation for them to come speak to her if they wanted, but they just went back to their work.

Emily felt the buzz in her purse, and then came the muffled, but familiar ring. She had begun to hate the Elvis Costello ringtone Jenna had downloaded as a surprise. What had once seemed so silly that it made them laugh until their sides ached now seemed derisive and a sad reminder.

"Hey Emily, can you come back to the office?" It was Kiplinger. His normally gregarious nature was masked by concern. "Marina Wilbur is here to see you."

Emily searched her memory, but nothing came up. She didn't know anyone by that name. Before she said so, Kip offered up more information.

"She's Peg Martin's sister. From back east. She's here to make arrangements."

"I'll be right there." Emily flipped her phone shut and sat in her car. The seat belt warning pinged, but she paid it no mind. She turned the ignition and looked in the rearview mirror, catching her own reflection for the first time. Her eyes were underscored with dark circles. *This is what a mother looks like who has lost her daughter. The face is mine.*

Emily engaged the seat belt, which stopped the pinging. She wanted to cry.

### Wednesday, 4:45 P.M.

Kiplinger was as grim-faced as Emily had ever seen him and they'd been through some pretty bad cases, though nothing of the magnitude of the Martin murders. He met her in the parking lot in front of the Public Safety building in downtown Cherrystone. His anxious countenance disturbed Emily to such a degree, she didn't turn off the ignition. The Accord idled. She pushed the button and the window slid down.

"I wanted to catch you before you came inside. Didn't want to have this conversation on the phone," he said. "Can I get in?"

Emily indicated all right with a quick dip of her head.

"What is it, Kip?" She called him by his nickname, rather than the more formal "Sheriff" that she used around the office. This felt exceedingly personal. "Have you heard something about Jenna?"

He shut the door and struggled to adjust the front seat to accommodate his six-foot, 200-plus-pound frame.

"No. Let's drive away from here."

Without speaking, she put the car in gear and it rolled from the lot to the main street.

"Let's go to the park and talk. And *no*, I haven't heard anything about Jenna. But that's what I want to talk about."

"You're scaring me," she said, her eyes switching from the road to Kip, then back again.

"Don't be scared. We're just going to talk and we just can't do it at the office. Too many people listening all around."

A spot under a willow that hung over the street like an archway. She parked and they walked over to a picnic table. A couple of preschoolers played nearby on a jungle gym, their mothers fixated on their every flip and twirl. A poodle was tethered to the slide. It barked sharply. It was a sunny morning and for a moment it seemed like any other day.

But that was all about to change. Kip lit up a smoke and faced Emily, his big brown eyes full of concern.

"Look," he said, "I know this is awkward. But I need to know how you and Jenna were getting along."

Emily knew where he was going and she didn't like it one bit.

"How can you even say that to me? You know we got along. Are you trying to suggest that she ran away?"

Kip narrowed his gaze. "That's right. There really

isn't anything to suggest that she left against her will. You *know* that. She wasn't abducted."

"We don't *know* that. We don't know anything for sure. And where is this coming from?" Emily stood up. She wanted to leave. It felt so insulting that her boss, *her friend*, a man that she trusted more than just about any other would sit there and utter such a cruel lie.

"I talked to David. He said that Jenna wanted to come live with him. You'd argued about it. Isn't that right?"

The poodle got off his leash and started running through the park. One of the mothers was frantically chasing him, while calling over her shoulder for her daughter to stay put.

The distraction was only momentary, and Emily's anger was a volcano.

"Goddamn that David! What an idiot! He thinks his backbiting comments against me are helpful in his daughter's disappearance? What kind of a man would put his hate toward his ex-wife over the love of his own little girl?"

"David *called* us. He talked to Jenna late last night. She called him. She's fine. She's—"

It was a molten iron spike to her heart. "What? He talked to her? Why didn't he call me? Where is she? What did she say to him?"

Kip motioned for her to be seated. "Take a breath. One question at a time, all right?"

Emily planted herself on the rough-hewn wooden bench, her heart pounding and sweat dampening her underarms. She was mad and relieved at the same time.

*Jenna was alive. She wasn't Polly Klaas. Jenna Kenyon was alive!*

"Please," Emily said, "tell me everything my daughter said."

Kip exhaled a stream of smoke. "David told us she called last night about midnight. Said she was calling from a pay phone—the caller ID indicated she used a calling card—I knew you would ask. She was a little shaken. She said she'd be home soon. She was helping a friend in trouble."

"What friend?"

"She didn't say. David pressed her for more details and she was pretty adamant that none would be coming. She did say one thing for you, though. 'Tell mom, I'm doing the right thing.'"

Emily flashed to the sheet metal sign that hung in her daughter's bedroom. It was the same sign that she'd displayed when that room was hers. It was made to look like a NO PARKING sign and read:

**DO THE**

**RIGHT THING**

**—EVEN IF**

**IT HURTS.**

"What else did she say?"

Kip shook his head. "Nothing. That's all. David said she was on the phone no more than a minute, if that long."

Distrust won over relief. "I don't believe him. That bastard's got her. My daughter is *not* a runaway." She didn't even care that Kip was right next to her and was going to hear intimate family business.

She flipped open her cell phone and punched the code for David. It rang five times then the recording came on. Jenna *must* be with him. If she was with anyone else, if that ridiculous story about a mysterious phone call was true, then David would be standing by waiting for another call or even news from Emily in case she had received a similar call. He would pick up right away. Unless he knew where Jenna was—safely at his side.

### Wednesday, 7:45 P.M.

What had happened at the Martin place on the Thursday before the tornado? It was after hours, but there was no going home. There was no reason to. Jenna was gone. The phone was forwarded. And there was the matter of the Martin murders. Emily Kenyon studied the Spokane coroner's autopsy report after it arrived bundled into one of those cheap accordion files. She'd always had a strong stomach and barely winced at the photographs that accompanied such files. But in the case of Mark, Peg, and Donovan Martin, Emily fixed her attention on the coroner's schematics— not the photos of their battered, bruised, and bloodied bodies. The schematics, the distillation of reality, were actually more telling. They were impersonal figures, no genitalia, no hair to suggest a woman or man's body. Just delicate black lines in the shape of a human form on a plain white sheet of paper. There were three of them. Mark Martin's wounds were the most severe.

His limbs were absent from the schematics. An X drawn by the coroner indicated where he'd been shot—in the upper back, probably at relatively close range. Peg Martin was next. Her wounds were beyond comprehension but it was there in black and white. She'd been shot in the chest. There was extensive damage to her torso—postmortem, the coroner noted. Finally there was the youngest victim, Donovan Martin. Like his dad, Donny had suffered a single gunshot to the back. A big black X marked the spot where the bullet had entered, another where it had exited his frame.

Emily set each of the sheets of paper across her desk. Muzak filtered in from the hallway and footsteps came and went, but never once did she look up. So much of what is routinely learned about what happened to each victim was quite literally gone with the wind. The tornado had swept away any trace evidence—fibers, hairs, even shell casings that had been left behind by the killer. *Why had Mrs. Martin been found nude?* Labs for the presence of semen came back negative. She hadn't been sexually active that morning, and unless the killer had used a condom, she likely hadn't been raped. The nudity was puzzling, however. Emily just couldn't wrap her brain around what had taken place. Maybe she'd just gotten out of the shower? Or was in her robe? She'd been bound—the only one of the three. From what Emily knew, Peg had called the schools and Mark's office with the urgent message to get home. Had the killer used Peg to lure Mark upstairs after he'd placed that call to Mark's office? There was no way of knowing.

But at least one person probably had an inkling, if

not a hand in it. Nicholas Martin. And Emily had only two questions to ask him: *Why had he done this? And what did her daughter have to do with any of it?*

Reluctantly Emily went home to the empty house on Orchard Avenue, full of memories, but missing the one spark of life that was her daughter.

*God, where is she?*

# CHAPTER THIRTEEN

When Marina Wilbur turned to greet Emily Kenyon, it was like seeing a ghost from an unsettled grave. The look of horror on the pretty detective's face could not have been more disconcerting—and tragically obvious.

"I'm sorry," Marina said, standing to acknowledge Emily as she entered her office. "I guess I should have told your boss to warn you. Peg and I are . . ." She caught herself and the tears she had held in check since the ride from the Spokane airport began to rain down her cheeks. "*Were*," she corrected herself as she fought to regain her shattered composure, "we *were* identical twins."

Emily, still caught off guard, set down her paperwork and lamely offered coffee. She was carrying her own from the coffee stand and felt awkward drinking in front of her.

"It's not bad for cop coffee," Emily said, looking

around for a tissue and hoping that Shali Patterson hadn't used the last of them.

Like her sister—*just like her sister*—Marina Wilbur was a thin and shapely woman with honey-blond hair and, given a much happier time, mischievous green eyes. Emily thought of the school carnival and how Peg had given a kid an extra cookie. Her green eyes literally twinkled. But Marina's eyes weren't all that mischievous now. They were wrought with worry, dread, and unimaginable sadness. She had flown from Dayton, Ohio, to face the worst possible scenario of any family—multiple murders at the hands of one of its own.

And now, sitting in Emily Kenyon's office, Marina was clearly losing her battle to maintain any semblance of control. She had started to sob softly. Maybe the first time, since Jenna's vanishing, Emily realized that others were suffering, deeper, irrevocable losses.

"I'm sorry, so very sorry," Emily said. "It is almost impossible to come up with any words that provide comfort at a time like this. I know it from losing my own parents not long ago. I liked your sister very much. She was a wonderful woman. This must be so hard for you."

Marina nodded. "Thank you. I heard about your daughter, and I'm sorry for what you're going through, too."

It was a kind gesture, but Emily found herself bristling slightly. *Jenna is not dead like your sister and your family. Jenna is with her dad and will come home.* But she said nothing.

"I appreciate that. Thank you." She lingered for a second, but there was nothing more to say. "Let's talk about your sister and her family, all right?" She pushed the Kleenex box toward Marina. "Do you need a moment?"

Marina crumpled a tissue and blotted her face. Her resolve was clear. She was as ready as she could ever be. The bodies of her sister, her sister's husband, and her youngest nephew were already in caskets, lined up for burial.

"I'm okay. I mean, considering everything that has happened this week. Has it even been a week? It was such an unbelievable shock. First, the tornado—which we watched on the news. When we couldn't reach Peg and Mark after the storm, we figured that the power and phone lines were damaged. We kept trying and trying, but never got through. I called Mark's office and they said he'd missed a day of work, which was odd for him, but I still didn't think . . ."

"How could you? I mean, really, no one could have," Emily said.

"I told myself that on the way over here. But you know it will take a lot of soul searching to figure out if I could have prevented this."

The remark was startling. Emily set down her coffee. The woman across from her wasn't there just to find out what happened to her sister, brother-in-law, and nephew. She was there for another reason. She felt guilty.

"How so?" Emily asked.

"Mark," she began, "had been troubled lately." She caught herself and stopped. Her words had come out all wrong. "I mean not to the extent that he'd do this . . ." She paused, and finally said, "I don't know."

Emily could feel her pulse race. "But you must know something," she finally offered.

Marina Wilbur looked out the window, across the parking lot of pickup trucks and late model cars. All needed a good wash. Cherrystone was not a wealthy town. She wondered why her sister would want to live in a place like Cherrystone anyway. She knew Peg loved Mark and always said that Cherrystone was "out of the way" and a "great place" to raise kids. What a crock that seemed now. She couldn't think of the last time an entire family had been murdered in Dayton, a far larger city than Cherrystone could ever hope to be.

"They were having trouble. Peg told me. Mark was upset about something. Work maybe, I'm not sure. That was the impression I got. She didn't say so, but I'm her twin. We don't need to spell out every little thing, you know. Peg said that he'd been under a lot of stress and it was causing trouble with the boys, both Donny and Nick."

"What kind of trouble?"

"She was vague about it. Said that there was a lot of arguing going on between Mark and the boys, particularly Mark and Nick. I don't like to pry and my sister's pretty private—" She caught herself, leaving the present-tense reference to her sister to hang in the air for a beat, but neglected to amend her words. "There had been some kind of knock-down drag-out, I guess, a couple weeks ago."

"No clue about what it was about?"

Marina reached for another tissue. The first one had been wadded to the size of a peach pit. She looked around for a trash container, but when she didn't see one, set the paper ball on the corner of the desk.

"This is very upsetting. And very private. But I guess I can tell you, I mean my sister's not going to get mad at me, you know." Her tears returned. "I think it had something to do with Nick's adoption."

"I didn't know until recently that he was adopted," the detective said.

"Of course not. Why would anyone need to know? He was their son in every way."

"Was Donny adopted, too?"

Marina dismissed the question with the shake of her head. "Isn't that always the way? They'd tried having one of their own for ten years—fertility clinics, counseling, you name it, they did it. They adopted Nick. They were so happy with a son to love. And bam, a couple years later, Marina calls up and tells me she's pregnant. On their own. No help from anyone. Donovan, Peg always said, was . . ." Her words stumbled from her lips, "was their miracle baby."

Emily opened her notebook and started writing, all the while keeping her eyes riveted to Marina Wilbur and her sodden tissue. She was unsure what this information meant for the Martin case, and what, if *anything* it meant for the subject that had most of her attention—her missing daughter.

She was going to get in touch with David and demand to talk to her daughter. Just what kind of relationship had she had with Nick anyway? Could she get in touch with him? Bring him in? Did David realize how vulnerable she was? He had to be warned that

Jenna might be mixed up in something very, very dangerous.

### Thursday morning,
### exact time unknown

The shack had been silent for almost two hours. Jenna Kenyon had sat quietly, alone in the shadowy building. Wind scraped the roofline and she pulled the cords on her hooded pale blue sweatshirt taut. *How much longer would he be gone?* She'd tried the doorknob, but it had been locked from the outside. The windows were too high up, and ultimately too small, even if she'd been able to hoist herself up there somehow. Her knee still throbbed. But more than pain, she felt a strange kind of uneasiness. It was fear. It was justified. She was alone in a strange place. Just waiting. Just wondering.

She heard the doorknob twist and she spun around; a bolt of light from the outside blasted its way inside. The silhouette of a figure stood in the doorway, stark and foreboding. Jenna put her hand to her mouth to muffle her involuntary cry.

"Sorry it took so long," he said, "but I had a hard time getting that beater going."

Nick Martin held a bag of food and a newspaper in one hand. He was pale and sweaty, but he tried to suck up enough courage so that he could at least appear to be calm. Jenna deserved that consideration. He didn't want her scared any more than she already was. Fear breeds like a virus in a small, confined space.

Jenna got up to meet him. "I don't like being left here alone," she said, taking the bag of food. "I won't

be left alone like that again. Trapped like an animal."
She indicated the lock on the door.

"I had to do that," he said. "I didn't want anyone
else finding you."

Jenna fished through the paper bag, found an apple frit-
ter, and started eating. Nick took the other. He unrolled
the paper and set it on the ratty sofa.

"Made the paper," he said. He indicated the front
page of the Warwick *Times*. The town was about ten
miles from Cherrystone. A headline ran just above the
fold:

### BOY MISSING AFTER
### FAMILY MURDERED

The article was accompanied by a color photo of the
Martins' flattened house—though it would be difficult
for anyone to comprehend that the debris scattered on
the image had once been a house. Jenna's eyes widened.
It looked like it had been bulldozed. A few telltale
pieces that indicated that the material had once been
fashioned into a home, but not much. She started reading and almost at once, her mother's name jumped off
the page. The story said that Emily Kenyon had gone
out to the residence after the tornado, only to find that
three family members had been shot and the fourth,
Nick Martin, was nowhere to be found.

"I can't believe your mother would say that," he
said.

"What?" Jenna hadn't made it that far into the article.

"That!" He punched at the newspaper.

"Hey! Knock it off!" Jenna yelled back. "I can't read it if you rip it up." She traced the columns of type with her now greasy finger.

> "Of course, we don't know what happened,
> but we're concerned about Nick. We want
> to find him before any more harm comes to
> him or someone else."

"See right there," he said. "She thinks I'm the one." His face was red and rage pooled in every fiber of his being. "Goddamn her!"

"Chill, all right?" Jenna reached her arm around his shoulders, now slumped and shaking. "This isn't good for you. You've been through so much. We just have to tell her what happened."

Nick extricated himself from Jenna's arm. "Your mom will *never* understand. No one would. This is such a lame mistake, Jenna. All of this is bullshit. My family didn't understand me. Your mom isn't going to, either."

"I'm here," she said. "I get it. I understand."

Nick got up and walked toward the fissure of light around the casing of the door.

"*Stop.* I'm here for you," she said.

He turned around. He was more handsome than menacing, with dark eyes that sucked the life force out of the room. His hair was curly, dark, almost black, though he'd cajoled his mother, Peg, into using one of those home highlighting kits. The highlights were supposed to be golden, though they looked more like brass. He wore blue jeans low on his hips, revealing the black band of Joe Boxer briefs against his very white skin. A vintage Metallica T-shirt and scruffy black Doc Martens completed the look. A closer examination would reveal twin pinprick scars through his eyebrows; the only reminder of a piercing look that he didn't think was cool anymore. Through the tears on his pallid face, he managed a smile.

"I know. Now and forever," he said. "You're the only one I can count on."

Jenna pulled him closer. It was tentative. Not in the way that a woman pulls a man closer, but as a girl comforts a brother.

"I have to talk to my mother," she said.

Nick pulled away, and took a step backward. His eyes followed Jenna as she slumped back down on the dirty sofa. "I don't trust your mother. You know what she thinks about me. Everyone thinks that about me."

Jenna Kenyon knew that Nick was right. She wondered how she had gotten herself into such a mess, but more urgently, she worried if she was going to be able to get out of it in time.

# CHAPTER FOURTEEN

*Thursday, noon,*
*Cherrystone, Washington*

Emily Kenyon hadn't eaten much in almost a week. Her last real meal had been the pasta that Jenna had made the night before she disappeared. Emily's clothes no longer flattered her figure; they draped limply. Her shoulders were wire hangers now. Aware of this, she smoothed out the wrinkles in the cotton blend skirt she'd put on that morning. But it was more than the forlorn fabric of the outfit that made her such a mess. It was her entire life. Her forever-marriage had been torpedoed by a husband who insisted his *needs* weren't being met—and found a way to rally in the arms of another, a *younger*, woman. She'd thought that living in Cherrystone among old friends and familiar surroundings would be a tonic for her troubles. But she was wrong about that, too. Even living in the family home, as lovely and as steeped in cherished memories as it was, had been somewhat of a mistake. Old homes take a lot of new money, and a detective's salary and the child support of a doctor-ex didn't add up to nearly enough.

Worst of all, Jenna was still gone. Emily had finally talked to David. She'd got her old friends in the Seattle PD to check it all out. And she was now convinced that David *had* been telling the truth. Jenna was on her own. Or worse. She was helping someone, she'd said. Emily knew it had to be Nicholas Martin.

Despite every effort of the sheriff, and of law enforcement all over the state, there was no clue where they were.

Emily had been adamant. She didn't want the public to know that her daughter was with Nick. That would make her personal involvement in the case a liability. It might tempt him to hurt her. So while there was a concerted effort to find Nick and ask him about his dead family, no one in Cherrystone except Shali and a few kids at school knew with certainty that Jenna was missing. Instead Emily had explained she was with her dad for a while.

When Randazzo's office at Cherrystone High demanded to know if Jenna was coming back, Emily said she would let them know what the situation was when she knew, that the family was working through some issues, and that her investigation of the Martin homicides had made the situation even more difficult. Randazzo had had the decency to back off.

So there Emily sat in her office, fishing through messages from the media, amid fermenting latte cups in the trash, and a legal pad headed with "Call Today" on her desk. She tapped her pen against the paper. She felt empty, depressed, and heartbroken. On some level the Martin case would have been a detective's dream—

a puzzler that required both wits and work, but she was short on both just then. Her litany of reasons to hate her life was topped off with the deep hurt she felt that Jenna had called David instead of her.

She had been a good mother. She was sure of it. She thought she and Jenna had been exceptionally close, a kind of personification of the old Helen Reddy chestnut, "You and Me Against the World." She wondered how she could be so wrong with her assessment. So blind. *What had been going on between them?* How could she have missed any warning signs that things were awry? She remembered all the times she'd passed by Jenna's bedroom and saw her typing away on her Mac. Emily had thought Jenna was doing her homework. Was she chatting with Batboy? Why hadn't Jenna told her about him?

She wrote on the pad in front of her: school, friends, teachers, neighbors. *Who held the key? Who knew?*

There was nothing in Nick Martin's background to indicate he'd be capable of killing his entire family. As Emily now worked her way through the rest of the rather thin green school district file, a reasonably positive picture of the missing teenager came into focus. His grade in Speech Communications was his lowest, a C+. He'd had mostly As and Bs. There were no teacher comments, but to Emily's way of thinking, Nick Martin was probably shy, uncomfortable in front of a group. *Most kids were.* As Jenna had told her, Nick was artistic; high marks in four different art classes bore witness to the idea that he was one of those creative types that are often ostracized in the high school culture that praised athletes over artists. In fact, nowhere on his transcript could she find that he'd been involved in sports. He wasn't a Columbine kid—one of those disenfranchised malcontents that stormed around the high school campus in a black trench coat bemoaning the world that had kicked him to the curb.

Emily's stomach growled and she pressed the palm of her hand against her abdomen to stifle a noise she was sure Kip could hear in the office down the hall. She'd had nothing but coffee all day. She thought of what Peg Martin's sister, Marina, had said about the problems that had seemed to be brewing between father and son. What was going on at home that caused both Nick and Mark Martin to leave school and work? Had a confrontation between father and son escalated into a bloodbath that wiped out the entire family?

Except one. Except Nicholas Martin, the missing.

The only thing that kept Emily from sinking into the floor in utter despair as she worked on the threadbare case was the phone call Jenna had made to David. That alone allowed her to sharpen her focus after Kip had suggested she drop the case because of "personal" reasons. Emily understood where the sheriff was coming from, but Kip had underestimated her—or what she wanted to be. Indeed, what she had been before returning to Cherrystone.

They talked after Marina Wilbur left the office to complete funeral arrangements for her sister, nephew, and brother-in-law.

"Look," he said, folding his big mitts on her desk, "I don't think Jason's ready for this by a long shot, but I don't know that you can take on what needs to be done here. I might need to, you know, elevate his role here."

"Jason?" Emily could scarcely believe her ears. "He's only a deputy and he's barely out of diapers," she shot back, knowing at once that she'd been on the borderline of insubordination. It was more of an over-reaction to demonstrate as clearly as possible that she was capable of doing her job. It was the one thing about which she felt confident at that moment, now that "wife" and "mother" seemed no longer in play.

"I've thought about turning it over to Spokane for an assist," he said. "We're not staffed for this kind of event here."

*Kind of event?* He was talking media-speak and it irritated her that much more. Her face grew hot.

"How can you say that? I have more experience than any of those grandstanders from Spokane. You know that. Jesus."

"Chill. Deep breath, Emily. Can't you acknowledge that you're under an inordinate degree of stress? Maybe so much that you really can't perform your duties?"

Emily bit her lip. What she wanted to say right then could get her fired and she knew it. She counted to three.

"Brian," she said, using his first name, a technique she employed while cozying up to a suspect she wanted to win over, "I admit I'm under stress. Okay? I concede that point. But I know I can do my job. Jason's not ready and since when did we ever want to get Spokane involved in our affairs? And—" She hesitated, realizing that she was on dangerous ground again. "I'm sorry. Give me a break, Okay?"

Kip groped for a pack of cigarettes in his jacket, and put an unlit cigarette in his mouth. It dangled from his lip as he started to speak, "I will. You deserve it. I'm going outside to puff and think. Let's talk about the case when I get back."

Emily turned her attention back to her notes and the file. "All right. I'll be ready." She knew a few moments cooling off were a gift and she was going to take advantage of it. She opened her case notebook and looked at her notes when the phone rang.

It was a reporter from a Spokane radio station.

"We've had a couple of sightings of the Martin boy," the young woman, with the unfortunate name, Candace Kane, said. "Care to comment? I'm recording now. Okay?"

"No, not okay," Emily said. "I don't know what you're talking about and I don't comment on anything I don't know about."

Candace barely took a breath, and then started chirping again. "But I need a quote for the news. Here's what we know. We got a call from a couple listeners who saw him shopping at the Riverside Mall at the Nordstrom."

Emily wanted desperately for it to be true but she didn't even attempt to hide her skepticism. "I doubt it's Nick Martin," she said. "Frankly, he doesn't impress me as the Nordstrom type."

There was silence from the other end of the line.

"Ms. Kane, are you still there?"

"Sorry. Yes. I was writing that down. Old school, since you won't let me record your comments for our air. Anyhow, that's what I thought about the Martin boy, too. The photo they ran of him in the paper made him look like a real space case. More grungy Mervyns than Nordstrom."

Emily didn't know that a photo had made it into the media. "Spokane paper?" she asked.

"Yeah, you can see it online. Pull it up on your computer. Just go to www dot—"

"Thanks," Emily said, but she was already tapping the keyboard as Candace Kane offered a minitutorial on how to access the station's Web site. She pulled down her "favorites" menu on her toolbar and clicked on the Spokane paper. An image of Nick in what obviously was a yearbook photo, the same thing that had appeared on *Good Morning America* when the sheriff stammered his way through that interview, popped into view. The portrait had a "painterly" background and the harsh flash of a photographer working on an assembly line. Nick's skin looked so pale, his hair nearly black. Emily leaned closer to the screen. *Was he wearing eyeliner? Didn't Jenna and Shali call it guyliner?* The quality of the image was pretty good, but she couldn't be sure. Her eyes progressed to the headline: SEARCH IS ON FOR KILLER. But then something else caught her eye. There was a sidebar to the main article: WHEN A BOY KILLS HIS FAMILY.

"You still there?" It was the voice of the radio reporter who interrupted Emily's immersion in the article. Her eyes continued to scan the content flickering on her computer screen.

"Yes, but I have to go," she said. "If I can make a statement later, I'll make it on your air first."

She didn't wait for the reporter to answer. She hung up the phone and looked back at the screen. It wasn't the main story that intrigued her—it was a mishmash of what neighbors had to say about how "things like that don't happen around Cherrystone" and some reminiscences about how kind Peg Martin had been to so many people. It fit what Emily knew to be true, not one of those post-death do-overs of someone's character. Emily didn't know Peg raised champion Russian Blues. Mark was a watercolorist. Donny had been named Cub Scout of the month by his pack, three times. None of that riveted her like the accompanying story. The editors had packaged the Nick Martin story with a broader theme: *Boys Who Are Bad*. They highlighted a case in Des Moines, Iowa, where, a month prior, a boy named Aaron Collins had shot and killed his parents before raising the barrel of a gun to his own temple. Emily remembered the story. There had been great controversy about the Collins case because school officials had seen some warning signs, but apparently disregarded them.

"That kid never fit in," the boy's maternal grandfather was quoted as saying. "He was so preoccupied with finding his birth parents in Seattle that he scarcely gave my daughter and her husband the time of day. He actually ran away a month before the murders. They should have let him run."

*Adopted?* The word hung in Emily's memory. She glanced at the clock; it was after six. Ordinarily she'd be hurrying for the door by then. Hoping that whatever she'd planned for dinner would still come together quickly for Jenna. She wondered if she'd put too much on Jenna. Too much responsibility. Too much of a need to excel and hold it together when her own life had crumbled.

The last face she expected, *wanted to see*, appeared in the doorway just then. It was Cary McConnell. He was a handsome man, with piercing blue eyes and wavy dark hair, the kind of coloring that had made Emily's heart beat faster even in high school. He had that handsome lawyerly look that made him the star of the courtroom. Nice suits cut by a Korean tailor in a time where almost everyone bought off the rack also distinguished him in style and attitude. Cary owned the ground he walked on. He was a control freak, sure. But a very handsome one.

"You haven't called me back," he said, inviting himself into a seat across from her desk. "I've been worried."

"Look," Emily said, "I've been through a lot. It wasn't personal." She lied, and Cary was too stuck on himself to sense it.

"I know," he lied right back to her. "Any news on Jenna?" He leaned back.

*He was getting comfortable. Damn.*

"She called David. She's helping a friend." Emily started pulling files together. She opened her briefcase. She was getting ready to leave, each cue was meant to tell Cary to back off. Go home.

"You want to get a drink and talk?" When Emily didn't respond right away, Cary pressed again. "Just a drink. Nothing more."

Emily didn't want to go home alone. She didn't exactly want to go off with Cary McConnell either. Kip had invited her to have dinner with him and his wife, but she felt that he just wanted to "observe" her to see if she was too messed up to carry on with the Martin investigation.

"All right," she finally said.

Cary McConnell flashed his faultless smile. "Good. *Just friends.*"

Later that night, after a couple of salt-rimmed margaritas and dinner at Rosario's Cantina, Emily Kenyon wondered how she'd been so weak, so foolish. Cary's stealthy charm and undeniably practiced compassion had worked on her frayed emotions. It was like sleeping with the enemy; a betrayal of what was really going on in her life. She buried her face against his lightly hairy chest and took in a deep breath. Her cheeks were damp from silent tears that predictably went unnoticed. Cary smelled of Calvin Klein's Obsession cologne. She found herself wishing that she actually loved him, but the thought was transitory. As the digital clock spun into the late hours, she had only one thing that was on her mind: Jenna.

*Where are you, baby? Come home. Come home.*

# CHAPTER FIFTEEN

*Thursday, 6:45 P.M.,*
*Ogden, Utah*

Spring and summer in Ogden, Utah, are hotter than hell, but few of those living there would ever deign to use such a vulgar metaphor when describing what they knew to be the Promised Land. Ogden was a burgeoning Mormon enclave of pristinely maintained homes set behind sidewalks that had never seen a chalk mark since the day Mexican workers poured them. Lawns were green and weed-free. Sprinklers on timers sprayed their staccato blast of water only at night. Everything was perfectly ordered and ordered perfectly.

But something was awry on Foster Avenue. Newspapers had piled up on the steps that set the stage for an imposing double front door. Tuesday. Wednesday. Thursday. Friday. The Salt Lake City *Tribune* was literally loitering on the ideal tableau of a good Mormon home.

The paperboy—a *girl* named Tracy Ross—told her mother that she was worried about the Chapmans at

4242 Foster Ave., an especially nice street of upscale homes with swimming pools and built-in barbecue pits. The girl, fourteen, had an excellent relationship with everyone on her route.

"They usually tell me when they go out of town," she said over a family dinner of roast chicken and mashed potatoes.

"Maybe it slipped Mrs. Chapman's mind." Tracy's mom, Annette, offered.

"That's right," Rod Ross said. "This is a busy time of year." He smiled broadly at his brood of six children, Tracy being the oldest of four girls and two boys. Dinner conversation was always pleasant. They didn't allow TV in the house. "Think about it. Think about how busy we are. Try not to worry, Sweet Pea. All's well in Ogden."

"All right, Father," Tracy said. She finished her meal, still worried about the Chapmans. There were only three of them. Mr. and Mrs. and their daughter, nineteen, a bookworm named Misty. *How busy could they be?*

# CHAPTER SIXTEEN

*Thursday, exact time unknown,*
*at the abandoned mine*

"I'm here. I'm not leaving. But you have to tell me everything." Jenna Kenyon had been patient enough. Up to that point, she had been too scared and confused to ask the really hard questions, but the article on the grease-marred pages of the newspaper begged for answers that only Nick could provide. She'd held him at night. She'd dried his tears. She'd even suffered the indignity of using an old Folger's coffee can for a toilet while he turned his back. It would be wrong to say she was a prisoner. She didn't think Nick would hurt her if she bolted for the door. But she had to know. She had to ask.

*"What happened?"*

His dark hair hanging like loose fringe over his hooded blue eyes, Nick sat on the dingy plaid sofa staring into the darkness of the old Horse Heaven Hills Mine hiring office. He pulled his legs up tight to his chest, his chin resting between his bony knees. Nick owed Jenna the truth. But he stayed silent.

"Tell me," she prodded once more. She put her arm gently around his shoulder. The smell of sweat and gasoline was pungent in her nose.

"All right," he began, slowly. "I'll tell you."


*It was just after lunch on the previous Thursday when Nick got a call from the school office that there was some kind of a family emergency and that he was needed at home.*

*"I just spoke with your mother," the dour secretary said, wire-rimmed readers on a chain from her slender neck. A worried look on the teen's face brought much-needed reassurance. She smiled and said, "She's fine. Your dad and brother are okay, too. I asked."*

*"What's happened?"*

*"I don't know. Go home. Call us if you need anything from here. Okay?"*

*"I guess so."*

*Nick signed out for the afternoon, slung his back-pack over his shoulder, and hurried to the Ford pickup his dad had given him for his seventeenth birthday. He checked his pocket for cash, but came up short. He should have filled up earlier in the day. He revved the engine; a cloud of exhaust poured from the tailpipe. The gas gauge indicated he had an eighth of a tank. Good. Enough to get home. He figured the "family emergency" probably involved grandpa or grandma. His dad's parents were already gone, and both Nick and Donny were close to their maternal grandparents.*

*They lived on a farm just south of Billings, Montana. Some of Nick's happiest memories were of visits to their farm, a place of long summer afternoons and quiet, star-filled nights.*

Pulling into their long wagon wheel driveway, Nick spotted his parents' vehicles parked in front of the house. There was also a black Buick, a Skylark. It was unfamiliar. The plates were framed in a rental car company's holder.

*Wonder who's here?*

The front door was ajar.

"Mom!" he called once inside.

There was no response. Natasha rubbed against his leg, and Nick bent down to pick up the cat. She immediately turned on her motor and started purring.

"Where is everyone?" he asked, petting the cat and moving deliberately through the house. The living room with its pair of antique love seats set off by an oval braided rug was empty. So was the kitchen. A drawer was open. Almost absentmindedly, Nick shut it with a push of his hip. The cat stopped purring and wanted down, but Nick held her. Next he made his way down the hall, but everything was quiet. Really quiet. On his way back from his dad's vacant office at the opposite end of the hall, he noticed Donovan's fifteen-pound, shoulder-bruising backpack by the front door. He was already home?

The Seth Thomas grandfather clock in the foyer ticked like a bomb.

"Donny? Dad? Mom?"

Natasha jumped from Nick's arms and scampered toward the door. Maybe they were in the backyard? The afternoon sun was blinding and a breeze wafted

*the scent of lilacs and mint through the air. Swallows
that had set up housekeeping under the eaves swooped
low over the grassy field that zoomed up the hill from
the driveway to the highway. He noticed that laundry
had been hung that morning. It fluttered soaking in the
smells of the country that his mother loved so much.
The serenity of the scene was utterly at odds with the
supposedly urgent request to get home. Something's
really wrong. Nick could feel panic rising.*

*He went back inside and stood at the bottom of the
honey fir–planked stairway.*

*"Mom?"*

*There was no reason to be upstairs. There were only
bedrooms on the second floor. With a visitor here, why
would they be up there?*

*Up he went, into a nightmare.*


Jenna found an old cotton painter's drop cloth, and
put it around Nick's shoulders. Each word of his story
sent a shiver from her neck to the base of her spine.
Like shards of glass stabbing. Like ice. Nick was looking at her then, measuring the impact of his words, not
sure if he was losing her or winning her over. What he
had to say was nothing, however, compared with what
he'd seen in his parents' bedroom.

"It was bad," he whispered. "It wasn't some movie
set or anything like that, but I wanted it to be fake. To
be like some big joke. But I knew that my mom and
dad would never play a joke like that."

Jenna held him closer. Her heart ached for what he
was about to disclose.

"You're going to be all right, Nick. You're going to be fine. I'm here."

He shot her a look that stopped her cold. He didn't even have to say the words. She felt stupid. Of course, he wasn't all right. How could he be?

"I want to smoke," he said.

"Later. I can't help you if I don't know what happened."

He drew in a deep breath and held it. He wished he didn't have to breathe at all. Breathing meant living. He'd wished to God that he'd been dead, that he'd never seen what was in his parents' bedroom.


*"Mom? Dad?"*

*The room was dark and absolutely still. The blinds glowed orange from the daylight outside, but the light was out and Nick couldn't see anything. He reached for the switch. The flash from an overhead bisque and brass fixture filled the room with creamy light . . . and red.*

*The red, he knew with the visceral response that comes with complete fear, was blood.*

*Not this. No. No. Please.*

*His mother was nude on the bed. She'd been bound with something on her legs and feet. His father, dressed, was beside her. A spray of blood spatter arced behind the bed. There was so much blood! He took each piece of the scene in like a Polaroid, not waiting to really see what he was viewing. Later the images would emerge from the fog of what he'd seen. His father's curly silver hair was caked in shiny whorls of blood. His mother's skin was tissue white. Everything had been touched by the dark red color of blood.*

*"Mom! Dad!" Nick lunged for the bed and tried to shake them into waking, though he knew they were dead. His father's dark eyes stared blankly at the ceiling. His mother had doll eyes, too. Open, but seeing nothing at all. He was crying then. His hands were wet with blood and he spun around, as the reality of what he'd seen sucked him deeper into terror. "Momma! Daddy!"*

*On the floor, he saw a foot, a leg, and then the rest of his brother. Still. Lifeless like his parents. Nick started circling the front of the bed. He was a caged animal. The door was open, he could leave, of course, but he just kept circling. He needed to call 911. Call the police. But he was paralyzed by fear. He called out, a wail of emotion, for his brother and his parents. Had Dad killed Mom, then Donny? Why? Nick felt his pocket for his cell phone, but it was gone. Must be in my backpack. Or the truck.*

*Family pictures looked on from the dresser. Among them was a shot of Nick and Donny grinning in cutoffs and Grand Canyon T-shirts standing against the celebrated red rocks of Sedona, Arizona. His mom and dad's wedding photo, his dad having to forever live down the white and powder blue tux that he'd put on because he loved Peg so much. Mom with her medallion for winning the Tri-State Cat Fanciers show.*

*Blood spatter mottled the mirror. Nick caught a glimpse of his own horror, a face he almost didn't recognize, so twisted in fear. He turned away to go for the phone when a guttural sound called out from the bed.*

*It was a plaintive cry, not quite human sounding. He wondered if Natasha had followed him upstairs.*

*The noise was a gurgling sound, but it wasn't the cat. It came from his father. Nick bent close. He could feel the warmth of his dad's breath.*

*Mark Martin was alive.*

*"Dad! What happened? What? I'm getting help now."*

*Mark Martin's eyes weren't tracking his son, but his lips were moving. Blood pooled from his mouth.*

*"Nick?"*

*Fighting back his tears, Nick wanted to tell his father how sorry he was for everything he'd done to disappoint him. He put his hand under his father's head, cradling him like a baby. He could feel the wetness under his dad's back that he thought at once had to be blood.*

*"I'm getting help. Going right now," Nick said.*

*Mark Martin tried to lift his head, he gurgled out another cry. He wheezed. "Closer . . . thought Donny was you." His words disappeared into the agony of his ebbing life.*

*Nick was near hysterics by then. He couldn't hear what his dad was saying. It just didn't make sense. Donny wasn't him. Of course, he wasn't.*

*"What, Dad?"*

*"Get out . . . son . . . go. Not safe. Angel here. Hide. Won't stop until you're dead."*

*And with that, Mark Martin's seemingly dead eyes rolled back into his head. He had taken his last breath to issue his son some kind of a warning. Hide. Not safe. Get out. Nick was in such a state of anguish and fear that he thought he might have dreamt the whole thing.*

*How he wished that could be true.*

*  *  *

Nick was crying so hard by then that Jenna knew her words couldn't console him. *Nobody*'s words could. He hadn't done anything wrong. He hadn't shot his mother and father and brother. She believed everything Nick said, not because she was some gullible young girl, but because the Nick Martin she knew, the one that she had fallen a little in love with, was the gentlest of boys. He would never hurt anyone. He never *had*.

It was as if all the emotion had sputtered out of him. Nick Martin was immobile. He'd relived the images of what he'd seen in his parents' bedroom. He wasn't even crying anymore. The lack of emotion was nearly as disturbing as what Jenna had heard him describe. She kept her arms around him, not sure what to say. He was like some kind of bird who had smacked into a window and slumped down to the ground. Stunned. Motionless.

"I'm all right," Nick finally said. "My dad saved me. He told me to get out. The killer might have been there. I don't know. I just got in my truck and drove. I didn't know where to go. I was so messed up. I came here."

"I'm so sorry," Jenna said. "We need to get help. My mom can help. You didn't do this."

He looked more hurt than distraught just then. "Did you think that I did?"

"No. I didn't. But Nick, I don't understand any of this. Who would have killed your family?"

Nick stood. "Do you think I know? Do you think that I would be sitting in this crap hole if I knew who did this? I want to make them pay! I'll kill them myself." His voice was rising with anger and it scared Jenna.

"Calm down, Nick. I'm here for you. I believe in you." She didn't let go, though her heart was pounding. Fear was filling the room. She wasn't really sure what had happened back at the Martin house, but she could accept that Nick hadn't played a role in it. "We have to think. We have to figure out what happened."

"A couple of weeks ago, my parents told me that my birth mother had wanted to meet me when I turned eighteen next month. She—I guess through a lawyer—contacted my dad through a lawyer here in Cherrystone—Cary McConnell."

"I know Cary," Jenna said, a disgusted look now on her face. "He's a jerk."

"You told me about your mom and him hooking up, so I didn't want to say anything to you. Basically I didn't want any part of this. I love my mom and dad. Sure I'm not exactly what they wanted, I guess. They are my parents. Not some woman who gave me up for adoption. Some guy who knocked her up and left her. Whatever her lame story is, I don't care. I told my dad that."

"Your mom and dad really loved you."

"My dad saved me."

"He called you his angel."

Another tear rolled down his cheek. Nick didn't bother to wipe it. He was lost in his thoughts. His father, mother, brother. *All gone.*

"What are we going to do?" he asked.

"My mom. My mom will help."

"She thinks I did this," he said.

"I'll tell her what happened."

"I don't trust her. I don't know what my dad wanted me to do."

"Let's talk to her. Let me call her."

# CHAPTER SEVENTEEN

*Friday, 6:30 A.M.,*
*Cherrystone, Washington*

Emily could not believe her ears. She was dripping wet from the shower and she risked an electric shock to turn up the volume on her bathroom radio. Candace Kane was reporting on the news that Jenna was on the run with a suspected killer. She didn't use her name, but might as well have.

"We're not identifying the girl, because she's a juvenile and out of respect for her mother, a county sheriff's employee," Kane said. "A source close to the investigation says that the girl disappeared the day after the Martin murders were discovered."

*I'll kill her,* Emily thought. *Why is she reporting this? How does this help any of us?*

Water pooled where her feet were planted on the slippery ceramic tiles. Emily just stood there, frozen, taking in each word and growing angrier by the nanosecond.

Candace went on, "Classmates at Cherrystone High said the girl and Nick Martin were close."

Static followed for a second, then the voice of a teenage boy came through the speaker.

"Yeah, they were both artsy. He was kind of a Goth, I guess. She's probably one of those goody goodies that like to hang with the bad boys. Pretty common knowledge around here they were seeing each other."

Another voice cut in. This time it was a girl.

"It was like Romeo and Juliet. It was like both parents didn't want them to date and maybe that's why he offed his family."

Emily reached for a towel. Her body was shivering, but mentally she was numb with anger at Candace Kane and her so-called news station. Her daughter was not "on the run" and there would be no more "updates to come." As far as Emily knew, there had been no Romeo and Juliet love affair. Not on Jenna's part. These kids were taking a tragedy and working it into some kind of overwrought teen romance. Jenna might care for the boy, but if she was in love with Nick Martin, she'd have told her mother. *Just what was going on?*

The calls had been coming in all morning. They were stinging wasps that couldn't be knocked away with a sledgehammer. One after another. Some were friends and family, worried about Jenna and where she was. Those came out of concern, but Emily Kenyon wished she'd been able to say more than, "Thank you for your concern, your love." It felt so useless, so damned weak. But the vast majority of inquiries flooding every phone line at the sheriff's office were from media jackals looking for a story. *The story.* Some got through to Kip and Jason, and by mid-morning the beleaguered dispatcher, Gloria, stopped patching anyone through. Lavender Post-it notes encircled the screen of Emily's computer monitor like a feather boa. *Call. Urgent. Third time. Important tip want to share.* Emily made a stupid mistake on that last one, calling back only to find that the reporter wanted a tip, he didn't have one.

*Thank you, Candace Kane, for your fantastic story*, Emily thought. *You've made my life even worse than it was. No small feat. Maybe you should be promoted to TV?*

Around noon, Gloria-the-dispatcher buzzed Emily on the intercom, a communications system so poor a shout down the hall would have worked better in most instances.

"Call for you, Emily. Line three," she said, her voice crackling under the strain of the failing speakers.

Emily jabbed at the answer button. "Message please, Gloria. I can't work with all this. Give the call to Kip or better yet, my detective in training, Jason." Her tone was decidedly sarcastic, which she regretted right away. "Sorry. Just take a message."

"Trust me, you'll want this one. Emily, I think it's Jenna."

Emily stared at the blinking white light on her phone. "Jenna?"

Gloria's usual cool demeanor ("gunshot vic on line two . . . incest perp calling again about computer . . . lawyer wants police report") ratcheted up ten times to over-the-top excited. "I think so, Emily. Talk to her. Pick it up!"

Emily pushed the flashing button and put the phone next to her ear. The room seemed suddenly small and dark. Closed in. The blinking light was now a solid glow. Just her and the phone, a lifeline to her daughter. Before she spoke, she heard Jenna's breath against the mouthpiece. It was soft and sweet. A mother knows when her baby is close. *But where was she?*

"Honey?"

"Mom? I'm sorry!"

"Jenna!"

"You're not mad at me, are you?"

"Of course not," Emily said, searching for a word that carried some measure of her pain. "*Worried*. I'm worried about you. Honey, where are you?"

Jenna fought to hold it together, but her grip on her emotions was spiderweb weak. "I'm all right," she said, her voice breaking. "I can't say where I am. But I'm safe. I'm fine. I told Dad to tell you that I'm okay."

A noise coming from the hallway cut into the conversation, and with the phone tight to her ear, Emily shut the door. "He told me, but why didn't you call me? I am your mother."

Jenna was crying softly into the phone. "Mom, you know how you get. Nick needed my help."

*Hold your anger. Keep calm. Jenna's okay.*

Emily heard a car with a bad muffler in the background; it seemed to pass near wherever Jenna was calling from. She could hear other voices, too. She wondered if Jenna was at a pay phone, maybe at a gas station or store.

"Nick needed you?" she asked. "Nick is in a world of trouble."

Another car passed by. *Was she outdoors?*

"I know what you're thinking, Mom. That's why I

didn't call you first. You are always too quick to judge. Nick didn't do what they're saying—what *you're* saying."

Emily wanted to yell into the phone for her daughter to get a grip. The boy was dangerous, unbalanced, a number of adjectives zoomed through her mind, but she knew better than to use any of them. "Jenna, you don't know what happened," she said.

Silence.

"Jenna?"

"I *do*, mom. Nick told me. He didn't do this. He isn't capable of anything like this. I know him." Jenna's words shattered into pieces and she stopped to compose herself. "He's scared, Mom. I'm scared."

Emily had never felt so helpless in her life. Jenna was her baby. She thought their bond had been stronger than anything she could imagine. From her side, it was. But there she was, about to beg her scared little girl to come back to her. The idea of such a plea would have seemed beyond inconceivable a week ago. But the world had turned over since the storm. Nothing was as it had been.

"Come home, Jenna. Both of you. This isn't safe. Don't you know that the FBI is within a hairbreadth of getting involved? They're thinking kidnapping here."

"Kidnapping?" Jenna wasn't crying anymore. Her mood had shifted. She was angry. "You wouldn't let them do that. You know I went with Nick willingly. I went to *help* him. I care about him."

"I realize that," Emily said, now lying. She hadn't even heard Jenna mention Nick Martin's name up until that phone call. She wondered how well she knew her only child.

Jenna went on. "I told Shali to tell you the truth, but she didn't think she could get through to you. That you wouldn't listen to her." Her voice now showed traces of exasperation. It was probably abundantly clear that Shali didn't tell her mom anything.

"You talked to her, too?" Emily felt foolish to feel hurt over that, but the feeling grabbed her too quickly for her to assess it and set it aside. "Dad, Shali? Finally, you call me?"

"Mom," she said, "don't be like that."

"All right. Now tell me where you are."

"I can't do that. I'm okay. That's all I'm saying right now."

"Jenna," Emily again struggled to keep cool. "Do you know what you're doing here? This is not right. His family is dead and he—"

"He didn't do it. I know him."

By then Emily was sure if she pressed the point any harder, her daughter—the real love of her life—would hang up. She'd get in some car with Nick Martin and disappear for a while. Emily had to think like an investigator, just then, not like a mother.

"Okay. Maybe I can help. I want to help. Can I talk to him?"

Emily heard Jenna put her hand over the phone and say something, though it was too muffled to make out.

Jenna got back on the line. "No, not now. But I can tell you what he told me."

"All right, honey, tell me. Take your time."

Jenna went on to describe how Nick had come home from school because of a supposed family emergency. He had searched the living room, kitchen, the yard, everywhere, but found absolutely no sign of his parents.

"Mom," Jenna started to sob again, "he went upstairs and found his parents and brother . . . they were all dead and stuff. I mean, his dad wasn't dead, but he was hurt real bad. He told Nick to get out. To run away. That there was someone that wanted to kill him."

Both ends of the line grew quiet for a moment. Another car passed by.

"Jenna? Are you still there?"

"I'm here, Mom," she said. "Oh, Mom, he's scared. He said his mom and dad and brother . . . they were all shot."

Emily wished she could reach through the phone line and put her arms around her daughter.

"Oh God, honey. I'm sorry. I'm sorry. Is Nick all right?"

"He's a mess, mom. He's scared spitless. We're both scared. Whoever is out there wants to kill him."

"Kill him? Why? Why in the world would anyone want to kill his mother and father and little brother, and then him?"

Jenna paused. She was collecting her thoughts, but Emily felt as if her daughter was sifting out what to tell and what to hold close.

"Nick thinks it has something to do with the adoption," Jenna said. "Ask Cary about it."

The name was a knife in Emily's heart right then. Maybe to her *back*, she wasn't sure.

"Cary?" She was incredulous. "What does he have to do with any of this?"

"I knew that would piss you off, Mom. Glad you dumped him. Nick says that Cary talked with his dad.

Made his dad really, really mad. Something about the agency or the birth mother wanting to see Nick, but Nick's dad didn't want anything to do with it. Nick and his dad fought about that."

Emily put her fingers to her lips. It just didn't compute. "But Cary? I don't understand how he was involved?"

A young man's voice said, "Let's go."

It seemed to distract Jenna for a second. "I don't know," she finally answered. "Nick said something about how Cary and his dad got into it one night, over the adoption. But he doesn't know."

"I'll find out. Now come home."

"No. We can't. Mom, we saw what you said in the paper. You said Nick's a killer. Everyone says so. But he didn't do it. And we aren't coming back until you know who did. Bye, Mom. I love you."

The line went silent so fast that Emily didn't have a second to plead for her daughter to stay put. *Help will come. I'll take back what I said. I love you. Don't do this. Don't be gone.* Her hand still frozen on the receiver, the room swelled back to its normal size. Gloria was at the door.

"Is she okay?" she asked, sticking her head inside.

Emily set the phone down. She turned to Gloria and nodded. "I think so. Gloria, see if you can get this call traced. Right away."

Gloria stood there expecting more conversation, maybe some details that could set her own worried mind at ease, but Emily didn't offer anything. Instead she scooped up some files, and put them in a drawer. Next she grabbed her purse and coat and started for the door.

"Where are you going?" Gloria asked, moving aside.

"I'm off to see a scumbag lawyer," Emily said, disappearing in the whirlwind of her exit.

### Friday, 1:14 P.M.

"Where's Cary?" Emily Kenyon refused to wait for a response from the latest in a long line of front desk girls at McConnell's over-ferned law office in the Old Mill Building. This one was blond and pretty, like the others. She was also completely out of her league when she tried to stop Emily. The detective would not be denied a meeting. *Appointment or not.* She kept walking toward McConnell's corner office in one of those industrial edifices tastefully reimagined by architects and interior designers into office space that said its occupants were hip and cool and cared about the history of their communities.

Without knocking, Emily pushed the office door open. It smacked into the doorstop with a loud thud. Cary McConnell, who was on the phone staring out the window at the street scene below, swung his burgundy leather chair around at the intrusion.

"Oh baby," he said. Seeing it was Emily, he put on a smile. His perfect teeth were blazingly white against his tanned face. "Miss me?"

"Miss you?" Emily wanted to lunge for him. "I could goddamn kill you."

Cary told the caller on the phone that "an upset client" had just arrived. "Unannounced. I'll call you later." He put the phone down, got up and shut the door behind Emily. She was seething.

"What's going on? Why are you angry at me?"

"Cary, look at my face. This isn't mad. This is furious. Why didn't you tell me you had information about the Martin case?" She felt her hands clench. She wasn't a person who ever thought of hitting anyone, but at that moment Cary McConnell nearly had it coming. If anyone ever did.

"Look, I can't talk about it," he said. "Anything I know is privileged."

"Privileged? My daughter is out there and you're going to use that law crap on me?"

"Emily," he said, putting his hands on her shoulders.

"Don't even think about touching me."

He removed his hands and took a step backward. He looked through the floor-to-ceiling sidelight next to his door. The young blonde was watching from the receptionist's desk. Cary slid out of view.

"I wanted to tell you, but you know I can't. You wouldn't respect me if I did."

"Respect you? I hate you. I can't believe that I slept with you again. That's a joke. I'm so stupid. God, I really know how to pick them."

"Let's not get personal," he said.

*Wrong words,* Emily thought.

"Personal? My daughter is off with some creepy kid. You know something about what's going on in his family. And you don't tell me? No. In fact you take me out for a couple of drinks and go back to my house . . . God, I'm so stupid!"

The blonde was standing up by then. She held the phone up and pointed at it, signaling to Cary that she could call someone if he gave her the word. She mouthed: *"Police?"*

Emily almost laughed at that. *Emily was the police.*

"You're not stupid," Cary said. "And I am sorry. You know me better than that. I care about you. I care about Jenna."

Emily could see this was going nowhere. Everything he said now was some cheap way of trying to calm her so he could get rid of her. *Get on with his day. Make some important deal. Screw the blonde. Whatever.*

"Okay," she said. "Can you at least confirm something?"

"Maybe. Try me."

"Was Nick's dad your client?"

Cary shook his head.

"Did another client talk to you about Nick's adoption?"

Cary, now sitting on the edge of his enormous mahogany desk, looked down at the floor. His face was completely grim. Saying anything was a breach of legal ethics.

"All right. I'll tell you this. My client is another lawyer, working for another party. I don't know the name. I can't give you the lawyer's name, either. But yes, it was about the adoption."

Emily moved closer. "Cary, *please*." She stared at him, imploring with her eyes to tell her what she needed to know.

"I don't know the client. But I'll tell you this. I think it has something to do with Angel's Nest in Seattle."

"Angel's Nest?" The name was vaguely familiar. Emily ran it through her memory. "Angel's Nest?"

"Yeah. Can you believe that? Talk about a blast from the past. That's all I can tell you I know."

Emily turned for the door. The fact that he held information that could have helped the case, could have shed light on Jenna's whereabouts, was bad enough. That he was so damn weak that he caved in and told her anything at all, was proof positive he was the biggest loser she'd ever slept with.

"Dinner tonight?" Cary asked.

Emily stopped and spun around and stood there. If ever she needed Botox it would be from the hostile glance she gave Cary McConnell. She held it longer than any expression she'd ever directed at anyone.

Finally she spoke. "Go screw yourself," she said.

# BOOK TWO
# A DESPERATE LOVE

# CHAPTER EIGHTEEN

*3:15 P.M., twenty-one years ago,
northern Washington*

It began like most grisly discoveries. A hapless individual wanders upon the unthinkable in a place where nothing sinister has ever transpired, where it is completely unexpected. The heart skips a beat. The eyes strain to see through the mind's protective shield of disbelief.

It was that way for Jeremy Landon, a seventeen-year-old from Meridian, Washington. He was paddling the Nooksack River, a meandering waterway that ran lazily from the crisp-edged Northern Cascades to Puget Sound, when a flash of white against a gray sandbar caught his eye. He paddled closer and maneuvered around a fallen cedar that dipped into the icy and swift-moving waters. Incredulity kicked in and adrenaline pumped like a spigot cranked on all the way. Jeremy knew what he'd seen before he poked the large plastic cocoon with a paddle. Hair protruded from an opening on one end. It was long and blond. A mahogany hand with fingertips still accented by cherry-red nail polish fell from a tear in the midsection of the cocoon. He rocked the large bundle with his paddle and yelled, this time, even louder.

"You okay?"

His kayak nudged the sandbar, a grating noise of gravel against the fiberglass hull and the rushing water was the only answer. He kept poking and calling out.

*But nothing.* The plastic-wrapped package just lay there. He knew. He'd found what everyone in the Northwest had been looking for, because it was clear the bundle contained two people. He felt a shiver deep in his bones. It was better than 80 degrees that sunny afternoon, but he was shaking like it was a midwinter snowstorm. The smell of death blew over the water, just under the summer breeze.

"Hey, you all right?" he said, his voice almost a prayer by then. Soft. Pleading. Yet, at the same time, knowing the worst had come to pass.

"Not sure why I called over to them," he told his dad, crying, some days later. "I know it seems stupid and wrong, but I really didn't want it to be those girls. I was hoping it was a couple of store mannequins wrapped up in a painter's tarp."

Shelley Marie Smith and Lorrie Ann Warner had been found.


Olga Morris moved methodically through apartment 703 in the monolithic redbrick building that Cascade University students called "Bucky Towers" or "BT." Buchanan Towers was the kind of building that could only have been dreamed up by architects working on a bare-bones state budget. Floors were warrens of studio and double units. Windows were tiny vertical slots and rooms were sparsely furnished with bunk beds, desks, and a pair of chairs. Upholstered love seats dominated the living room/kitchen combinations.

Olga Morris was a detective for the Meridian Police Department and the irony of the task at hand weighed heavily on her. She was there investigating the murder of two coeds, across the hall from the same apartment that she had lived in when she was a student.

Olga was barely five feet tall, a sparkplug of a woman with short-cropped blond hair and a confident presence that always made her seem taller. Even though a decade had passed since she had lived in the building, it felt exceedingly, and painfully, familiar. The faucet dripped in 703 as it had in her apartment. Blue mineral deposits corroded what was supposed to be a stainless steel sink. The ventilation was poor and she cranked open one of the narrow windows. A faint breeze moved the miniblinds.

Morris retreated to the bedroom. Shelley had the bottom bunk; Lorrie, the top. The bedding had been removed by the crime scene investigators and had been processed for fibers and hairs. Semen and pubic hairs that weren't Lorrie's were found on her sheets, a cheery lemon and orange percale that her mother had bought for her junior year.

*Her mother,* Morris thought as she pulled a desk drawer open, *seemed more upset that her daughter had a boyfriend and was sexually active than the fact she was missing.*

But she was no longer missing. She and Shelley, or rather their remains, had been discovered by a kayaker on the Nooksack River.

"Find anything?" It was Tammi Swenson, the resident aide, who apparently had the uncanny ability to come into any room unnoticed. "How's the case going?"

Olga looked up and managed a smile. She shut the drawer. Tammi was one of those upbeat young women who talked in the peppy cadence of a cheerleader.

"Fine, Tammi. We'll catch whoever it was that killed the girls. You can count on that."

Tammi sipped her lemon-flavored Pepsi Lite, her blue eyes widening. "I hope so. I mean, I know you will. I feel like I'm way out of line, but my supervisor wanted me to ask you again—*nicely*—when you're gonna release the room. I have two girls on the wait list and they're really nice. I mean, a good fit for the floor."

Detective Morris nodded. "I see. Well, tell your manager—"

"—he's just a supervisor. He thinks he's a *manager*, though."

"As I was trying to say," the diminutive detective continued, "the room is available. We've processed everything. Nothing left. This wasn't the crime scene—be sure to tell the new girls that, okay?"

Light streamed through the slashes of glass and the blinds moved once more. Music rumbled from down the hall. It was Fleetwood Mac with Stevie Nicks doing her best to rock Bucky Towers.

Tammi brightened for a moment. "Good to know. Thanks! Can I ask you a question?"

Olga nodded. "Sure, I'll try to answer."

Tammi took a deep breath. The detective had seen that move a time or two, usually when a suspect is being questioned and is suddenly ready to reveal something they think will help throw the interrogator off the track.

Tammi wasn't trying to do that, of course. Instead, she was summoning the courage to ask a question to which she had no business knowing the answer.

"Was it true what the papers said about Lorrie and Shelley?"

"What, specifically?"

"They were, you know, violated."

The detective looked directly into Tammi's vapid blue eyes.

"Dear," she said, "we can use the word rape."

Tammi sighed. She seemed emboldened by the detective's clarification and her precision.

"Okay, were they raped? Because that's what I read."

It dawned on the detective that the girl wasn't in search of salacious details. The look on Tammi Swenson's face was utter fear.

"I can't say one way or another; the case is ongoing. But I will tell you this. Don't go out alone at night. Check your car before you get in it. Don't talk to people you don't know."

The college student stepped backward, toward the door. Olga Morris continued her litany of warnings.

"Be careful. Tell your friends. Tell every girl on the floor, okay? We'll catch him, but we won't catch him until he makes a mistake. And, Tammi, we don't want that mistake to be any more dead girls, okay?"

Tammi gulped hard. Her bulging eyes shifted nervously away from the detective's piercing gaze. "Okay."

What neither Olga nor Tammi knew was that the mistake had already been made.

Coffee rings and a spherical grease spot indicating a doughnut had been consumed while someone reviewed the autopsy report turned Olga Morris's stomach. She wondered if she'd ever get to the place where'd she be so callous as to be able to eat breakfast over the kind of descriptions and images that came with such reports. In her office at the Meridian Police Department, she spread the pictures and documents across her desk. Photos of Lorrie here. Shelley there. A stack of the medical examiner's reports, the interviews conducted by the police in the early stages of the case—when it had been a missing persons case and not yet a homicide. She squared up the edges of each pile of papers and photos. It dawned on her as she moved from one stack to the next that it almost looked like she was playing some freakish version of solitaire.

She knew then the images would never leave her. The bodies, wrapped in plastic, and out in the sun had swelled and burst. Water had chilled the exposed body parts—Shelley's right hand, in particular. Clumps of hair had fallen from her head. Decomp was a nightmare far beyond the imagination of anyone who'd never seen a rotting body.

*Who had the stomach to eat an old-fashioned doughnut and look at these?*

As she scanned the color 8 x 10s, Olga noticed that a ligature of some kind—the ME thought that the marks, smooth, but with a single striation down the center, indicated an electric cord—had cut so deeply into Shelley's wrists that her hands were nearly severed. Lorrie's body had incubated in the plastic wrap, so it was harder to tell. It appeared she'd suffered the same fate. Both had been brutally raped and shot in the back of the head in what laypeople always called execution-style.

*Some execution,* Olga thought as her unblinking eyes scanned. *With what these girls went through they probably were grateful for it to end.*

The ME suggested that both women had died about the same time—but not right after their disappearance. It was tough to pinpoint exactly when they did die. Because of the plastic tarp, the sun had literally cooked their bodies, the greenhouse effect accelerating the decomposition process.

Based on the ME's guess—blowfly larvae, tissue decay, and a copy of the Meridian *Herald* dated July 18, the girls had been dead only a month when discovered. Maybe six weeks. The newspaper, Olga and others surmised, had been used to absorb a puddle of blood—probably at the scene. Since neither victim's head held a single bullet, ballistics would be of no use in tracking the killer. The gun was probably in the bottom of the river, or somewhere. Olga was fixated on the cording used as the ligature.

*Find the cord, find the killer.*

The detective knew that in most instances when a killer used electrical cording it was either an extension cord or some cut from a table lamp or other small household appliance. It was usually just the right length—three feet to tie up a victim.

She looked around her office. A poster of Mt. Baker

hovered above her desk, its white conical form silhou-etted against a fiery sunrise. The bookcase behind her was overstuffed with training manuals, some photos of her cats, and two notebooks that kept cold cases always within the swivel of her office chair. Her credenza was set up as a mini hot beverage bar, with an electric teaket-tle, a wicker basket of dried noodle soups, hot choco-late, instant coffee, and teas. She eyed the teakettle and its electrical cord, but thought better of it.

*What can I use?*

Olga ran her fingers through her short hair, ponder-ing the scenario she was about to employ. She could go down to Property and get a spool of twine, but that was a hassle and she was the type of woman who wanted to do what she wanted, *when* she wanted to do it. The an-swer was on her desk. *The telephone.* She unhooked the wire from the jack and disconnected the phone. Just then Stacy Monroe appeared in the doorway.

"Phone problems?" Stacey, a patrolwoman with a husky voice and warm demeanor, poked her head in-side Olga's office. "That happened to me last week."

Olga smiled. "No. No problem. But you're just in time to lend me a hand—*literally*—with a little experiment. You game?"

Stacey's eyes moved over the photos and files on Olga's desk. Clearly she was intrigued.

"Warner and Smith?" she asked.

The detective nodded, and stepped around from be-hind her desk, the phone wire now coiled in her hand. "I'm just playing around," she said. "I'm glad you're willing. Why don't you sit here?" She pointed to the edge of the desk. "I'm going to tie you up."

Stacey let out a nervous laugh and sat down. "Not like I haven't done that before."

Olga gave the officer a slight wink. "Oh really?"

"Kidding! God, you know my life. You know my husband."

"Yes, I've met Frank." She smiled. "Just how did we get on this topic, anyway?"

"I don't know. You were about tie me up."

"That I was. Put out your arms." Keeping the end of the length in her left hand, Olga started wrapping the beige wire around Stacey's outstretched wrists. Once. Twice. Three times. She stopped and craned her neck to better view the photograph of Shelley Smith's disfigured and decomposed wrists. "Looks like he wrapped around five or six times," she said, almost to herself. "I expect pretty tight, too, but I won't do that to you."

"Good," Stacey said, suppressing a smile. "Something to look forward to later."

Olga played along. "Aren't you just full of surprises?"

The women laughed, cutting the tension of what they were really doing. Olga was mimicking the actions of an unknown killer while poor Stacey who'd just wandered onto her shift had made the mistake of coming by to say hello.

Olga stepped back and admired her technique before unspooling the cording. Stacey stood up and rubbed her wrists. As gentle as Olga had been, the wire still hurt a little. Her wrists were red.

Olga fished a ruler from the top drawer of her desk. "Almost twenty-four inches," she said.

"Good? Bad?"

By then, Olga had started for the door, scooping up her black saddlebag purse, detective's shield, and a tan Gore-Tex coat that was all about function rather than fashion. It was raining outside.

"Bad, I'd say. Bad for someone who works at Builders' Center."

"Huh?"

"You'll see. Thanks, Stacey." With that, her coat swung over one arm, Olga Morris was gone.

# CHAPTER NINETEEN

*1:05 P.M., twenty-one years ago,*
*Meridian, Washington*

The sky was a colander. Olga Morris scanned the parking lot of the Builders' Center off Railroad Avenue as she sought a vacant spot close to the door. Her coat, while waterproof, lacked a hood. Her short hair guaranteed a chilly splash on her scalp. She maneuvered her dark blue Chevy into a reserved parking spot. She did so somewhat reluctantly, but the thought of getting drenched won out over the prospect of being caught taking advantage of the silver and gold shield she carried in her purse.

Inside, she rushed past the contractor's help booth, and a swarm of shoppers filling their carts with caulking, lumber, and the miscellaneous provisions of home repair. The detective was grateful that she was an apartment dweller and hadn't been forced into the nest-building trap so many homeowners had embraced unwittingly.

*Forget a caulking gun; I'd rather carry a Glock.*

She made her way to Arnold Davis's office, a small room behind a ten-foot-wide two-way mirror that allowed the fiftyish manager with gorilla-haired knuckles and a tuft of troll- doll hair protruding from his open collar to keep an eye on the selling floor.

"I'm back, Arnie. Miss me?"

She took off her coat and shook it slightly. Rain puddled the linoleum tile floor. "And I'm soaked!"

Davis looked up from his Tupperware bowl of macaroni salad. Mayonnaise collected at one corner of his tight mouth, and Olga's gaze zeroed in on it in such an obvious manner that he scrambled for a napkin. The room smelled of garlic.

"I assume you're back to talk about Lorrie and Shelley," he said. "We're having a memorial after hours, now that . . . now that we know."

"May I?" Not waiting for an invitation to sit, she pulled up a visitor's chair. "I hadn't heard about the memorial. That's nice. When is it?"

"Saturday at nine."

"Okay, I'll be here."

"If you didn't come about the memorial, then what's up?"

"We're looking into the manner of death," she said, her tone shifting from warmth and concern, to cool and dead serious. "This is very important. I want to talk to you about some of the products you sell."

"What do you mean?" Davis leaned closer and looked toward the open door. Several customers standing in line were looking inside. "Let's shut the door," he said.

Olga nodded and reached over to the knob, teetering on the cheap plastic molded chair, and pulled it in tight. The air was sucked out of the room. Behind the two-way glass the people who'd been staring turned away. There was nothing for them to see, just a silver void and their own gawking images.

She noticed a couple of flyers, slightly balled up in the trash. She knew what they were. Anyone in town would have. Since the girls went missing more than four thousand handbills had been stuck on telephone poles, Laundromat bulletin boards, and anyplace where college students congregated. Across the top of each page was the word MISSING. Underneath those big block letters were Lorrie and Shelley's photos. Both had been employed part-time at Builders' Center.

"None of this has been in the media," Olga said, "and I expect it to stay that way."

"I understand," he said. His eyes looked watery and she wasn't sure if the store manager was tearful or overdosed on garlic, which, judging by the overpowering smell in the room, was Mrs. Davis's chief ingredient in that macaroni salad she'd packed for her husband's lunch.

"Two things turned up by forensics indicate the killer might have had access to a special kind of wire and a clear plastic tarp of a fairly large size. Of course I thought of your store."

"I see." The color drained from his face. "You don't seriously think the killer shopped here?"

Olga shook her head, but it was halfhearted. "No, I'm not saying that."

"Good." Relief washed over Davis's face, but it was only momentary.

Olga Morris dropped the bomb.

"I think he might have worked here," she said.

"Look, Detective," Davis said, rising and suddenly turning his salutation into something formal. "You and your people have talked to *everyone* here. There isn't an employee here who didn't love those girls."

"I'm sure, but this is a crime of sexual brutality, Arnie—and sometimes there is a fine line between love and brutality. In some people, it's a hair trigger between the two."

Davis's face was now red. "You know what I mean. We're like a family here. No one here would ever hurt Lorrie and Shelley."

"Let's hope so. Now I'm going to show you something that might be upsetting. I've cropped out the girls, but I want you to look at two pieces of evidence."

"Oh God," Arnie Davis said, slumping back down, the crimson draining from his face. "What is it?"

"Two pictures. That's all." From her purse, Olga removed two color photographs. She had used strips of copier paper to mask off any bits of human flesh. With her eyes riveted to Davis's she put them on the desk, scooting the Tupperware bowl to one side with her other hand. Davis dropped his gaze to the desktop, a perplexed look on his face.

"What is it?" he asked. "May I?" He indicated the desire to turn the first photograph at another angle. The exposed photographic image was narrow on that one, with the other being broader. Still unsure, he looked up at Olga.

"It's Shelley's wrist," she said.

Davis gasped. It was an involuntary response, one he wished he'd felt coming. The color of Shelley's skin looked so gray for human flesh it almost seemed as if it had been taken with black-and-white film, yet there was a hint of color in the form of thin bands that marked her wrist. He peered closer and felt the macaroni rise slightly in his stomach.

He tapped the photo. "What are those?"

"Ligature marks. Look closely. Do you have anything for sale that might leave that kind of indentation?"

Davis pulled reading glasses from his breast pocket. "It looks like a double line, each mark."

"That's correct. The wire or tubing used to bind the girls' wrists and feet, we think, though I admit it has been difficult determining just whcre they were bound because of the decomposition of the bodies."

"It could be 45V9, electrical," he said. "It's dual wire and is about that thick." He tapped the photo once more. "Pretty flexible, too."

Olga wrote down the stock number. "You sell it here?"

Davis looked up, queasy, but emotionless. "Yes. Not often, but we keep it on spools."

*Spools, good. The killer needed lengths of it to tie them up.*

"All right," she continued. "Before you take me to it, look at the other photo. I'm concerned with the plastic tarp."

"Is that a leg?" he asked, looking closer at the larger of the two images on his desk.

Olga didn't answer him directly. "Focus on the plastic," she said. "Anything like that around here?"

Davis shook his head and rapped his hairy knuckles on his desk. Nerves were kicking in and beads of sweat had collected and started to roll from his temples. "No, I mean . . . I mean it is just clear plastic. That can come from anywhere. It could be Saran wrap for God's sake. Maybe the Safeway people next door can help you."

Olga stood, picked up a Builders' Center pen and directed him back to the photo.

"I realize that," she said. "But look *here*. Look at the edge of the material. It is as plain as day and I don't need to blow it up to prove to you that there's something distinguishing about this tarp."

Davis narrowed his gaze back to the unpleasant business at hand. Just past where the form of the human leg ended, he could make out some whitish cross-hatching. The tarp was at least three millimeters thick, and the edge of it had been embossed with three rows of $X$'s. They ran the full length of the seam, and then disappeared under, what Davis now apparently allowed himself to accept, was one of his part-time cashiers' dead bodies.

"I think I know what that is," he said. He lifted the photo and brought his gooseneck desk lamp closer. He turned the fixture to better illuminate the image. "Looks like Crossbeam's Triple D painter's tarp. The edge is embossed to stop tears."

Olga wrote that down, too. "DDD?"

"Dense, durable, and defect-free. And yes, we sell it here. Not much. It's expensive. Top of the line, but we do sell it. Oh God, no . . ." His voice trailed to a soft whimper as the realization of what it meant set in. "You don't think the killer got his supplies here?"

Olga gathered up the photos and tucked them back inside her oversized purse. "As I said, I don't think he shopped here. But I'd bet my life he works here." She reached for her coat and started for the door. "I want to see Dylan Walker. Is he working today?"

* * *

If there was a more handsome man working at the Builders' Center—in all of Meridian, for that matter—Olga Morris would have been hard pressed to give up a name. Everything about Dylan Walker was perfect. His teeth were whiter than plaster of paris. His eyes were dark and sparkly. At thirty-three, he had a thick mane of dark brown hair that any woman would have killed for. His body was that perfect V: broad shoulders that were square without being too angular and honest-to-goodness six-pack abdominal muscles that revealed themselves whenever he reached for a can of paint on a higher shelf. More than one Meridian woman asked for the eggshell tint base, when she really wanted a flat paint because, well, Dylan Walker had to move that body to reach it.

Olga moved past the plumbing supply section, sinks and toilets displayed with pencil-point lighting that made them look like objets d'art. The smell of gardenias from a shipment of plants in the nursery hung in the soggy air of the rainy day. As she rounded the corner at the end of the aisle, she could hear a woman twittering about something.

". . . Oh really? I thought it would be so much harder to do."

"Depends on how hard you want things."

Olga interrupted Dylan Walker and the now red-faced suburban mom who'd been caught flirting over a stack of travertine tiles.

"Dylan, I could use some help, too," Olga said.

Even though he knew why she was there, he flashed his blazing white smile.

"That's what I'm here for," he said.

The woman with the shopping cart of travertine started to back off slightly. Olga was tiny, blond, quite pretty, and best of all, carried a badge. The shopper must have realized that those attributes easily trumped over-weight, mousey, and an upper lip in need of bleaching.

"Thank you," the woman said, her smile now sagging and her cart inching down the aisle. "If I have any questions, can I ask for you, Dylan?"

Walker stuffed his hands in his pockets; his jeans were loose around his thirty-four-inch waist. He turned and fixed his gaze on the detective. "What do you want now?"

Olga's eyes remained steely, completely unflinching. She let a slight smile part her lips. It was merely for effect and had nothing whatsoever to do with how she felt about him. They'd had it out during the first week of the investigation when he tried to suggest the missing girls were promiscuous.

"They were always coming on to me," he had said.

Olga knew the guy was a creep and just looking at him sent a shiver down her spine.

"You," she said. "Dylan, just like everyone else around here, I want *you*."

# CHAPTER TWENTY

*9:15 A.M., nineteen years ago,*
*Meridian, Washington*

The Whatcom County Superior Courthouse was the jewel of a revitalized Meridian, Washington. It was an old terracotta castle, with five gold-tipped spires that held court over a downtown that had seen a recession come and go, and a kind of renaissance emerge. The art museum had scored a major postimpressionists show—a coup for a city of Meridian's size. Nordstrom store officials had vowed to keep their location just where it was, thus ensuring that the mall going up in the hinterlands of the county would never be more than a second-tier destination.

It had been more than a year since the two Cascade University students were found on the sandbar. It had become a touchstone moment. Nearly every resident could recall where they had been when the news broke. The college had tightened security. The police stepped up neighborhood patrols. In a sense, the city dusted itself off and continued moving forward.

There were problems in the courthouse with the Dylan Walker double-homicide case. What had seemed to have been an exceedingly strong case was imploding. Olga Morris, who'd made the collar for Meridian Police Department, sat stone-faced while lawyers argued about whether or not the defense's theory of another perp could be heard by the jury. Ordinarily that wouldn't have been much of an issue. Blaming someone else had always been in the hip pocket of any half-good—and sometimes desperate—defense lawyer. But this one was tricky. No one could depose Tyler Ticen. No one could get him on the stand. This particular "I-didn't-do-it-he-did" target was stone-cold dead—a suicide without a note.

College student Ticen also worked at Builders' Center. Detective Olga Morris wondered who *didn't* work for Builders' Center. Ticen let several coworkers know that he was interested in Lorrie. An examination of his room on campus showed an overt interest in criminology, sociology, and true-crime books—one of which was about a killer with the same ligature and torture MO.

But he was dead. The suicide, the defense postulated, was a direct result of his growing guilt over the arrest of all-American charmer Dylan Walker. Walker enjoyed the volley of words as the lawyers pitted their wits against each other and case law. He sat somewhat smugly, Detective Morris thought, shifting his weight from one side to the other while keeping a slight smile on his handsome face. His hard brown eyes followed everyone in the courtroom like a roadside artist's painting of Jesus, only creepier. There was nothing soft about Dylan Walker. Hard body. Heart of stone.

*All of that but no place to go but prison.*

Olga hoped Walker would be off at the state penitentiary in Walla Walla as someone's bitch by month's end. But the petite detective was nervous. Her blond hair was longer now; she absentmindedly pushed it behind her ear. She leaned closer to capture every word being said by the lawyers with their backs like a wall in front of the crammed courtroom of spectators. The judge was actually listening to the public defender, a windbag who made grandstanding look like a classy move.

"Your Honor, it is my client's right to present an alternative theory of this case and you know it."

The judge, an old-timer with a bird beak nose and halo of gray hair, frowned. She turned to the prosecutor, a veteran of the worst criminal cases the region had seen, but who wanted to win this one to cap off a relatively distinguished career.

"I don't like this one bit, but I'm allowing it."

The prosecutor kept up a front of righteous indignation.

"Your Honor!"

"Can it!" The judge didn't bother looking at him; she turned her attention back to the bailiff and sighed. "Now let's bring out the jury and finish this case."

Olga felt her stomach dive. *This BS is coming in?* When there was so much that wasn't going to be presented to the jury. It was the system, she knew. But it still felt like a hard kick to the memory of those who'd come across Dylan Walker never to be heard from again. Although the case of the two dead college girls had led him to that courtroom, there were three others that hovered like apparitions throughout the proceedings. One was only twelve years old, a redhead named Brit Osterman.

Her case didn't fit the profile that the FBI had originally crafted for Meridian PD when the two Cascade coeds first went missing. Too young, they insisted. But then again, Olga knew, Dylan Walker was sixteen at the time. *Maybe she was his first? The first sip of bloodlust had to come from someplace.* Olga was all but convinced he killed the sixth grader.

The strongest link between Walker and a victim was a Seattle woman who went out for a jog in Walker's neighborhood. Tanya Sutter never came back. Her body was found a week later in a thicket of blackberries and fireweed off the old highway between Seattle and Tacoma. She had been wrapped in plastic. Bound. Shot. Dumped. Too much time had passed on that one and though interrogators tried to break Walker to force a confession, the man was Teflon. Nothing seemed to faze him. His gaze was cool, smug, almost indifferent. Not one ounce of indignation.

"I'm not a guy," Olga Morris had told the chief after that interrogation, "but if I were, I'd want to pop anyone who even made the suggestion that I brutalized some woman for kicks. But not this self-absorbed charmer. He just smiled those pearly whites and shrugged. It was like we were cutting into his time to kill."

There was suspicion of another victim, a girl named Steffi Miller who went missing while Walker attended a church youth camp in Nampa, Idaho, the summer of his senior year in high school. Her body was never found. In all, Dylan Walker had been linked to five

dead or missing: Brit, Tanya, Steffi, Lorrie, and Shelley.

*Unluckiest man in the world or serial killer?* The press
had already decided. More than a hundred reporters had
descended on the gold-pinnacled courthouse to write
about the nation's most handsome killer. Most were
women. All wanted an exclusive interview, but Dylan
Walker played hard to get.

"I'd love to, Connie," he'd say, "but my lawyer is
dead set against my talking to anyone right now. But if
I did give an interview, I'd do it with you."

He'd used the same line, or a variation thereof, over
and over. "There's plenty of me to go around, once I'm
exonerated," he said more than once.

Olga Morris sat still in her spectator's chair just behind the prosecution's table, her blood boiling. She'd
already testified so she had nothing more to say officially. But she could barely contain herself as she
overheard the twitters of Walker's burgeoning fan
club. No one called him "Dylan Daniel Walker" in the
three full-names fashion that was usually accorded to
the suddenly notorious.

Instead they dubbed him "Dylan" or "Dashing Dylan,"
which finally morphed in to just plain "Dash."

The adulation made her skin crawl in unqualified
revulsion. She knew that part of the problem was
America's fascination with a handsome killer. The
media fostered that kind of twisted thinking. Victims
were pretty. Killers were ugly. But every once and a
while the good-looking stumble. Ted Bundy was often
described in press accounts as handsome and charming. But Dylan Walker was no Ted Bundy. Or rather,

Ted Bundy was no Dylan Walker. If a photo lineup was made of Tom Cruise, a young Robert Redford, or Paul Newman, Dylan Walker, and Ted Bundy and a woman was requested to pull out the most handsome and least handsome in the array, Bundy and Walker would be the ones pulled—and Bundy would be on the losing end of the deal.

Even though there had been endless discussion about Walker, most of it was based on his looks, not his life. Not much was known about him. He'd been raised by a grandmother in Seattle. He was an only child. He had excelled at school, but barely graduated. He'd been deeply religious. And after those formative years, the trajectory of his life became exceedingly murky. Olga dug in deep but since he never held a job very long, never filed a tax return, didn't have any credit cards, and never had any close relationships, no one could really track where he lived at any given time.

*Or what he'd been doing.*

Olga thought of him as one of those sharks she'd seen at the Vancouver Aquarium about two hours' drive from Meridian. He commanded the tank with stunning and relentless evil, cold eyes following every twitch of movement in the swirling clear waters of the expansive tank. Slowly he swam, almost bored and disinterested. He worked alone. Quietly. Stealthily. It was as if he wasn't even paying attention to anything at all. But he was. He did what he was born to do: *kill*. He did so quickly, effortlessly, and then moved on, crimson staining the water. As if it was nothing. He was an evil thing of beauty; lean and streamlined. That's what Dylan Walker was, the detective believed, a cunning predator with no attachment to anyone or anything. He was a killing machine.

### 7:15 A.M., twenty-one years ago, Seattle

"You know you want to go with me tomorrow."

Tina Winston was shy about going to the Walker trial all by herself. Sure she was an independent woman, but she also knew that joining the media circus was out of character. She thought she could summon the courage only if one of her best friends, Bonnie Jeffries, came along. Plus the long drive, about two hours, would be more fun with Bonnie in tow. She even dangled an offer of dinner at the new restaurant just south of Meridian.

"Come on," Tina pleaded. "It will be fun. The place is absolutely spectacular. The chandelier in the lobby is made of one thousand Waterford goblets turned upside down. It sparkles like diamonds against velvet."

Bonnie made a face. "Oh, I don't know," she said. "I have a lot to do around here tomorrow." Carrying her handheld phone, she wandered her living room, and then down the hall to the laundry room as she listened to Tina try to convince her. Even so, her mind was elsewhere. She wondered how one person could make such a mess. She worked four 10-hour days to ensure that she'd have Fridays to get the place ready for the weekend.

"My days off are precious, you know."

Tina pressed Bonnie. "What have you got planned?"

"Nothing much. I've got a ton of cleaning to do."

"Precious days off? So you want to spend it cleaning your house?"

Bonnie let out a little laugh. "Not everyone can afford a housekeeper." It was a bit of a dig. Bonnie was a low-level manager. Tina ran her own gift-basket business and she was making big money doing it, having landed an upscale retailer as a major account.

"Not fair. You could have joined me, you know," Tina said referring to her offer of a partnership four years ago.

"Don't remind me." She pinned the phone between her chin and shoulder and reached for the laundry basket. She turned on the water.

"Don't you ever feel you're in a rut?" Tina was going for the kill. She knew that Bonnie's life was work and nothing else. She didn't have a boyfriend. No kids. No social scene to speak of outside of church.

Bonnie watched the washer tank fill. She measured the detergent.

"Okay, you got me," she said. "I'll do it. Let's go check out Dylan Walker. He's cute for a killer."

"Stop *that*. He's not convicted. And I don't think he will be. He's a victim of an overzealous police department. You know the type that wants to put someone— really *anyone*—behind bars."

Bonnie dumped her clothes into the washer. The lid bounced shut. "That's your theory."

"Yes, and I'm sticking to it," Tina said, her mood now elevated because Bonnie had agreed to go. "See you at seven."

Bonnie looked at herself in the mirror. She dropped her robe and stared hard. She was fifty pounds overweight, with a roadmap of stretch marks across her abdomen. In the dim light of evening, she tried to imagine herself as someone prettier. Like Tina. But Bonnie knew that the god of good genes had saddled her with her mother's nondescript features and her father's big-boned frame. She had a plain face, pleasant brown eyes, and dark curly hair. Tina was pencil thin and strawberry blond. Whenever they went out together, men gravitated toward Tina. Bonnie had tried all diets from Weight Watchers to a liquid protein shake to the Scarsdale diet. She'd try in earnest for a couple of weeks, but in the end she'd give up. She'd been to so many free makeovers at cosmetic counters across downtown Seattle that she probably could work for any of the big makeup manufacturers. She hated how she looked. Part of her also hated Tina.

What does one wear to a murder trial? Bonnie Jeffries mulled it over for a minute, searching for control top underwear and her best bra. She selected a pair of black slacks and an aqua blouse; both were loose enough to make her have that just-lost-weight sensation that she welcomed above anything. Loose clothing was like dieting without having to do without. Bonnie was barely thirty, but she looked like someone's middle-age mother. She stacked up her clothes for the next morning on her dresser and trotted off to the kitchen. Rum Raisin ice cream out of the carton sounded so good.

# CHAPTER TWENTY-ONE

*12:25 P.M., twenty-one years ago,*
*Meridian, Washington*

It was as difficult a call as a detective can ever make, aside, of course, from the bone-chilling one that comes in the middle of the night and begins with, "I'm sorry to be phoning you with this news. Your child was involved in a very serious car accident . . ."

Olga Morris had never imagined the verdict would have been split, though the four long days of deliberation had sent a surge of worry through her system to the point of near overload. Dylan Walker was guilty; she knew it with every fiber of her being. He was a cold-blooded killer. He was a killing machine in an appealing package. Dylan Walker was no more human than that. He'd been found guilty, thank God, but despite the best efforts of a prosecution that had done its homework, he was only convicted of a lesser charge—two counts of second-degree murder.

*This is ludicrous,* Olga thought. *Since when did binding a couple of women with wire, wrapping their*

*bodies like pupae, and dumping them in a river to es-
cape detection look like anything but first-degree murder?* The TV and newspaper pundits exalted the defense
for punching holes in the case by bringing in the other
possible suspect, but even more so for getting it into
the heads of some jurors that Dylan Walker had never
planned to murder anyone. That it was some kind of
accident. What were they thinking?

When the jury filed in, Olga nearly did a double
take in the defendant's direction.

For a nanosecond she was all but certain that Walker
had winked at juror number 4, a leggy brunette who
drank in the defendant with her big blue eyes.

*What in the world is going on here?*

That and the verdict were a sucker punch to the gut.

*How did this happen?*

Olga didn't speak to any of the reporters hovering
around the courthouse stairwell. Not that any really
wanted to speak with her. After the flurry of gasps and
running for the doors, those with mics and notebooks
wanted to talk to the defense—not anyone associated
with the prosecution. The man with the trail of dead
beauties was a bona fide star, the big media "get."

Olga retreated to her office on the first floor of the
Meridian Police Department. She was almost in tears
as she pulled out the Walker case file. It was thick,
dog-eared, and dirty a year after she'd compiled most
of its contents. The pictures of the bodies as they were
first found along the sandbar still roiled her stomach. It
was all so utterly senseless. Inside, she found Shelley's
mother's phone number in Olympia. Mrs. Smith was
shaky when she got on the line.

"I'm afraid the news is mixed, Mrs. Smith. I'm terribly sorry. I didn't want you to hear it on the TV first."

There was a long pause. Olga could hear the mother of a dead girl brace herself by sitting down. It was a good idea.

"I heard they came back with a verdict," Shelley's mom said. "What did they say?"

Olga Morris felt like a complete loser, like she'd failed the woman on the other end of the line. She had promised to call with the verdict, but now regretted it. At the time she was sure the verdict would have gone completely in the prosecutor's favor. That was before the defense used the tragedy of the Ticen suicide to diffuse the truth.

"Like I said, mixed," she began, tentatively, still searching for words that would ease a broken heart. None, she knew, could ever be found. "Two counts of second-degree murder."

Olga waited, but Mrs. Smith just breathed softly into the line.

"I'm so, so sorry. Shelley and Lorrie deserved so much more than that."

Mrs. Smith finally spoke. Her words were measured, but there was an underpinning of loathing coming from deep inside. She was fighting it, the kind of churchgoer that she was. But it was undeniable. "Both girls are in heaven now. And after seeing how the world is up in your part of the state, I'd say they're both better off for it. Shame on a system that lets a man steal two beautiful lives as if they were nothing."

The words pierced Olga's broken heart. She knew they'd failed those girls. Now the worst kind of human being—the kind who can only mimic compassion or approximate the affect of humanity—was getting the biggest break of his life.

"As I said, I'm so, so sorry."

The line went dead. Mrs. Smith had hung up without saying good-bye.

Two weeks later insult was added to injury when sentence was passed. Twenty years to life for each girl's death. The absolute blow: The sentence was concurrent. Dylan Walker would likely see the light of day.


"Ready?" Tina Winston looked suspiciously at Bonnie Jeffries standing in the doorway wearing her nearly threadbare quilted bathrobe. "You don't look it."

Bonnie was perplexed. She drew her robe belt tighter and opened the door wider to let Tina inside.

"God, you can be so obtuse, Bonnie."

Tina breezed into the foyer and shut the door behind her. "We're going up to Meridian today, right?" Tina put her hand on her hip and regarded her friend impatiently. She was nearly giddy. She tried to fake a frown, but she was obviously so excited about something she couldn't even be in a teasing mood.

"Dylan Walker wants to meet me. He sent me a personal letter." Without taking her eyes off Bonnie, now sitting on the living room sofa, Tina unclasped her Louis Vuitton handbag. With the flourish of a waiter presenting some fabulous meal under a crystalline dome, she handed Bonnie an oversized envelope.

It was addressed to Tina Winston. The return address was D. Walker, c/o Whatcom County Jail, Meridian.

"He actually wrote to you?"

Tina grinned broadly. "*Finally*. I sent him at least three notes of encouragement throughout that travesty of justice up there in Meridian." She slid down next to Bonnie and, unable to wait a second longer, pulled the letter from the envelope like it was a Christmas present she'd been dying to open.

"This is stupid, Tina," Bonnie said flatly.

"Maybe you won't think so when you read it."

Bonnie was skeptical, but she put on her red-framed readers anyway. Dylan Walker's handwriting was surprisingly crisp, nearly feminine. It looked almost as if he'd never developed a style of his own after learning penmanship in third grade. Ascenders and descenders were perfect in form and angle.

*Dear Tina: Your letters have been so welcome and I'm sorry there has been delay in my response. You cannot believe how much mail I get here. There's no way I could answer each and every note, but your sincerity and genuine interest in my case really touched me. I've suffered more than any man I've ever known. I'm not one for pity, but I have no idea why God would do this to me. All I've tried to do is live a good, honest life. See where it got me? Thank you for the photo . . .*

Bonnie looked over the top of her glasses and made a face. "You sent him your picture?"

Tina shrugged as if no defense was needed.

"So? Even if he's guilty—which he's most definitely *not*—he's headed to prison. He's not going to hurt anyone from there. I'm more worried about him than anything. I don't have to remind you that famous people are victimized in prisons across this country every day. They're targets of the riffraff incarcerated there."

Bonnie kept her mouth shut. *What could she say? Dylan Walker was not some innocent man pulled off the street and tried for a double homicide on a whim. He* was *the goddamn riffraff.* Tina Winston was smitten with Walker, and he was playing her for all she was worth, which was considerable. She went back to reading the note. She breathed in, catching a slight whiff of cologne, which surprised her. She didn't think prisoners were allowed to wear cologne.

> *. . . you are lovely, if you don't mind my saying so. You also look like the kind of person who can see into someone's soul. I long for a friendship with someone like you. I've added your name to the visitation list. If you come, please tell them you are a lifelong friend. I am not allowed to meet with anyone I didn't know before my arrest. I hate to ask you to lie, but it is the only way. Fridays are good. I'll be here another month before being transferred to the prison in Shelton.*
>
> *Peace, Dylan Walker*

Bonnie took off her glasses and shifted her quilted bulk. The couch creaked. She was fatter than she'd ever been and she hated herself for it. She looked into her friend's eyes with utter disbelief. Tina was a stunner. She had a successful business. Her figure? She loathed it when Tina showed up in some crop top and shorts in the summertime weather. Her legs were impossibly long. She actually had ankles. As far as Bonnie Jeffries could imagine, there was no one on the planet who had more going for her than her friend, Tina Winston.

"I'm uneasy about this," Bonnie finally said. "I don't think this is a good idea whatsoever."

"Are you judging me?"

"No, I'm worried about you."

"Worried or jealous?"

"Jealous of your relationship with a serial killer? Jesus, Tina."

Tina reached for the envelope and Bonnie handed it over.

"Look, I'm going up to see Dylan and I need your support. I've been there for you, haven't I? When you had problems with your car, who picked you up and drove you to the grocery store?"

"That's hardly the same thing," Bonnie sniffed. "We're talking about hanging out at a jail, not going to Safeway's frozen-food aisle."

Tina giggled. "Come on," she said. "It'll be so fun."

"I can see it will be fun for you. But what do I get out of it?"

"Lunch at the new restaurant . . . and better yet, you get to live vicariously through me."

The last words almost made Bonnie cry. She'd lived vicariously through Tina Winston for most of her adult life. But the promise of the advertised ninety-nine-item salad bar won out over her good sense and bruised ego.

"Okay. Okay. I'll go with you."

Tina flashed her disarming smile. "You won't regret it," she said. "I promise."

The jail trusty was a man in his fifties who had practically made a second home of the Whatcom County Jail. He'd never done anything that sent him up to Washington's prisons in Walla Walla, Monroe, McNeil Island, or Shelton. He was what the jail called the ultimate boomerang. In time, he was known merely as Boomer, a name that was laughable considering his rail-thin frame. *Sticks* or even *Humpback* would have been more apropos. He pushed a metal library-style cart with the day's mail from one cell to the next, passing out love letters, legal missives, and even the penny shopper.

"Want this magazine?" he said to a hollow-eyed kid in on a drug possession charge, a misdemeanor.

The kid accepted the rolled-up magazine, a copy of *Discover*. "Hell no, I don't like that shit. Science kept me from my GED. Besides, isn't that a federal offense?"

"Huh?" Boomer said, his cart now squarely in front of the punk's cell.

The kid poked the magazine back through the bars. "Giving out someone's mail, man?"

Boomer let out big laugh. "What are they going to do? Send me to jail?" The kid had set him up with a joke. *Nice*.

"All that shit for Walker?" The kid pointed to a bloated canvas bag resting on the bottom shelf of the cart.

Boomer nodded. "Yeah, Mr. Hollywood gets more fan mail than that twink Tom Cruise. Sends out more than anyone here, too. Should probably have a personal postmark by now. Maybe even a stamp with his mug on it?"

The kid did his best to look cool and tough. He was neither. "Yeah, you lick the back of it and die."

Halfway down the corridor, Dylan Walker could hear the exchange between the trusty and the young inmate. It didn't make him angry, though if he was in closer range and he thought Boomer and the punk knew he heard them, he'd have put up some kind of a fight. *But not then*. Instead, he hurried to finish the letter he was writing. But he was neat. He didn't like to rush. Every stroke held some kind of power.

> *. . . I long for a friendship with someone like you. I've added your name to the visitation list. If you come, please tell them you are a lifelong friend.*

> *Peace, Dylan Walker*

By the time Boomer arrived at Walker's holding cell, he had finished addressing the envelope. He wanted it to get out in the day's mail. The letter was addressed to a woman in Acton, California.

"Here you go, Boomer," Walker said, his smile reflecting the dim light of the buzzing fluorescent tubes that hung from ceiling chains over the corridor. "Just ten to go out today. I'm behind." He laughed a little and handed over a stack of letters, envelopes of varying sizes, postage affixed by the senders in response to the jail's request for self-addressed, stamped envelopes for inmate mail.

Boomer opened the canvas bag and started feeding mail to Walker. "If you thought you were behind before, meet your future bout with writer's cramp."

Walker beamed as letter after letter was passed through the bars.

"This is stupid," he said. "You should just give me the damn bag."

"You know the rules. They consider you a suicide risk. The drawstrings might be too tempting for a guy like you."

"Tempting? Why would I ever want to hurt myself? I've never felt more wanted in my life." He topped off his revelation with a big smile.

*I'll bet you do, you psycho,* Boomer thought. Instead he said, "That's it for today. Better get busy. The mail train from Seattle's running tonight. You're getting another load tomorrow, hot stuff."

# CHAPTER TWENTY-TWO

*Friday, 2:26 P.M.,*
*Cherrystone, Washington*

**E**mily knew the name, Angel's Nest, because it had been in the news intermittently when she was a student at the University of Washington in the early 1980s. In the almost twenty years since then, she hadn't given it a single thought. She turned on the teakettle and waited for the whistle. *Angel's Nest. What was that all about? Cary had said it was a "blast from the past." She remembered that the agency had been in the news. There had been some kind of scandal.* When the boiling water rumbled, and then whistled, she dropped a bag of chamomile and a squeeze of honey from a plastic teddy bear bottle into a cup. Steam rose up from the spout as she poured. Everything that could be wrong, was just that, *wrong.* She was still jittery and angry at Cary, heartbroken that Jenna wouldn't just come home, and a wreck over the whole idea that she didn't know her daughter as well as she thought she had. *How could she have been so blind? How can they seem so* *close one day, and the next be separated by a triple homicide? Herbal tea, something her mother prescribed for everything from a broken date to a hysterectomy, sounded good.*

She sipped it from the cup Jenna had painted at the Ceramic Castle; orange poppies spun around the rim. She was unsure exactly what had been the source of the agency's troubles. She'd called David to see if he remembered anything, but she got his answering machine—his voice sounding puffed up and all-important, even when he wasn't there to speak. She left a message. Next she did a quick search of the Internet, which only turned up the scantest of information. Angel's Nest was an adoption agency shut down in the mid-1980s over charges that its president had not only misappropriated funds but also somehow snipped through government regulations when it brought babies into the country. One woman from Tacoma even had to give her baby back.

*But how would Nick Martin have been involved with this agency, anyway?*

Taking her steaming cup down the hall to her office, Emily lingered in the doorway of Jenna's bedroom. *Her old bedroom.* The screensaver on the Mac was a digital aquarium with a pair of pink kissing Gouramis doing what they did best, over and over. Emily flopped herself on the pineapple-post bed, patting the pink-and-yellow quilt her grandmother had made. Memories of her daughter flooded the room. She could smell Jenna's Vanilla Fields perfume, a gift from Shali that Christmas. Over the bed was a framed print of The Little Mermaid, a souvenir from a trip to Disneyland. Beanie Babies left over from the long-abandoned col-

lecting craze took refuge on a shelf. A purple Princess
Diana teddy bear was the prize, a plastic "tag protec-
tor" dangled from its paw. *So innocent then. All of us
were.* Jenna was smart. She was capable. She cared
about doing the right thing. Emily sat still, breathing in
her daughter, then went to her office and sat in front of
her computer.

*You'll be home soon,* she thought. *I'll never be too
busy to listen.*

The screen snapped to life and she typed in the web
address for a Seattle daily paper and clicked on the link
for the archives. She typed in "Angel's Nest," hit Search,
and two small items popped up. One was a brief mention
in a column, quoting a detective who had worked a
homicide case that had tangential ties to Angel's Nest.
The other was an item that indicated that all the assets
seized by the government had been dispersed at auc-
tion, five years after the scandal. Emily thought there
would be more; it had seemed like a bigger story. She
searched again, but nothing more came up. It was then
that she noticed the archives only went back to 1990.

*What was it?*

She tapped out the name of the detective quoted in
the article: *Olga Morris.*


**Friday, 3:39 P.M.,**
**Salt Lake City airport**

The reader of the newspaper wadded it up and threw
it into an airport trash receptacle. A teenage girl chatted with her boyfriend on her cell phone. A woman
scrounged through her purse to come up with enough
change for an Orange Julius. A businessman's fingers

worked over the keyboard on his laptop, something apparently so important that it couldn't wait. Amid the blasé world of the airport concourse, the reader of the newspaper wanted to scream. The article that so enraged the reader was an account of the Cherrystone murders, discovered after the tornado had swept through parts of the eastern Washington town. The story recounted how Mark and Peg Martin, and their son, Donovan, had been shot and left for dead. The storm had taken what was likely a family rampage and twisted it into a perfect crime.

*Perfect crime? Not even close. Perfect screwup was the real truth.*

Missing from what had once been the Martin family home was the eldest boy, Nicholas. Also missing was the chief detective's daughter, Jenna.

*Find the cop's daughter. Find the boy. Finish the job.*

*Friday, 6:50 P.M.,*
*northern Washington*

Running a rototiller at fifty-one was not easy. With a smile on her face, Olga Morris-Cerrino cursed her late husband's idea that they should move out to the country, till the land, raise exotic sheep.

"It will make us more interesting," Tony Cerrino had joked when he sold her on the idea of the mini farm on the outskirts of Whatcom County. "You know . . . gentleman farmer types."

*Easy for you to say,* she thought back then. *Even more so now.*

Olga brushed the sweat from her brow, leaving a

muddy streak on her already tanned forehead. How she missed him. How she wished that he hadn't taken that business trip that icy November.

"Damn you," she said softly, standing in the cookie-batter soil of what would have been her husband's best year ever gardening. "I loved you so much." Her arms ached, but she wasn't unhappy about what she'd accomplished. Her eyes ran over the plot of creased earth behind her. The rows were perfectly straight.

"No need for strings if you have a good eye," he had told her that first day they'd planted. "And you have a good eye, my dear."

She'd sowed popcorn, sweet corn, and a brand-new variety of buttercup squash that early evening. She'd planted more than she could use. That was by design. She knew the old women at the Whatcom Food Bank would be pleased when harvest came that fall. She'd arrive with a red wagon of produce fit for the tables of the finest restaurants in the county. But it would be for those who really needed it. Doing that would be hard this fall. It would be the first without him.

Olga Morris-Cerrino watched the sun dip below her white clapboard house, as a chilling breeze worked its way across the meadow, then closer, to the garden where she stood. She zipped up her jacket and checked the tiller for gas. It was getting dark, but once she got going it was hard to stop. Evenings in the country were like that. Tony knew it. He loved it. And despite everything she had once thought about herself, she'd grown to love it, too. Yet the breeze right then was like an icy hand on her neck. When she heard the phone ring she set the tiller down and used the intrusion as the excuse she needed to go inside.

She swung open the gingerbread-framed screen door and went to the antique wall phone that Tony had re-outfitted for the modern age. The change kept with the integrity of the home, he'd say. But it was wall mounted and hard to get to. So much for modern.

"Hello?" Olga said, into the mouthpiece, out of breath.

"Olga Morris?"

She pulled the zipper on her jacket. "Who's calling?"

"I'm Emily Kenyon, sheriff's detective, Cherrystone."

Sliding off one sleeve, then the other, Olga sighed. "Oh, I'm sorry, but I've already made my donations for the year."

"Detective Morris, I'm not collecting for anything. I'm calling for your help."

"It's Cerrino now, and I'm retired." The cat jumped on the kitchen counter and Olga frantically shooed it down. "Down, Felix!"

"Huh?"

"The cat. Never mind. You're calling about?"

"It's about an old case you worked," Emily said. "Do you have a moment?"

The cat was now on the floor, and Olga was at ease. She took a seat on the old oak stool and absentmindedly started straightening the paper clips, tape holders, and scrap paper she kept by the phone. Felix yowled, his Siamese lineage coming through loud and clear.

"They're *all* old cases," Olga continued. "I'm retired, as I said. Now is not the best time, can you give me a few? I have a cat here that if he doesn't eat he'll scratch a bloody groove through my leg."

Emily laughed. "I know the type. I'll call you in say, a half hour?"

"Fine. And what case was it?"

"Angel's Nest."

There was a long silence and for a second Emily assumed that Olga Morris-Cerrino had hung up.

"You still there?" she asked.

Again a short pause.

"Yes," Olga answered, sounding a little rattled. "I'm here. Yes, call me. I don't know how I can help you, but I'm glad that someone is looking into that mess."

Olga Morris-Cerrino was still all that she had been years ago. She was still blond without the help of a bottle. She was still tiny, with a trim figure unchanged by childbirth or bad eating habits. Faint lines collected at the corners of each eye, but no one really noticed them. *How could they?* When her eyes sparkled as they always did, no one saw anything else. She fed the cat and took a Diet Coke from the refrigerator, popped the top, and filled a water glass. She sliced a lime and dropped it in; fizzy pop bloomed over the sides. The call hadn't really surprised her. She had no idea what case the detective from Cherrystone was working just then, but she never thought Angel's Nest or any of the people associated with it would just fade into dust.

*The world just doesn't work that way,* she thought. *Evil doesn't really die.*

While she waited for the phone to ring, Olga meandered around the first floor, a space filled with antique furniture and carpets. Over a settee with a pin-point gallery light on timer was her husband's most prized possession—an original Norman Rockwell portrait. It was a schoolgirl standing outside of a gymnasium as a group of cheerleaders practiced. It was called *Dreamer*. It was the image of his mother, who had posed for Rockwell when she was a girl in Stockbridge, Massachusetts. The painting had been a family heirloom and was worth tens of thousands.

Olga pushed the pager button for the cordless phone she kept in the den—the one thing she'd done that defied her husband's wishes, but he was gone and there would be no arguing about being "true to the house." The phone handset called out to her from a sofa cushion in the living room. She fished it out, put her feet up on an ottoman, and waited for the earthquake that was sure to come when the phone rang again.

It had been only a matter of time.

Jenna finished the conversation with her father, cut short by a cheap cell phone they'd stolen from a man at the counter of the minimart. The theft was completely impulsive, but after being called a murderer, a kidnapper, and an "artsy" high school student, just about anything went by then. Jenna looked at Nick with disapproving eyes. His new look would take some getting used to. Nick had shaved his head earlier this morning and a slight rash had developed, making his pasty white scalp look something like a bruised strawberry. He sat glumly on the curb, the light of day eclipsed by the hour.

"My dad said my mom called about us," she said.

"No surprise there. I knew we couldn't trust her."

"She's my *mom*. And we *can* trust her. She called my dad, not the FBI."

Nick lit a cigarette, his last one. "As far as you know."

That hurt a little and Jenna didn't try to hide it. "Don't be like that. Look, both my parents say the same thing. We need to turn ourselves in. We didn't do anything wrong."

Nick wasn't buying any of that. He slumped back down on the curb. The mine building was rancid, creaky, and drafty. His family was gone, his house was gone. His life was over.

"Nobody's calling you a killer," he said.

Jenna pushed her long dark hair over her shoulder. He had a point. Words were so stupid, so hurtful, and at that time, so useless. They could hurt, but not calm.

"In her message," she said, finally, "my mom asked my dad if he knew anything about Angel's Nest."

Nick exhaled and his eyes followed Jenna as she moved closer and sat next to him. He turned his gaze to the grimy floor and searched for words.

"My dad warned me about that," he said while patting his irritated scalp. "He said to me . . . before he died . . ." Nick let himself go back to that upstairs bedroom, back into the depths of the worst memory he'd ever hold.

*"Get out . . . son . . . go. Not safe. Angel here. Hide. You're in danger. Won't stop until you're dead."*

"Angel?" Jenna asked. "He called you angel?"

"He never called me that. He called me NickNack, but not *Angel*. I thought it was some weird comment, you know, like seeing an angel before you die."

Jenna couldn't make the connection. "What do you think he was saying?"

"I don't know, but I thought he was warning me about an angel now."

"Or Angel's Nest?"

Nick nodded, it seemed to make sense. "My dad said that was the name of the adoption agency in Seattle. It was what he and Cary McConnell argued about. We're going there."

"We can't." Jenna could feel fear rising in her.

"I need to know," he said. "You can stay. You can go back to your mom." When he said the word "mom," his voice cracked slightly, almost imperceptibly. "I'm going."

Jenna knew then that it was too late for her. She'd lost any choices she could make when she decided to help Nick. She cared about him. She trusted him. She thought that he could even be right about her own mother. Maybe she couldn't understand. Maybe she wouldn't really believe them.

"I know where Shali keeps an extra set of car keys," Jenna said.

# CHAPTER TWENTY-THREE

*Saturday, 6:26 A.M.,*
*Cherrystone, Washington*

**E**arly Saturday morning two cars were headed out of Cherrystone. One, a bland Honda Accord driven by the detective in search of her daughter and a killer, and the other, a VW bug with a flapping ragtop driven by the suspected killer and the same daughter. Neither of the drivers or the sole passenger knew the other was on its way to the same destination, for the identical purpose. Getting out of town hadn't been an easy prospect for either. One had to steal a car; the other had to squirm a little.

Emily Kenyon didn't exactly argue with Sheriff Brian Kiplinger to leave the investigation, but he wasn't thrilled about it. "I know you have personal problems, Emily," he had said, "but we're up to our necks in alligators here and we need you to wrestle a few."

It was a lame metaphor, but Emily knew what he meant. Her investigation had been stymied by her daughter's inadvertent involvement, the FBI had offered to step in, and the Spokane police had drawn their line in the sand, too.

"I get that." Her dark eyes flashed. "But, look, I think that some of the answers to what happened at the Martin place will be found in Seattle."

Kip crossed his burly arms and narrowed his gaze. "And maybe your daughter, too?"

Emily bristled at the mention and wished she'd just called in sick. "Jenna is not a runaway. She's not a victim here. I know she's just trying to help a friend. I believe that. Why is that so hard for you to accept?"

"Emily, I'm your boss." Kip shifted his frame in the chrome-accented chair that was the only luxury in his office. He rocked backward and steadied the chair by putting his foot on the leg of his desk. "You're talking to me like I'm your ex. I don't know what happened. I'm glad you think Jenna is all right. But I just talked to a woman who buried her sister, brother-in-law, and nephew out at Green View two days ago and she's none too happy that we haven't picked up Nick— guilty or not."

The dialogue played in her head as she climbed the mountain pass where yellow flashing lights advised drivers to watch for falling rocks. The remaining snow piled on the shoulder was coated in gray sludge and had almost disappeared. She could see the conical yellow and pale green forms of skunk cabbage as it fanned out along the swampy edges of a waterfall-fed bog. The AM radio talk show that had kept her somewhat entertained, out of her own head for almost an hour, began to crackle. The blowhard's voice faded.

She pushed FM and the radio scanned through several Latino stations before landing on Celine Dion singing that song from *Titanic*.

*Jenna loved that movie when she was a little girl. She thought that Leonardo DiCaprio was the cutest boy ever. Cute and artsy. Maybe that's how she views Nick Martin?*

As Celine worked her vocal chords into an unqualified frenzy, Emily began to wonder once more why Olga Morris-Cerrino had changed her mind and would only speak to her in person.

"Some things are better covered face-to-face," she had said when Emily had called back that evening. "Come up here. I'll pull my files. I might even fix you lunch."

"Lunch would be good," she said, before saying good-bye.

She didn't know it, but a half hour ahead of her Honda, Shali Patterson's stolen VW sped down the mountainside, the radio playing the same Celine Dion song.

### Saturday, 10:45 A.M.,
### Mercer Island, Washington

Mercer Island, Washington, barely felt like an island. It was pinned to Lake Washington by Interstate 90 and a pair of bridges, one of them floating on the surface of Seattle's Lake Washington on enormous concrete pontoons. The lake was so deep and a suspension bridge so costly, that at the time of its conception a floating bridge seemed a good idea. Mercer Island was named for Asa Mercer, who'd famously brought women from back east to marry the loggers carving out the great forests. It seemed that Mercedes Benzes, BMWs, and Jags were the only cars that exited the interstate to the island's addresses.

David Kenyon was a surgeon making big bucks, but not so much that he had been forced to live on the island with Microsoft millionaires, sports stars, and the very few that actually carried a whiff of old money from the lumber and gold of Seattle's past. His girlfriend, Dani, however, was a social climber of the highest order. She stretched the doctor's income like a tube top on a stripper—to near breaking. But she got the island house. Not waterfront, but view. And not peak-a-boo view, either. The house was a 1960s rambler that if plunked down somewhere in the Midwest wouldn't cost more than $150,000. On Mercer Island, it was a cool million dollars.

It wasn't all that early in the morning, but Dani was in bed and David was padding around the house when he heard a knock at the door. He found Jenna and Nick, standing outside, looking scared. Instinctively he went to Jenna and wrapped his arms around her.

"Oh, Jenna," he said. "You've scared the hell out of us."

"Dad, I'm sorry. But we needed a place to go," she said. Tears puddled her eyes.

"Nick?"

Jenna nodded and he put his hand out to shake.

"Who else could it be?" David wanted to ream the kid for getting his daughter involved in this mess. He saw how Jenna looked at Nick and knew that any kind of harsh words, threats, promises to put him away, would only make her defensive. Maybe angry. She was safe now. That was all that mattered.

"We're calling your mother," David said.

"Dad, *please* don't do that just yet. I came here for help. *Your* help. Nick didn't do anything wrong."

David reached for his phone. "But kidnap you," he said tersely.

She grabbed her father's free hand. "That's not fair and that's not the truth. Don't call."

"I didn't, sir," Nick said, wishing he hadn't used the word "sir" but it just slipped out. It seemed so false, though it hadn't been meant that way.

David didn't know if he should call the police or his ex-wife. Or listen to his daughter and the stranger that accompanied her.

"Listen, Nick, I don't really know what happened," he said. "But I'll be blunt. Your family is dead and the police are looking for you. I'd put this at the top of anyone's list when it comes to troubling. Wouldn't you?"

David didn't wait for an answer, which was fine, since it didn't appear as if Nick was going to say anything. He stood mute, stepping backward toward the door. His eyes were full of fear and, maybe, David thought, *remorse*.

"And somehow, God knows how, you've got my little girl involved in this mess—"

"What's going on here?"

It was Dani. The noise of the argument rousted her out of her feather bed. Her blond hair was surprisingly tangle free and she even wore—at least Jenna thought so—a little lip gloss. Her bathrobe was a Vera Wang knockoff, all creamy and flowy. It didn't conceal much.

The teenager stood there, her big blue eyes wide.

"You're pregnant," Jenna said. She looked over at her father. "She's pregnant."

Dani pulled on the belt tie of her robe and like some kind of floating cloud, took a seat next to David.

"I was going to tell you," he said, his eyes riveted on his daughter. Embarrassment swept over his handsome face.

"*When?* When my brother or sister was born?"

"It was something I wanted to tell you—"

"*We* wanted to tell you," Dani interjected, her hand now caressing her melon-sized abdomen.

"In person," David continued, finishing his thought.

"We want you to be here for the wedding, too." Dani's words were meant for Jenna, but she seemed to say them in the direction of her future husband, now sitting on the couch. "I was hoping you'd be in the bridal party. If you don't think that's too weird, you know. It would mean a lot for me."

Dani was carrying on like she was talking to a wedding planner, not a teen that'd just found out that she was going to be a big sister.

"You know," Jenna said, "I thought that I had the worst week ever. Let's see. A tornado rips up our town, Nick's family is murdered, I'm sleeping in a shack, my mom is pissed off at me, and now my dad's girlfriend is knocked up."

"Enough!" David stood up. His face was red with anger. He was walking a fine line and he knew it. In front of him was his nearly grown daughter and to the left his pregnant girlfriend. He knew he needed to let her vent, but the "knocked-up" comment was too much.

"I'm not saying I'm perfect," he said stiffly, holding his temper.

Jenna went to Nick, who was standing with his hands in his jeans pockets looking around like he wanted to escape. "No Dad, you're not," she said, fighting back tears. "Far from it. Some family we are."

No one said anything for a few long seconds, when Nick finally broke the ice.

"Can I use your bathroom?" he asked. "Been a long drive."

Dani smiled, though she had fanned the flames of the little altercation, she knew things in her perfect home were not so ideal after all. Regrouping was in order and she pounced on the opportunity

"Down the hall, Nick. Let's all get some coffee," she said, looking at the other two still frozen in their anger.

Jenna followed her dad and his girlfriend into the kitchen, an enormous room of hanging pots and pans and a gas-fueled fireplace.

"Does Mom know?" she asked softly, once more feeling the hurt of a secret revealed.

"Yes," he said. "I'm afraid she does."

Dani feigned a preoccupation with brewing coffee, and Jenna summoned the courage to speak her mind. The words came in a rush. "Dad," she said, "if you call the police and say anything about Nick, I'll never speak to you again."

He clearly didn't like her attitude. "Don't push me," he said.

"You know, I cried for a week when you moved to Seattle. Make that a month. And all along you probably had *her*. Like she was waiting in the wings. I thought that your leaving us was something that you needed to do to practice your specialty. Spokane wasn't big enough."

David remained mute. He figured at the very least in some small way, he had it coming.

"And you know what, Dad? Seattle had everything you wanted," she said, again thinking of Dani. "But it didn't have *me*. It didn't have Mom."

"It is more complicated than that. You'll see when you live your own life."

"Complicated? What I'm going through right now is complicated. I need you to be there for me. I need you to help me. Nick and I need your help."

*Saturday, 11:15 A.M.,*
*north of Seattle*

Traffic was uncharacteristically light as Emily Kenyon drove northward from Seattle. Her back ached from the long drive from Cherrystone, and her car smelled of a cinnamon scone she'd picked up from a Starbucks drive-through. She told herself to ignore the exit off the freeway that led to the home she and David had shared when they were first married. It was a classic Craftsman in the University District. It had more built-ins than they had things to stash. David was doing his residency at the University of Washington Medical Center back then. She was finishing up her stint at the police academy south of Seattle. All was good. *Too good. Too short.* She knew that the fragmentation and ultimate destruction of their marriage had been shared by both, but even so she wished she'd given in more often. For her daughter's sake, and deep down, she knew, for her own.

She glanced at the Mapquest printout of directions to Olga Morris-Cerrino's address and pulled off the freeway onto a two-lane road along the creamy green waters of the Nooksack River. A grove of cell towers flew by the driver's window. She passed a small dairy farm and wondered how much longer it would be there. New homes were pushing the countryside farther and farther away. It was true of just about every populated part of Western Washington. In time, she knew, there would be no more farms. That would never happen in Cherrystone, of course. As David had pointed out time and time again, "Nobody with half a brain would want to live there."

*If it was home, you would*, she'd thought.

She passed by an emu farm, its sentinel of birds standing along a wire fence line like prehistoric creatures. All turned their heads in unison as her Accord drove by. Emily thought they were ugly, but considered stopping to snap a photo with her cell phone. Jenna would think they were cute. She thought opossums were *adorable*. Emily turned right up the long dirt driveway, a tuft of grass separating two parallel grooves. The mailbox: CERRINO.

Olga Morris-Cerrino was already waiting out front of the big white house, the chief benefit of a very long driveway. Standing over the sink in the kitchen window, one could see a car coming two minutes before it arrived. There was always time to do a little urgent straightening of the house and a cursory check in the mirror to see if the hair looked all right.

"You made good time," Olga called out, walking toward the car. "Perfect timing. Minestrone sound good?"

Emily shut the car door and extended her hand. "You must be Italian."

Olga ignored the hand, and embraced Emily with a warm hug. "Don't let the last name fool you," she said, with a laugh. "I married into that one. And the minestrone? It's my mother-in-law's recipe. I claim nothing."

"It is so beautiful here," Emily said, looking around at the garden as they walked toward the open front door.

Olga bent down to pick up the cat.

Emily smiled. "That must be Felix."

Olga nodded and the cat purred. "He's probably the only one who knows the *real* me. I'm not a cook. Not Italian. And until I married Tony, I thought dirt was something disgusting. Now look at me. I can't keep my fingernails clean." She flashed her nails, edged in garden soil. "I never wear gloves. Love the feel of the soil on my hands. You'd laugh if you knew me before I ended up all the way out here. Couldn't keep a houseplant alive."

"My silks even die," Emily said. And they both laughed.

The kitchen was authentic in every way. It wasn't one of those new homes that tried to look old with beat-up butcher blocks and retrofitted stoves from the 1930s. An enormous pine table commanded the entire wall of windows on the south side. Light streamed in, bending and twisting as it flooded a row of colored bottles lined on a shelf that passed through the top third of the windows. It was like a prism, sending shards of color everywhere. A wooden bowl with apples sat in the middle of the table. Not wooden apples out of a Pottery Barn catalog, but the real thing. Above all, the kitchen smelled wonderful.

"Sit, eat," Olga said as she scurried to bring Emily a bowl of the steaming soup. Then she handed her a dish of powdery grated parmesan. "Sprinkle some of that on top. And if I overdid the oregano, shoot me with the gun on your hip." She looked at Emily's gun, revealed on her waistband as she sat down. "Just kidding."

"Thanks for that, and thanks for seeing me. I'm not too proud to tell you that I'm grasping at straws here, but, well . . ." She stopped and looked down at her soup.

"I read about your daughter after we talked," Olga said. "Let's see if we can't sort out some of this together." She looked over at pile of file folders. "That's Angel's Nest and Dylan Walker. We'll get to that after we eat."

"Dylan Walker?" The name had come from nowhere. "What's he got to do with this?"

Olga's expression flat lined. "I'll get to that." She got up and retrieved a pitcher of ice tea from the counter and set it on the table. Emily shook her head when Olga indicated if she wanted some. "But since I'm retired, I don't ever discuss politics or work at the table. Let's eat. Now tell me all about your daughter. Did you bring pictures?"

# CHAPTER TWENTY-FOUR

**W**hile Olga cleared the old table of the lunch dishes, Emily excused herself to return the flurry of calls that had kept her phone vibrating throughout the meal. Felix followed her out to the front porch, the screen door snapping on its rusted spring.

She scrolled through the call list, Shali, Kip, David, Cary, and Candace Kane had called.

*That one's not getting a call back. Neither is that one.*

She called Shali first, on the off chance that Jenna had made contact with her.

"Not exactly, Mrs. Kenyon. She basically stole my car," Shali said from the school cafeteria where she was stuck eating lunch. "Borrowed it, I guess. She did leave a note."

"Oh no! When?"

"Not sure, but I think early this morning."

"What did the note say?"

"'You need to take the bus. Be back soon. Love, Jen.'"

"Are you holding out? Now's not the time, you know."

"I know. And I'm not."

Emily thanked her for the information, and just before she hung up, Shali Patterson added the little piece that she was, in fact, holding out.

"My mom called the police. I guess you should know that."

*Perfect.*

"All right. Call me if you hear from Jenna."

"She's going to be okay, right?"

"Yes. She's going to be fine."

Emily didn't believe her own words, but she didn't want Shali Patterson running around talking to the police, the media, her *mother*.

Next she pressed the speed dial for David, still set at number One. *Need to change that.* When he didn't answer, she figured he was at the hospital in surgery or at one of those endless admin meetings. He'd never screen her calls. She left a short message.

"I'm near Meridian. Call me. Jenna took Shali Patterson's car."

She skipped most of Cary McConnell's message.

"Hey, sorry about everything. I'm in Seattle. We really need to talk—"

*Delete.*

When Kip didn't answer his cell, she called Gloria, the dispatcher, who told her that Kip was talking with "a herd" of reporters. An FBI profiler was coming in that day to help with the case.

"This is getting big," she said. "The stuff they are saying around here would make you puke."

Emily scanned the garden. She could see where Olga had tilled and planted. She also noticed muddy footprints on the porch. *Jeesh, the country's messy.*

"Try me," she told Gloria.

"It's this whole Romeo and Juliet thing. Emily, they are putting this off on Nick and saying that Jenna knew about it ahead of time or was even involved."

"That's such bullshit," Emily said.

"You don't have to tell me that. I've known Jenna since she was three feet tall. The only thing she's guilty of is having a good, trusting heart."

"Tell Kip I called. I'm with Olga now. We're going over some of her case files. Might have something later. I'll call him. Promise."

Emily looked around for the cat, but when Felix was nowhere to be seen, she went back inside without him.

"I let the cat out," she said, when she found Olga at the table, papers and folders spread out all over. "Sorry."

"That's all right. He lives for the freedom of messing up my garden."

Olga motioned Emily to sit. She pointed to the ice tea and Emily shook her head.

"Remember Dylan Walker?"

"The serial killer? That Dylan Walker?"

Olga nodded. "Is there any other?" She picked up a folder. "I'm going to give you the background first. Then we'll see if we can connect the dots with what you've got happening over there in Cherrystone. Fair enough?"

"Fair enough."

Over the next hour, Olga told Emily about the Meridian murders of Shelley Marie Smith and Lorrie Ann Warner. Although it had been years since it all happened, Emily could see that the retired detective was channeling deep, dark memories—as if she was watching a movie unwind in her mind. Everything, it seemed, was as vivid to Olga at that moment in her country kitchen as it had been back in the days when she first looked at the dead bodies of those college students, wrapped in an expensive plastic tarp on the sandbar of the Nooksack River. She talked about Dylan Walker and the other women that had crossed his path only to turn up dead. There was Brit Osterman, twelve; Tanya Sutter, twenty-four; and Steffi Miller, seventeen.

Olga sipped her ice tea and pointed a finger at one of the news clippings in the file. "All these girls murdered by him—I don't have to say *allegedly* now because I'm retired and I know what I know—and he turns into some kind of Lothario for the lost and lonely."

Emily let out a breath. "I remember now. My girlfriends at the UW talked about how much more handsome Walker was than Ted Bundy."

"Bingo," Olga said, no longer smiling. "I had to live with that during the trial."

Emily felt a little embarrassed. "But no one wanted to date him. It was just more like it was *such a waste.* Dumb, I know."

Olga sighed. "You were young. Others were older and should have known better. That brings me to Angel's Nest."

"Right. That's why I'm here. I don't see the connection." Emily looked at the papers as Olga spread them out. There were many. Felix, who'd managed to let himself in, took a spot on her lap.

"He likes you," Olga said. "Does that bother you?"

Emily shook her head and massaged Felix under his chin.

"Now," Olga went on, "let's discuss Angel's Nest, which we nicknamed 'Devil's Best' back at the office when the news first broke. God, we hated that place."

Olga recounted how the Seattle agency had been seen as a model of its kind, matching pregnant college students with prospective parents and generally living up to its business card motto: WE CREATE FAMILIES. No one knew exactly how many families were created through the agency, because even despite the court cases that ruined the place, such numbers were elusive.

"Confidentiality laws work for criminals, too," Olga said. "Keeps everyone in the dark. Even the grand jury that heard the case was clueless as to how big the scandal was."

"The scandal?"

"Oh yeah, you want the good part."

"And the connection?"

Olga nodded. "Right. I'll jump right to it. Randall Wilson, the president of Angel's Nest, was indicted, and convicted, on procuring babies for a fee. Big fees. He and his office had more demand for their services than babies, so over a six-year period—we don't know for sure—they placed more than twenty babies for big bucks. They sold babies to desperate people."

Emily remembered the name Randall Wilson. "This was the 'buy a baby' case?" she asked.

"That was what got the attention from the media. In the end it was true that we—and it was never *my* case— only convicted on those cases. They were just so much more obvious. The prosecutors in Seattle didn't want to rip apart families that they didn't have to and expose birth mothers who were local girls. It seemed too big and too wrong. Shutting down the agency was the ultimate goal."

"Look, Olga, I get that. What I don't get is how you're involved and how does any of this connect the dots?"

"I'm sorry. I digressed. I don't get many visitors out here."

Emily wished she hadn't been impatient just then and she apologized. "It's just that I'm worried about my daughter."

"I know." She put her hand on Emily's and patted it gently. "I'm sorry," she repeated. It was clear that she meant it. "Okay, when I read about your case, I wasn't thinking Angel's Nest—you brought that up when you called. I was thinking about the signature of the crime. Mrs. Martin, nude, tied up, and shot. Maybe even strangled. It reminded me of my girls."

*Her girls,* Emily knew, *were Lorrie and Shelley.*

"I didn't think anything about it until you called."

"But I don't see the connection," Emily finally said.

"During the Dylan Walker trial, and afterward, women from all over the country wrote to him. They came here. They visited him. One of them was a woman named Bonnie Jeffries. I would never have given her a second thought except that she worked for

Angel's Nest and was one of the chief witnesses against her boss."

"Where is Bonnie?"

"Not sure. She faded away after the trial. Stopped going to see Dylan Walker at Monroe. She just disappeared. I made a couple of calls before you came, but no one knows what became of her. She hasn't filed a tax return for years." Olga looked through her notes, faintly yellowed with the passage of so much time. "I do remember one thing; she had a cohort that came with her to the trial. Let's see. I have the name here somewhere." She kept looking, flipping pages and at times getting lost in the memories of the case.

Emily could not have been more disappointed. It seemed so thin. But it was all she was going to get.

"Tina Winston. That's her." She tapped her finger on a page. "I remember reading about her a few years ago. Almost wanted to call her husband when I read in *Seattle Magazine* they had gotten married. In fact, I clipped the article."

"Who is he?"

"Rod Esposito. The software guy. Big bucks. Wonder if he knows that she was once smitten with a serial killer?"

Emily's mood lifted; a slight smile came to her face. It was the part of detective work she loved the most— finding the leverage needed to get someone to talk.

"Let's see," she said, letting her smile fade as Jenna's whereabouts pulsed once more. "I have to make a stop at my ex-husband's. Never fun, but I have a feeling he's got a houseguest."

### Saturday, 4:00 P.M., on the interstate
### just outside of Seattle

Kip was meeting with the FBI—a male and female agent from the Seattle field office—who had been the first to arrive to help with the Martin investigation. Gloria, stuck at the phones while all the excitement unfolded around her, assured Emily that he'd call as soon as he could break free.

"They're all over him like a dirty shirt," she said, mimicking one of the sheriff's favorite sayings.

"Is Jason around?" Emily asked, wishing she had a hands-free phone as she dodged the Seattle traffic.

"Nope. He's hanging around the FBI, too. Says it's a golden 'training' opportunity."

Emily turned off on the second Mercer Island exit, and drove south. Everything about the island said *money*. She couldn't imagine David actually wanting to live there among the train of Mercedes and Lamborghinis that snaked along the surprisingly forested roads that passed from one McMansion to the next. His values had flipped. Long gone were the days when he measured success with the lives he'd saved, not the money he made.

"Gloria, do you know if an APB went out on Shali's car?"

"Didn't David tell you? His squeeze Dani called earlier. Said the kids were with them and she'd see that they were brought in. The APB is out, but Kip said we'd follow David's lead. The FBI lady says they don't think the Martin boy was the shooter."

"She said *what*?" The mention of David's bride-to-be stung more than it should have. Emily thought she was over it. She looked for a place to pull over. What made her angry just then wasn't the comment about Nick Martin not being the killer of his parents and brother, though she'd get to that. It was Dani's interference in their lives.

"First off, she's *not* his wife. And second, what did she say?" Emily parked the Accord in front of a shady driveway that led up a steep, fern-fanned incline to a faux chateau huddled next to a tennis court and pool.

"She said she was concerned for her safety. Jenna and Nick had showed up and she felt uneasy, you know, *scared*."

"Jesus," was all Emily could say. If she needed another reason to hate Dani Brewer, she had one now.

Gloria sighed sympathetically. "Anyway, I said that you were en route to Seattle and you'd handle things. I told her, 'isn't it better to keep things in the family?'"

"That was good." Emily was still fuming, but she'd take care of Dani soon enough. She put the car back into drive and got ready to exit back onto the road. "Okay, what about Nick?"

"The FBI's being cagey—you know how they are— all I've been able to pick up is that the killings match the signature of some other family murders out of state."

"Did they say how?"

"I'm the dispatcher, remember. All I get around here is what I pick up on the radio or when Kip is telling me to bring him coffee or a Payday bar."

"I know. I'm sorry. Have him call me. One more favor, okay?"

Gloria let out an exaggerated sigh. "You want coffee, too?"

Emily laughed. "Do me a favor. Contact Parole and find out where Dylan Walker is living now."

"Kip told me about Walker. Kind of blew me away. You know, that he got out of the Jersey prison after that prison bed swap completely under the radar," Gloria said. "I'll dial up Parole and see where he's at."

She thanked Gloria and looked at the directions she'd printed from the hotel's front desk computer. Another turn and she'd be at David's.

"Take it easy, Emily. Hang in there. Dani fits the profile, you know. A second wife is always a bitch. I ought to know. I'm one myself."

Emily laughed a little more, said good-bye, and snapped her cell phone shut. Gloria had already married Dani off to Dave.

*Dani? Let see. Serial killer. New wife. Serial killer. New wife. Toss-up.*

Dani Brewer opened the front door with a stenciled-on smile that could have not been more false. *Lancôme Retro Rouge?* Emily suspected that Dani had seen her car pull up and hurried to the mirror to see what kind of affect she should wear on her reasonably pretty face. She had long blond hair, tousled in a messy bun. In all fairness, her pregnancy did give her the characteristic glow that made plain women appear pretty, and already pretty women undeniably ravishing.

*She's somewhere between pretty and beautiful on her very best day.*

"Oh, Emily, please come in," Dani said, stepping back and letting the door skim her bulging belly. "I talked to your office. They said you were over here."

Emily hadn't really waited for the invitation; she was already inside. The foyer was cold gray stone, slate. Cold like Dani.

"Is Jenna here? Nick? How about David?" Emily's words were rifle shot and she scarcely allowed a breath to intercede.

"David's at the hospital." Dani closed the door. "The kids came and went. Coffee? A soda?"

"This isn't a social call."

"Can't we just get along?"

"Get along? I couldn't care less about getting along. I want to find my daughter. She was here. Now where did she go?"

Dani frowned and for a second Emily thought she'd rolled her eyes in annoyance. "I thought we were past that."

"Dani, don't mess with me. I'm a mother, and I also carry a gun."

Dani led Emily into the kitchen. The stainless gleamed. A set of chef knives stuck in an oak butcher block. "Are you threatening me?" Her eyes were filled with what Emily was sure was an exaggerated affect of terror.

Emily turned her anger down a notch. She'd pushed too hard. "No, I'm sorry. I just want to find Jenna."

"Okay. I'm not a mother yet, but I get that. Mineral water?"

"No thanks." *Enough with the refreshments! Where's Jenna?* "Where are the kids?"

"I think they went to the library or something. Maybe an Internet café. They had that car, the one from Jenna's friend. They were full of questions about Angel's Nest. David told them what he remembered."

"Are they staying here with you?"

"Yes."

"And you expect them back later."

Dani nodded.

Emily glanced down at Dani's bulge. Anger had given way to worry. "I guess Jenna found out about your baby."

Dani turned away and opened and poured a San Pellegrino. "I thought you would have told her about it."

"You asked me not to," Emily said. "You and David wanted to break the news yourself."

"I know I—*we*—said that, but I thought for sure you'd let the cat out of the bag. I would have."

"Good to know," Emily said. "It was on my mind, but I just never found the time."

"Well, she knows."

"How'd she take it?" Emily asked, though she hated any assessment coming from Dani.

"She's angry. She'll get over it." The remark was so glib, so unaware of how a teenage girl would deal with the realities that her father, *her idol*, had impregnated another woman—*before* marriage.

Emily couldn't let it go. "Look, Dani, you and I don't need to be friends. We don't have to spend any time together whatsoever. I'll probably never see you again—except at my daughter's wedding."

Dani set her glass down and looked out at Lake Washington. The water was ice blue. She shook her head slightly, looking wounded. "I don't know why you hate me so much."

*God, you're better than I thought. David's in for a wonderful life with you.*

"I don't hate you," said Emily. "But I don't imagine

I'll ever have warm feelings toward you. That's just the way it is."

"I'm sure all of this is hard for you." Dan had let a softer tone into her voice.

*I don't want your sympathy. I used to babysit kids older than you.*

"Thanks," Emily said, stiffening as she set aside the urge to shove a pregnant woman.

She started for the door, planning to find David at the hospital. Suddenly she noticed that the house was decorated in a kind of spare, contemporary way, with stark, simple lines and a lot of leather and chrome. David hated contemporary furnishings. She allowed a slight smile to come to her face.

*Good. He's getting everything he never wanted.*

On her way to the car, she tried to calm down. At some point, Emily knew she could never really forgive David for the affair. She wanted to. Even though the marriage was "irretrievably broken" as the lawyers said, she knew they were connected forever. Although they'd be apart, they had a little girl to raise and love. It hurt so deeply that they would not do that together. Her vision for her life had been the same one she'd grown up with in Cherrystone. Two parents. A stable home. A place where birthdays would be celebrated. Holidays observed. Memories made together as a family. But that was all fractured when he betrayed her with a student nurse.

"She meant nothing," he had said at first. "I screwed up."

As Emily's anger grew, his story changed. Soon after the impetus for the affair belonged to her. "You weren't there for me."

To some degree, he'd had a point. That crushed her. Playing a role in the disintegration of her family was almost impossible to bear. The only joy she could allow herself was when she learned that he'd cheated on his girlfriend with a young office assistant, Dani. *Once a cheater, always a cheater.*

As Emily slid behind the wheel, Dani called out, "Emily, I really do want us to be friends." Her voice was intentionally loud enough for her well-heeled neighbors to pick up on her troubles. Dani liked a little drama, it seemed.

Emily pretended not to hear. She just slammed the car door shut. There was no need to fan the flames, and nothing out of her mouth would seem anything but venomous. She glanced over her shoulder as she backed out. Dani was there by the front door, holding her mineral water, and looking either sad or mad. It was hard to say.

Her phone rang as she pulled away. It was Olga's number.

"Hi there," Olga said, her voice cheerful. "I've got something for you. I set up a dinner date for you."

For a moment it flashed through Emily's mind that she'd probably talked too much about not having found a decent man. She was like bloody chum tossed in a shark cage. Desperation must have oozed from every pore.

"A dinner date," she said, sighing. "I don't know . . ."

Olga laughed. "Not that kind of a date, my dear. A date with Tina Winston. You're seeing her at Embers on Stewart downtown."

"Oh really?"

"Yes. Tonight."

"Tonight?"

"Yes. And one more thing."

Emily hung on Olga's words. *This is going to be big. Olga knows something.*

"Order the fish."

### Saturday, 4:42 P.M., Seattle

Nick Martin and Jenna Kenyon stood outside 1225 Stone Way and looked up at the four-story red brick building with green awnings that looked like eyebrows over the street level windows. It was an edifice with a past. Several in fact. At the turn of the previous century, it was the home of the *Seattle Bulletin* and its considerable printing operations. Today, an old letter press with brass fittings gleamed like a museum piece in the front lobby. After the paper folded, it became apartments, then offices, and now it had gone condo. It was its incarnation as an office building that interested the teenagers standing before it.

That's when it had been the home to Angel's Nest, an adoption agency.

"I guess this is where I came from," he said.

Jenna, still angry at her father about keeping Dani's pregnancy secret, stood quietly before saying, "Let's go to the library."

Her father had said that Angel's Nest had been in the news in the early 1980s. He had rounds to conduct "or I'd go with you."

Jenna saw that as just another lie. When she pleaded to let her and Nick try to find out a little information before turning themselves in, she lied, too.

"Dad, we'll go to the police this afternoon. All of us. When you get back from hospital rounds."

David Kenyon took the bait then. Too easily, she thought. Jenna knew that he had already crossed over that invisible line between new family and old. He didn't care about her. Maybe Dani wouldn't let him care. She was pregnant. She was young. She held all the cards.

"I promise, Dad. See you later," she said.

"Okay, later then," he said

*Much later, Dad. Like never,* she thought.


The basement of the Sullivan Library on the campus of the University of Washington is one of those cavernous spaces where footsteps echo like thunder. After negotiating a labyrinth of shelving, Nick Martin and Jenna Kenyon spoke with a librarian in the research periodicals department, a cheerful man of about fifty with a soup-strainer moustache who agreed that it was silly that no newspapers of the 1980s were yet archived in a searchable electronic format.

"If it didn't happen after 1992," he said with a wink, "it just flat didn't happen. Writing a paper?"

"Yes," Jenna said, "We're from West Seattle High and our teacher sent us here. We're doing a team project." She was proud of her quick response and Nick shot her a quick glance indicating he, too, was impressed.

The librarian smiled. "What's the subject? We have an excellent reader's guide to our periodical collections."

"Angel's Nest," Nick said, testing the notoriety of the name.

The man didn't flinch. "Oh, *that* one. Should be interesting."

He directed them to a massive row of gunmetal-gray cabinets, and they searched under Adoption, Seattle Scandals, and Criminal Cases of Puget Sound. After twenty minutes of digging, they only found one scrap of ephemera on the subject.

It was a postcard mailed to college campuses in the 1970s. It showed a picture of a pregnant young woman, sitting on a swing in a playground. Underneath her name it carried the words: "Make a Future. Make a Family. Give Your Baby to Angel's Nest."

"That's creepy," Jenna said. "The girl looks like she wants to jump off that swing, ditch the baby, and get back to class."

Nick didn't know what to make of it. "Why didn't she just get an abortion when she could?"

"Times have changed," said the librarian, still hovering nearby. "You two are bound to find more info on the microfiche rolls of the paper." He jotted down some suggested dates and pointed to the south end of the building. "If you have any trouble working the equipment, let me know."

Nick had threaded the first tape and began to spool through the images of the 1980s as presented in the pages of the *Seattle Times*. Jenna pulled up a chair and retrieved a pad and pen from her purse.

"I think this is the part where they play some cheesy electronica," she said.

Nick glanced over at her with a blank look on his face. He didn't have a clue what she was talking about.

"You know, as we zip through the pages, a loud instrumental track plays," she said. "God, Nick, like *CSI*, don't you ever watch TV?"

Nick grinned. It was the first time Jenna had seen him smile in days. *Since it happened.* For a fleeting moment, it gave her just a little hope. *We'll be okay. We'll all be okay.*

Jenna put her hand on Nick's shoulder as the grainy images of the microfiche flew through the reader. Every once in a while, she'd drop a quarter into the coin box and push the button. A slightly damp photocopy of the worst possible quality came from the printer. Headlines were gray instead of black. Photos were milky. One headline, despite its ghostly shading, screamed for attention:

## ADOPTION COORDINATOR:
## "NO IDEA WHAT WILSON WAS DOING"

It was accompanied by an artist's sketch of a plump woman with long dark hair. She was in the witness box testifying. The caption read: *Defense lawyers tried to discredit Bonnie Jeffries by questioning her about her pen-pal friendship with noted serial killer Dylan Walker.*

*Saturday afternoon,*
*Ogden, Utah*

It was the smell coming from 4242 Foster Avenue in Ogden, Utah, that finally got local police inside the beautiful home with the tall paneled doors. It wasn't the pile of newspapers on the stoop, or the concerns of a fourteen-year-old paper delivery kid. Just the fetid stink that cops knew immediately as the scent of decomposing human flesh. Maggie and Jim Chapman, and their daughter, Misty, a freshman at BYU, were found in a back bedroom, bound, gagged, and strangled to death. The cord from a miniblind from the laundry room had been used to asphyxiate the daughter. Mrs. Chapman had been strangled with a phone cord, and it appeared that Mr. Chapman had died from the pressure of his own necktie. The autopsy conducted by the medical examiner's office downtown would make the determination, of course.

The *Salt Lake City Tribune* ran the story on the front page. The article was picked up by the Associated Press and dispatched across the country:

**PARENTS, GIRL, SLAIN BY INTRUDER IN OGDEN**

CNN ran a video version the next day, flashing images of the murder house and the neighborhood. One viewer in Seattle paid particular attention, satisfied that the mission had been accomplished.

*There was Ogden, Des Moines, the Cherrystone screwup, and the last one close to home.*

Armed with their stack of damp microfiche printouts and a genuine need to get away from the Johnny-on-the-spot research librarian, Jenna and Nick retreated from the basement and found a quiet corner and some soft upholstered chairs on the third floor. A trio of engineering students studied for a test nearby. Otherwise, they were alone.

"What exactly are we looking for?" Jenna whispered.

Nick divided the copies in half and handed a stack to Jenna. "I'm not the detective's daughter."

"Thanks," she said, her tone anything but thankful.

"Sorry," he said. "I didn't mean anything by it. Really. I guess we're just looking for whatever we can find about Angel's Nest."

As they worked their way through the material, they learned that the agency had a sterling record for its first decade or so back in the 1960s. Randall Wilson had helped reinvent the whole concept of adoption. At least, according to one article, prior to Wilson agencies were often viewed as shameful dumping grounds for unwanted babies. Wilson's brilliance was marketing. Through ads on TV, he was able to turn that thinking on its ear, and make an unplanned pregnancy something positive and heartwarming. Wilson, a genial fellow of forty, saw adoption as "a golden opportunity to build new families." Instead of selling the idea of taking in an unwanted baby, he sold hard to the birth mothers, making them feel like cherished heroines instead of shameful losers.

A photo of Wilson showed him outside the building on Stone Way. He had his arms crossed over his chest and a broad smile on his face. *"No child is really unwanted," says Wilson. "They just need to find their way into the right family. That's my job."*

"What's the big deal?" Nick asked. "I mean, I'm adopted. My parents wanted me."

Jenna looked up from the papers. "You're a guy. You wouldn't get it. But back when our parents were young, getting pregnant out of marriage was the biggest sin of all. Not like today when every movie star has a baby without ever getting a husband. In the 1960s women actually went away and hid out until their babies came."

"So?" Nick pushed his chair back from the table. "Big deal."

The remark surprised Jenna. "So? This was huge. Wilson was one of the first to turn that thinking around, I guess. He helped promote the idea that having a baby and giving it to someone else was a great gift."

Nick shook it off. He put his head down and kneaded his eyes with the palms of his hands. He seemed exhausted and hurt. But he wasn't about to cry in front of Jenna again.

"When I was a kid, my mom and dad told me I was adopted," he said. "They said that they had 'chosen' me. I guess that was good enough for me. I never thought of myself as a bastard or anything like that."

"I'd hope not." Jenna continued scanning the page in front of her. "But what if it wasn't good enough for your birth mother or father?"

Riffling through the stacks of news stories quickly, the headlines told the story. By the 1980s, the agency was buying babies from shady operators overseas and selling them to rich, childless couples. There were also hints in the story that they were also buying babies from girls here in the United States and selling them in quickie private adoptions.

Randall Wilson had been tried and found guilty. The agency had been shut down. And apparently the star witness against him had been an employee of Angel's Nest, Bonnie Jeffries.

"I've read enough," said Nick. "We can get the fine print later. You have that calling card?"

Jenna pulled it from her purse.

"Let's call your mom's boyfriend. He's the only one who knows anything."

"Good idea," Jenna said. "But he's not the only one. I'd say one of these two might know something." She tapped the top page of her stack of clippings with the eraser end of a pencil: first the photo of Randall Wilson, and next the courtroom artist's image of Bonnie Jeffries.

"Okay," he said. "They're next."

She had McConnell's office phone number on her speed dial, from when he and her mom had been dating, and she gave it to Nick. They walked past the three engineering students, sullen and bored in their studies, and found a bank of pay phones, relics of the pre-cellular era.

Nick dialed and a law office administrative assistant answered.

"I need to talk with Cary. It's urgent," Nick said, doing his best approximation of mature and demanding. He'd hoped his voice carried even a hint that he was a money-paying client. He wasn't sure what he was trying to be.

"Mr. McConnell is away on business," she answered. "Can I take a message?"

"When will he be back?"

"He's on the coast," the young woman said, employing the term those east of the Cascade Range used for the entire region west of the mountains.

"This is important. I'm working on the Angel's Nest situation. I need to talk to Cary."

"Who's calling?" she asked.

Nick offered the only name that popped into his head—it came from the news clippings. "This is Randall Wilson," he said. He was sure he didn't sound anything like Randall Wilson. Randall Wilson would be nearly seventy by now. But given the circumstances, and the lack of any real plan for his call, it was the best he could do.

The young woman apparently heard the hesitation in his voice.

"Just *who* is this and what do you need?"

"I . . . I . . ." Scared and feeling a little stupid, Nick abruptly hung up.

"Well, that went great," Jenna said.

Nick would have laughed just then if nothing important had been at stake.

"No kidding. I totally choked."

Jenna started back to the table. "Okay, let's figure this out."

Nick looked beat up. His big moment as a macho take-charge guy had fizzled. Jenna nudged him on the shoulder.

"Cary McConnell knows something but he's a lawyer—"

"And a jerk." Nick added, brightening somewhat.

"Right. Trust me, I know!"

Nick stared at the photocopies. He placed his index finger on the image of Bonnie Jeffries.

"She's the one," he said. Jenna leaned closer to get a better view of the photograph. "She's the one we ought to talk to. She's kind of a whistle-blower type and they always want to help."

Jenna agreed. "Let's go see if she's still around. I think we can get on one of those computers over there."

"If we have enough money," Nick said.

"This is a library," she said with a smile, "some things just have to be free around here."

# CHAPTER TWENTY-FIVE

*Saturday, 6:30 P.M.,*
*Seattle*

"That's a part of my life I don't like to discuss for fairly obvious reasons," Tina Winston Esposito said, curled up like a cat in a darkened booth in Embers. When fire flashed from the restaurant's grill, it lit up her face. She was still thin and beautiful. Her blond hair was cut in a bob that made her look chic and rich, which she was. She no longer had her own business, or the need for one. She'd married a wealthy software executive and lived the good life in a high-rise condo downtown. Her bag was Prada. So were her shoes.

"I can imagine," Emily Kenyon said. "And I'm sorry for the intrusion. Thanks for meeting me."

"I must admit I practically lost it when you mentioned Dylan's name," Tina said, sipping a Death Valley dry martini that was delivered to her without so much as a request.

*This lady's on home turf.*

"Water, for me," Emily said. "No lemon, please."

Nerves were getting the best of her. Her stomach growled.

"You know, I hated that detective up in Meridian. Could have scratched out her eyes. Now I wonder why? Everything about those days seems like a dream. A nightmare, really."

The waiter, a young man with a tattoo bandaged to hide it from restaurant patrons, returned to take their order. Tina selected the salmon.

"It's wild, not that horrid farm-raised Atlantic fish," she said.

"Yes, Alaskan," the waiter said, turning his inquisitive gaze toward Emily.

"I'll have the same," she said.

The waiter nodded, disappeared, and the kitchen flashed more fire.

Alone with the detective and her martini, Tina Esposito's demeanor shifted. The warm, nearly genteel manner turned to stone.

"Look," she said, "I'll help you any way that I can. I don't even want to know why you're here. That's your affair. The less I know the better."

Emily said nothing. She knew when to keep her mouth shut. Sometimes the less a detective says, the more she'll get in an interview. The tactic always served her well. *Let the subject fill in all the uncomfortable gaps in a conversation.*

"You just have to promise me that you'll keep me out of any of this," Tina went on. For a woman who had a purse worth more than Emily's monthly salary, her tone was surprisingly pleading. "I have a pretty good life now. I can't ruin it."

Emily felt sorry for her. "If you haven't been a party

to any criminal activity" she said, pausing slightly for emphasis, "I'd say that's a promise I can keep."

"Criminal activity? Good God, *no*. I'm guilty of one thing. Being stupid." She finished the last of her martini. "Really, *supremely* stupid."

"We've all done stupid things," Emily said, thinking of Cary McConnell. At least Tina's stupidity was decades, not *hours*, old. "Tell me. Tell me about you, Dylan Walker, and Bonnie Jeffries."

"All right," she said. "But be prepared. I warn you. It's pretty messy."


Ensconced behind prison walls, Dylan Walker hardly faded into oblivion, as the prosecutors and detractors had predicted following his trial for the murders of Shelley Marie Smith and Lorrie Ann Warner. He wasn't lonely, either. He had a full roster of visitors and an endless supply of pen pals.

Tina Winston started making the drive to the prison two months after Walker was convicted. She'd wanted to go right away, but she had to wait until after the state ran him through diagnostics and a battery of sessions with a counselor to determine how he'd fit into the prison population. Even more to the point, how he'd survive. He was considered "high profile" which really meant "high target."

Walker wrote to Tina a week after he'd been moved from Administrative Segregation or Ad Seg, to his "permanent" cell in Block D. His cell mate, a firebug from suburban Seattle, was the perfect fit. He was younger and a follower. That was good. A narcissist like Dylan Walker preferred being the star of his own show. Everyone else was a supporting player. That meant his cell mate, and those who wrote to him, like Tina.

Tina didn't know it, of course, but she was being played. He wrote to her that his loneliness and need for her understanding heart and unconditional love was the only thing that kept him alive. She alone could free him from the mental torture of his prison sentence.

*I sit here, alone, and desperate. I feel broken.*
*Not for what I've been accused of doing. Not for*
*what the world thinks of me. I feel broken*
*because you are so far away. The walls that hold*
*us apart seem insurmountable. You might think*
*that I'm counting the days to my appeal, but*
*really, I only count the days until I see you.*

Tina always stayed at the Windsong Inn, only ten minutes from the prison. It was a sterile little motel room with cardboard-thin walls and a lamp that was bolted to the nightstand. She could have afforded better accommodations, of course, if there had been better. Despite the jittery and excited feelings—the kind that come with a first date—that came with seeing Dylan, she knew it wasn't a real romance. She also knew her visits were not to a resort town. The prison town was stark, lonely, and bitter.

Tina arrived in town Friday night, so she'd be dressed and ready at the prison by 8:00 A.M. Saturday. It took about an hour to get through the examination process to ensure she wasn't smuggling anything in. By 9:15, her heart would stop when she first saw him line up in the visitation room. His dark eyes sparked with recognition. Even in the drab attire of an inmate's daily wear—a T-shirt and jeans—he was godlike. If the clothes just hung on the SOBs that other women were there to see, they clung to his ripped body like a second skin. If he hadn't been a prisoner, a convicted murderer, no less, Dylan Walker could have been a male model or film star. He sauntered to the table, a big white-toothed smile set off by dimples chiseled into that unequivocally handsome face.

They'd kiss and sit down. Quick and passionate. The second kiss would have to wait until the conclusion of a "date" Tina never wanted to end.

"I hate that we can only be together twice a month," she said on more than one occasion.

He leaned as close as the guards would allow. "I feel the same way."

And so each visit went. Tina promised to stand by Dylan. He said she was the only one who understood what he was going through. They talked about each other's lives. Friends, family—all of the things that held any real importance. In some ways Dylan Walker was the perfect man. He could charm. He was gorgeous. He made her laugh. Best of all, she didn't have to live with him.

*The only downside,* she thought, *was that part about him being suspected of being a serial killer. So harsh. So wrong!*

The salmon was perfect, just as Olga had promised. But Emily Kenyon only picked at it as Tina Esposito went on with her story of unrequited prison love. The combination of a woman in love with a creep—handsome as he was—made the detective's skin crawl.

"How long did you keep it up? Visiting him?" Emily asked.

Tina swallowed and dabbed her mouth. "Too long. I think I saw him for about a year and half. And that's when Bonnie came into this."

"I thought she came to the trial."

"She did. She came a few times, only because I didn't want to go alone. I think I was starstruck or something and wanted someone to blather to about Dylan."

She finished her second martini and it was clear as she looked about the darkened restaurant that Tina Winston Esposito was contemplating a third.

"What happened with Bonnie?"

"I really can't blame her. Not exactly. I told her to write to him. She was lonely and he liked getting mail. So she did. I had no idea that it would turn out the way it did. I was in love with him and I trusted her. I know that it is crazy," she said, her voice rising a little, "but I'm *still* mad at her. Ultimately she did me a favor, I guess. But my blood still boils when I think about how I found out."

"What? What happened?"

"I'm going to have one more drink. Then, as the kids say, I'm going to rock your world."

"I'm ready to be rocked," Emily said. "And I think I'll have what you're having, too."

Tina plucked the olive off her toothpick and smiled.

\* \* \*

The display on the dessert cart at Embers Restaurant was to die for, but Emily Kenyon stopped doing dessert when she turned thirty-five and knew her cheesecake days were out the door along with low-rise jeans and tummy-baring tops. Tina Esposito, however, ordered a Grand Marnier–infused chocolate torte. Considering all the slender woman had consumed during the meal, it did cross through Emily's mind that she was not only the ex-squeeze of a serial killer, she was likely bulimic, too.

Emily looked at her watch. They'd been talking—or rather Tina had been talking—for more than an hour and fifteen minutes. And they weren't getting very far.

*Have to wrap this up*, Emily thought. *Jenna's out there with Nick. The police are probably looking for Shali's car by now.*

"What happened with Bonnie?" Emily finally prodded.

"Oh that bitch," Tina said, swaying tipsily. "She double-crossed me. She took away my boyfriend."

"But your boyfriend was a sociopath," Emily said, amused by the absurdity of their conversation.

Tina tilted her head and slurred, "Touché. But isn't every successful man just a little bit sociopathic?"

Emily didn't say so, but she almost agreed. The concept fit David. It fit that jerk Cary McConnell. Most of the men that had come in and out of her life were more sociopathic than altruistic. Tina took a forkful of the dark chocolate ganache and twisted it upside down in her mouth. She closed her eyes, savoring the dessert or remembering a moment with Dylan Walker. Emily wasn't sure.

"I guess it is my fault, too," Tina said quietly when she came up for air and swallowed. "I introduced them."

As the torte disappeared, Emily listened as Tina spun a tale of being jilted by Dylan Walker. He'd convinced Tina that he cared about her friends and family and wanted to meet them.

"Family was out, of course," Tina said. "You don't think I was completely out of my mind." She stopped and thought better of her remark. "Don't answer that."

"I didn't say anything," Emily said, playing along.

"Okay, so I told him all about Bonnie. She was sweet. Single. Lonely. How she could use a friend. He soaked it all up. Made notes about her, for all I know. Anyway, the next thing I knew she was coming to the prison on *my* Saturdays." She looked through her purse, Emily assuming that she was getting her credit card to pay the check. Instead she pulled out an envelope.

"You can have this," she said, handing it to Emily. "I don't even know why I saved it."

Emily noticed that Tina's eyes had watered. *Was she going to cry? Jesus, tell me that I'm not this pathetic when it comes to men. To David. To Cary.*

The return address was the prison, in care of Dylan Walker.

*Dear Tina,*

*This is so hard for me to write. But I'm in an impossible position here. I've fallen deeply in love with someone else. Please don't hate me. Please don't think our time together was without deep meaning. In many ways, I owe you the very*

*fact that my heart is whole enough to love
another. Moreover, I owe a debt of gratitude
that can never be repaid. You have brought me
the woman of my dreams. Thank you, dear Tina.
Thank you for my Bonnie.*

*Love,
Dylan*

Emily folded the letter and slid it back into the
frayed envelope.

"What did Bonnie say about this?"

Tina sighed and shook her head. "Nothing. Not a
peep. I called her. You bet I did. I even went over to
have it out with her. It was so silly. Fighting over
Dylan Walker? So idiotic. But Bonnie and I never
really talked again. When the Angel's Nest thing made
the news a few years later, I called her, you know, to
give some support. But she acted like she'd never
heard of me. She treated me like some crank caller.
Later the prosecution came to me about Dylan and
Bonnie and her being mixed up with him. I was married then. I said I didn't know who either of them
were." She took another deep breath and smiled. "That
felt so good."

"I can imagine. What were they getting at?"

"I don't have a clue. As I said, I never saw her again
after Dash—I mean Dylan, dumped me."

"What became of her?" Emily asked.

"I ran into her cousin or something at Westlake
Center one day and she said Bonnie had fallen on hard
times. She was working as a janitor, I think." She thought

for a moment, and her face brightened once more. "Yes, that's right. A janitor for the Seattle School District."

Tina grabbed her Prada bag and opened it once more.

"My treat," she said.

### Saturday, 9:40 P.M.

Emily Kenyon checked into a room at the Westerfield, an expensive Seattle hotel that ordinarily wouldn't have been on her list of places to stay. Not without one of those half-price coupons she got out of a school fundraiser book, anyway. She was too exhausted to drive another mile for the cheaper rates of a suburban or airport hotel room. Sure, the county would pay for the room, but rack rates suggested by written travel policy put a night's stay at $78 a night, not $190. *I'll add this to the list of things I'm never going to deal with,* she thought, as she set her overnight bag on the travertine vanity. She'd been through so much that day, from Cherrystone to Olga to Tina, that she needed a little time to regroup. She took a diet soda from the minibar and perched herself, shoes off, on the edge of the bed.

A moment later, Emily found herself succumbing to sleep. She didn't fight it. She just let go.

# CHAPTER TWENTY-SIX

**Sunday, 7:40 A.M.,**
**Seattle**

It was early, but not too early for a call to Brian Kiplinger. It wasn't like he was a churchgoer. Emily Kenyon opened her cell phone and called her boss, an act that she dreaded.

"Where are you?" Kip said, his gruff voice not quite loud enough to hide the TV playing in the background. Emily thought it was a gardening show, which was a predictable choice for the sheriff. He was known around Cherrystone as the "Sheriff with a Green Thumb and a Load of Fertilizer." He acted like he didn't think it was funny, but those who knew him understood Brian Kiplinger loved any kind of attention.

"Seattle, at the Westerfield," she answered. "You *know* that."

"I didn't know you were on a freaking vacation."

"That's not fair. I'm beat."

"And?"

"What do I have to show for my day?"

"That's right. Tell me." Emily heard a beer can pop.

Emily could imagine the irritated look on Kip's face as he settled into his leather recliner. She hoped by the end of the conversation, they'd be back to what they were before the Martin murders—friends with a mutual respect for each other. She told him about Olga and the links among Tina Winston, Dylan Walker, Bonnie Jeffries, and Angel's Nest.

"Interesting, of course. I remember the Walker case. But it sounds like a stretch," he said.

"I get that, but there is something here. Look, Cary McConnell told me that someone connected to Angel's Nest had made inquiries about the Martins. I haven't been able to confirm it, but I'd bet my detective's shield that Nick was an Angel's Nest baby."

"And you think this is going to shed some light on our triple homicide?" He sounded gentler now, but still skeptical.

She ignored him. "Gloria told me that you have the Feds en route?"

"They should be in Spokane about now. Coming on a flight from the Seattle Field Office. Two of them." He paused. "How about Jenna?"

"I have a feeling Jenna and Nick are at David's. I'll call you when all this gets settled. In the meantime, can you get Jason to do something for me?"

"What's that? Feed your cat?"

*Soft as butter. Kip couldn't stay mad.*

"That's an idea, but not what I had in mind. I need someone to tell me if Dylan Walker's in Monroe or Walla Walla."

"I can answer that," Kip said, an air of satisfaction permeating each syllable. "Neither."

Emily acted dumbfounded. "Really?"

"You just don't keep up on your golden oldie serial killers. He was shipped out to a prison in Jersey a dozen years ago or so. He'd been too much of a distraction for our local systems. I'll call my buddy in corrections and find out where he's at."

Emily thanked him and hung up. As she made her way to the shower she had thought of visiting Dylan Walker, maybe out of curiosity as much as anything. But that wasn't going to happen now. New Jersey was out. She'd focus on finding Jenna and Nick, and Bonnie Jeffries. She turned on the hotel shower. Steam poured into the room and she stepped inside. As the water rushed over her, she imagined all her troubles going down the drain.

*Jenna, how I love you. I let you down.*

### Sunday, 8:50 A.M.

"Why are you ignoring me?"

In the crystal-chandeliered lobby of the Westerfield Hotel, Emily Kenyon, making her way to the coffee shop for a quick breakfast, turned around to the sound of a familiar voice. It was not the voice of someone she wanted to see. *Then or maybe ever.* But there he was. The blood had pumped Cary McConnell's face into a mass of red and blue veins. Even his eyes seemed rosy, instead of blue. If he'd ever been handsome in his life, it would have been impossible to say for sure just then. He looked like a pinstripe-suited monster, puffed up and in a fury. His red tie was a blood-hued spike that hung from his neck.

"Are you stalking me? I said it was over," she said.

Emily Kenyon stood face to face with her former lover and she felt nothing but revulsion. He'd never been what she thought he was—the knight in shining armor who was going to save her from her fractured marriage, the whirlpool, sucking her down. Drowning her. As he stood there in the hotel lobby, the concierge, a thin, fey man with wing-shaped sideburns looking on, Cary McConnell was nothing that she thought he was.

"You sleep with a woman, you think she cares to know you," he said. His words were angry and possessive but his expression was one of worry.

"I don't know why you're here." Emily hurried toward the elevators and McConnell followed. "I have enough on my mind. There's no room for you."

He touched her shoulder and she spun around.

"Emily, I'm here to tell you I'm sorry. And to tell you something you need to know."

She stopped and turned toward him. His anger had ebbed slightly. "What is it?"

"It's about Dylan Walker."

Emily had never mentioned the name to Cary. He'd had no clue that she was searching for Walker. "What about him?"

"He's my client."

"The serial killer is your client?"

"Look, I'm not sure he's a serial killer. But even if he is, he's entitled to legal representation. I can't disclose why he contacted me. I'm in murky ethical waters just telling you he's my client."

"You're unbelievable," she said. "What did you do for him?"

"I'm not playing games here. I'm telling you . . . more than I should. I care about you, Emily. I do. You know that. I wanted to warn you."

"Warn me? About what?"

"About Walker. Look, I can't be any more blunt than this. He asked about you. About Jenna."

By now Emily was furious. "What did he want to know?"

Cary took a step back. His face was flushed now. He appeared embarrassed, like a kid caught doing something wrong and lying about it. He muttered something ineffectual, but Emily couldn't quite grasp it.

"What are you saying?"

He looked at her. He seemed almost sorry.

"I can't say. But be careful."

She wanted to threaten to call the police, but she *was* the police. "Go. Get out of here." The elevator door glided open and she stepped inside. As the two brass-plated halves began to come together she saw Cary for what she hoped was the last time. He stood staring with what seemed like a genuinely remorseful look on his face.

*Remorseful, but pathetic. That's what he was. Truly pathetic.*


The dark heart of true evil is a hammer on the soul. With each beat, it pulses and sends the tainted blood throughout a killer's body. Like a virus. Or a deadly and dangerous toxin. Some killers know his or her bloodstream is poisoned with wickedness. Most don't.

Not far from the chic comforts of the Westerfield Hotel, one such person pondered the next move. The internal struggle against the heart of evil had been fought and lost. The end was near.

# BOOK THREE
# SINS OF THE FATHER

# CHAPTER TWENTY-SEVEN

*Sunday, 10:30 A.M.,*
*Seattle*

Emily Kenyon held her breath as she drove over the two-tiered viaduct that swept several stories above Seattle's waterfront alongside its shimmering harbor. It had long been viewed as an unsound structure, destined to pancake if there was a major earthquake. Given the tornado, the Martin murders, and the sad state of her personal affairs, Emily felt that if the time had come for a big shake, it almost certainly would occur when she was on that disintegrating elevated highway. She held the steering wheel in a death grip.

Emily looked straight ahead, her peripheral vision barely capturing views of a pair of ferries and a container ship as they maneuvered in Elliott Bay. She was headed south to an address in Georgetown, a scruffy but slowly gentrifying neighborhood on the concrete edges of Seattle's industrial district. Bonnie Jeffries's address, given to her by a resourceful Olga Morris-

Cerrino, was a dark brown two-story that along with a half dozen others were the holdouts of an old family neighborhood that had seen far better times and hadn't yet been restored and revitalized. Black wrought-iron bars—more county jail than French Quarter—fortified the first- floor windows of each house. One set of iron security grilles apparently hadn't been enough of a deterrent; one window had been replaced by a sheet of heavy plywood.

Emily pulled up next to the weedy sidewalk. *These people should sell to some energetic young couples who want to restore these places and will put up with crime and grunge while they wait for the neighborhood to come back*, she thought as she made her way up the buckling front steps. What could have been the world's oldest dog, a Norwegian elkhound mix, barely looked up when the detective knocked on the door and waited. *No answer.* She pressed the doorbell but the silence that followed indicated it was out of order. She strained to hear. She leaned close and pushed the ivory button a second time. The door was ajar. She knocked and it creaked open.

"Bonnie? Bonnie Jeffries?"

Silence. *Maybe she was at church?*

Emily entered the small foyer, startled by the sound of broken glass under her feet. She turned to look behind her, and for the first time noticed a small glass pane had been shattered. Broken glass glittered on the shabby shag carpeting. *What's going on here?* She made her way toward the living room. The residence smelled of one of those carpet cleaning powders. *Vanilla and lavender*, she thought. The house was deathly quiet.

"Ms. Jeffries? Bonnie? Are you home?"

Emily entered the living room, a cramped space of floor-to-ceiling bookshelves, knickknacks everywhere, and too much furniture. It was tidy, but overloaded. It passed through her mind that the furnishings were all from the overstuffed 1980s. Bonnie hadn't always bought quality, and apparently had never bothered to update.

Rust and green competed with mauve and gray as dueling decades fought for her sense of style. Emily instinctively patted her side, checking for her gun. She'd been in law enforcement long enough to get that sixth sense that something was awry. The feeling was akin to paranoia, but it had been always so deeply rooted in reality that she never disregarded it.

*Something's wrong here.*

Among the books that competed for space on Bonnie's overflowing living room shelves were volumes about psychology, forensic science, and true crime. In other circumstances, Emily wouldn't have thought twice about that collection. She'd seen a best-selling crime author, a woman with an exceedingly sweet voice and a gentle manner, on a television show talking about the psychographics of her readers. They weren't a pack of blood-lusting housewives. *Far from it.* She insisted that they were the "gentlest" people one could ever hope to meet. "The kind of people who take a spider outside in a tissue," the author had said.

*Never hurt a spider? But maybe fall in love with a killer?*

Books and a tray table had been knocked to the floor. A door in the sideboard that Bonnie Jeffries apparently used as a secretary—bills and letters were stacked neatly on its luminous pecan surface—was open. Papers from within were scattered. *Someone had been looking for something.*

Emily quickly sifted through the papers, but nothing grabbed her.

The kitchen was next. It was clean and orderly, decorated in a red apple motif that showed all the earmarks of a collector's chief problem. Once collecting an item—owls, Scottie dogs, and apples—every gift one receives is tied to the theme. Bonnie Jeffries had framed apple crate labels and apple-shaped platters on the wall. Even the kitchen clock was faced with an apple tree design. There was so much red in the room, Emily didn't notice the red spatter on one of the McIntosh apple-crate label prints, a variety from a farm called Blossom Orchards. And there was an apple-shaped cookie jar on the counter next to a big wooden knife block, just like one that Emily had.

"Bonnie?" Emily's voice was now a whisper. She walked down the narrow hallway, drew her gun, and turned toward the open bedroom door. The room was still and dark. Music from a bedside radio played low. The windows that faced the street had been covered in sheets of aluminum foil, presumably to keep out the light. Emily knew from her conversation with Tina Esposito that Bonnie worked nights as a janitor. She slept during the day.

She clearly lived alone. Emily felt sorry for her. For a second, Emily felt the air move, then the hair on the back of her neck prickled and rose. The sense of foreboding was palpable.

*Something is terribly wrong here.*

Emily flipped on the lights. In a sudden flash of illumination, there she was. Bonnie Jeffries, all 250 pounds of her, was laid out on the bed. The sheets were streaked with so much blood it made Emily gasp. Bonnie was facedown, her nightgown-clad torso painted with her own blood. Adrenaline flowing, Emily scanned the room. Just Bonnie.

"Jesus Christ," Emily said, automatically reaching for her cell phone and dialing 911.

*What the hell happened here?*

Emily spoke to the emergency dispatcher, identifying herself as a detective from another jurisdiction. Though her heart pounded, her tone was surprisingly cool. She could act like what she'd seen didn't upset her—thought the truth was far the opposite.

"I'll secure the scene until Seattle PD arrives," she said.

"All right. Your name? Your affiliation?"

"Emily Kenyon. Cherrystone, Washington, Sheriff's Office."

"All right. Sit tight. Officers en route."

"I'll wait outside," Emily said. The smell of blood made her nauseous. "Bring the coroner. No need for lights. This lady's dead." Sadness swept over her. A woman's life had been taken in the most brutal way imaginable. Emily had never been so hardened by the experience of her job that she didn't feel jabs to the heart at the sight of a murder victim. The cramped house in the rundown part of Seattle's southern city limits was now a crime scene.

On the way out, Emily noted that baby pictures

stared down from the walls, and she spotted a basket of yarn and an unfinished sweater. Every outward indication of what Bonnie Jeffries was in life was at odds with her devotion to serial killer Dylan Walker. She was the Suzie Homemaker type, but robbed of the joy that comes with it.

*Maybe that's just the kind of person he wanted. Someone he'd be able to control?*

Emily hurried to her car.

The story had been told often enough that Emily could almost live the rest of her life nearly believing that she'd moved back to Cherrystone to take care of her parents, the house, save her marriage, whatever had come to mind when someone asked why she'd returned.

But the reality was darker than that. As dark as night. Emily sat behind the wheel in front of Bonnie Jeffries's sad little house and knew that her past was about to catch up with her. She had toyed with the idea of leaving the scene and not making the call to 911. *I could have left Bonnie for someone else to find. But who? And when? Bonnie lived a solitary life. Maybe she'd lie on that bloody bed until the blowflies came and went, raising generation after generation?*

Calling 911, doing her sworn duty to uphold the law, was her only possible choice. Yet it came with a price. As the swarm of vehicles converged all around her, Emily knew she'd have to face head-on what she'd fought so hard to leave behind.

"Emily Kenyon?" the voice came from behind her.

Emily turned around to see a familiar face, an older one, but recognizable nevertheless. It was Christopher Collier, a detective she knew from her days in Seattle. They'd shared many of the biggest and toughest moments of her professional life. Seeing him would be tough, too.

"I couldn't believe it when I heard your name," he said, coming closer with a friendly smile on his handsome visage.

"Hi Chris," she said, letting the uneasiness that had gripped her pass. "It has been forever."

"Yeah," he said, reaching out to shake her hand. Like her, he had been nothing but green when they first knew each other at the academy. His still-dark and wavy hairline had receded and he'd added some weight, but overall Christopher Collier looked no worse for wear. "I heard you got your shield. Read it in the *Police Bulletin* a few years back. Over in Spokane, are you?"

Emily nodded. "Near there. In Cherrystone, where I grew up. It's quiet. Nice place for me and Jenna." Saying her name just then was hard, she hoped that it didn't prompt a question: "Saw that there's an APB out for your daughter, Jenna. What's the deal with that?"

Thankfully, it didn't.

The pair went for the front door, as two blue uniforms started unfurling plastic ribbons, yellow crime scene tape.

"So you called this in? What's goin' on?"

She liked Christopher. In a very real way, it was a gift from the Almighty that he'd been the one to respond to the Jeffries crime scene just then. He wouldn't hurt her. He wouldn't bring up any of the unpleasantness that had made her flee Seattle. At least not to her face.

"Working a triple homicide back home." She could tell by the look on his face, he already knew about all of that, but she continued anyway. "One of the victims had a connection with Jeffries and . . ." She stopped as they went inside the front door. "Watch for the glass."

He looked down and acknowledged the sparkling shards. "So, what's this Jeffries woman's deal?"

Christopher Collier was a patient man, a broad-shouldered six-footer with a gentle countenance. He could be fierce when needed, but generally was the kind of man who deliberated on everything. *Carefully. Thoughtfully.* He never rushed. Emily liked him for that very reason. But as she struggled to come up with a good reason why she was there in a house with a dead body, it felt a little as though he was letting her twist in the wind. She told him about the Angel's Nest connection with her homicides in Cherrystone and how she'd seen Olga Morris-Cerrino, then Tina Esposito, which had led her to Bonnie's house.

*Bonnie's corpse.*

She led Christopher into the hazily lit living room. "I found her down there in the bedroom. My guess is that she was killed in bed. She sleeps days, works nights. The assailant got in by breaking that window and turning the knob."

"Okay," he said. "Let's have a look."

Emily stayed where she stood. "Your case," she said. "I'll stay here."

The Seattle police detective disappeared into the darkness of the hallway. Emily heard him speaking to another of the detectives, a younger man, whom she did not know.

"Emily Kenyon," he said, his voice somewhat lower than normal. "She used to be one of us. Got her butt kicked hard by the Kristi Cooper case."

"I remember studying that case at the academy. That's *her*?"

"Yeah, she's okay. Been through a lot. I'll handle her. Let's look at the vic."

*Kristi Cooper. Kristi.* The name nearly stopped Emily's heart. If she lived to be one hundred years old, she'd still never get over what happened with Kristi. It was clear that others hadn't forgotten the name either. No one ever would. *Jesus, the police academy taught that?* As Emily remained frozen in the living room, a dead woman on the bed, a half dozen police officers and detectives moved in and out of the tattered brown bungalow. She found herself wishing she was invisible.

But she wasn't.


*What in the world?* Emily stood in Bonnie's over-stuffed living room and tried to catch her breath. She shut her eyes tightly and opened them. Something so bewildering it couldn't be real. She couldn't believe her eyes. The coin purse on the credenza was pink and beaded with the design of a flamingo standing on one leg. It was so familiar. The flamingo was missing its eye. *Couldn't be.* She picked and pulled on the zipper and opened it. The missing eye bead was still inside.

*Jenna was here.*

Emily steadied herself, resting the palm of her hand on the back of the oak desk chair. She felt the floor move a little. It was the sensation that she'd endured during the Cooper case so many years ago. She hadn't felt the shifting floor like that in years. *Not a panic attack.* Her throat felt constricted and her breathing grew shallow. *What happened here?* Her sense of control fluttered. It was like the days after Kristi when she couldn't move, couldn't even drive. It was all she could do to get behind the wheel of a car back then, only to find she couldn't turn the key. No one who'd ever experienced a panic attack could ever understand how powerful it could be. *Get over it. Pull yourself together. None of that worked.*

As Christopher Collier started down the hall, Emily did the only thing that came to her fragile mind just then. She put the tiny coin purse in her jacket pocket. She breathed in deeply. She heard Christopher and the other detectives as they moved about the back bedroom. She heard a photographer taking pictures. *What had happened here? What had Nick and Jenna done?* She closed her eyes.

"You all right?" It was Christopher. His voice snapped her back.

"Fine. Thanks."

"You look as pale as a ghost."

Emily tried to shake it off. "I don't know. I guess you just never really get used to this stuff. Not if you're human," she said. The pink edge of the purse protruded slightly from her pocket, and she gently pushed it out of sight. Her heart was a bass drum. She felt sweat work its way down her temples.

"Hear, hear." Christopher tilted his head in the direction of the front door. "Let's get you some air."

"Thanks. Turn up anything back there?" she asked.

"Yeah. One thing. The kill was fresh. Probably within the last hour or so. The ME will know better. I'm just stating the obvious of course. The blood on the floor had barely coagulated. Slippery mess in there."

Emily didn't say anything. She didn't know what to say.

"When did you get here?" Christopher picked up the slack in the conversation, the light of a sunny day now flooding the yard in front of the dull brown house. A flowering cherry tree Emily hadn't noticed was like a mushroom cloud of pink over the garage. "About what time?" His tone wasn't exactly accusatory, but it bothered her. But not for the reason Christopher Collier would have dared to imagine. She thought of the coin purse. *When had Jenna and Nick been there?*

"I was here no more than five minutes before Cen Comm took my 911 call for help."

"That's what I thought. Sure is something that you'd find another body when looking for answers to those three back in Cherrystone."

"Yes, I guess so." She didn't know what else to say. He was right.

"Are you going to be okay?"

She nodded.

"Drink later? I have to stay and process the scene."

Emily didn't want to, but saying no right then might appear like she was pushing him away. Better to have him close just then.

"At the Westerfield downtown. Call me there," she said.

Emily put her car in gear and started to leave, and watched the scene in her rearview mirror. Christopher Collier walked back inside. Four more cops and techs had arrived, as had the tricked-out truck of the local 24/7 radio news crew. The TV people would probably be next on the scene. Yellow plastic tape now stretched across the front of the house like a banner for a soldier's homecoming from Iraq. Emily had no intention of going back to the hotel. *Not now.* Now more than ever, she needed to find her daughter. *No more mistakes.* She drove east to David's house on Mercer Island. The image indicating a new message played on the tiny LCD screen of her phone. A text message from Sheriff Kip that nearly caused a pile up on the I-5 and I-90 interchange.

Walker released last year. Returned to WA. Tacoma area.

Emily took her cell phone to the sitting room adjacent to the bedroom. It occurred to her that the space would have been a better work area than her bed. *A lot better.* She sighed and punched the speed dial number for David. It went immediately to voice mail. *He was on the phone.* She sighed and dialed Olga's number.

"Emily?" Olga answered. "Is that you? Are you all right?"

"It's me. I'm sorry it took so long to call you back. The day has been a nightmare."

"I know. I heard about Bonnie turning up dead."

"Oh," Emily said, slumping into a chair. "What's the media saying?"

"It hasn't been on the news," Olga said. "A friend of mine from Seattle PD called me. Gruesome. *You* found her?"

"Yes," Emily said, softly, unable to stop the images of what she'd found from playing once more. The blocked-out windows. Bonnie on the bed. Everything soaked in blood. The little pink purse. The baby pictures. They rolled, one after another. She changed the subject to save herself from reliving it even more.

"Do you know anything about Bonnie's family?" Emily asked.

"What family? She was an only child. Her parents disowned her when she went head over heels over Walker. I talked to them one time, very briefly. Ran into them at the Angel's Nest trial. I was going to testify that she was a nut job, but I was never called."

"There were baby pictures in the hallway," Emily said. "She must have had someone in her life. No sibs?"

"None that I ever knew about. Best friend was Tina Winston and the love of her life was Mr. Wonderful, Dylan Walker."

Emily's phone indicated that David was calling and Emily told Olga that she'd get back to her as soon as she could. She said good-bye and pushed the Talk button.

"I tried calling a moment ago."

"I know," David said, his voice cool. "What did you want?"

"Our daughter, of course. God, do you have to be such an ass about all of this?"

"You haven't exactly made my life easy."

"Easy? Let's not go there."

David exhaled. "All right. Jenna's not here. We haven't seen her all day. I left you a message to call me."

"I've been busy." Though she felt defensive just then, Emily also felt a wave of panic. She'd hoped that Jenna was home with her father. She didn't see the need to tell him about the Jeffries murder nor about Jenna's coin purse being found there. Neither could she admit that she'd reconnected with Christopher Collier, albeit at a crime scene. The name would enrage David. He'd been the source of many of their arguments in the past.

*"Why don't you just confide in your cop buddy?"*

*"You have your own little girl now. Kristi Cooper has been dead for years. Get over it. I'm your husband. Christopher Collier is married to someone else."*

*"Christopher called. He's worried about you."*

There had never been any real reason for the jealousy. Their relationship had never been sexual. But David didn't see it that way.

"David, we've got to find her. Jenna's in trouble."

"Besides her boyfriend with the dead family, what do you mean? Jesus, Emily, what is going on?" His patience was maxed out and the familiar timbre of his irritated voice was in full force.

"Look, I don't know what's happening. I don't have a goddamn clue right now. But this is bad. This is serious. You need to act like her father. You need to make her safe."

"Don't start lecturing me. She was living with you when she ran off."

"You know something? I'm glad that you have Dani. She's a bigger bitch than I could ever be."

Emily snapped the phone shut. And it felt good.

# CHAPTER TWENTY-EIGHT

*Sunday, 2:10 P.M.,*
*Seattle*

Emily felt her pocket. *The little pink change purse.* Jenna and Nick had been at Bonnie Jeffries's house. They'd probably found her in the phone book or in some Google search at the library. *What had they seen? What had they done?*

The "Watching the Detectives" ringtone sounded. Emily reached for her cell. The number was local, but unfamiliar. She answered.

"Emily? It's Christopher Collier. We're wrapping up the scene. Pending notification, this is going to make some news. The media will probably want to talk to you."

Her heart sank. It would take two seconds for even the worst Seattle reporter to make a connection with her name and past news items.

"Can't you leave me out of this? I've got my own problems right now."

"You know I can't. You found the vic. That's the first question anyone is going to ask about."

"How much time do I have?" she asked.

Christopher hesitated. "I don't know. We're trying to track down her family."

"All right."

"You know where they're at?"

Emily turned the Accord onto the freeway headed west toward the hospital. "I didn't know she had any kids."

"The pictures in the hall. The baby pictures."

Emily remembered. A trio of black-and-whites of a newborn were framed among a montage of other photographs. Some of Bonnie. Some of her pets. They hung in a row of cheap drugstore frames, the golden finish tarnished and flaking.

"Sorry," she said. "Can't help you." Her mind throbbed with worry for her daughter and what might have happened to her. It was all that she could process just then. His next words snapped her back into the moment.

"Drinks tonight? Like we talked about?" he asked, almost hopefully.

Emily caught the vibe. And her own response surprised her.

"Sure," she said. "Love to. I have some things to do."

"Jenna will turn up," he said.

"I'm going to see David."

"Right. I'd tell you to say hi, but I know how that would go over."

Emily disregarded the comment. There was no point in going there.

"See you tonight," she said.

She called David and begged him to meet her at his office.

"I don't know where Jenna is," he said. "Dani and I are busy today, anyway."

"Be there. I need you."

Her message must have come through. She didn't think she was pleading. She didn't think his heart could open to her anymore. But for a second, the walls came down.

"Okay, I'll be there."

### Sunday, 3:30 P.M.

"After what you said to Dani, I should never speak to you again without a lawyer." David Kenyon was as angry as Emily had ever seen him. His face was red and his eyes were narrowed so tightly they threatened to merge into a single lens.

"You can hate me all you want," she said, knowing full well she'd crossed the line. *Hell, jumped over it.* She'd come to his office prepared to eat a bucket of dirt because what she was about to do went against everything she knew her by-the-book ex-husband stood for. She wanted him to break the law. "But this isn't about me right now, David. It's about *our* daughter."

David didn't soften one bit, at least outwardly. His anger was deep and invoking Jenna's name wouldn't fix it. Even so, he knew that he had to help.

"I don't want to be like Rick Cooper," he said. It was a cheap shot—a reference to her freefall from grace—but Emily let it roll off her. She didn't offer a retort that punished him for something that he'd done.

*Like screwing Dani and getting her pregnant when we're trying to raise a daughter into a decent young woman.*

She held her tongue.

Just then, David's assistant Lindsay McKee entered the office. She was young, single, pretty—a deadly combination for any doctor.

"Working on a Sunday?" Emily gave David a knowing glance.

He ignored it.

"Doctor, I had some things to do," Lindsay said, shashaying into the room, in a short skirt and three-inch heels. "Some problems with the insurance on your Tuesday surgery." Lindsay rolled her big green eyes and David smiled.

"All right," David said, letting out an exaggerated sigh. "Did any of us think insurance companies would run our lives when we were back in med school?"

Lindsay laughed. "God knows they run this hospital!" She nodded at Emily and waited a beat to see if Dr. Kenyon would introduce them, but he stayed mum. As soon as the girl left, Emily came around the desk to face the computer screen. David started typing his password: Dani21.

It wasn't hard to see the keys he was hitting, especially the last two.

"Is that her age?" Emily's words were drenched in sarcasm.

David made a face, but said nothing.

"Kidding."

David hit the Enter key and the system flashed into life. A blue-and-white screen displayed various fields

for names, socials, addresses, and insurance information.

"Okay, to search the database is pretty easy," he
said, looking at Emily. "If I can do it, you can do it."

"Okay. Remember you're talking to a woman who
still thinks blackberry is a pie filling."

"I remember." He softened a little. "Records from
all Seattle hospitals are held on separate servers that
share the same interface and same security protocol.
The only hitch here is that I'm a surgeon, not a records
clerk. I have access, but it will log that I've looked at
records that I probably have no need to review. It will
send a report up to the IT people and I'll have some explaining to do."

"You'll think of something," Emily said. "You can
be a good liar when you want to be." She hated herself
for saying that, but the words just slipped out. David
was doing something that she needed done. *Desperately.* A court order would take too long.

*Jenna won't be another Kristi Cooper.*

"Where's your printer?" Emily asked.

"You didn't say anything about making copies. I
could get in deep shit for this. *No copies.*"

"You want me to be here all day? Do you want me
to get to the bottom of this?"

David eyed his office door. He wasn't entirely convinced, but he was willing to consider what Emily was
saying. His assistant Lindsay dropped off some corre-
spondence. She smiled at David. It was a slightly flir-
tatious smile, not quite come hither, but far past
cordial.

*The look for a single doctor.* Emily figured she didn't

know that Dani was at home, pregnant and destined to be the doctor's wife.

After she left, David spoke.

"Okay, the printer is next to Lindsay's workstation. I'll tell her you are printing out some tax stuff for us, and to keep people clear of the printer. She'll listen."

"Yeah, she's in love with you."

David blushed slightly, but he didn't deny it. "Just do what you need to do. For Jenna." He left his expansive office, letting the door shut slowly behind him.

Emily stared at the screen and began to type: Angel's Nest + Agency. The system's hourglass timer began to spin as the computer worked through the thousands, if not hundreds of thousands, of records. Emily looked around and noticed for the first time a photo of Jenna and David taken at the Grand Canyon. She was missing from the shot. Not because she'd held the camera—as she did on most of their travels—but because he'd cropped her out. She could still see the shadowy form of her arm over Jenna's shoulder. Emily shook her head. The computer kept grinding. Through the frosted glass panels alongside his office door, Emily could see Lindsay's silhouette moving around her cubicle.

The search screen popped up.

*What the—?*

It was packed with entries for Angel's Nest. Bonnie Jeffries's name leapt off a few of the citations. There must have been more than a hundred. Emily started scanning them when Lindsay decided she needed to come in with a mug of stale hospital coffee.

"Want some? Dr. Kenyon told me you're his ex-wife," she said, though there was no reason except the medical assistant's apparent need to confirm what her boss had told her.

"I'm fine," Emily said. "I'm printing out some private tax records."

"David told me," she said.

*David? Hmmm. Poor Dani. I almost feel sorry for her. Almost.*

"I'll get those pages for you."

"No," Emily said firmly. "I'll get them. They are, after all, private."

"Oh that's okay," the assistant said with a smile. "David trusts me with all of his private affairs."

"But *I* don't." Emily got up, pushed past the dumbstruck young woman and went to the printer. She guarded it as page after page rolled out. Finally, a moment or two passed, and the machine stopped. She retrieved the stack and started for the elevator.

Lindsay stood there with her hands on her hips. She was talking to another medical staff member. Emily could read just one word on her lips.

"Bitch."

*You don't know the meaning of the word,* Emily thought. *But Dani will teach you.*

# CHAPTER TWENTY-NINE

**Sunday, 5:10 P.M.,**
**Seattle**

It was very late afternoon when Emily returned to her
hotel room. She'd practically lived on her cell phone
since leaving David's office with the medical records
tucked into a Macy's shopping bag next to Lindsay-in-
love's desk. She'd talked with Gloria at the sheriff's
office back home. No news. She left a message for
Olga. She had even talked with Dani to try to patch
things up. The conversation played in her mind and
she felt her anger rise.

"I am sorry," Emily had said, gritting her teeth
somewhat, but making a valiant effort. An outboard
motor went by. Dani was out on the deck overlooking
the lake.

"I'd like to believe you," Dani responded, coolly.
"For Jenna's sake."

*Why do you insist on being such a bitch? You've got*
*the view home. You got the surgeon. You can have all*

*of that. Just don't bring up my daughter's name like she means a damn thing to you.*

"That's right," Emily said, swallowing the bile in her throat, "for Jenna."

She slipped out of her shoes and made a beeline for the minibar, which to her dismay didn't have a drop of tequila. She'd had a taste for the Mexican booze all day. She settled for gin and tonic. After talking with Dani Brewer, it just seemed especially good right for the moment. She noticed the light on the hotel phone blinking and she punched in the code for the message center. There were two. Both from Christopher Collier.

"Hi Emily. Chris here. Dinner tonight? I've tried your cell twice. You must be out of range. Call me and let me know if you want to meet up at your hotel." Drinks had become dinner. That was fine with her. A kind face would be a welcome change.

The second call was a hang-up.

She dialed Christopher's number, this time getting the Seattle Police detective's voice mail. In a way it was a relief. She felt anxious, foolish, tired. But she was also lonely and in need of company. Maybe even in need of validation that she hadn't screwed up her entire life or lost her daughter.

*Hadn't been the victim of bad karma.*

"Chris, dinner tonight sounds lovely. How about eight? See you here at the Westfield."

Seeing Christopher, she knew, was something she had to do. She sipped her drink and remembered what until Jenna's disappearance, had been the worst episode of her life. It was long ago and Christopher had been there.

### Long before the tornado, on the Washington coast

The summer wind blew cool moist air over the driftwood along the Pacific shore. A few seabirds dove into the surf, and about a hundred yards down the beach, a couple of beachcombers looked for their elusive prize—Japanese glass fishing floats. Emily Kenyon was alone; her partner Christopher Collier was searching the area from the south side of the beach. She wore street clothes—khakis, open-toed shoes, and white cotton blouse. A heavy woolen sweater concealed her weapon. Sand and beach grit found its way inside and was grinding the soles of Emily's feet. She cursed the fact that she wore those completely impractical shoes.

She and Christopher were looking for a little girl named Kristi Cooper. The Northwest had been riveted by the story of the little girl, who had last been seen by her mother in one of those gigantic bins of multi-colored plastic balls at a Seattle fast food restaurant. *Last seen.* It had been a while. Kristi had been missing for almost three weeks. She was blond and pretty. She was also small for her age. In a media-driven world that had embraced the concept of bland American adorable, Kristi fit the bill to a T. Her picture was everywhere—newspapers, flyers, even a billboard along the interstate just north of Olympia. Certainly her face was a key reason that Kristi captivated the hearts and minds of residents around Washington State. But it wasn't the only reason. She also was the daughter of a wealthy car dealer—one who made his fame by appearing on cheap TV commercials smashing cars with a sledgehammer and screaming that only his insanity could explain the low prices he offered.

*"I'll smash up this car to make a deal with you!"*

It was a clear case of kidnapping when a $250,000 ransom demand quickly followed. That, of course, made it a federal case handled under the auspices of the FBI, with help from the Seattle Police Department. Seattle PD was stuck in a supporting role, while taking most of the heat from the media as the story unfolded. Rick Cooper, Kristi's used-car-magnate father, followed the FBI's request to withhold the ransom while they tracked hundreds of potential leads. None, however, seemed to get any traction. A week after it started, the kidnapper stopped calling.

Emily, who up until that point had peripheral involvement in the case, volunteered for extra duty the day of the beach search—another low priority follow-up from an anonymous tipster.

Those days always played in her mind like a bad dream. There were many images that came to mind. *The girl, of course.* But the one that held the tightest grip was the face of her father. Emily could never forget seeing his bitterness, his deep hurt, his complete and unmitigated rage.

All of it had been directed toward her.

"Does she know what she's done?" Rick Cooper asked a local TV reporter, the microphone so close to his angry mouth that he could have swallowed it in one gulp. "We don't know where Kristi is and Emily Kenyon is the reason why."

*The reason. The cause.*

Emily didn't reach for the bottle like some cops who'd made mistakes they could easily live with. She did see a doctor and took some meds for anxiety, but only for a short time. She didn't fall apart, at least not outwardly so. She had a husband and daughter who needed her. There was an investigation over what happened in the Cooper case. There were more media reports. She gave up her shield for thirty days. She tried to keep her mind on Jenna and David, but a girl she never met would not leave her mind. Even when she was engaged in a conversation with David, thoughts unspooled. She had screwed up. She hadn't meant to, of course. But when she looked down at her hands, she knew they had been the inadvertent instrument of a little girl's demise.

*God, please forgive me. God, give me the chance to make this right.*

Reynard Tuttle was wheezing, his lungs pierced by a single bullet from Emily Kenyon's police-issue gun. It had all happened so fast—a racing speed that allowed not a second for introspection about what had just occurred. A dark spot of blood bloomed on his food-and sweat-stained white cotton T-shirt, and then oozed crimson to the cabin floor. He was only twenty or so, barely a man. Emily knelt beside him. He was trying to speak. She pushed his gun away and she leaned close.

"Shouldn't have done that," he said, barely able to form his words.

"Where's Kristi?"

"That's for me to know and you to find out." His voice was a soft rasp.

Emily knew he was dying, but his death went far beyond the tragedy of his own wasted life. He had to live to tell her what she needed to know. Adrenaline pulsed. She shook him. "Don't fuck with me."

"You'll never find her." Tuttle turned his head slightly and looked up. His eyes were beginning to roll.

"Don't leave!" she said. "Stay with me. You don't want this to be what you're remembered for. You don't want to hurt Kristi. Where is she?"

Collier rushed through the opened doorway. "Jesus, Emily, are you all right?"

She glanced over her shoulder and with one quick nod, indicated she was unhurt. When she looked back down at Tuttle, his eyes had been emptied of life. They were the eyes of a cold, dead animal.

"Come back here!" she said, tugging on his shoulders. "Goddamn you!" His head thumped on the cabin's planked flooring. *Hard*. "Where is the girl?"

"Emily, stop!"

She couldn't and Tuttle's head smacked against the floor over and over. But he was gone. *So was Kristi*.

A helicopter outfitted with an infrared camera worked a precise grid of forest and beachfront acreage in the vicinity of the Tuttle shooting. Tourists and homeowners watched the sky as the aircraft's whirling blades rattled their windows. Everyone knew what the Seattle Police and FBI were looking for—the telltale hot spot that indicated Kristi Cooper, dead or alive. At one point, a team was dispatched for follow-up on a glow of red picked up near Foster's Pond. Working shoulder to shoulder in a squared-off line, almost fifty FBI agents, police, and Boy Scouts trained in a process of a detailed grid search marched lockstep toward the hot spot.

"Anything and everything gets tagged," a Seattle sergeant yelled across the front of the line as the teams began to walk. One kid dropped a marker at a smoked cigarette; another found a rotted sleeping bag.

*"Tag it!"*

About twenty-five minutes into the march, a female volunteer caught an acrid whiff of the instantly recognizable scent of death. She started coughing. She was sure that she'd found Kristi Cooper's remains. Any hope that she was alive was erased by that terrible smell. That stench could only mean one thing. *It was over.*

"Over here, my end of line," the young searcher called. Two CSIs moved methodically toward the call for help. They stepped on the existing tracks of the search team. Each step was a shadow behind those who'd walked ahead.

In front of the young woman, now doubled over in anticipation of vomiting, was a mass of undulating maggots.

A CSI in a dark blue jumpsuit, bent down. "Dead fawn," he said, not masking his disappointment. "No tag, but steer clear. Damn it. This must be our hot spot."

For nearly two years, the dead deer was the closest anyone really got to finding Kristi. Emily had left the Seattle Police Department by then, moving David and Jenna into the old house on Orchard Avenue. She'd told everyone that her parents were ailing, but the truth was she could no longer face the reminders of what she'd done. Being exonerated by the department's Internal Affairs meant nothing.

Not when a missing girl with blond hair and blue eyes haunted every dream.

### Sunday, 7:10 P.M.,
### Seattle

Emily finished a drink from the minibar and looked in the mirror. All the makeup in the world wouldn't make her beautiful just now. Christopher Collier would have to see her for what she was—a middle-aged mother heartbroken with worry about her only child. *Where was Jenna? What had happened at Bonnie's?* She filled the sink and splashed cool water on her face. She'd hoped it would reduce the puffiness of her eyes, but she doubted it. She patted herself dry and put on a touch of makeup and some lip color. She was about to try something with her hair when the hotel phone rang.

"Emily, I'm downstairs. Want to eat here? I checked out the dining room menu. Looks good."

"Sure, Chris. Be down in a minute."

"Good. We have lots to talk about."

Emily buttoned up a fresh blouse and slipped on a simple linen skirt. She ran a brush through her thick, dark hair. She fished through her bag and found a gold bracelet that Jenna had given her for Mother's Day the year before her marriage crumbled. She dabbed on a little blush. This was as good as it was going to get.

*Christopher has seen me at my worst. He won't mind.*

**Sunday, 8:00 P.M.**

The dining room at the Westerfield was all cream and gold, with ceilings soaring thirty feet above candle-lit tables spread with linen, silver, and crystal. The menu was a haute cuisine mix of Pacific Rim cooking. The feature that evening was Chilean sea bass prepared with sesame, garlic, and scallions. Emily and Christopher both ordered it, along with a bottle of Chardonnay from a small Washington vintner that had won raves from *Wine Spectator*. A little awkward small talk reigned for a while. Christopher had been divorced for ten years. His kids lived with his ex and her new husband on a ranch in Boise. He lived in a downtown condo overlooking Puget Sound and Seattle's Pike Place Market. He still loved hiking and made frequent treks in the Cascades and Olympics.

"You still hike, Emily?" He speared a bite of flaky white fish.

She touched her napkin to her lips. "Yes, but we don't get out as much as we'd like," Emily said, obviously referring to her and Jenna. Every sentence seemed to be constructed that way. It only served to remind her of the deep emptiness she felt, the fear she had for her daughter's safety.

After a pause, she said, "Thanks for not making a big deal about me being *the* Emily Kenyon at the Jeffries scene." When she'd overheard him talking about it, he'd seemed forgiving—more forgiving than she had been over the years about what had happened back then.

He swirled the wine in his glass. "No problem. That

case has followed you much more than me. I mean, I was there, too, you know."

"Yes, I remember." Emily sipped her wine, reminding herself she'd already had what amounted to two shots of tequila. Though grateful that he understood, Emily took the opportunity and changed the subject. "Did you make the notification about Bonnie Jeffries? Should I brace myself?"

"No," he said. He set his fork down. "That's one of the reasons I wanted to see you. Catching up with you, as pleasant as it is, wasn't my sole motive."

Emily felt a flash of embarrassment. "Of course."

"We can't find any record of Bonnie having any family," he said.

She thought of the papers up in her room. Tina hadn't mentioned any children, either. "What about the pictures? Maybe a nephew?"

"No family. Seems Bonnie's parents were killed in a car wreck back in ninety-one. No sibs. No husband. The woman lived alone after the Angel's Nest scandal. Hardly ever went out. Her neighbors didn't even know her last name or where she worked."

Dinner continued with some shop talk, some family stuff. When the dessert cart scooted by, both took a pass. Christopher pulled out what looked like an old photo album. It was scuffed black leather, with red corners. Emily hadn't really noticed that he brought it along until then. She looked at it inquisitively.

"From Bonnie's place," he said. "I think you should see it."

She put her hand out, but Christopher didn't give it up.

"Not here. Let's take it somewhere private. Your room?"

If it were any other man, Emily would have shot down the suggestion with a laugh and a quick retort. But she trusted Christopher. And more than that, she saw the concerned look in his eyes.

*Or was it something more?*

# CHAPTER THIRTY

"**D**oing some clandestine research on the case?" Christopher asked as they entered Emily's hotel room. She nodded in the direction of the stolen stacks of hospital records she'd laser printed off David's office computer.

"And, *no*, I didn't have a warrant," she said.

"I didn't log this baby into evidence yet, either," Christopher said, setting the photo album on the corner of the bed. "Nice place," he said. "They must have big expense accounts in Cherrystone." He surveyed the plush surroundings, deep coppery hues on the pillow-overloaded bed, a gas fireplace, an oil painting that appeared to be original—not a mass-produced phony like most places have. He walked over to the floor-to-ceiling windows. The Olympic Mountains off in the distance were nearly indigo and the city lights of Seattle twinkled in the foreground. "My place is right over there."

Emily stood next to him, feeling the effects of too much Chardonnay. "Where?"

He pointed to his condo, but when she didn't spot it, he reached over and turned her head just a touch. "There."

The moment begged for double entendres along the lines of I'll show you mine, if you show me yours—*evidence, that is*. But both parties resisted. There was too much at stake just then, and the teasing near-romance of their friendship was years ago.

The message feature on her cell phone pulsed and Emily took the cue to break away from Christopher and the window. She dialed and learned that David and Olga had phoned. She'd call both of them back after Christopher showed her whatever it was that he'd brought to dinner.

Christopher took the opportunity to dial in for an update on the Jeffries case. His face was stone. No smile. None of the charm that he'd shown during dinner. Whatever he was hearing, it was unpleasant and dark. When he ended the call, he told her that he'd been talking with the medical examiner's assistant about the Jeffries murder.

"Overkill, for sure," he said. "I guess even a rookie could tell that by the scene. Jesus, talk about blood-soaked. ME says that Bonnie Jeffries was beaten and stabbed. Either could have killed her. She was hit with a hammer or something like that—tool marks on her skull are being reviewed now. Looks like at least a half dozen times. She was stabbed with a serrated blade probably thirty-five times."

The possible circumstances of her last breaths were more than bone chilling. They were arctic.

"She had a big set of knives in the kitchen," Emily said. "I have the same set."

He nodded. "Right. I saw them. Not yours. Hers."

"I got that."

"The ME says she was probably out cold when she was stabbed. Not a single defensive wound."

"But she bled out, so she was still alive when the killer stabbed her," Emily said.

"Sliced and diced is more like it. The ME says that whoever killed her was driven by rage and contempt. Hatred to the nth degree. He drove that knife into her no more than a half inch, as if he wanted to tease her to death."

"Or enjoy it. Make it linger."

"Yeah. We know the type. Some twisted psycho who gets off on torture."

"Any trace? Anything at all to tag her assailant?"

"Assailants, with an S. Had to be at least two. She's a big girl as they say. ME says she was first hit in the kitchen, then finished off in the bedroom. Posed there."

The brutality of the attack made her sick. Emily studied the skyline, searching for words and trying to find some kind of calmness in the moment. The idea that there were two assailants was like an ice down her spine. *Nick and Jenna? Not possible. But they had been there.* Her mind was racing, but she fought to stay cool. She had no choice.

"Anything on tox?" she asked.

He shrugged. "Clean."

That surprised her somewhat and she turned to look at Christopher. She remembered seeing a bottle of vodka on the kitchen counter and an array of pills. *She'd expected something.*

"Whoever killed her caught her unaware. She didn't see it coming," she finally said. Her mind transported her back to the gruesome scene. She'd been in the bedroom only a minute, but the images of what she'd seen would never fade. Foil held the room dark. The radio played. The sheets—cheerful daisies were the print— were colored in ropes and slashes of blood. Bonnie was in a pale blue nightgown.

"She was facedown on the bed," she said. "Hit from behind?"

"Maybe, but she was stabbed in the chest and the back. He or *they* moved her around on that bed a bit."

Christopher picked up the black album. "This is from Bonnie's place. We found it wedged behind the desk. I don't know if it was hidden there, or if it just fell." He indicated a wingback chair he scooted next to the bed where he'd taken a seat. "Sit here. There's some weird stuff in this book."

Suddenly the Macy's bag of hospital records seemed irrelevant.

Emily edged the chair closer to Christopher, who'd opened the book with his eyes fixed on hers, gauging her reaction. It was a compendium of news articles, neatly cut and pasted on black sheets of construction paper. Whoever had set up the book, clearly did so carefully. There wasn't a crooked edge or scissor slip. The headline on the opening page was unfamiliar to her.

**MISSING ONE WEEK:**
**WHERE IS BRIT?**

Now holding the book across her lap, Emily scanned the yellowed, brittle clipping. It was an article about Brit Osterman, a twelve-year-old girl who'd gone missing on her way home from school in her cozy Seattle neighborhood.

"What's this?" she asked.

Christopher just looked at her and shook his head. "Read on. And like I said, be prepared. I think there's something here."

The article on the first page was followed by one with a picture of an adorable girl with cat-eye glasses and a nose splashed with freckles. She had not been found. Her parents were quoted as saying they'd "never give up . . . until our little girl is home safe and sound."

Another item recounted how the girl was never found.

### FIVE YEARS AGO,
### LITTLE GIRL VANISHED

Emily looked up at Christopher. Her mind was racing for a connection. "Bonnie?"

"Oh God no," he answered flatly. "Not at all. Flip to the next one."

The headline on the next page was an absolute screamer. The letters were at least two inches tall, centered smack under the masthead of the Nampa, Idaho, *Daily Express*. The words were utterly heartbreaking. Emily touched her lips, as if doing so would stop her from tears as she read.

**STEFFI MILLER'S MOTHER:**
**WHY DID GOD ALLOW THIS?**

The article was about the disappearance of a teenage girl from a religious camp on a lake near Nampa. A couple of campers were quoted about how much Steffi had enjoyed canoeing and theorized that perhaps she'd suffered a fatal accident. But the reporter pretty much put that to bed with a quote from the ever-PR-minded camp director: "If she took a spill in the lake, she did it without a canoe. All of our canoes and skiffs are accounted for. We just don't know where she went." A photograph of a half dozen boys and girls sitting around a campfire had been the interest of at least one person. In red pencil, someone wrote: *"Me"* with an arrow pointing to the back of one of the boy's heads.

Emily met Christopher's knowing stare. He half smiled in that way cops do when something really devious is about to be sprung on an unsuspecting partner. Emily felt like a partner, back in the old days . . . and right then, too.

"Are you having fun yet?" he asked.

"Actually, I'm not." She frowned, knowing that he knew more and was holding out on her. "You know how I hate it when anyone withholds information."

"I remember," he said. "Oh yeah, I remember. The Miller case was never solved. No body ever found. Turn the page."

There were additional clippings. These featured a Seattle woman named Tanya Sutter. The name seemed somewhat familiar to Emily, but she couldn't quite place it. According to the news articles—and there were four pages of them—Tanya's body was discovered by a roadside cleanup crew one week after her disappearance. She was swathed in a plastic wrapping and dumped near an off-ramp outside of Tacoma.

The light went on. Emily pointed a slender finger at Tanya's photo. "Didn't they tag Dylan Walker for this one?"

"Bingo."

She scanned the articles and was reminded about Olga Cerrino and how she'd told her that the plastic wrapping had been a signature of Walker's. Since the other victims' bodies were never recovered, no one could say for sure if they'd been murdered, how the killer had done it, or if Walker had indeed been the killer. The bodies were the missing evidence.

"Are Shelley Marie Smith and Lorrie Ann Warner in here?" she asked.

"Yup. But that's not why I brought this to you."

Emily looked at him, puzzled. She started flipping toward the back of the book.

"Stop! Back up," he said. "You know better than to read the back of a book first."

Startled by his initial command, Emily missed the playful sarcasm of his last words. She started going backward, page by page; the headlines replayed the story of the Meridian murders from conviction to the discovery of the bodies. It was like a videotape on rewind. Pictures of Dylan Walker looking snarky and charming, handsome and devious. The high school photos of the victims showed them in all their youthful glory. Long hair. Braces. Wide smiles. Hand-wringing headlines covered every aspect of the story. An image of Olga Morris-Cerrino caught her eye and Emily lingered on the photo. *She was so lovely then. So young. So unaware that she'd marry and be a widow before fifty-five.* Emily started flipping the pages once more.

"There," Christopher said. "Right there."

She stopped. The black pages framed four news clippings. Emily put her hand to her chest. Her eyes were fastened to the pages in utter horror. She felt the air rush out of the room. She could barely breathe. The photos and words were so familiar, but the context of the book that someone had created was all wrong.

"What in the world?" she finally said. Her eyes glistened with the beginning of tears. "Chris?"

He leaned closer to her and put his hand on her knee.

"I know. I thought the same thing."

Emily started to cry. It was more than she could take in. "You know what this could mean?"

"I know and I'm sorry. But it might be wrong, a hoax. A mistake. Maybe wishful thinking on the part of Bonnie Jeffries. Maybe she wanted Walker to be responsible for every unsolved murder case."

Emily swallowed hard. It was quick gulp for air. She looked once more at the headlines. They were knives stabbing at her eyes, but she couldn't turn away.

**GIRL ABDUCTED FROM RESTAURANT**
*Search Continues For Kristi Cooper*

**COP KILLS KIDNAPPER**
*Girl Still Missing*

**BOY, 12, FINDS MISSING GIRL'S BODY**

The last article brought a torrent of memories. None of which had ever been anywhere but just beneath the surface. The slightest scratch, a twitch, the wrong word brought her back to the autumn of Kristi's discovery. With Christopher holding her close, Emily spun her way back to that day.

In every way, Christopher Collier was there, too.


The vine maples were on fire, colors so deep red and bright orange they looked like some set decorator's fantasy of what autumn should look like in a 1950s movie musical. All that had transpired was indelible, a memory tattoo.

Two Bentonville, Washington, boys with a new BB gun worked their way through a trail as they searched for squirrels and birds to shoot. The older of the two, Tyler Preston, was fourteen and the gun was a birthday present from his father. The other boy was twelve-year-old Mason Davidson.

"When am I going to get to shoot?" Mason asked for what must have been the tenth time.

"Not very patient, are you? I guess you can have a turn," Tyler said, finally handing over the BB gun. "You know how to shoot? See that robin over there?" He jabbed his finger at a bird about twenty-five yards away, a close enough target for him to hit, but not for the younger boy.

"Yeah."

"Watch this." Mason aimed, fired, and to Tyler Preston's sheer amazement, the robin fell from the branch. He looked over at his buddy with a gleeful smile and handed back the rifle.

"That's how it's done, bud!"

He ran to get the fallen bird. Tyler looked down at the shiny barrel of the BB gun and shook his head. *Beginner's luck.* He heard a noise and looked up, but Mason was nowhere to be seen.

"Mason?" he called. "Where are you, bro?"

A faint cry came from twenty yards away. "In here!"

Tyler set the gun down and ran. He ran to what appeared to be a big hole in the ground. A well? A sinkhole? He leaned over to get a better look.

"Tyler! Get me out of here!" Mason didn't sound hurt, but he sounded scared spitless.

"Hold on, dude!" Tyler looked for a branch or something he could use to extricate his buddy from the darkness below. "Hang on!"

"Get me out of here! Tyler!"

As his eyes adjusted to the dim and dank surroundings, Mason's terror escalated. He was unsure of what he saw at first. *Was it real? Was it a joke?* He moved closer and gasped.

"There's a bed down here and some other stuff. Hey, I think there's a dead body down here."

"No shit?"

"Yeah, there are bones," he said, cupping his hands to amplify his voice in the darkness. The makeshift covering of rotting boards shoved aside, a stream of light found its way to the floor of the twelve-foot-deep hole. "There's blond hair, too!"

"Whoa! Cool!"

"You wouldn't think so if you were stuck down here. Come on!"

Mason Davidson didn't know it right then, of course,

but he'd solved a mystery that had haunted the Pacific Northwest for two years.

He'd found Kristi Cooper.

### *Sunday, 11:00 P.M.*

In the same red pencil Emily noticed that someone had underlined Reynard Tuttle's name in an article that detailed how Emily had shot him in the ill-fated raid on the cabin. There was also an annotation. The words were tiny and in grammar school–perfect script: *Poor Dope.*

Emily found her footing and spoke. "I don't know what to say."

"I don't know what any of these means," Christopher said, releasing his slight embrace. "And you know how much I hate to admit that."

"I'll never forget the day those boys found her."

"I know. Whenever I see fall colors, I think of her, too."

"Whoever wrote in this book—Bonnie, I guess—wants us to think that Tuttle wasn't Kristi's captor."

"But he *was*," Christopher insisted.

Emily had always had her doubts. It was something she never spoke about to anyone, not David, not Christopher. It was the small voice she'd heard in the back of her head whenever she thought of Kristi and how she died. The voice she heard was never answered out loud. To do so, would bring home what she'd done.

"As far as we knew," she said. "I mean, there was nothing that tied him to the body, once we found her. No trace. No DNA."

His eyes were penetrating. "We can't second-guess what we did now."

"But you've brought this to me for a reason. You think there's something there."

"There's a link between Bonnie and Walker."

"She was his number-one fan," Emily said. "I talked with her girlfriend, Tina Esposito. She said she and Bonnie were best friends and had a major falling-out over Walker. Bonnie basically stole Walker from Tina. God knows why. They hadn't spoken in years."

This clearly interested Christopher. "Fighting over a serial killer?"

"You could put it that way. It wasn't that he was a serial killer. They believed he wasn't. Both of them. In fact, there was a legion of Bonnies and Tinas out there that lined up to see Walker during and after the trial."

He let out a sigh. "Another prison groupie, Jesus. What's with these women?"

Emily narrowed her gaze. "It isn't simple. I fought over a two-timer," she said, letting her guard down a little. "I lost. Some women love a guy they can't have." Emily looked over to the minibar. Another drink was against her better judgment, but the memories of Kristi Cooper and the possibility that she actually hadn't shot her captor called for something to thwart her creeping doubt. She opened the minibar.

"I'll have what you're having," Christopher said.

She opened a couple of mini Chivas Regal bottles. "No ice. No mix. Okay?"

He agreed and she poured. They sipped the smooth, smoky whiskey. "Perfect," he said. "Now let's get down to business. I've saved the best for the last."

"Better than Kristi?"

"Better."

"What are these?" Emily asked. Christopher was holding several slips of paper that had been kept in the back of the black album as precious souvenirs.

"Letters from Bonnie's boyfriend."

Emily pulled them out and looked at the signature on the last page of the first missive.

"Dylan Walker?"

"Yeah, and it's the typical sick stuff that these creeps send to women on the outside."

"The lonely and desperate or the desperately lonely." Emily started to scan the pages. "The handwriting appears consistent with the penciled notations in the album," she said, flipping back to the "*Me*" and "*Poor Dope*" written on the news clippings.

"That's what I thought. I mean, we're not allowed to speculate—*rush to judge*—and everything goes through the lab." He rolled his blue eyes and smiled.

Emily started reading, mostly silently, but as she moved through the pages she caught a few choice lines and looked up at Christopher.

*Feel me take off your clothes, one button at a time . . . lingering as they fall to the floor. Your hunger for my touch, insatiable . . . but I try.*

"Can you believe these women fall for this?"

"I know. Remember when the Shadow Murderer Bill Canton got married?"

Emily nodded, a disgusted look on her face. "You mean that Baby Jane–type blonde who went all over TV professing her love."

"Yeah, her love for a man who stalked and killed eight young women and dumped them all over LA like they were garbage."

"I guess Bonnie was that type of woman. Willing to believe anything, do anything, for love." She looked down and started reading, cherry-picking another line to read aloud.

*. . . You stare back, longing for us to become one. Your hands slip between my legs . . .*

# CHAPTER THIRTY-ONE

*Monday, 6:45 A.M.,*
*Cherrystone, Washington*

Jaws dropped to the floorboards as Shali Patterson climbed aboard school bus number 227. She managed to make it to the bus stop that morning when she found her car missing and a message from Jenna Kenyon. One of the kids she'd smoked with her tailpipe every morning couldn't resist making note of the occasion.

"Your ride in the shop, Shali Patterson? Have a seat. Anywhere."

Shali scanned the front, then the back of the bus. *This sucks.* Right now, she wanted to strangle her supposed best friend. She found a seat next to a freshman girl and slid next to her.

*Jenna thinks she's got it bad, but she doesn't know what bad is.*

***Monday, 9:00 A.M.,***
***Seattle***

Christopher Collier's resonant voice filled Emily's ears and jolted her like a slap in the face. She nearly dropped the phone. She'd always been an excellent judge of a witness's veracity. She listened, assessed, and without fail was right on the money when she determined whether or not she could trust someone. She'd believed Tina Esposito when they shared lunch and a smattering of true confessions at Embers restaurant. As far as Emily could see—and her instincts were always flawless—Tina was a gracious woman who'd made a horrendous mistake many years ago and suffered for it. Yet she was a survivor, a woman who'd completely extricated herself from Dylan Walker and Bonnie Jeffries. But what Christopher was telling her now indicated all of that was a big lie.

"Five calls this week alone," he said. "More when we go back a few weeks. There was even a call from Tina the morning Bonnie was murdered."

Emily was stunned. "She told me they hadn't spoken in years."

"She's a liar. I'm going to see her," he said.

With the cell phone snug against her ear, Emily looked for her cream-colored jacket. "Not without me, you're not. I can meet you at her place or you can pick me up and we can go together. Your choice."

"I figured that. I'm calling from downstairs."

Emily managed a smile. Christopher Collier knew her better than anyone. She liked him, trusted him, but she'd had more lapses in judgment when it came to men. Something about last night bothered her, but she'd had too much to drink to be sure about *everything* that had transpired. Sunlight streamed between a slit in the hotel curtains she hadn't remembered drawing. In fact, she hadn't remembered much of what happened after she'd started pouring the Scotch.

"Chris?" she asked.

"Yes?"

"Last night . . . we didn't, did we?"

"God no," Christopher Collier said. "Do you wish we did?"

The mosaic of what had transpired the previous evening started coming together. The dinner. The drinks. The revelations. The scrapbook. She noticed that it remained on the desk next to the hotel phone.

"You left the album," she said.

"I know. Bring it when you come downstairs."

Five minutes later, Emily was in the lobby. Christopher, looking dapper in a blue blazer and red tie and khakis, was waiting with Starbucks in hand.

"Vanilla latte?" he said, handing her the hot cup. "I just guessed."

"You're a mind reader, thanks."

A moment later, they were in his Audi—where the scent of cigarette smoke could not be refuted. He saw the look on her face.

"Yeah, I haven't quit yet." It was a preemptive strike against Emily's expected rebuke.

"I didn't say anything," she said.

They drove from the hotel toward the exclusive waterfront high-rise that Tina Esposito called home, Harbor Court. It was twenty stories tall and had been the source of much resentment from upland locals for blocking their waterfront views. But money and zoning talked. It always did. The Espositos owned the top floor.

"She's there," Christopher said, turning down the hill toward the waterfront. "We have an unmarked car down there with a couple of guys babysitting for me. We wouldn't want to miss her."

"You love this, don't you?" Emily asked.

He turned from looking at the street in front of him, his handsome face now overtaken by an almost impish smile. "Don't you?"

She had to admit that she did. "Better than a traffic stop in Cherrystone, that's for sure." But deep down, she thought that the recent events in Cherrystone had been anything but routine. *Mark, Peg, and Donny Martin had been murdered and that was the reason why she was in Seattle.*

### Monday, 10:15 A.M.

"My husband can't know about any of this" were the first words out of Tina Esposito's perfectly painted mouth as she opened the penthouse door. She was referring to Rod Esposito, the software developer who had earned millions when he developed a computer program that quickly became the gold standard of the airline industry's reservation systems. The joke was that he was afraid of flying. "He's away on business in Vancouver." She looked at her diamond-encrusted Cartier Santos watch. "His train arrives in three hours." With a sweeping gesture, she escorted the detectives into a living room with an absolutely breathtaking view of Elliott Bay to the west and Mt. Rainier to the south. Everything about the space was luxe. The carpets were Persian, and not from some flim-flam rug store featuring a two-year going-out-of-business sale.

*Not like mine back home,* Emily thought.

The furnishings were all antiques, of the most simple and elegant style. None of that ridiculous rococo French crap that most Americans clamored for once they had a few million to rub together. Emily noticed a landscape behind a settee, but suppressed the urge to get close enough to study it. She was sure it was a Constable, but she wasn't about to tip her art history class hand by saying so. Few residences in Seattle could make the pages of *Architectural Digest,* Emily mused to herself, but this one could.

*The Espositos might be new money, but their taste— or their hired interior designer's—was decidedly old school.*

Ensconced in her grand living room, Tina put up her hostess facade. It was merely a mask. Beneath her fine silk blouse, it was clear that her heart was beating at an accelerated rate. She was scared.

"Can I offer you some coffee?" She pointed to a mohair sofa. "Please take a seat."

"No coffee, thank you," Emily said. "We're not here on a social call, Tina. We're here to talk about the murder of a close friend of yours."

The remark brought a hard stare from Tina, then a curt response. "Bonnie and I *weren't* friends." She poured some coffee into a dainty china cup and proceeded to sprinkle a blue packet of sweetener into the dark brew. Then she stirred.

*The wheels were turning. She was buying time.*

"But you were," Emily said. "You called her five times this week."

Tina continued to stir like she was paddling a river. Christopher glanced at Emily. They both knew what was going on.

*Buying more time. Time to think.*

"I don't know what you're talking about," Tina said stiffly. She picked up the tinkling china cup and saucer and drank.

"Why are you making us treat you like this?" Emily said.

"How so?"

"Like you're a liar. We have the phone records. We *know* you called her."

An overweight longhaired mini dachshund waddled in and jumped up on Tina's lap. "Millicent," she said. Tina seemed grateful for the intrusion. She started stroking the dog's fat belly.

Emily leaned forward. "What did you talk to Bonnie about?"

Tina said nothing.

"If you'll look at the duration of the calls," Chris interjected, "you'll see they were very short."

Tina stammered, pretending to be unhappy with her coffee, her dog, her maid taking the day off. She was beginning to unravel. Her face was red now and she was petting the dog with such pressure, both detectives were sure the poor animal would yelp in pain if she didn't stop.

Chris pressed harder. "What was the nature of the calls? We have to know."

Tina just sat there. It was almost as if she wasn't listening.

"Do you get this?" It was Emily taking charge. "The woman's been murdered."

"Right. I know," she finally answered. Millicent the dog jumped to the floor and Tina stood up. "But if I tell you what I know you'll think I killed her."

Emily glanced at Christopher. This was the money shot. "Try us," she said. Her words were a command, soft, but not without some very real force.

Tina bent over and set her coffee on the table tray. "I didn't kill her. I *couldn't* kill anyone."

"All right." Christopher was standing now, too. "Talk to us."

With her arms wrapped around her like she was fighting off the chill of the air conditioner, Tina started across the room. She wasn't having any of it just then. "I think I might need a lawyer."

Emily indicated to Christopher that he stay put. She took Tina by the arm and they moved to the breakfast room off the kitchen. "Look, Bonnie was a big girl. I doubt you killed her and moved her body around that house. But you do know something. If you get a lawyer involved it'll just make things messier and more public. You don't want that, do you?"

Tina's hands were trembling then. She tried to steady them by clasping them together.

"I just don't want my husband to know."

Emily nodded. It was a false assurance, but she needed to nudge the woman into saying what she knew. "I can't guarantee anything. But trust me. I will do what I can to keep your name out of this. Tina, what do you know?"

Tears were streaming down Tina's face and she looked for a tissue. Finding none, and not wanting to go back out to the living room and be seen by Christopher Collier, she took a linen napkin from a sideboard drawer and dabbed at her eyes.

"I had a baby." She stopped talking as she fought to form the words that would reveal her darkest secret. "I gave it up for adoption."

Pieces were falling into place.

"Through Bonnie at Angel's Nest?"

"Right. Bonnie helped me."

"A lot of young women have given up babies when they couldn't care for them."

Tina set her napkin down and flattened and folded it. "That's not what happened. I had a job. I wasn't some dumb girl."

"But you did what you thought was right."

Tina was crying so hard now, she could no longer speak with any clarity. A few words tumbled from her lips, but they were nearly unintelligible. Whatever she was about to say had been buried for a long time. It wasn't going to come out without a fight. Right then, Tina Winston Esposito was fighting a losing battle. She could not hide it any longer. She was in quicksand.

"Take your time. It'll be all right."

Tina steadied herself. "Please," she said, "don't tell Rod. *Promise*. Promise me. Don't tell anyone." Her pretty eyes were pleading. Her hands were now held like she was praying.

*In fact, she was.*

"I'll do my best. What is it?"

"My baby's father was Dylan Walker."

It took almost half an hour to calm her down. By then, Tina Esposito had been ravaged by her emotions. Her blond hair was entirely limp, her carefully applied makeup had left her face for the folds of a linen napkin. She no longer looked like the woman who lived in that fabulous penthouse, but a stranger at odds with all of her surroundings. She was frightened and ashamed. She seemed short of breath in the way that an asthmatic might while confronting the last flight of a staircase.

"Relax. We'll get through this."

"I can't."

"You can. You will."

Emily went to the refrigerator and retrieved some bottled water. *Tina's getting ready to talk. Just have to keep at her. Give her the space she needs.*

"My Xanax is in the cabinet to the left of the sink, behind the Earl Grey," she said.

By then, Christopher had joined them, but with the shock of the revelation, he abdicated the role of lead interviewer to Emily, who was doing all she could to reassure Tina.

"There's no need for this to come out," she said. "But we do have to know everything."

"How can I be sure?" Tina suddenly looked like a middle-aged woman with a past that finally caught up with her. "My husband will leave me."

"He wouldn't do that," Emily said.

"You don't know Rod. He's all about appearances. This is his home. His money. It all comes from his carefully manufactured image. It matters."

"Tell us everything and then we'll go," Christopher said. "If we need to talk with you later, we'll arrange a discreet location. We're not here to ruin your life for something stupid you did a long time ago. Okay?"

Tina shook her head. "I can't say that I thought I'd be able to live my whole life having swept this under the carpet. The truth is, I've never gone a day without wondering if someone would come knocking on my door and asking, 'Are you my mother?'"

Christopher sat next to Emily, facing Tina. "Tell us what happened." His calm, understanding tone seemed to say, *don't be embarrassed. Don't hold back. You can trust us.*

Tina stayed silent, collecting her thoughts. She closed her eyes. Emily could see how hard this was, that Tina was fighting the compulsion to stay closed up. *To lie.*

"All right. But I want you to know that whatever I did, whatever stupid mistake I did, I've regretted it for a lifetime. It isn't me. My therapist has taught me not to let it define me. So I won't. I just won't."

Tina told them how it started, how the whole love affair with Dylan Walker had blossomed into something sexual.

"God, I know, you think I fell for him because he was so handsome. But it wasn't like that. It was through his words. It was like he could see into my soul. I know that sounds completely ridiculous, but the man had a gift. He was one of those rare people who could look right at you and know everything about you. Everything that mattered to you."

"I know the type," Emily said. "The world is full of charmers."

The disclosure seemed to calm Tina. She brightened slightly. "Maybe you do understand? I have beat myself up for almost twenty years. You'd probably be surprised to know that it wasn't until very recently that I've been able to put the blame on him, rather than myself."

Chris shot Emily a look, but she ignored it. Chris was the kind of man who never once considered that any actions were the result of another's control. He was all about personal responsibility.

Tina told them that when she first wrote to Dylan Walker, it was on a whim. But within a few months, she was in so deep that when he asked her to have his baby, she said yes.

Emily prodded, though she did so as gently as possible. "That's a huge leap, Tina. How did it happen?"

Tina stared at her smudged napkin. "I said yes, because I knew it wasn't possible. We weren't married before his conviction and therefore there'd never be any conjugal visit. Not in Washington, anyway. It was all a fantasy love affair. I believed in him—I never thought he'd killed *anyone*, let alone those girls from Meridian. I mean, I *knew* that to my bones. My love and support for him just masked the reality of what I was about to do."

Emily drew her in with a knowing smile, a look of acceptance. "Sometimes we do things that when we look back, we can't imagine that it was us at all." It was the kind of comment that made her such a good interviewer. Reveal a little something of yourself—or at least let the subject *think* you are. It builds trust and trust leads to further disclosure. In this case, Emily's thoughts were on Reynard Tuttle and Kristi Cooper.

"It was me," Tina said. "And I've thought about it every day. For years I tried to set it aside. When the Angel's Nest scandal broke I was just sure that it would come out. I started going to church. I prayed every night. I got on meds. Each moment closer to trial

I just knew my life was going to implode. But it didn't. I was home free. Until you."

"Back up," Christopher said, apparently comfortable enough to interject. "I'd like to be sensitive about this, but I can't think of a better way to say it. Just how did you manage to get pregnant?"

Tina Esposito stood and walked to the dining window. It was a slow, purposeful walk. The sunlight on her face showed every flaw. She had been beautiful once, but right now she looked old, tired, and scared. She spoke to the window, refusing to face Christopher or Emily.

"This is very embarrassing," she said, her voice a whisper. "During our visits, he'd pass me a sample."

She hesitated.

"A sample?" Emily asked.

"Oh God, you're going to make me draw you a picture, aren't you? Of his semen, you know. I'd excuse myself and use the bathroom." She searched for the most genteel words to describe what she'd done. Her embarrassment was etched on her pretty face. "I put it *inside* of me."

"Jesus," Collier said, his tact evaporating with the outrageousness of her disclosure.

She started crying, and turned to face the detectives. "Don't judge me."

"No one is being critical of you," Emily said. "We just need to know what happened."

Christopher pushed it. "How did you get a sample?" He tried to make his affect as flat, as *nonjudgmental*, as possible. "The semen sample."

"This is the embarrassing part," she said, hesitating

while she tried to come up with a way of relating the information as clinically as possible. But there was no way to do that. "He ejaculated into empty ketchup packets."

Neither investigator needed Tina to draw "the picture." They could see it very clearly now. Walker ejaculated into the packets, smuggled them to Tina, and she found her way into a bathroom stall and inserted the tomato-flavored semen into her vagina.

"It isn't as if I did this dozens of times," she said, seeing how unseemly as it all must have appeared. "I got pregnant on my third or fourth attempt. Are we done here? Do you have enough of what you need to know?"

"Not really," Christopher said. "What were the plans for the baby? And how did Bonnie get involved?"

"By the time I was pregnant and past the point of an abortion, I knew that I'd made the worst possible mistake of my life. When I came to visit Dylan one time to talk about his appeal and our fantasy future together, I had met another woman at the motel. Her car broke down and she had to stay another day, otherwise we never would have met. We started talking about our men on the inside. About fifteen minutes into it, we both realized our men were the same man. She'd been seeing Dylan, too. He'd told her that she was his soul mate. I wised up fast." Relief washed over her face. She'd told her story and it seemed to calm her for a moment.

"And Bonnie?" Emily asked. "What about her?"

"Look, Bonnie was my friend. She was visiting with Dylan, too. Nothing going on there. I mean, she was never his type."

Emily caught Christopher's eye. *The black album of clippings and letters surely indicated otherwise.*

"Anyway, she knew I was pregnant and she promised to help me by putting the baby up for adoption. That's what I did. I couldn't continue the friendship with Bonnie after that. Every time I saw her, I was reminded of what I'd done." She looked at her watch. Her husband would be home soon. "Are we finished?"

"No. Why the calls to Bonnie? And where were you yesterday?"

"Don't even go there. I was at the gallery all day. And the calls to Bonnie, that's the real reason why you're here, right?"

"That's right," Emily said. "Why were you talking to her?"

Before she answered, Christopher cut in. "We'll have to verify your whereabouts, you know."

Tina nodded in his direction. "Verify, if you must. I have no reason to lie. At least not anymore. Seeing how you know everything."

"Not everything. Why the calls? Why did you reconnect?"

"Because of this," she answered. She went to her Prada purse and retrieved a slip of paper. She handed it to Emily. It was a white card, better paper than a standard index card, but about that size, with just five words printed in a now-familiar handwriting.

*I miss you. Love, Dash*

Christopher looked over Emily's shoulder, then over to Tina. "Dash?"

Emily answered for Tina, who by then had slumped back into a chair.

"Dylan Walker. He was called Dashing Dylan by some of the media during the trial. It became his nickname for a time."

Tina nodded in solemn agreement. "That's right. Bonnie and I shortened it to Dash. He liked it. God, we were so screwed up."

"You think this is from him?"

Again, another nod.

"Where's the envelope?"

"There wasn't one. It was slid under the door. He got into the building."

"Did you tell anyone? Your husband? The police?"

Tina didn't have to answer. The look on her face was transparent. She hadn't told a soul.

"I called Bonnie about it," she said. "She told me she'd heard from him, too. She was positively giddy. It was as if she'd been waiting for him all these years, and he'd come home to her. She was the keeper of the flame. He was in love with her. She was the chosen one. She was dieting to get into a wedding dress she'd picked out. The woman had lost it. Talking to her made me sick, but she was the only one who I *could* talk to. Rod doesn't know any of this and I need to keep it that way. I didn't know what Dash wanted with me, anyway."

"Or if this really was written or delivered by him at all," Emily said, setting the card down on the table. "Did Bonnie have any kids?"

Tina shook her head rapidly. Clearly the concept was beyond absurd. "Absolutely *not*. Never. She was too busy brokering out those babies for Angel's Nest. She had two things in her life. Dylan and that job."

"No family?" Emily asked.

"None that I ever met or heard about."

Christopher leaned closer. "We have reason to believe that Nick Martin, the boy who survived the family homicide back in Cherrystone, could be your son."

"Oh, no," she said. "That's absolutely not possible."

Emily had seen the look of denial countless times. So much of what people believe is what they *want* to believe, not necessarily what is true. Denial is the defense mechanism of first resort. Anger usually follows such confrontations, and Emily prepared herself for it.

"I know all of this is hard on you," she said.

Tina shook her head. "No. It can't be." Her tone was confused, but relatively calm. "You don't understand. Nick Martin couldn't be mine. I had a baby girl."

# CHAPTER THIRTY-TWO

*Monday, 12:10 P.M.,*
*Seattle*

Chris Collier played tug-of-war with the hotel valet as he insisted he didn't want to give up his keys.

"I'm dropping her off. She's a hotel guest."

"Key card, please?" the pimply-faced kid asked.

Emily showed the card and disappeared inside the revolving door. A florist had delivered a new table arrangement, teddy bear sunflowers and spikes of blue delphinium. Freesia filled the air. Ordinarily she'd stop and take in the beauty of the flowers. But not then. All she could think about was Jenna, Tina, Bonnie, and the serial killer that had somehow brought all of them together. She and Chris would talk later, but right then she was on her own. David was mad at her. Kip wasn't answering. Even Gloria was too busy. She felt a flash of paranoia; a feeling that came from making a major mistake and never being able to rectify it.

"FBI here. Can't talk," Gloria whispered. "Call back in an hour."

"All right." Emily shut her phone and looked at the black album. The image of a little blond girl came to mind. She was laughing. She was on a swing. She was running in a field. And she ended up in the cold darkness of a hole in the ground, a root cellar, a grave.

If Dylan Walker was responsible for Kristi's death, then how was Reynard Tuttle involved? She flipped through the pages. What happened?

*But more than anything, where was her daughter?*

Christopher's number lit up the LED display and her phone vibrated.

"I'm on my way back to the hotel," he said. "Em, I have some news." His voice was mixed with dread.

"What is it?" Emily asked.

"Better if I talk to you about this in person."

"Chris," her unsteady voice was ten times louder, now. "Don't do this. Tell me. Am I in trouble?"

Christopher hesitated. "No, not you. Not directly."

"*Please.*" Emily was begging then. She never begged. *"Is it Jenna?"*

"All right. Be calm. Sit tight. I'll tell you." His words came in a machine gun fashion, a breath between each staccato utterance. "Shali Patterson's car's been found. The one Jenna and Nick Martin were driving. There's blood on the steering wheel."

"Were they in an accident?" The remark was merely her best reaction to what he was saying, partly a cover for what she already knew. It was also hoped. The color had drained from her face. "What hospital?" The phrase ended with the up tick of a question. It was spoken by a mother with hope—at least a mother wanting to believe that everything was all right.

"Jenna and Nick are *missing*. The VW was found behind a grocery store not far from Jeffries's place."

There was silence. He waited for Emily to say something. "Are you all right?"

"Dear God," she said. "Where are they? What happened?"

"There's more, Emily."

"Yes?" She steadied herself. *What more could there be?*

"There was a note."

"A note?" *From Jenna?* "I don't understand."

"We'll figure it out. I'm turning in to the garage now." Silence followed and Christopher thought maybe the phone had lost its cell.

"Emily?"

"Yes. Yes," she repeated.

"You need to know something. The note was addressed to *you*."

Emily put her hand out for the card. There was a slight tremor in her grasp, but she kept her eyes riveted on Christopher Collier as he entered her hotel room. There was a strange look on his face, and she couldn't quite determine what it was. *Look at me*, her dark brown eyes pleaded. *Show me.* She took the card. It was plain, white, and carried in a clear glassine envelope.

On its slick surface it read:

*EMILY KENYON: YOUR TURN NOW*

The words were handwritten, with a distinct and printing cursive combination that looked like what they'd seen at Tina Esposito's house and in the black album. She noticed some smudges on the other side. It had already been processed for latents by the crime lab.

"When did you get this?" she asked.

"Two hours ago. Yes, it's been processed. Unfortunately, it's clean."

Still holding the card, Emily sat down. "How could you? Why didn't you call me right away?"

Christopher moved closer. "We think it's about Jenna's disappearance."

The air was sucked out of her lungs, and she could barely speak. She forced the words from her lips. "No. No it's not."

Christopher shook his head and tenderly took her hand. "Look, Em, it seems to be. The card came for me. It was in my mail slot downtown. No one saw who brought it. It had no envelope, just the card." He could see that Emily was crying then, though she was doing it silently, in that way that he came to know when they worked together. *When the case went bad. When the murder scene involved children.* She was tough and smart, but she had her breaking point. A lot of cops did. Some reached for the bottle. Some smoked like there was no tomorrow. Emily Kenyon cried it out, very quietly.

"Look, there's something else you should know," he said. "The blood in the car was Bonnie's and another person's."

"Jenna's?" Her face froze.

He shook his head. "We typed her through your old HR records. Not her. We think Nick Martin's, but that's just a stab in the dark." He regretted his word choice right away and backpedaled. "You know, just preliminary. Could be anyone."

Emily got up and opened a bottle of water. She took a couple of aspirins.

"All right," she said. "The card is the same as the one we saw at Tina's. The writing is the same."

He nodded and let her talk.

"Someone wants to hurt me, right?"

"That's what I'm thinking. That's likely the message here, about it being your turn."

"Right. My turn to suffer? My turn to die?"

"Maybe. But we don't know."

"But we do know one thing. My daughter is missing. Some sicko is playing some game with me. I don't know if it is Nick or Dylan or Tina's husband or who might want to do this."

She went for the crumpled Macy's bag and pulled out the papers she'd smuggled from the hospital. It was all she had. Doing something always won out over tears and frustration. She and Christopher spread them out on the hastily made bed.

"I've started dividing by year," he said, "I found the one with Tina Winston's daughter listed." He held up a printout. "Says the father is Eddy Bunt, thirty-three, born in Tacoma."

Emily took her notebook to Christopher and wrote down the name. She reached for one of the papers and started scanning.

"We'll figure this mess out. We always could, you know."

She looked up and smiled. "I know. I just want to know where my daughter is."

"Me, too."

Her eyes stopped cold on one of the printouts. The mother's name was listed as Bonita Jeffries. The father was Herb La Sift. But that wasn't what nearly cut off her air supply. The birthday was Columbus Day, October 12, the same year as Nick Martin's birth date.

She pointed to the document. "This could be Nick. Same birthday. I know that from the school records I looked at."

"No shit? There's another here. Bonita Jeffries is the mother and Johnny "Ace" Wage is the father. Same DOB as La Sift."

"Boy? Girl?"

"This one's a boy."

Emily set down her pen, her eyes fastened on Christopher's. "There's someone else with that birthday, you know."

He nodded. "Dylan Walker."

"That's right."

"What a lonely woman won't do for love."

The remark made Emily bristle slightly. She'd made some bad choices, too. "What a cruel game a sick manipulator like Dylan Walker plays with a lonely woman."

Christopher seemed to understand. "The only problem with this is that Bonnie Jeffries never had any kids of her own. Black market babies?"

"I'm not sure. But she did have those baby pictures. Remember? There were photos of kids that meant something to her."

"A lot of adoption agency people keep a wall of fame. You know the place where they can stick up all the photos so they can feel good about what they've done."

"Yes, but this was at her home. That makes it even more personal."

Emily looked down at the names in her notebook: Herb La Sift, Eddy Bunt, Johnny "Ace" Wage. "Maybe there is a little game of sorts going on here." She and Jenna had played Scrabble every night when Jenna was in seventh grade and going through that awkward "no one likes me" phase that afflicts so many prepubescent girls. That all changed, good or bad, when Shali Patterson decided to make Jenna her "new" best friend.

"Eddy Bunt is an anagram for Ted Bundy," Emily said.

Bundy, of course, was the superstar serial killer of the 1970s, having been the prime suspect in dozens of murders of pretty young women from the Northwest, Colorado, and eventually Florida where he met his fate strapped into Old Sparky, the electric chair. She glanced over at Christopher, who had a dumbstruck look on his face. "Remember her book collection? How her reading material seemed to indicate a preoccupation with serial killers?"

He did—the mostly red and black volumes filled the dead woman's shelves—*Lethal This, Deadly That, Fatal Whatever*. "To know one is to love one, I guess. And yes, I remember. You get that by just looking at the letters?"

Emily shrugged; it wasn't exactly a gift, but merely a practiced ability.

"Yes, but the others are more difficult. Nothing's popping out at me. She tore some squares of paper and wrote one of each letter of Johnny "Ace" Wage's name. "You work this one."

He took the pieces of paper and stretched them out on the floor.

"I'll do Herb La Sift," she said.

"You're not going to time me, are you?"

"No."

He grinned. "Good, because I'm not a right-brain guy."

"I know." Two minutes later, Emily had her puzzle figured out. "I think I took the easy one," she said. "This one's Albert Fish."

"Fish?" Christopher looked at her blankly. "Doesn't ring a bell."

"He should. Think fava beans and a nice Chianti."

"Hannibal Lecter?"

"Yeah, the original. He was convicted in the thirties. Killed a dozen or more boys and ate them."

"Lovely."

She looked over Christopher's shoulder. "I ought to be on *Wheel of Fortune* or something. I've got yours done."

"Thanks for nothing," he said. "Who's this gem?"

"John Wayne Gacy."

"Jesus, everyone's favorite clown, that one."

He was right. At least every psycho's favorite clown. Gacy was the suburban Chicago serial killer who had raped and murdered thirty-three young men and boys. While he was hobnobbing with the Jaycees and donning his clown costume he wore to visit sick children, he was burying body after body in his crawl space.

"Seems like Bonnie was the creative type," Emily said.

Christopher scooped up the slips of paper. "More like deranged."

\* \* \*

Emily searched Christopher's dark eyes. If she was looking for comfort, she found it. *Understanding, too.* But she also felt something just then that she hadn't counted on. For the first time, she saw him as man, not a coworker. A supporter, not a colleague helping her because he'd been paid to do so. She knew the rest of the world viewed law enforcement as one big club bound forever in blue, but that wasn't always so. As in any profession, insecurities, competitiveness, and jealousies play a role in how those with a badge treat one another.

After the Kristi Cooper debacle, Emily Kenyon had learned how frail support and loyalty really could be. It was like a thin string, stretched and snapped. Several of her friends made derisive comments about her during the investigation, which ultimately exonerated her. In a way she learned how hard it was for a defendant to recover his or her good name after an acquittal. Once the bell has rung, it can never be completely silenced. Even David made cruel remarks about how she'd let the heat of it all steal her wits, how she shouldn't have done what she did.

But never Christopher. He was true blue from the moment Reynard Tuttle was shot, to the dreadful discovery of Kristi Cooper's body by those boys out with their BB gun, to the departmental investigation by her supposed friends and colleagues.

"What is it about you?" she asked. "Why did you stick up for me?"

Christopher set his hand on her shoulder. "Look, what happened to you could have happened to me. *To anyone.* You were doing your job. You have always been a million times better than that one incident. What happened never defined you for a second. Not to me. Not to anyone who really knows you."

*But to David, it was the crack that grew to a chasm.*

Without saying a word, her eyes now cast downward, Emily started to sob. She didn't want to cry in front of Collier just then, but her emotions were so jagged, she just let go.

Christopher put his other hand on her opposite shoulder and gently turned her to make her face him dead on. "Don't do this," he said. "Don't beat yourself up again."

She shook her head slightly. "I don't know." She knew she couldn't change what had happened to Kristi, but she wondered how much that played into Jenna and Nick's disappearance. She was thinking of her daughter just then, not Kristi.

"What if we don't find Jenna?" she asked.

Christopher wrapped his strong arms around her. He didn't hold her too long, or too tightly. "We will," he said softly in her ear. "We're going to get her and bring her home."

A voice called out into the darkness. It was indifferent. Barely louder than a whisper. A voice of ice. Just words strung together. "Hey. *You.* Hey?"

It came from a slit of light, across the blackened space.

*Is this God? Am I dead?*

In an instant the light was snuffed out with a thunderclap, like a trapdoor into another world. Darkness consumed the space. Jenna Kenyon couldn't move. She hurt everywhere. She wanted to touch the back of

her head; she was sure she'd been injured somehow.
The pain was disorienting. The darkness didn't help.
*Maybe hit over the head? Blacked out?* But she didn't
know. When she went to move, she found her arms,
and then her legs, were paralyzed. She was supine on a
cot or mattress, smelly and damp. She was so unsettled, so confused, that she had no clue where she was
or how she got there. After the light went out, she felt
the presence of another, somewhere in the room, the
cave. *Wherever* she was.

"Hello?" she asked, her voice trembling with fear.
She heard something, but it was behind her and she
was unable to turn. "Hello?" She twisted her body and
tried to squirm into a sitting position, but it was no use.
Her limbs were bound tightly by rope or cording.

Then he spoke. "Jenna?" His voice was recognizable, but her thoughts were so hazy, Jenna couldn't say
who it was just then. "Are you all right? I'm over here."

She tried to follow the sound with her eyes, searching through the blackness of the smelly black place.
She knew for sure that she wasn't alone, and she wasn't
sure if she should feel relief or fear. Her memories
were hazy and as she slowly regained consciousness,
her terror began to spike.

"Nick?" she asked, barely able to keep from crying.
His name came from her lips with more hope than confidence. "Are you here?"

A muffled noise. Then an answer.

"Yeah," he said. "I'm over here. I'm tied up with
some tape or something. I can't move. You free?"

Jenna let her tears flow. It wasn't possible to hold
them any longer. Not there in the dark. "No. No, I'm
not."

"Can you move?" Nick's voice was stronger just then. He was being stronger for her.

"I don't think so. I think my legs are broken." She heard scraping sounds above. Maybe they were in a basement somewhere and someone above was moving furniture about the house. "Where are we?"

She could feel him, his breath, his voice as his words came to comfort her. He was maybe five feet away. *Close*. The space wasn't as large as she'd first thought.

"I don't know. I think we're underground somewhere. I can feel dirt against the palm of my hand."

Jenna was shaking. "I'm cold."

"I know."

"I'm scared, Nick."

"I am, too," he said. "We'll get out of here."

"Who did this to us?"

"I didn't see," he said. "Did you?"

Just then, a brilliant flash of light flooded the space, and something skidded across the floor. She could see Nick, though her eyes were burning and she was crying. He was supine, too, about four feet away. In the same flash, she saw the walls were concrete for the most part, but bricked over in sections. It was so fast, like a flashbulb exploding in someone's face and blinding them temporarily, that she couldn't be sure of what she'd seen. She thought she caught a glimpse of a bucket, a hammer, and some baling wire. Maybe a ladder and some rope, but it all happened so fast it would be hard to say for sure.

In the same flash there was the echo of breaking glass. Someone had thrown something into their prison. *Maybe a bottle shattering on the hard, stony floor?* Then a strange odor. Jenna had smelled that scent. And then nothing. Everything was in the darkest shadow as though a heavy curtain had been hastily thrown over the entire space. The light was gone. The air was still.

Not far from Nick and Jenna, there was more scraping, followed by the rapid thud of hurried footsteps, and then absolute silence.

# CHAPTER THIRTY-THREE

*Monday,*
*exact time and place unknown*

A pinprick of light like a tiny star came from the doorway. Jenna lay still and stared at it for the longest time, her mind trying to focus on where she was and how she got there. She felt woozy and nauseous. *Look at that pretty little star*, she thought. *Twinkling*. A nursery rhyme streamed through her consciousness, but she shut it out of her mind. She tried to concentrate on what she last remembered. But it was all foggy, drowsy.

"Jenna? You awake?"

It was Nick's voice, huskier and raw.

"Yeah. What happened?" Her voice was a whisper.

"Someone chucked something in here. We passed out. Are you okay?"

"I'm sick," she said. "I feel like puking."

"Me, too. I've been awake for a while. Whoever put us here hasn't been back."

"Who is it? Where are we?"

Thinking, Nick hesitated. Then his voice pierced the darkness. "I don't know. I'm totally messed up on remembering. Last thing I knew we were at Bonnie Jeffries'."

Jenna dug through her memory, but between whatever made her sick and the fear that wrapped around her, she could recall very little. "Yes, in her living room talking. She went to the back door, the kitchen door."

"Yeah," Nick said. "I can't put it all together. Anything after that?"

"No."

"Me, neither. We have to get out of here. and I've been working on that. I might be able to cut this tape. I've found something sharp, a nail or something, and I'm kind of rubbing through it. I think it's working."

Jenna couldn't move at all. "We have to get out of here." She shivered in the cold, damp air. She could not have been more frightened or more grateful that she wasn't alone. Nick was there.

"We will. And we're going to kill whoever did this to us."

Another wave of nausea hit her. "I feel sick. Going to close my eyes." When she did, nightmares of the mining shack and the rats, the tornado, the bloody scene that Nick had seen back home came at her in a seamless reel, over and over. Blood. Gunshot. Bonnie. Angel's Nest. Dani's pregnancy. It rolled on through her strange, almost drug-polluted subconscious. It was a storm. Each memory shaking her, scaring her.

A flash of light. It jolted her. Her eyes snapped open. Then she slammed them shut. She was so scared. She just wanted to sleep.

*Monday, 3:15 P.M.,*
*Tacoma, Washington*

Dylan Walker's house was one of those grand-styled Victorians with a large bay window that at one time overlooked Tacoma's Commencement Bay. Trees and buildings had risen to block the water views in the decades since it was first built. It had a broad front porch that had been painted gray. The rest of the house was gray, too. *But not by design.* Years of neglect had allowed the dirt and grime of the city to steal the luster of the oyster-white paint. Flakes fell like snow onto the front porch. The place had been carved into apartments, a further indignity to what had been a fine, old home.

Emily parked the Accord around the corner, a half block away from the house. She looked at her watch. She thought that she might be early, but, in fact, Christopher Collier was late. *Must be some trouble with the judge.* She turned on talk radio and listened to some blabbermouth host yak about the rising price of gas and how the middle class would never recover from what the current administration had put it through. If she had been with someone she would have rolled her eyes. If she had been with someone she trusted, like Christopher, she'd have threatened to call in to the show.

*Who cares about the price of gas when our lives in general are so screwed up? Who cares about anything when your daughter is missing?*

Refusing to wait with her daughter's safety on the line, Emily knocked on the door marked with a black plastic label—703½—and held her breath. She'd never seen Dylan Walker except in photographs. It had been a long, long time. Prison years were like dog years—times seven or ten. She doubted he'd still live up to his nickname: *Dash.*

"Are you looking for Dan?" A voice came from a graying man with rounded shoulders, a bright pink nose, and wire-framed glasses that gave him the distinct countenance of a skinny Santa. He was cutting grass.

"Dan?" Emily looked puzzled.

"Yup. Dan Walker. He's not there."

*Dylan Daniel Walker.* She processed the information. It would be a violation of his parole if Walker had taken on another name—to hide who he was. But using his middle name was fair game.

"He's been gone for a while. Lost his job at the hospital a week or so back. Maybe he's out looking for work. Hope so. I'm his landlord, I can take a message."

"No message." Emily showed her detective's badge and the old man acknowledged it. "Just waiting for another officer to arrive."

"Let me know." He didn't ask any questions, which surprised her. Instead he brushed his sweaty brow, nodded, and went back to his yard work. "Might rain soon," he said.

Emily was about to take a seat on the railing by the front door when her cell phone rang. She flipped it open. The voice wasn't familiar at first, but her words were.

"Can I put you on the air?"

It was Candace Kane, the reporter from the Spokane radio station.

"No, you cannot," Emily said, wondering how the

reporter got her hands on her cell number. The number she always gave out went through dispatch—a land-line. "I'm in the middle of something here."

"I know. I heard about Bonnie Jeffries. You found her," she said. "That's why I'm calling."

Emily felt some relief. *The call hadn't been about Jenna.* "Candace, I know you're just doing your job, so I know that you'll understand that I'm just doing mine. I can't comment on the investigation. For one thing, it's not my place to do so—this is a Seattle case."

"Yes," Candace said, "I understand that. But you're over there in Seattle because of a connection between the Martins and Angel's Nest. Bonnie Jeffries worked for Angel's Nest. Right?"

"Look," Emily said, her patience rapidly evaporating, "you apparently already have better sources than me."

She noticed Christopher parking out front, and very abruptly the phone call was over.

"Sorry, I'm late," he said, coming to her. "Got the warrant here."

"He's not here," she said. "Landlord's over there. He'll let us in."

On seeing them talking about him, the landlord ambled over.

"Now there are two of you," he said, squinting into the sun. He looked at Christopher only—one of those men who are blind to a female cop when there's a choice between a man and woman with a badge. "What can I do you for?"

"We have a warrant to search this apartment," Christopher said, holding out the folded papers.

He waved the warrant away. "No need. I follow the law. When you've lived in this neighborhood you see a fair amount of those. Of course it wasn't always that way. We're supposedly a neighborhood in transition. To what I ask?"

"Sir, I can only imagine," Emily said as he fished in his front pocket for his keys.

"Found 'em," he said. "What's Dan done to get all this fuss?"

Christopher started to answer. "We can't say—"

He cut off Christopher with a quick, "yeah, yeah . . . I know the drill. I'll wait outside. Leave the place as you found it please. Otherwise the wife and I will have to clean it up. We can't afford to call in any more help, you know. Fixed income."

"All right," Emily said. She put on her rubber gloves. Christopher did the same.

"You won't find anything nasty in there," the landlord said. "Dan is the neatest fellow you'll ever meet."

Christopher held the door and the pair retreated inside. The apartment was in perfect, almost boot-camp-barracks order. Nothing suggested that Dylan Walker was anything but the neatest tenant since Felix Unger. Shoes by the front door were matched and in perfect alignment with the baseboards. A stack of magazines—mostly automotive, aerospace, and, oddly, gardening—were set with such precision one would have thought the place was being previewed by a real estate listing agent.

The furnishings were simple, not expensive and not upholstered.

"You'd think he'd have a pillow around here. Jesus, who could watch television on that?" Christopher pointed to an old mahogany church pew that Dylan Walker used for his sofa. A small TV sat on an antique wire-and-wood egg crate on the other side of the room.

Emily agreed. "Not exactly the cozy type, that's for sure. Maybe those years in New Jersey gave him a taste for a spartan lifestyle." She let her eyes wander over the room, noting that there was not a single photograph or picture on the walls. The sole bit of wall art was a hardware store calendar with a small picture of an apple orchard. Emily went over to a Formica desk and opened the drawers. The first two were empty, save for a couple of pencils and some legal-sized envelopes. The third and bottom drawer held a shoebox of photos. Emily sifted through its contents, hoping to find some images of Bonnie, Tina, *someone* whose face she'd recognize.

*Any ties to the case? To Nick? And by extension, Jenna.*

Instead, the photos were all of Dylan Walker, albeit an older and decidedly tired version of the man that had prison groupies hearts atwitter so many years ago. Most had him wearing a T-shirt or a chambray shirt. A small tuft of gray hair poked from the V of the collar. His face was still quite handsome, his features still chiseled, though somewhat softened by the passage of time. *Maybe sun in the prison yard?* Despite that, his eyes remained a pair of lasers to the camera lens. On the back was his signature: *Love, Dylan.*

"This guy thinks he's got game. Even in prison," Emily said. "He must have kept a stash of photos to send out to the lovelorn who wrote to him."

"Jersey said his fans faded after some time," Christopher called from the other side of the room. "Got up to a hundred letters a week in the beginning. By the end, only Jeffries was a regular."

"She visited him?" Emily asked, slightly miffed that the information hadn't been disclosed until that moment.

"A time or two," he answered. "Not much. He was pretty much done with her."

She put the photos in a plastic bag. She couldn't let it go. "What else do you know that you haven't told me?"

Christopher looked over at her, not answering, just staring. "I'm not holding out on you. Why would you even think that?"

"Sorry." She didn't say anything more. Emily moved into the kitchen and opened the cupboard doors. The shelving had been marked with permanent marker in the shapes of cups, glasses, and plates, a guide to exactly where every object should be set. She'd seen this on a pegboard tool storage system in a basement workshop, but never in a kitchen. She opened the drawer next to a wall phone. It was the proverbial junk drawer. But in this apartment there was nothing junky about it.

"Check this out," she said, pointing with her index finger at the form of a pair of scissors portrayed on the particleboard bottom of the drawer.

Christopher peered over her shoulder. "Neat freak, all right."

"No it isn't that, but you're right. What I was getting at is that if this guy's so neat then where are his scissors?" She looked at Christopher and he shrugged. "And what do you suppose this is?" She indicated a circle drawn in the bottom of the drawer. It was about the size of a softball.

"You got me." Christopher touched his gloved fingertip to the drawer bottom. The latex adhered slightly. "My guess is a roll of strapping tape. Something sticky, anyway."

The bedroom was next. It was stark in every way. With the sole exception of a small gilt cross next to the window, the walls were white and empty. The bed was queen-size, but lacked a comforter or spread. Instead it was covered with an army blanket and a turned-back white top sheet. Two pillows in perfect, pristine condition sat next to the wall. No headboard. No nightstand. Christopher opened the closet. Dylan Walker's clothes hung in perfect, color-coded order.

"Was Dylan in the military?" Emily asked, poking her head inside.

"Nope, just prison."

"We'll he sure learned how to keep things in order there," she said. "Let's get out of here. There's nothing here."

"That we can *see*. I'm going to have the tech guys come down here and take a look."

"What about his vehicle?"

He nodded. "DMV says Walker drives an old Chrysler sedan. We've got an APB out on it now."

The cool basement apartment belied the hot hour of the afternoon. Going outside in search of the landlord brought a furnace blast to Emily Kenyon's face. A jasmine vine pumped perfume into the air, now further scented with fresh cut grass. It was heady and sickly sweet. She went around to the side of the old Victorian where she'd heard lawn equipment buzzing while she and Christopher were inside conducting a search. She found the old man on one knee bent down and rolling up the Day-Glo orange cord to his electric edger in the front yard.

"Another day, another dollar," he said, this time smiling. "Find what you're looking for?"

"As you know, we're looking for Dylan, I mean *Daniel*. Any ideas where he might be?"

He got up, brushed at the grass stains, grousing that his wife was going to kill him. "He's usually pretty good about telling me where he's going. Yeah, I know he's an ex-con. I know about his troubles with the IRS."

Emily shook her head. "Sir, I'm not with the IRS. But I do need to find him."

"He's a good tenant. Why are you people hassling him?"

She brought out her badge again. "I told you this is a police matter and I don't want to bring you in for hindering our investigation. Understood?"

He folded his burly arms around his sweaty chest, his genial nature now gone. He was irritated and angry. "He has a cousin who has some beach property. He goes there once in a while. Not often. But given the weather, I'd say he's there. Probably working his ass off painting or doing yard work if I know Dan."

*You don't know him, sir. But that's another story.*

"Do you know *where* it is?" she asked. *"Exactly?"*

He turned and started for his front door. "Sure. My wife keeps all the addresses of everyone she's ever known. Tenants become like family, you know. I'll get it. Wait here."

*If he's not back in two minutes, I'm going inside.*

She heard the voices of the landlord and a woman, presumably his wife.

"God, I hope we don't have to re-rent that unit," the woman said, "it's so hard getting decent folks."

*If you only knew who you had rented to,* Emily thought. *Your wife wouldn't have had a decent night's sleep in months.*

A few minutes later, a smile on his face, the landlord returned. By then, Christopher had come over.

"Everything okay?" he asked.

With a nod, Emily indicated the returning landlord. "He's coming now with the address of Dylan's relative's vacation place. Says there's a good bet he's there."

"Nice."

"Here it is," the landlord said. "Told you she'd have it in her book."

He pressed a small white card into Emily's hand.

*4444 Copper Beach Rd. Copper Beach, WA*

She felt a wave of recognition and dread. "Where did you get this?"

"From my wife. She keeps everybody's address in her book."

"No, not the address. The *card*. Where did you get the card?"

The man shrugged. "It's just old photography paper I cut up. I went digital and closed out my old darkroom a year ago. I have boxes of the stuff I stupidly bought in bulk from some guy who was smart enough to unload it on me because he went digital. Cut it all down into index cards."

Emily looked at the address. It was familiar, too. *Deadly familiar.*

"You all right?" The landlord was staring at Emily. "You look like you've seen a ghost or something."

Emily handed the card to Christopher.

"I guess you could say that," she said, trying to avoid revealing too much of what she was feeling. She looked into Christopher's eyes, now full of an awareness of their own.

"Yeah," he said. "We know the address."

*Reynard Tuttle had breathed his final breath there.*

"I'm not sure what's going on," Emily said, as they walked to their respective cars. "But I'm going there right now." She fumbled for her keys. "There's something I haven't told you. I don't know what it means. But I think I'll find Jenna at the cabin."

Christopher stopped and looked at her. "What are you talking about, Emily?"

"I think Jenna and Nick are in serious trouble." She felt awful just then, knowing that she'd withheld information from a man who had been nothing but kind to her. *Interested in her. Cared about her.* "They were at Bonnie's."

"At Bonnie's?" He was stunned by the disclosure.

"Yeah," she said, her voice ready to shatter. "I found this." She pulled out the purse. It was tiny, pink, and sweet. "It's Jenna's. It was by the desk. She left it there."

"Why didn't you tell me? And wait a minute, this could be anyone's."

Emily shook her head. "No. It's hers. I'm certain. Her dad bought it for her. Even though she'd long since outgrown it she kept it because it was from him."

"What were they doing there? I mean, how?"

"They'd been researching Dylan Walker, Angel's Nest. Don't you see? Nick Martin was an Angel's Nest kid. Bonnie put him in the Martin home. They're all connected."

Emily got behind the wheel and turned the ignition. "We're going to find him, and then we can find Jenna. Walker's playing some sick game. He's using Kristi Cooper's case to mess with me. I don't know why. But I do know this—I'm not going to let him hurt Jenna. Not one hair."

"I'm right behind you," Christopher said. "I'll call the desk and tell them what's up. But let's get going."

# CHAPTER THIRTY-FOUR

*Monday,*
*exact time and place unknown*

Jenna woke up, shivering. Her hands and legs were still bound together. Dried tears had formed a glue-like crust on her eyes. She rubbed her face against the fabric on which she lay. She tried to lift her head and breathed in. *Good.* The sickly sweet smell that had left her dizzy, then asleep in the darkness, had abated. The air was damp and heavy, but it did not have that strange odor. To her left the crack of light had narrowed to the thinnest of slits. *Where was she?*

She called over to Nick. "Can you hear me?"

There was no response, so she tried again, saying his name in a louder voice, though still a whisper.

*But again, nothing.* She worried that he was still overcome by the fumes of what had been tossed into the dark space. She rolled over on her right side. As she did so, the mattress beneath her buckled on its rusted frame. For the first time, she realized she was on a bed of some kind. It had springs and batting. She wriggled her torso to get on her side so she could see Nick. He'd almost been free when she passed out. *He'll get us out of there.* He was cutting the tape that bound him.

"Wake up," she said, urgency rising. "Nick, I need you." She could feel the ligature around her wrists. *Was it her imagination?* It seemed looser than it had been before the curtain of utter blackness fell. Before the sound of the crashing, breaking glass. The smell. It was all in her memory as she twisted her body. In shifting her position, she'd been able to reduce the tension of the binding. It no longer cut into her flesh. Instead she felt she could move her wrists. They hurt. The raw edges of her sliced skin stung. She did not cry. Instead, she could feel something else rise within her. *Resolve. Hope. Courage.*

*I'm going to get out of here,* she thought. *Nick and I are going home. Please wake up.*

### Monday, 4:05 P.M., Seattle

Olga Morris-Cerrino knew she wasn't on the case anymore. She knew that she'd long since exchanged her love for the law for the joy she'd found tilling the soil and making fruit leathers from her own apricots and her husband's prized golden raspberries. But when she heard that Bonnie Jeffries had been murdered, Jenna Kenyon was missing, and Dylan Walker had been released from prison, she went into Seattle and sought out the one person she thought might have some answers.

"Hi Tina," she said, as she stood in front of a floor-to-ceiling painting, an abstract of a waterfall, at the Winter Gallery, where the former prison-groupie-turned-society-babe volunteered two days a week.

"Do I know you?" Tina looked blankly right into Olga's penetrating eyes. She was scanning for recognition. *A party perhaps? Probably not, the jewelry's from Macy's. A patron? No, the shoes are cheap.* She tilted her head and looked suitably confused.

Tina looked as good as though only a few years had passed, not so many more. Olga put on a reasonably warm smile. It wasn't easy, but it was necessary. They were in a public place. "We met years ago," she said, "through a mutual friend, Dylan Walker. I'm Olga Cerrino. I used to be Detective Olga Morris."

Tina's flinty eyes flitted nervously around the gallery. Patrons stood in front of enormous contemporary paintings that mimicked the splattered work of Jackson Pollock. They stared as if there was meaning in the chaos of the artist's wanton spray.

Olga said, "Is there a place we can talk? Or should we just do it here?"

"Oh no," Tina said quickly. "Let's go back to the docent's office."

"Then you do remember me?"

"Yes," Tina said, leading her past the sculpture gallery and into a long white-walled corridor. Her Pradas smacked hard on the marble.

Olga didn't say anything as Tina took a brass key and turned the lock on an office door. Some African tribal figures stared from one corner. Supplies nearby indicated that they were in some state of repair. One of them was a large woman with a protruding belly. She was obviously some kind of fertility goddess.

"I call her Trader Vicki," Tina said, noticing how transfixed Olga had been by the statue, "I think she belongs in a bar and not a museum." She smiled nervously.

Olga didn't see the need for small talk. "Look, I know about you and Bonnie and Dylan."

Tina turned away from the carved ebony goddess and faced her interrogator. "You're going to ruin my life, aren't you?"

Olga remained expressionless. "I don't know what you're talking about."

"I see the way you look at me, judge me, envy me."

"Trust me, I don't *envy* you."

Tina looked away. "Whatever."

"Listen, Tina, I just want to know what you really know. Not what you think you can get away with withholding to keep your own involvement minimized."

"Involvement with what?"

"You *know*," Olga said, though, of course she really didn't. *God, this feels good*, she thought. It had been so long since she'd had the opportunity to face off with someone who had something more precious than gold—pieces to a puzzle.

"Did you know Bonnie was dead? Murdered?"

Tina looked frightened. "Yes. It was on TV. But if you think I had anything to do with Bonnie's murder, you're crazy."

"I didn't say that. But I do think you know more about what Bonnie was actually up to."

Tina was less nervous now. "You do? Well, then, good for you."

"My friend at the *Times* would love to know."

"Are you blackmailing me? I have the best law firm in town on my side."

*The haughtiness might work if you didn't know this lady's backstory,* Olga thought. She decided to press Tina, *hard*.

"Are you so incredibly self-centered that you don't care about a dead woman?"

"What do you want to know? Am I supposed to stand here and spill my guts? Is that how you want it?"

"Be truthful." Olga paused for emphasis. "About Dylan, Bonnie, and Angel's Nest."

"I knew this day would come," Tina said, tears welling up in her eyes, "When Bonnie came here a month ago . . ."

Tina Esposito almost didn't recognize Bonnie Jeffries when she accosted her outside of the gallery, earlier that spring. So many years had passed and they hadn't been kind to Bonnie. She was older, and dumpier. Seeing Bonnie was like revisiting a bad dream, one she'd finally been able to suppress.

"You've done well for yourself. I hope you've been happy," Bonnie said. Her voice was cheerful and *overcharged*, like the phony inflections of teenage girls who act as if they are *so so so* happy to see each other.

Tina barely put on a smile. "Thank you. I can't complain. You look well, too," she lied. "I'm late for an appointment," she lied once more.

"This won't take long," Bonnie said, her own smile now waning. If she had expected there was a happy re-union of old friends, she'd been mistaken. She stood in front of Tina, almost blocking her.

"Obviously," Tina said, "we can't talk here." She directed her back to the docent's office. "Five minutes. But then I really have to go—a benefit tonight."

"I knew you were up there," Bonnie said, seemingly impressed. "I've seen your picture in *Seattle* maga-zine."

Tina nodded, but she didn't smile. She didn't want to give Bonnie Jeffries any more insight into her life. The magazine article had been a risk, and until just then, no one from her past had come after her. The ar-ticle was as close as she wanted Bonnie to get.

"I'm a custodian for South Seattle schools," Bonnie said. "After the trial, no one wanted to hire me. Thought I was a whistle-blower. But all I was doing was com-ing forward to protect us."

"Us?"

"When I made the deal with the prosecution, they agreed to keep my pregnancies out of the papers."

"Your pregnancies?"

"And yours."

Tina appeared mystified. "I didn't know *you* had a baby."

Bonnie's lips curled to a smile. "I had *three*." There was more than a hint of pride in her voice.

"I don't understand. I never knew." Tina Esposito was a good actress, she'd been playing rich and happy for years. But even she couldn't suppress her surprise just then. *Who could?*

"Jesus, Bonnie," Tina said. "I don't know what to say. Except, why are you telling me this now? What does it have to do with me?"

"My babies are your daughter's brothers."

The look on Tina's face was shock, then horror. "Dylan?"

"Yes. When you left him, he took me on as his soul mate. It was the happiest time of my life. I was continuing on with something you started, bringing life and love to a world that needed it."

"What I did was not about life and love. It was about being foolish and desperate."

"Call it what you want." She took some breath mints out of her purse and extended her hand to Tina.

"No thanks," she said. "Now that you've ruined my day, *my life*, what do you want?"

Olga sat breathless, only just believing all that she heard. The idea that these women had conspired to have a murderer's babies was beyond comprehension, though she knew other women had done it. She recalled how serial killer poster boy Ted Bundy managed to get a woman pregnant while he was incarcerated in Florida. A California student nurse who'd been caring for Charles Manson made headlines when she revealed she'd had the *Helter Skelter* killer's boy/girl twins—six years *after* he'd been sent away for life.

"What was her visit all about? What did she want?"

"At first I thought maybe she was lonely. Maybe she had a boring life and she read about me in one of those magazines and thought I had a more glamorous

one and wanted to rekindle a friendship. You'd be surprised how many people read those stupid publica-
tions. But not Bonnie. She didn't want to look me up to
be best pals. For Bonnie, it was always about Dylan. I
guess she wanted to reconnect with me because Dylan
had been our connection. And she wanted to tell me we
were connected through his babies, too." Tina sighed.
"She never saw through him. She'd been convinced
that he'd been innocent of the murders of those girls in
Meridian."

"Lorrie and Shelley," Olga said. "They had names,
you know."

"Don't you think I know that?" said Tina, suddenly
angry. "And I know Dylan Walker killed them, too. I
know because he told me so."


The prison visiting room had been their sanctuary, a
place where they could cement their love. Talking for
hours, making plans that never really had to come to
fruition. But in a very real sense, it had also been a
tomb. There was no escaping it. It was in that vault that
crying mothers, angry fathers, and deceived wives met
with the men who had done humanity the greatest
harm. It was a sad little play that repeated itself every
week. Tina Winston never really saw herself as one of
the foolish. *The tricked.* She viewed herself as woman
enough to love a man she couldn't ever really have. It
was a great and beautiful sacrifice.

But all of that changed one Saturday afternoon
when he told her.

"I know people—reporters, cops, *people*—talk about

me," Dylan said over a microwave-heated burrito that she bought with four quarters. "They don't always get it right, you understand."

"Certainly," Tina answered, "I know that."

"Do you?" His surprise was exaggerated.

She could barely take her eyes off his. It was that way whenever he spoke. She nodded and sipped her Coke from a paper cup.

"You are the only woman who really knows me to my soul, aren't you?"

"Of course." She adored how he leaned on her, confided his deepest feelings. *He completely trusted her.*

Dylan looked over at her pregnant belly. At four months, she was starting to show. "You've proven your love," he said. He couldn't touch her just then. Kissing and hugging were reserved solely for the hello greeting and the good-bye. He put his hands on the table, just a whisper from hers. She could almost feel the heat from his fingertips.

"I did it," his words coming to her like the soft, sexy talk of a lover. But the content didn't match the tone. Not at all. "I killed Lorrie and Shelley," he said. "Neither of them understood me. Not really. I mean, not the way that *you* do."

In a split second of clarity, Tina Winston understood for the first time that Dylan Daniel Walker was a monster. She said nothing more to him that day or any other day. She knew that whatever she carried inside her was the spawn of evil, a child she could never love. A mistake she could never obliterate.

\* \* \*

Olga listened intently as the words tumbled from Tina's trembling lips. She stopped and blotted her eyes, careful not to smudge her makeup. "You know, that's the first time I've said his name in all these years. With Bonnie I just used 'him' or Dash. I didn't want to give his name life, he was so dead to me after what he'd done.

"But that's not all," Tina went on. "He said there had been others. Others no one—you, the police—didn't know about."

"Did he say *who*?"

Tina shook her head. Droplets of her tears hit the shiny marble floor. "No. And I didn't ask. I just wanted to get out of there and throw up."

Olga waited for Tina to get a grip. It would take a while. Tina had gone from stunning and confident to haggard and limp like a wrung-out dishrag in about a half hour. Her eyes were puffy. Her nose was red. Every wrinkle on her face had suddenly etched itself deeper.

*Something nagged at Olga. Something Tina had said before she had told her story. That's it. When she'd asked why Bonnie had sought her out she'd said "At first. At first I thought."*

"Why *did* Bonnie come and find you?" she asked.

Tina took a deep breath and swallowed hard. Her eyes looked downward. "She said Dylan had gotten out of prison and was back in the Northwest. He was in Tacoma. She'd waited for him and he for her. She came to me to gloat, I guess. She was rather smug. As if we'd been in some competition and she'd finally had the upper hand. She'd been the chosen one. She'd been the one all along. You know what her last words to me were?"

Olga didn't have a clue and said so.

"Our son—that's what she said—our *son* and Dash and I are going to be a family."

"Anything else?"

"Yes, she used the phrase, 'there are some flies in the ointment' and she said she was sorry."

*Monday,*
*exact time and place unknown*

Jenna Kenyon had worked her hands free. The release of her wrists and arms sent a quake of pain through her body. She expected that she'd feel her pain diminish, but the opposite had been true. She let out a little soft cry and called over to Nick.

"I think I can get loose now," she said. "Nick, how are you coming?"

When she didn't hear anything, she pulled herself up, and moved her feet like she was dolphin kicking at the Cherrystone community pool. At last the cords that held her ankles together slipped to the earthen floor. It was too dark to see, so Jenna crawled on her hands and knees to where she'd last heard Nick's voice. She touched the floor lightly, timidly. *No broken glass. Thank God.* She didn't want to allow the thought to take hold, but it managed to slip inside her brain: *What if he's not asleep? What if he's not drugged? What if he's dead?*

She wondered where her mother was, if she was looking for her at all. She found herself praying to God and Jesus that she'd be able to wake Nick up, and they'd get out of the cruel darkness and she'd find her mother. *My mom will get us out of here. My mom won't let whoever is doing this get away with it. My mom is the toughest woman I know.* The thin line of light in the black, which she now assumed was a doorway, had been dimmed. It seemed so far away.

On her stomach, feeling the hard, muddy floor, she slithered in the direction where she had last heard Nick's voice. *Groping. Reaching.* She put her hands out, touching a damp, soiled blanket. Her fingers were extended like claws. She was Helen Keller, probing with her fingertips to find something. To find Nick.

"Where are you? God, Nick, where are you?"

But once more, no answer. Jenna could feel her heart pounding deep inside her chest. It was thumping hard. But there was nothing to answer it back. No call for her to be calm. "Where are you?" She spun around and called in every direction, but nothing.

Jenna Kenyon was completely alone.

*Monday, 7:45 P.M.,*
*near Meridian, Washington*

Olga Morris-Cerrino returned to her farmhouse, fed Felix, and put the teakettle on. She'd dialed Emily three times, but kept getting "customer out of service area." She turned on her computer and let the old PC rumble to a live screen. She logged on and the dial-up connection choked and coughed before she could log on to the archived files of the Retired Police Officers Association of the Northwest and put in her password.

She found Reynard Tuttle and started printing. Olga

never doubted that Dylan Walker was a killer, despite her failure to have him put away for the rest of his life. It hadn't been her failure alone. The police in Seattle, Tacoma, and Nampa, Idaho, had also come up with nothing. Even the FBI had been unable to do what was needed to catch a killer. But no one, not a single law enforcement organization, had thought that the Reynard Tuttle/Kristi Cooper case had been related to Dylan Walker. In many ways, it didn't really seem to fit. None of the victims had been held captive anyplace—at least not that they were aware. When Olga pondered the Idaho case of Steffi Miller, she wondered if the girl hadn't been found because she'd been hidden somewhere. *Somewhere besides a grave.* Kristi had likely been disregarded because she'd been so young. But Olga knew that Walker was a cross-generational killer. He killed women of all ages.

She began scoping the Tuttle printouts. Now it was her turn to see photographs of Emily Kenyon when she was younger, before her downfall. There was no mention of Walker, of course, but there was a very small detail that leapt off the laser-printed page. The address of the McDonald's where Kristi Cooper had last been seen: 513 Winchester Avenue. Olga almost did a double take and then immediately went to the phone.

"Answer. Answer," she said, as Emily's phone rang and went to voice mail. "Damn it."

She waited for Emily's greeting to give way to the beep. At least she could leave a message, all staccato and full of excitement. "Emily, Olga. I've been poking around some. Got some interesting info from our favorite society gal, Tina Esposito. Bonnie had three kids, at least that's what Tina says. Three by Walker. Ugh. Anyway, call me. Also, found something interesting about Walker and your Cooper case. He lived a block from the restaurant . . ."

Olga wanted to say more, but the phone connection failed. *Cheap piece of garbage,* she thought. *Hope she got all of that.*

# CHAPTER THIRTY-FIVE

*Monday, 8:35 p.m.,*
*on the Pacific coast of Washington*

It had started raining early in the day and hadn't let up. *Couldn't let up.* The sky was a pewter lid smacked down over the ocean and the coast. Dunes with cockscombs of sea grasses held off the foamy surf. Rain pelted the windshield with relentless force as Emily followed the two-lane seaside road to the address on the card. She turned on her wipers to maximum speed, but she could barely see. The defroster was blowing at full bore, but it couldn't keep up with the damp air that circulated through the soggy Accord. Emily opened the driver's-side window to suck out the warm, moist air, but it just sent needles of rain against her left cheek. With her eyes fixed on the road, she leaned over and pulled some tissues from the glove box and started to wipe. *Better.* A sign flashed by the window: WELCOME TO WASHINGTON'S COAST. She looked in the rearview mirror and squinted at the bright headlights that had trailed her since she left Seattle.

*I'll need to tell Christopher to get those lights adjusted.*

Whenever Emily thought of Kristi Cooper, she thought of Reynard Tuttle. That was long before she had any inkling that Dylan Walker could have been involved. So sure was she of Tuttle's guilt that she completely dismissed the Tuttle family's feeble protestations that he was innocent. Reynard Tuttle's sister and ex-wife were united in their insistence that Tuttle, who was diagnosed as schizophrenic when he was twenty-two, was innocent of the Cooper kidnapping. "He's not capable of hurting an innocent little girl," Delilah Tuttle Lewis, his sister, told a TV reporter not long after the shooting. "He was crazy, but a gentle crazy."

Tuttle's background had suggested as much. He'd been arrested only once for loitering in front of the King County courthouse. With the ACLU by his side, the charges were dismissed. His lawyers said that since he usually was seen holding a placard espousing hatred for the police whom he accused of conspiring against him, he'd been unfairly and unjustly singled out for prosecution. The day they picked him up was the *only* day anyone could recall in which Tuttle had been without his little sign. Tuttle had never been violent in his life. He'd never hurt a soul. Crazy, his family said, didn't make him a kidnapper and a killer.

There was no wrongful-death suit from the Tuttles, however. The reason for that was cruel and simple. Tuttle, as a mentally ill man, had no worth. The loss of his life could not be equated to future earnings of any kind. It was as if he didn't exist.

After she'd killed him, Emily Kenyon never allowed herself to think for one second that he'd been anything but a killer.

*Crazy or not, he did it. Because if he didn't, then that meant his blood was indelibly on her own hands.*

But that was before. Now she had doubts that gnawed at her soul.

Emily turned off the highway toward the Pacific, and the tourist community of Copper Beach. The sun had dipped into the ocean, but even at high noon, it would still have the dark gloom that makes the water and sky a seamless wall. Copper Beach had been platted in the 1980s as Washington's great answer to the coastal communities that brought retirees with fat pensions. Two golf courses were built. Tribal land nearby also factored into the plans. In Washington, gambling was illegal. But Native American tribes who owned vast stretches of the state operated as sovereign nations. Tribal casinos would soon spring up. It was the yin and yang developers had long dreamed about: Wonder bread communities on the coast with the naughty fun of the bad-influence-neighbor just down the road.

One problem. *The weather.* Washington wasn't California, or even Oregon. Rain kept the place from really taking off. As Emily drove though the town, motels and saltwater taffy shops competed with moped rentals and sad old horses that had never seen better days—Sea Nags—hired out for beach rides. Alongside the road beach houses were draped in necklaces of fishing floats and flanked by chainsaw effigies of New England fishermen wearing yellow slickers and spinning ship's wheels. Sand dunes threatened the roadway. Despite the ocean's waves crashing against driftwood, the world outside her car seemed so silent. *So lonely.*

Emily Kenyon thanked God that Christopher Collier was right behind her. *Following her.* How familiar it all felt.

She remembered the heavy tangle of driftwood that lined the beachhead and protected the road, wooden limbs clawing into the damp marine air. The stream of light from her perpetually-on high-beam headlights brought the snags and roots to life.

A last turn, and Emily was almost there. Adrenaline, the drug of working cops, skydivers, and mothers in search of their endangered children, pulsed. It nearly flooded her system when she saw it. A black mailbox carried the number on its silvery weathered driftwood post: 4444 COPPER BEACH ROAD. She pulled over and kept the car idling until Christopher opened the passenger door and slid onto the seat.

"You drive like a maniac," he said. "I could barely keep up with you."

Emily faked a smile. "That's because you drive like someone's grandpa."

Christopher shrugged and allowed her the upper hand. He cracked the window. The car was warm inside. "You ready to do this?" he asked.

"What about backup? Did you call the local blues?"

"Nope. We don't need them. We're just doing a little surveillance."

"What if we're wrong and she—*they*—aren't here? What if Walker's playing some kind of mind game?"

"There's no *what if* on that one. He *is*. He's got to be."

Emily opened the door; the soft ping of the warning sound faded into the stormy air. "Let's go."

The cabin had been remodeled in the years since they'd both been there. People with money had taken the place with the idea they'd be able to turn it into a bed and breakfast. They'd had intermittent success. During his drive from Tacoma, Christopher had contacted the owners, now living in Seattle and the place was vacant. It was not owned by Walker's cousin after all.

"Worst investment we ever made," the gruff-voiced man said. "The place is cursed. Can't keep it booked more than half the season. Go ahead. Have a look around. If you like it, I'll make you a deal on a rental."

That would never happen, of course. The Seattle detective could think of nothing more unlikely than vacationing at the scene of the Tuttle shooting.

"Key's under the gull by the front door," the man had said.

# CHAPTER THIRTY-SIX

***Monday, 11:30 P.M.,***
***Copper Beach, Washington***

When Emily and Christopher got within ten yards of the cabin's front door, a porch light—a floodlight, no less—went off like a paparazzo's camera. *Flash!* They blinked back the sudden, silent explosion of brightness. *Who was that?* Their eyes had barely adjusted to the flash when a figure, the silhouette of a man, appeared in the doorway, then disappeared.

"Come on in," a voice called out from somewhere in the pool of light. "I've been expecting you."

*It was a familiar voice: the voice of a thousand cheap documentaries with prison interviews over which he presided whenever a pretty producer would call. It was Dylan Walker.*

"Put your hands where we can see them, Walker." Christopher used his don't-mess-with-me voice. It was a far cry from the tough voice he'd use on a garden-variety suspect.

For a cop, Dylan Walker was the unholy grail.

"Why should I?"

Walker lingered for a beat before turning his back and sauntering farther into the cabin, out of view. It was as if he hadn't a care in the world and loved the attention of two guns pointed at him. "You arrest me," he called out. "You shoot me in the back. Either way, you'll never see your daughter again."

Both guns pitched in front of them, the two went up the steps. Emily knew that if Jenna wasn't there—and she knew that possibility was next to nil—then only one person would know where Jenna was. The man who would be king of the serial killers was the only one who could save her daughter.

Dylan Walker was a man without compassion.

Emily, just behind Chris, whispered, "We're going in."

The wind howled behind them. Chris gave a slight nod, as if to say everything would be fine.

"Stay close," he said.

She wouldn't have it any other way. *He always could read my mind,* she thought.

The pair stepped out of the windy night and through the open door. Sand moved under their feet like fine grit sandpaper. A carving of a seagull on a piling crouched in the space next to the doorway. Dead houseplants lined the entryway, a kind of graveyard of neglect that indicated no one lived in the cabin full-time. Neither could see Dylan Walker just then. Flames crackled through the driftwood logs in the river rock fireplace that went from the floor to the ceiling like a stone temple, hollowed by fire. It was a cozy scene.

*Cozy for a serial killer.*

Walker appeared, coming out of what Emily was

certain was the rental's tiny kitchen. She'd been there. She knew. Dylan Walker held a beer and a gun.

"Thirsty?" he asked. "I have some Doritos, too."

Christopher almost shook his head at the remark. "Maybe you're blind and you don't see the guns here? Drop yours now."

Dylan shrugged at Christopher, but addressed Emily. "Maybe you don't know how to have a good time? Do you, Emily? I mean, you haven't had a good time since Reynard Tuttle went down. Since Kristi Cooper." He set the beer on a lamp table and grinned. "Didn't you shoot Tuttle right here?"

Emily stayed mute. She wanted to speak, but she was fighting the memories he was callously flinging at her. Walker pointed to a spot on the worn pine floor-boards. "Still stained."

Emily glanced at Chris who kept his weapon punched toward Dylan. Then, almost reluctantly, she cast her gaze downward. The wood floor was scuffed and scratched, but its color was golden, a perfect Swedish finish. There were no stains. No blood. By the time she looked over at Walker, she knew he'd gotten what he'd wanted. His self-satisfied grin told her everything.

"Made you look," he said.

"You're a real piece of work, Walker," said Christopher.

"Oh, you really scare me."

"I mean to." Christopher's mouth was a straight line of anger.

Dylan laughed and patted his firearm. He backed into a chair, stretching out his sinewy legs to meet a tattered, upholstered ottoman.

Emily tried to gather her wits. She willed her heart

to slow its rapid pace. *Where is all of this going?* The scene was surreal with the three of them, guns drawn at each other in a bizarre stalemate. She and Chris both knew that if Jenna and Nick weren't in the cabin with Walker, they could be anywhere. The man with the perfect body and piercing, cold eyes was the only one who knew just where that could be.

"Where's my daughter? Where's Nick Martin?"

"Not here, if that's what you're asking. Look around."

With Chris covering her, Emily moved swiftly from the main room, to the kitchen, to the single bedroom. A window was open and she could hear the roar of the Pacific, but no sign of her daughter. *Why is this happening? Why is God doing this to me?* Emily fought to push all of the things that spoke to her being a mother to the back of her consciousness. *Let the cop take over,* she thought. *Let the cop find the girl.*

"Last chance. Where is she?" Emily's gun, once more directed at Dylan Walker, wavered just a little. She moved her finger on the trigger.

Chris looked at her with abject horror. *Not again, Emily.* "Let's keep cool here, Walker," Chris said, though his words were really meant for Emily.

Walker knew it.

"Tell that to Ms. Rambo."

Emily didn't say anything. She let Christopher take over. She knew she'd lost her perspective just then. She was a mother more than she was a cop.

"Let's all stand down, all right?" Christopher asked, his voice cool and commanding. "No one needs to get hurt here."

"Good idea. If I get hurt, Jenna dies. So I'm game.

And if you don't think I can keep a secret, you don't know me at all. But I'm willing to talk. Maybe. Just point your guns to the floor." Dylan lowered his gun slightly, his eyes fastened on his adversaries, who both ignored his request.

Emily had wanted to kill Dylan Walker for all that he'd done. But trumping all of that, of course, was Jenna's whereabouts. *Her safety.* Sucking up to a monster could save her. It was the only thing she could do. But there was another presence in the room . . . Kristi Cooper. Emily knew that Kristi was the reason for this horrific reunion.

"Where is she? Where is Jenna?"

"At first, I thought the Tuttle shooting was a godsend," Walker said, ignoring her question. "You'd killed an innocent man. I'd gotten away with something. Your murder of Tuttle made mine a perfect crime—"

"The shooting was an accident."

"Incompetence, I'd say. But you call it whatever helps you sleep at night."

"Where's my daughter?"

"Poor Kristi. And now, poor Jenna. I won't ask you again, lower your weapons."

Christopher moved toward Dylan, just a step or two. Just enough to let him know that he was unafraid.

"Where is your son?"

The words brought a smile, but Walker said nothing.

Christopher pushed harder. "Are he and Jenna together? If you're here . . . and they are off somewhere, doesn't that leave you without the prize?"

A blank look came over Walker's face. "The prize?"

"Your son. All of this is about him. The smuggling

of your semen? The babies by Tina and Bonnie. All about your legacy, right."

Walker let out a long insidious laugh. It was the kind of laugh that chills a body to the marrow, Freon in the bloodstream. An evil laugh that had nothing to do with anything being amusing. "For all of your reading about serial killers, all the stupid classes you've taken for your somewhat checkered career, you don't understand me one bit."

"I do." It was Emily this time. "I get you. You're all about control and power. That's why you pick on young girls, trusting women. You like to be in charge, don't you?"

"Ooooh," he said, "I like it when you act smart."

"Don't patronize me, Dylan. I *know* you. I can see through you. You're nothing but a guy who thinks the world revolves around him. You're a narcissist."

Walker laughed again, this time it was brief like a release of gratification.

"As if that label would sting a little," he said, sitting back. "I'm a narcissist because I look good. People like me. *Women* like me."

"Not this one," she said. "Now, let's give this up. You can be reunited with your son. I can find my daughter. You can go quietly and safely."

Walker looked confused. It was the first time he'd seemed out of sorts, as though what Emily said finally touched a nerve. Finally she was able to penetrate the facade, the mask.

"You don't get it, do you?" he asked. "You don't understand me like Bonnie did—"

"Before you killed her?" Christopher cut in. The fire crackled and sent embers across the pine floorboards.

Dylan Walker was agitated. The coolness of his demeanor was draining before their eyes. "Like Bonnie did. She was smart. Fat, but smart. Weak, needy, and smart. My favorite combination. She knew I was a mimic. She knew I didn't care one bit about her or anyone. Nick included. I didn't care whether any of them took their last breaths. That made her want me even more." The heinous grin returned, but this time it seemed fake. Practiced. Bravado.

"Where is Jenna Kenyon?" Christopher asked.

Just then, without warning, a shot pierced the small space of the cabin. Almost on instinct, Emily checked her own gun. *Had it gone off? Had she pressed the trigger when she hadn't meant to?* She wondered if that's what happened years ago with Reynard Tuttle. *Had that been a serious misstep or an accident?* All of that passed through her mind as the realization came that it was not her gun that had fired and that Dylan Walker had not been shot.

Dylan was standing, having jumped to his feet, his gun in his hand. Smoke curled from its shiny black barrel. Emily heard the sound of a body falling, a heavy thud. She turned.

Christopher Collier was on the floor, blood oozing from his chest. His life draining from his body, one red drop at a time. He was so pale; he looked like one of those Elizabethan courtesans, all white with a gash of red for his mouth. The blood was flowing. In the split second of the shot to the realization that Dylan Walker had shot Christopher, Emily Kenyon let her guard down. She could have fired back at Dylan, but she didn't. She'd been trained to do so. *Officer down! Fire back! Stop the shooter!* Everything she knew from the police academy failed her. The knowledge was there. The skill, too. But when she learned how to deal with a cop shooter, she hadn't been a mother.

She hadn't needed to know where a serial killer had stashed her daughter. The only link in the chain of evidence to save Jenna was the evil force with the gun pointed at her.

"What did you do?" She dropped to her knees and held Christopher.

His breathing was labored. His handsome face, pallid. "I'm going to be all right," he said. Christopher's voice was soft, but he tried to show confidence.

"Of course you are," Emily answered, not sure who was lying just then. *Her? Him? Both of them.* She blinked back her tears. "We need to get medical attention here."

"Not so fast." Dylan Walker now stood by the doorway. "Aren't you forgetting something?" He hesitated. "Someone?"

*Jenna.*

Emily pointed her gun. Walker smiled at her and in doing so, it rushed through her mind that he'd never been handsome in his life. *Evil like that never could be.* His features were symmetrical, classic, and well proportioned. He'd been likened to a "Greek god" by magazine writers who fantasized for their readers what being with the ultimate bad boy, the King of the Serial Killers, might be like. *The sexy mix of danger and good looks. So damned stupid.* But just then, he looked hideous, a twisted kind of handsome.

"I'm going to leave just now. You can call 911. Detective Collier just might live. You might be able to find your daughter. You stop me. Shoot me. Whatever's going through your mind right now, isn't going to happen. Because if you stop me, you'll never find her."

Emily knew he was right. She pressed her palm against Collier's heaving chest. She'd stopped the syrupy red blood flow. *For now.*

Walker scanned the room, surveying his work. He seemed so satisfied that it repulsed Emily all the more. As he walked toward the door, red clay particles fell from the soles of his shoes.

"Please," she said, "where is she?"

"In the dark," he said. "Just like Kristi." His gaze was the dead-eyed stare of a shark. "She's alive, for now. But remember poor Kristi . . . she waited for someone to find her."

Anger and fear converged. Emily thought she might lose control and just lunge for him. Instead, she pleaded.

"Please."

"Jenna Kenyon. Kristi Cooper. Two peas in a pod. Pretty girls. The kind I like to—"

"Just shut up," she said, finding her voice, breaking his rhythm. If he had meant to hurt her deeply, he'd done so. The wound was deep. "I want my daughter and Christopher needs a doctor. *Now.*"

Dylan stepped backward, once again that dead, cold stare fixed on her like the scope of an assault rifle. "I'm going now. If I stay, your daughter will be just like Kristi, a bag of bones in the dark somewhere. That is, if they ever find her. Remember they've never found Steffi or Brit."

Emily closed her eyes to shut out Dylan's words. When she opened them, she focused on Christopher. She leaned closer. The color of his face was slightly better. She could feel the faint warmth of his breath against her cheek. He wanted to speak, and he fought for it. "Let him go. We'll find her." His voice was a rasp. Emily gently squeezed his hand, telegraphing that she believed him; she trusted him. Despite the gunshot, despite the turmoil of the moment, Christopher Collier was what he'd always been—calm and direct. He lived up to every promise he ever made.

"I hope so," she said, her voice a soft whisper. She brushed his wavy hair with her fingertips. If there was a better man, a stronger and gentler man, she'd never known him in her life. Tears rolled down her cheeks, and she tucked her chin down to wipe them from her face.

When she looked up, the door was open, and Dylan Walker was gone.

She punched 9-1-1 on her phone's keypad.

"We're going to be all right," she said as the call went through. "All of us. Walker's not going to get what he wants."

Deep down, she wasn't so sure. She told the dispatcher where she was, and she uttered the words that no cop ever wants to say: "There's an officer down . . ." She gripped Chris's hand and told him once more to hang on, help would be there.

"You're going to make it, Chris."

He nodded.

The bars on her phone flickered and the call to help was gone. She'd told the dispatcher all she could. Emily Kenyon sat on the floor and cradled his head in her lap. The fire crackled, the overstuffed sofa beckoned. But everything about the scene was wrong for the events consuming her. It was not a romantic getaway for two. It was a crime scene redux. Reynard

Tuttle. Christopher Collier. *God, please help me. Help me. Help Chris,* she thought.

A whisper from Christopher stopped her prayer.

"I have an idea where Walker is," he said.

Emily wasn't sure if he was delirious or not. His eyes were hooded and his voice weak. "Closer," he said.

She pressed her ear to his warm mouth, nearly grazing it.

"The red clay. I've been there . . ."

"Where?"

"Red—"

Nothing more came from his lips. Chris slipped into unconsciousness.

"Where?"

But nothing.

Emily felt for his pulse. Nothing. She was panicking and could no longer tell if she was feeling her own heartbeat or his.

"Chris! Don't leave me!"

Again, nothing.

Emily tried harder. She shook him. *Was he breathing?* She felt a puff of air flow from his lips. *Last breath? God, no!* Finally, she felt the thump, thump of his heart. It was weak, but steady. She wanted to cry. It was more than her missing daughter, as if there could be any more. It was also this man, this gentle, smart, and caring man that seemed so vulnerable and so much in danger.

It passed through her mind and she fought it: Was this all her fault?

"Don't leave me," she said, her words desperate and loud, as if the volume of her concern could snap him out of the darkness. The clock above the fireplace inched later and later.

Emily heard the roar of a thunderclap and the pounding of gale force winds off the roiling Pacific. But the evenness of the noise indicated something else, something so welcomed. It was the answer to a prayer and proof that the dispatcher had taken down all the information. Emily placed Christopher's head on the floor and ran toward the door and began to flash a message to the pilot by flipping the switch to the flood-lights.

She didn't use Morse code. Just a quick succession of light and dark to signal the message that could save Chris Collier: *"We're here!"*

A hospital helicopter landed on the wide beach in front of the cabin and two EMTs and a nurse were on the ground and in the cabin in less than a minute. Within five minutes, Emily and Chris were onboard; she saw their cars parked just down from the cabin, a bright light pouring from the picture window facing the ocean.

It was silly and she knew it, but Emily wished she'd thought to turn off the lights.

The helicopter lifted and was sucked up into the black sky.

"Officer, you need to be belted in," an EMT, a man of no more than twenty-four, told Emily as she hovered over the sagging frame of a man she cared deeply about, a man who was there in harm's way for her.

*For her daughter.*

"I'm not letting go of Christopher. You understand?"

The young man acquiesced. There was no messing with Emily Kenyon right then.

"All right," he said, "I'm going to pretend I didn't notice."

"You do that. And you tell your pilot to get to the goddamn hospital as fast as he can."

# CHAPTER THIRTY-SEVEN

***Wednesday, 3:30 P.M.,***
***Seattle***

Emily sat in a plastic chair in a grim hospital room in Seattle's Harborview Medical Center, the region's prime trauma unit. White walls and floors had not yet seen the mauve and taupe makeover of most hospitals. It was cold, antiseptic, and anything but homey. But for Emily Kenyon, it felt like the greatest place in the world just then. Christopher was drugged up, but peaceful. *He was alive!* Flowers from friends in the department filled the deep sill of the window. A banner generated by someone's ancient dot matrix printer spelled out GET WELL CHRIS! over his bed. A nurse in a blue-and-white smock fiddled with one of the tubes that connected Christopher Collier to an array of bags— saline, pain meds.

"You all right? You really ought to go home, Officer."

"I'm fine. I'm not going anywhere."

"Suit yourself," the nurse said. "His vitals are good. Should be waking up any time now. Might as well get some coffee. Machine's down the hall."

Even machine coffee sounded good. Emily studied Chris's face for a clue about his consciousness. But he was still. *A minute away wouldn't matter.* When she returned, she nearly dropped the Styrofoam cup full of what she now considered the world's worst coffee.

"Emily. Are you here?" Chris said, his tired eyes lighting up just a little when she came into view.

She hurried to his bedside and patted his hand. "Where else would I be?"

"Did you find Jenna?"

For the first time, tears came, rolling down her cheeks. But there was no whimpering, no sobs, just the release of a nightmare. She knew his question was out of genuine concern, but it felt wrong to pounce on her missing daughter's case the second the man woke from surgery.

"No, Chris. No. You had me so worried." She bent over him, "You feel better?"

"I'd feel a lot better if I could get out of here to help you find your little girl and hunt down that asshole."

His voice was a near wheeze. He was a big man, but he looked so small and helpless it nearly broke Emily's heart. *Had this been her fault, too? Had she led him to disaster once more?* The bullet missed Christopher's heart, but had to be surgically removed from his lungs. He'd be breathing like a leaky tire for quite some time, but he'd recover. That was the one bit of good news that came that day.

"I'm going back to Copper Beach," she said.

"To find her?"

"Yeah," she said. She touched his hand. "I have to do something."

Christopher looked up at her and nodded. "Emily, I've an idea where to look."

Emily's eyes widened and she felt herself sink closer to him, to capture what he said. She almost assumed that he'd been hopped up on morphine, but the look in his eyes was clear. He did have an idea.

"Where?"

"Remember the red clay dust Walker tracked around the cabin?"

She did. "Yes. You mentioned it before you blacked out."

"There's a formation not far from Copper Beach. Red clay isn't all that rare near there, but there is a place that might be the kind of hideaway a piece of garbage like Walker might like. I remember going there a few years ago with the kids."

Emily recalled the events of the evening of the shooting. She remembered how the red clay had clung to the soles of Walker's shoes. It had been wet, then dried and flaked off.

"Where?"

"There's an old World War II bunker near Copper Beach. Maybe ten miles away."

Emily's heart started to race. *A bunker? Underground?* She gave him a quick kiss on the cheek, his beard's growth pricking her lips.

"I need a place to start looking," she said.

As she turned to leave, she thought she heard Christopher say something more. The words were a complete surprise, though not unwelcome.

"What, Christopher? What did you say?"

"I love you, Emily."

And just as she hoped his suggestion of where to look for Jenna, she hoped that his last words were also rooted in reality—not the steady drip of the drugs that kept him comfortable and half asleep.

"I love you, too," she said. She went back to him, bent down, and kissed him on the lips tenderly. "You already know that, don't you?"

He managed a smile. "Yeah, I do."

# CHAPTER THIRTY-EIGHT

*Thursday, 12:22 A.M.,*
*place unknown*

Emily parked in front of a weathered chain and stepped outside, her flashlight's narrow beam barely a match for the heavy shroud of weather, an approaching storm. But, of course, none of that bothered her. Nothing could stop what had fueled her hunt since it all began—her daughter. *Where was Jenna?* Before the last bars on her cell phone died, she'd talked to Olga Morris-Cerrino about what had happened and where she was going. Olga told her that she'd heard through her pal at Seattle PD that local cops had requested infrared flybys to search for Jenna.

"My daughter is alive," she said. "We don't need to look for a goddamned hot spot."

No one could steal her hope. Though some tried. The worst had been her ex-husband. His last remarks could not have been crueler. His words were like wedding rice in the face, spiny and sharp, unexpected. How she had ever loved him was lost forever as his vitriolic words came back to her.

*"This comes down on you, Emily. You've really messed up this time. With our own daughter!"*

Only Olga had seemed adamant that Jenna would be found. "To think otherwise, is to lose her," she told Emily when she saw her outside Christopher's hospital room.

"I know." Emily's voice was soft and her emotions fragile.

"You need to get a grip," Olga said. "You're stronger than this and your daughter depends on you." She looked around the hallway; several other cops with coffee hovered nearby. "Do you want to count on them?"

Emily shook her head. "Absolutely not."

Olga went on, her voice no longer hushed. "All of his vics were taken in close proximity to where he'd lived. He's good looking *and* lazy. That's the standard combination of any straight guy with a hot body and pretty face." She tried to get Emily to smile, but she couldn't. Instead, she hatched a plan. "I'll work some things around here. The cops are all over this, but they're no match for you."

Emily knew Olga was right.

"There's an old World War II bunker not far from the cabin. Chris thinks I should go there. I sure can't just wait here."

Emily felt her way along the iron chain, so heavy and rusted. Probably a relic from a shipwreck, the chain was meant to keep interlopers and vandals from the bunker. She was nearly out of breath, though she had barely exerted herself. *So hard to breathe in this wind.*

The weather could not have been worse, and for once, the radio weather report could not have been more accurate: "Gale force winds on the coast; small craft advisories in all Washington coastal waters. . . ."

She pulled her coat tighter and followed the length of the chain, searching for a bolt or a latch of some kind, but found none. *I don't want to have to walk up there,* she thought, eyeing the impossibly steep and rain-washed road to the top of the bluff and the bunker. She kicked at the chain, but it stayed anchored by the four-foot creosote pilings that had been jammed into the sandy soil. She'd have no choice but to completely brave the elements and walk. She went back to the car, turned off the engine, dimmed the headlights, and grabbed a heavy Maglite from the glove box.

A second later, the flashlight's beam poking through the darkness, Emily was over the chain and in search of her daughter. She had gone directly from Christopher's hospital room to this desolate spot. If Jenna was in there, she didn't want her to wait one minute longer than she had to for her mom. She had to get her out of there as soon as she could.

*Before it's too late. Before she dies. Before my life is over.*

The bunker had been built on a promontory above the Pacific in World War II. It was one of several positioned around Washington state in the event that the Japanese had somehow launched a secret offensive to invade the West Coast. After it had been abandoned for decades, the locals had tried to make it a tourist destination but as the concrete interior that had once housed a pair of sixteen–foot cannons began to crumble, the state shut down the site and posted a series of WARNING and DANGER signs.

As Emily trudged her way up the darkened bluff, she could see that the heavy chain had not been a complete deterrent—several beer cans and even some paper plates indicated that the bunker might have been a party spot; charred logs indicated a campsite. Tire tracks from motorcycles and all-terrain vehicles had slashed the sandy soil with ruts that now collected water. A dozen little streams ran down the hillside, the wind roared, and she pulled her jacket closer. The cold air sliced every inch of her exposed skin.

*Jenna*, she thought, *where are you?* She didn't call out. The noise of the storm made any kind of utterance completely impractical. And if that had not been the case, Emily would have kept her mouth shut as a precaution. She worried if Jenna's captor was within the sound of her voice. If he was, there was no need to tip him off. Surprise and her Glock—warm from her constant touch—were among the things she had going for her. But neither were her greatest source of strength and power; finding Jenna stood above all.

*My daughter's out there and I'm not leaving until I find her and bring her home.*

Something screamed. Startled, Emily looked up and into the night sky, a boiling brew of clouds. *Just a seabird.* She was almost there. The bunker was twenty yards away, behind a hedge of sea grasses and spruce trees so tortured by the elements they looked like alarmed figures fleeing the waves of the Pacific. The trek to the top of the bluff had taken no more than ten minutes, but with each step she felt as if the sinking sand would steal her feet. *Here. I'm here. But where are you? Where is the bunker?*

Emily steadied herself on the grassy and sandy layer that covered the concrete slab roof of the secluded bunker. She looked around with her light, finally tracing the edges of the roofline beneath her feet. Waving the flashlight's beam toward the ocean, she could distinguish the crisp edge of the bunker's camouflaged covering. Bracing herself against the elements, she moved slowly toward its face.

Emily could hear the surf of the Pacific two hundred feet below, pounding the embankment with a relentless fury. Gooseflesh consumed her body. Since she could barely see, she climbed down a ledge backward, facing toward the edge of the cliff. She expected it was no more than ten yards away. There was no other way down, at least none she could see with a flashlight that only produced a strong beam when she rocked it back and forth, shifting the weakening batteries.

She bent down, her back to the ocean, and slid. Her hands were frozen and wet, but she barely used them for grasping; they'd become more like hooks than hands. She dropped ten feet, feeling the relief that came when her feet rested on the packed red clay and sand of the earth.

*The red clay.*

She was close. Close to finding Jenna. Her heart pounded with such a hurried force, she worried that she might have a heart attack. She'd die right there. No one would find her. No one would find her daughter.

Her lips were blue, and vapors curled from her mouth as she frantically searched for a way in. All the while, a fierce wind pummeled her.

The bunker had three openings, not really windows, but more the size of very small doors. Each had been fashioned with bars by the state's Fish and Game Department to allow access for bats, but to deter visitors of the human kind. A sign proclaimed the bunker as a protected habitat for Townsend's Big-eared Bats. On closer inspection, she noticed that one of the bars could easily be removed. It was clear by the color and condition of the bar—darker and smoother than the others—that it had been handled. It had been moved. She tucked the flashlight under her armpit, its beam scattering in the wrong direction. She pulled and twisted and the middle bar came loose. She dropped it and it fell with a thud into the sand.

*This is the way in,* she thought, hoisting herself up to the opening and fishing her feet through it. She swiped her light at the floor to make sure the drop wasn't so severe as to cause an injury. She slid herself into the opening, and slumped to the wet concrete floor. She dropped to her knees. She was inside.

Once more, her light moved across the floor.

*Blood? Oh God, no!* she thought as she caught the sight of red spatter that had marked the middle opening. *Oh no, please.* The words nearly slipped from her lips as her freezing fingertips felt the red color. *It was hard.* Even under the layer of wetness from the rain, Emily Kenyon could feel that it was a dried pigment. *Not blood. Paintball,* she thought, momentarily relieved.

She pointed the beam into the depths of the bunker. It looked empty, dark, hollow. The space was surprisingly large—maybe as much as two thousand square feet. She trained her light all around. There were sodden boxes full of garbage. It smelled of bat guano. A rat or maybe even a raccoon lurked on the other side of the darkness.

"Jenna?" Her voice echoed in the darkness. "Are you here?"

"Help me! Get me out of here," called a faint voice— *her daughter's voice.*

Emily felt a jab at her heart. Toward the back of the bunker, the wall farthest from the ocean, there was a steel door. The voice was coming from there.

"Honey, I'm here."

The wind howled outside, the storm was moving at breakneck speed from the gloomy waters of the Pacific. She wondered if she'd heard *anything* at all. The wind was messing with her. A whistle, then a shriek. There had been no answer to her call.

She tried again, inching toward the door. "Jenna?"

"Mom? Mom?"

*It was her!* "Yes, it's Mom!" Her gun now drawn, Emily reached for the door and lifted the lever handle.

"Help me," said the weak voice as Emily swung open the door to a small room. File boxes filled with county records were packed in rows that had once likely been neat. Right now they were a shambles. *More paintball spatter.* The smell of moldy paper permeated the air.

"Help me," came a voice once more. It was male this time. *Young.* A teenager.

*Nick? Or was it Dylan, toying with her once more?*

Emily aimed her light at the direction of the voice and scanned the room. A leg. A torso. A face. It was Nick Martin. He was on the floor, his legs bound by cording. His skin was ashen, and his eyes glittered like wet stones. His gaze sliced through the air. He looked so different from his photograph, even more so, Emily thought, from when she'd seen him last. *With his mother*. His dark hair, so carefully highlighted by Peg, was gone. Even his youth failed him right then; his handsomeness was no longer evident. He was caged. Angry and weak at the same time.

"Mrs. Kenyon, help me." His voice was a rasp. "We gotta get Jenna out of here."

"Where's my daughter?" Adrenaline was now a flood through her body.

Brown eyes stared back. "Get me out of here," he said.

Emily bent down and began to untie the ligature that was wrapped around his surprisingly muscular body. She'd thought that he was slighter. A runner or something. But he was bulkier than she remembered. Much more so. She started to loosen the cording, but something struck her as terribly wrong. It was already loose. Oddly so. *Anyone could take this off. A kid this strong could break this cord with a half-assed tug.*

"Mom! Don't!" It was Jenna's voice, this time muffled.

Emily peered over Nick's shoulder. *Was Jenna right there?* She looked into his eyes, but it was already too late. A pipe or steel rod came down on her, grazing her temple and striking her shoulder. Then another, this time dead on. The small musty room closed in. And as she began to fall only one thing came to mind: *Jenna and I are going to die.*

From the other side of the bunker, a cigarette glowed.

# CHAPTER THIRTY-NINE

*Thursday, exact time unknown,*
*in the bunker*

When Emily regained consciousness, two things were on her mind. Her daughter, and a gaping hole in her right temple that sent a rivulet of blood down her clammy skin. She shook her head, trying to startle herself into being fully awake. *Where am I? Where is Jenna?* Her mouth was like cotton, so dry, that at first she thought she'd been gagged. *What happened?* She tried to speak, but her words came out in a whisper. *"Jenna?"*

A voice came at her like a dream, like the sweet song of an angel. If words could be uttered like a hymn, they had been just then.

"Mom, I'm here."

The phrase brought a smack-down bump to Emily's awareness. It was a spark. It rekindled a flash fire of memory. *She'd been in the bunker. She'd been tracking Nick and Jenna. Jenna was there. She'd been help-*

*ing Nick get free. Then a curtain of darkness, sudden and complete.*

A battery-powered lantern glowed a few yards away. Within the yellow light was the silhouette of two fig-ures. One was standing, a cherry ember hanging from his lips as he smoked. The other was sitting on the ce-ment and clay floor. It was a much slighter figure. *Jenna*.

Emily found her voice again. "Nick, what's going on here? What are you doing to us? Jenna, are you all right?"

"Shut up!" Nick said. "She's okay. But she can't talk."

Emily tried to lean forward to get a better view, but her body was frozen. "What have you done with her?"

Nick sucked on his cigarette and exhaled, sending a sliver of smoke into the air, then, like a whirlpool, out into the drafty bunker. "Nothing. Nothing compared to what's been done to me."

Emily struggled even harder to stand, to get a better look, but it was useless.

"What are you talking about? Let me help you."

Nick looked at her, blank eyed. "I'm not helping anyone. No one ever helped me."

He continued to smoke and Emily strained to get a better view of her daughter. Jenna was within a few yards of her, and she could see in the dim light that her breathing was rapid and shallow. But she was alive. Relief mixed with the fear that seized Emily. She wrig-gled in the cording, but it was too tight. "Look," Emily said, her tone gentle, "I know about Bonnie and Dylan. No one will blame you for any of it. You've been through so much. I'll help you."

"You don't have a clue about what I've been through. I've been alone my entire life."

Emily was unsure how to play it. *Play him.* Her instincts failed her. Her head hurt. Her heart ached. *What to say?* "That's not true. Your parents loved you. They wanted you. They chose you." It was weak and she knew it. She was firing off a list, hoping that she'd trigger something that would bring him back to what she hoped was really there. "You were wanted."

"You didn't live in my house with my family," he said. He dropped the cigarette butt and twisted it with the heel of his shoe.

"I know. But I did know your mother."

"You *think* you knew her. She was ten times worse than my dad. Everything was about Donny. Donny reminded Dad of his father. Donny had Mom's eyes. Donny was a chip off the old block. I was nothing to them. I was the boy they picked up from an agency because Mom couldn't get knocked up."

"Don't talk like that, Nick." Emily felt wetness at her temple. She couldn't reach it, of course, but as it dripped down she wondered if it was blood or sweat. She was unsure of how badly she was hurt by the scuffle. She saw a length of rebar by his tennis shoe–clad feet.

"Why are you doing this to me, to Jenna?"

"Dan says that Jenna's collateral. Just like you. He's just pissed off at you for screwing up everything."

"What? His place in the serial killer hall of fame?"

Nick laughed. "It's a little like that. Dad says that God told him that he had a special plan for him and that his son, me, would help him get there. I'm willing to do for him what needs to be done."

"But killing Jenna, me? What's that?"

"Collateral, Mrs. Kenyon. You ruined my dad's rhythm. You cost him what was rightfully his when you killed that dumbass Tuttle."

"What are you talking about? That was an accident. I was trying to save Kristi. She was just a little girl. She didn't deserve to die."

Nick Martin was unmoved. His eyes, cold like a doll's eyes.

*Like his father's.*

"Maybe so," he said. "But you're really the one responsible for her death anyway. You killed her by killing Tuttle. When you did that you messed with my dad. You stole from him."

"Stole what?"

"His rhythm, his plan to be more famous than Bundy."

There was no point in arguing the merits of his bio dad's sick run to be some kind of serial killer superstar. She'd heard of people like that, people who sought infamy over fame. People who cared to make a mark, no matter how dark, how evil. There was no arguing. No defending the other side of it.

Emily changed the subject. "Jenna needs water," she said. "Please give her some."

"Water? She's gonna die. Why make her comfortable? That's stupid. You researched me. You know I'm no dummy. Yeah, my grades weren't as perfect as Donovan's, but he wasn't an artist."

The wind whistled through the bunker. Emily didn't want the conversation to track there. Talking about Jenna not making it was not anything she'd even ask about. *No fuel for whatever sickness drives this boy.*

"Nick, that's right," she said stiffly. "You're special. You're an artist. What's going on here isn't you. I know that."

His eyes, his *father's* eyes, were black voids. "But it's who I want to be."

"No, it's who you've been forced to be. This is wrong. It doesn't have to be. I'll help you. We can repair all of this. Nothing's gone too far. Yet."

Jenna's breathing had appeared to slow and muffled sounds of her coughing came through the gag. Every neuron in Emily's body fired. She was hyper alert, with the kind of rush that allows a desperate mother to pick up a car crushing her child.

"Nick! Take that out of her mouth right now! Jenna can't breathe!"

He dropped his cigarette. "Jesus. Where did that come from?" He winced at the increased volume of Emily's voice—the "mom" voice that women can summon when they needed it. "All right. I'll get her some air. She's gonna die anyway, but you don't have to yell at me."

He loosened the gag and Jenna coughed.

"You don't have to yell, you know. I can hear all right."

Emily detected the tiniest fracture in the teenager's practiced veneer and she went for it.

"Yelling? Did your parents yell at you?"

He blinked. "No shit. Every chance they got."

"How did it make you feel?"

"Like I was worthless."

*Chipping away. Making him feel something. If not for Jenna, for himself. Good.*

"You aren't worthless. You know it. Didn't Jenna see it in you? See your worth? Your talent?"

Nick's eyes were downcast. "I don't want to talk anymore," he said. "You're not some school counselor trying to make me happy. My dad's coming. My *real* dad. We're getting out of here." He sat down next to Jenna, her pale, pasty skin now alarmed her mother even more.

"Please," Emily said, "let my daughter go."

"Shut up. That's not the plan."

"What is the plan, Nick? I wasn't aware of a plan."

He shot her his best FU look. His eyes were cold, his stare hard. "Wouldn't you like to know?" He allowed a brief smile to come to his lips. "You're gonna die. Just like Kristi Cooper. You're gonna die because no one can find you."

"You know about Kristi?"

"I know what my dad tells me."

"Which dad?"

"The one that matters, Dylan Walker."

"Don't you know he killed all those people? Doesn't that mean anything to you?"

"*You* killed someone."

He was referring to Tuttle, of course, maybe even Kristi Cooper. But Emily didn't go there. *She couldn't.* She had to keep him talking so that just maybe she could find a way to talk them out of the bunker. To daylight. To freedom. To safety. The wind sent another blast of air against the bunker's openings. It sounded like the whistle of a train, the rolling of the tracks.

"I never meant to kill anyone."

"Good for you. I never killed anyone."

"Not even Bonnie."

"Dad took care of her."

"But she was your biological mother."

"She was a breeder and that's all. She was stupid, too. My dad tried to get rid of her for years. I would have killed her, but instead, I just helped clean up the mess. Dad never liked working alone."

Emily was reeling. It was as if all that Dylan Walker had done was now being revealed by his biological son, a son no one knew about.

"There were others, too. Bonnie took care of them. Just like she did to the Martins. Other mistakes he made that he wanted cleaned up."

"What others?" It struck a nerve that he now had referred to his family by its surname. His split from them was so complete. Emily wondered if he held any emotion for Peg, Mark, or Donovan.

"What happened to your family," she asked, hesitating, before shifting her words, "to the Martins?"

He looked downward. A trickle of feeling? Emily studied him through the murky light of the bunker. *What was he thinking? What was he feeling?*

"It was planned," he said. "Everything. But the storm. The storm wasn't planned."


Jenna was wide awake, listening to Nick Martin spin a slightly different—*and darker*—version of what had happened in the hours before the tornado. She listened without moving a muscle while her mother surreptitiously struggled to break free. Jenna knew she'd been played. It had been a setup from the beginning. Nick hadn't just come home to find them dead.

*Nick had known what he was going to find.*

"Okay," he continued, "I didn't know that Donny was going to be home."

As she fought her binding, Emily's eyes beamed through the darkness at Nick. It was as if she willed his attention to hold on her face only, not her hands. "But your mom called him to come home," she said.

"No. Peg didn't call him. Bonnie did. Dylan, *Dad*, said that Bonnie really messed up. She came to get me. Take me out of Cherrystone. My dad was important. Famous. She was my birthmother, but the Martins didn't want anything to do with her."

*He called his parents by their names,* Emily thought, *no longer Mom and Dad. It was like he'd dissociated himself from them. No ties. No connections.*

"By the time I got home, they were all dead."

Tears welled in his eyes. Emily saw it as a hopeful sign. *Maybe this kid has a soul after all,* she thought.

"I don't know why that bitch called Donny home," he said, sniffing a little.

"Maybe she didn't want any loose ends to worry about?" Emily tried to sound unthreatening and helpful. She was more mom than cop just then, at least she hoped that's what Jenna's friend-turned-captor would think.

Instead a little defiance followed. "He wasn't a loose end. Even though the Martins couldn't stop yapping about how great he was, he was my brother."

"Right. And you loved him."

"I love my dad. He's coming for me. We're going to live in Mexico. He says I get my creativity from him."

*And your taste for blood*, she thought. "He's not coming for you. You were a loose end. All of them. The kids. The families."

"You don't know anything," he said.

Emily caught Jenna's eye. She could see that Jenna

had made some progress. No words were needed, just the look of desperation giving way to hope.

"I know enough," she said, her calming tone barely in check.

"Too bad. You're gonna die, Mrs. Kenyon. Jenna, too. 'Cause you're my loose ends."

"No," Emily said firmly. She wouldn't allow one drop of fear to color her words. He was just a goofy kid. A mixed-up, goofy kid. In another time or place he could have been a Columbine student skulking under a table as bullets sprayed over a cafeteria. He could have been a chess champion, making his final move, winning the prize. Or just a plain old kid waiting at a bus stop or laughing and pushing and shoving his friends in a movie line at the Cherrystone Cinema. *Anything*. Anything—but a monster.

He was a lost boy.

"Yeah, that's what you are," he said, looking for a smoke, then pulling one out of a twisted pack and poking it into his mouth. "A loose end." He spat out the words as he felt for his lighter.

Jenna's hands were free now. She tried not to let her excitement show on her face, or become audible through her breathing. As quickly as she could, Jenna untied the bindings that held her legs. The cords had cut so deeply into her skin that the wave of pain that came with their release was nearly unbearable. It felt as if she'd been cut with the jagged edge of a hunting knife. Her feet were numb. *Had she lost blood? Had gangrene set in?* She wanted to cry. It took every bit of strength she had to just swallow that pain as she scanned the darkened space of the bunker.

*Where did Nick put my mother's gun?*

Jenna saw the rebar by Nick's feet. While his hands were in his pockets searching for his lighter, she lunged for the metal rod.

"Jenna!" Emily screamed.

Still on her knees, Jenna grabbed the bar, started to swing. Nick looked down, his eyes fixed with terror as the bar smashed into his kneecaps.

"Hey! Damn you. Leave him alone!" a voice, a man's voice called from the other side of the bunker.

It was Dylan Walker. He'd been there the whole time, watching as if the whole series of events unfolding were some kind of a performance. A play. A crazy, horrific skit.

Nick let out a scream. But he was clearly more than startled. He was also hurt. His face was warped with pain and he finished the little scream with a growling moan.

Dylan Walker leapt across the bunker. But he didn't really intervene. It was as if whatever was happening was just fine with him.

Jenna didn't stop, even after Nick fell to the cement floor, doubled over in pain. There was enough adrenaline pulsing through the teenager's veins to keep her going. He had sounded weak. She knew she could hurt him more. Hurt him enough so that he couldn't hurt her or her mom. She closed her eyes and she pounded him with the steel bar, not like some girly girl who'd been featured in ballet recital back in Cherrystone.

Far from it.

"You're a liar," she said, tears streaming down her face. "I hate you. I wish you were dead." Now, as he crumpled over his stomach, she brought the bar down hard on the back of his skull. Suddenly there was a lot of bright red blood soaking his hair. Jenna remembered hearing her mother talk about head wounds being "big bleeders." *Good.* She'd open up that wound even more.

Nick was a limp heap but Jenna kept waling on him.

"Jenna, stop it!" Emily struggled to free herself, to stop her daughter from doing what she had done once. There would be no more blood on their hands, no matter the reason. "Honey, stop!"

Jenna froze in a semicrouch, her bloodied weapon held like a baseball bat, droplets of blood dotting her face like scarlet freckles. She looked at her mother with wide, scared eyes.

"Stop, Jenna. *Now.*"

"But, this is my fault . . ."

"Now! Drop it!"

Jenna let the bar fall; its heavy steel clatter echoed. Nick lay still on the dirty cement floor. He was curled up in a fetal position. A rivulet of red ran from his blood-matted hair down onto his pale, white cheek. His breathing was labored and raspy.

Jenna was sobbing now. "I want to go home, Mom."

"You're not going anywhere." Dylan kicked the rebar out of the way and brandished his gun, the gleam of black barrel visible in the dark bunker. "Nice work, kid," he said to Jenna. "Nick told me you were tough. Tough like your mom."

"Dylan, Nick is your son. He needs help." It was Emily. She knew it was a last-ditch effort to try to wheedle some sympathy from the man. Was there anything in his DNA that tied him to his son? A bond? Any connection whatsoever?

"You're confusing me with someone who gives a

shit. Nick served his purpose. I don't care if he lives or dies."

It dawned on Emily that Dylan Walker might be one of those serial killers who didn't like to get his hands dirty. Killing someone only brought a rush when he could manipulate someone else to do it. It was a coward's way to kill.

*Killing Tuttle had been a manipulation.*

He pointed his gun at Jenna.

"Leave her alone!" A familiar voice called out.

Emily looked up and saw a figure backed by a halo of light coming into the bunker.

"Leave her alone!" the voice repeated.

The figure was carrying a gas-powered camping lantern. Its fiery mantle hissed in the darkness. As it moved closer, the smaller figure appeared to be a woman.

"We're over here!" Jenna called out.

"Shut up," Dylan said.

Emily rested a hand on her daughter and tried to feel for the steel bar. How far had he kicked it away? She tilted her head to look into the streaming light.

"Don't even think about it," he said.

To Emily's relief, the light ran over the startled face and tiny torso of Olga Morris-Cerrino. Her eyes were round and terrified. It was just a quick strobelike image, but Emily could see that Olga's gun was drawn.

From near Emily's feet, Nick moaned.

Olga lowered the lantern. "Are you okay?"

"We're all okay," Emily said. "But he needs a doctor."

Olga stared at the crumpled boy while Dylan moved the gun barrel around the room, unable to see where anyone was.

"Let us go!" Emily yelled. "Olga, be careful. Dylan has a gun."

The lantern was steadier, casting a ghostly light over the bunker. Olga could see the little tableau now. Jenna was crouching down low, crying softly a few steps from Nick, who was on his side curled in the fetal position. His hair was matted with blood. His eyes were slits of white. The light swung again slowly, including Dylan and Emily in the composition.

*Hang on. This isn't over.*

"You miserable piece of garbage," she said in a low rasp.

"Wow, scary," Dylan answered with his washed-up, has-been, serial killer laugh, underscoring his contempt.

Emily shifted her attention to Dylan. She meant to distract. "Look what you've done. None of this was necessary. What's the point of it all?"

"Mom, I'm scared," Jenna said. "I want to go home."

"You're all going now," Dylan said, in a still, uncertain voice. "But not home. You messed with my legacy."

A cry came from the floor of the bunker. It was Nick.

"I hate you!" Nick pulled himself up, leaning on his palms, turning a bloodied face to his biological father.

"You ungrateful kid," Dylan yelled back.

"Why did you let her hurt me? You told me you'd protect me if I did what you wanted."

"You get your stupidity from your mother's side of the family," Dylan said. There was no irony in his statement.

Olga dropped the lantern and rolled it toward Emily,

spinning light in the cavernous space like a cop's strobe. And there it was. *A gift.* The Glock. Emily lunged for it, aimed the trigger at Dylan's chest, and fired. No warning. Just three bullets firing in rapid succession.

*Pop. Pop. Pop.*

Dylan slumped down onto the cold floor.

"You shot me, you bitch!" he said, a gurgling sound coming from his windpipe. Blood trickled from his mouth slowly, like red candle wax. "Three times! You shot me. You didn't even tell me to drop my weapon!"

Emily took one step over and kicked the gun away from Walker. Then turned back to Jenna and Olga.

"Yeah," she said. "One time for Kristi and"—look-ing at Olga—"one each for Lorrie and Shelley. I hope you feel each one, you piece of garbage."

"Call an ambulance!" Dylan coughed out. "Please!"

Emily lifted Jenna to her feet, and then when she was steady, she turned to Olga. It was as if Dylan Walker was already gone.

"Thank God you got here," Emily said. "How did you? How did you know where we were?"

Olga smiled. "A smart guy who thinks the world of you told me."

Emily smiled back. She knew it had been Chris. He'd always promised to look out for her.

"Mom, I love you." Jenna wrapped her arms around her mother. "I knew you would come for me. I'm so sorry. I was so stupid. I shouldn't have gone off with Nick."

None of that mattered. "Honey, we're all okay. You're okay."

"What about me?" It was Dylan Walker again, weak

and pathetic on the cold, hard floor. "I need you to get me help!"

Olga shrugged. She no longer had a smile on her face. "We'll call all right," she said. "After you've died." Olga looked over at Nick Martin, now unconscious. "What about him?"

Emily shook her head. "He's a basket case. He's pretty badly beat up, too. But he'll live and he'll go to trial." She looked at Dylan Walker as he slowly writhed. Life seeped from him. She stared at him. Kristi. Lorrie. Shelley. Jenna. All victims past and yet to be flashed through her mind.

"Emily?" Olga asked. "You all right?"

Snapped back into the moment, Emily put her arm around her daughter and pulled her tighter.

"Yes," she said. "Let the monster die."

# EPILOGUE

*Six months later,*
*Cherrystone, Washington*

It had been months since the "sexiest killer alive" had been dispatched for eternity in the dark confines of the bunker. Media attention had died down. "He died instantly and thank God for retired Detective Cerrino. Without her intervention we'd have all been on his grisly tote board," Emily said when she talked to *People* magazine about her daughter's kidnapping and the connection between Dylan Walker and the murders in Utah, Washington, and Iowa.

"Nick Martin told his lawyers that you and the detective purposely let Dylan die. You didn't get him help because you wanted revenge," the magazine reporter said.

Emily sighed. "Poor Nick, he's such a mixed-up kid."

Olga had been over to Cherrystone twice; her friendship with both Emily and Jenna was built on a terrifying night in utter darkness that the three of them shared.

"No one will miss him," she said to Emily over coffee at the kitchen table one afternoon during a visit to the old house on Orchard Avenue.

"Except his Internet fan club," Emily said. "I feel sorry for those people."

Olga's flinty eyes sparkled. She suppressed the urge to smile.

"Dylan got what he deserved."

Emily nodded. "Guess so."

Olga sipped her coffee. "My girls, Lorrie and Shelley, can rest easy now. So can Kristi."

Emily looked over at Jenna who was watching TV in the living room. She swirled some artificial sweetener in her coffee. "We all can."

In many ways, they could.

Nick Martin was in county jail awaiting trial for his role in kidnapping Jenna Kenyon, but mental health advisors said he wasn't sane enough to stand trial, and figured he'd be a shoo-in for an insanity defense. The kid was screwed up. If he was aware of what he was doing—which they implicitly denied—the defense was sure it was the result of a mental breakdown brought on by the murders of his family. He had no hand in the events that brought him to the bunker. He wasn't a murderer. Bonnie and Dylan had cooked it all up.

The rental car from the Spokane Airport tied Bonnie to the locale, though the tornado had swept away any real trace that she'd done it or if Dylan had been with her. The same had been true with the Utah and Iowa murders—a paper trail indicated Bonnie, not Dylan Walker.

Yet Emily knew that Dylan Walker never worked

alone. Olga was able to pry some information out of Nick Martin that suggested supposed suicide victim Tyler Ticen had, in fact, been involved in the double homicide of the two college girls from her jurisdiction. But those cases would never be officially solved. The Ticen suicide was a cover, she was sure, a way for Walker to silence his accomplice.

Using schizophrenic Reynard Tuttle had been a master stroke. Handsome, brilliant, and evil: the trifecta of serial killer superstars.

And dead.

The house on Orchard Avenue in Cherrystone had seen its occupants find their way back to a closer, more loving relationship than they had before mother and daughter were held captive by the serial killer's son. It had been a slow climb back to their normal lives. Jenna obsessed about her father's new baby, his betrayal, and the nightmares of the bunker. But she was determined to get over it as was Emily. In many ways, David had become part of her past, just as he started anew with Dani and their daughter, Cassandra. Custody gripes involving Jenna were no longer an issue. David didn't fight for his daughter to visit, and she didn't balk when the time came.

They found balance in forgiveness.

Emily had worked out the loose ends—a phrase that caused her to wince—with the help of Christopher Collier, who'd made a rapid and remarkable recovery from the gunshot wound to the chest. They talked on the phone and even dated a couple of times. Where all of that would lead was beyond the point right then.

"I just want to heal and move on," Emily told him

one night late as they were talking on the phone. "But when I do, I want you there."

"Promise?" he asked.

"Promise. Definitely, a promise."

One fall evening, the air crisp as a freshly laundered man's dress shirt, Jenna was in her bedroom, pink keyboard and mouse in hand. On the screen was a chat window with best-friend-forever Shali Patterson, who by then had a new VW, and was delighted with all the attention her part in the ordeal had brought her. She was the best friend of a kickass girl, one who saved her mom from a serial killer's kid. *Nice.* The girls chatted about their senior year and who would be crowned homecoming queen later that week. Jenna dared to dream that it would be her. In no small way, she felt she did deserve it. Saving her mom was a bigger deal than being yearbook editor.

With its characteristic chime, her Instant Messenger account announced a name she'd almost forgotten—Batboy88. She could scarcely believe her eyes. A wave of panic hit her.

Batboy88: Hey Jengrrl!
Jenna froze at her keyboard.
Batboy88: You there?

*Nick was in county jail. He didn't have access to a PC.*

Batboy88: Missed U!

Jenna found her voice. *"Mom!"*
Emily was in the kitchen soaking a dreadfully dried-

on lasagna pan when she heard Jenna's scream from down the hallway. The timbre of her daughter's voice suggested trouble and fear shot through her. There had been screams for her before, night terrors, as she recalled the dark hours in the bunker. The idea that she'd been so close, a hairsbreadth from evil. But this was too early in the evening.

She found her very still, in front of the screen, staring at it with disbelieving eyes.

"Mom, it's an IM from Nick."

Emily's face went pale. "It can't be." She peered over Jenna's shoulder. "This is someone playing a game." Emily gently pushed her daughter aside and sat down. She started typing.

Jengrrl: Who is this?
Batboy88: Who do U think?

Emily looked up at her daughter, her keys tapping slowly. She hit the ENTER button again.

Jengrrl: You aren't Nick. I know that. Who r u?
Batboy88: When I get out, you want to go to r place, u know, the mining camp?

Without even thinking, Emily reached over and quickly yanked the plug from the outlet. The screen sputtered and went dark. The computer's tiny fan slowed, then whirled to a stop.

Jenna looked horrified. "Mom! Why did you do that?"

Emily stayed quiet for a second, her mind trying to catch up with what she'd done. Finally she spoke and when she did so, the words were more a promise than a statement. "It's over. He's *over*," she said. She put her arms around her daughter, in the bedroom where she grew up. It was over. Nick Martin was gone from their lives.

And so was Dylan Walker.

# ACKNOWLEDGMENTS

I wanted to take a moment to thank some of the people who have been so amazing with their support and advice as I wrote *A Cold Dark Place*. Naturally, none of it is possible without the support and love of my family—Claudia, Morgan, and Marta.

Thanks also to the best thriller editor and the best thriller agent in the business: Michaela Hamilton, executive editor of Kensington, and Susan Raihofer of David Black Literary. What a team you two make!

I'd like to acknowledge the writers that have been so helpful to me recently. All of the Killer Year members and friends have been great, but I especially want to spotlight JT Ellison, Bill Cameron, and Sandra Ruttan for their wonderful support and partnership over the past year. My Killer Year mentor, Allison Brennan, has no peer when it comes to writing pulse-pounding suspense *and* encouraging new (even old!) authors.

Thanks to Kathrine Beck, Tina Marie Brewer, Charles Turner, Bunny Kuhlman, and Matt Phelps for their much-appreciated guidance along the way.

There are many behind-the-scenes people who helped shape the final product that you now hold in your hand. I want to publicly thank Lou Malcangi for his terrific cover design and Diane Burke for her thoughtful copy-editing. If I wore a hat, I'd take it off to you!

Finally, to my readers. Thanks so much for following me from true crime to fiction. Your e-mails, letters, and posts on Crime Rant mean the world to me.

Don't miss Gregg Olsen's next exciting Waterman
and Stark thriller

# JUST TRY TO STOP ME

Coming from Kensington Publishing Corp. in 2016

Keep reading to enjoy an exciting excerpt . . .

### The day Brenda and Janie vanished

Janie Thomas looked at the laptop she'd been ordered to transport to her second-floor office at the Washington State Corrections Center for Women in Purdy, Washington. It was against prison protocol to bring any electronic devices inside the secure facility, but Janie *was* the prison superintendent. When she started to breeze though the checkpoint, she told her favorite officer, Derrick Scott, that she was running late.

"Rough morning," Janie said, an exaggerated look of displeasure on her face. She glanced at her phone. "Have a call with the governor's office in five minutes."

"He's never on time," the officer said. "Not with a meeting or getting a budget approved. But if you ask me, a crying baby in the middle of the night is at the tippy top of the 'rough morning' scale. I didn't sleep a wink last night."

"Tell me about it," Janie said, going through the detector. "I haven't forgotten those days. You'll get through them."

The African American man grinned, showing white teeth, and passed Janie's briefcase over the counter instead of through the scanner. The superintendent was always so nice, asking about the kids, sharing photos of her family from her phone.

Later the officer would say that the briefcase weighed more than usual and he probably should have opened it, but she was, after all, the boss.

"She runs the prison," he said. "What was she going to smuggle in? A set of keys? A file?"

A half hour later that same morning, Brenda Nevins was in Janie's office, purportedly to take on a special work assignment to help other inmates with life skills. Other prisoners saw an irony in that, but didn't say a word. Speaking up against Brenda meant getting cut in the shower with a shank made of a mascara wand and the sharpened edge of a Pringles' can top. Or poisoned at lunch with meds ripped off from the infirmary. Or, worst of all, cut off from visitation with family.

"I run this place," Brenda had said, when a new girl—a meth head from Black Diamond with more body tattoos then brains—challenged her. "You keep that in mind if you piss me off."

In her office the day she disappeared, Janie opened the laptop for the benefit of the woman who had told her to bring it.

"Nice. Does it have video capabilities?" Brenda asked as the pair moved from Janie's office to the records room—the only location in the institution that did not have the prying eyes of security cameras.

They stood face-to-face, a worktable separating them. Brenda had done her hair in the way she knew Janie liked—down, with slight curls that brushed past her shoulders.

The two of them were there to plot the escape. Janie's *and* hers.

"It's an Apple," Janie said. "Top of the line. My husband helped me set everything up."

Brenda watched a flicker of emotion coming over Janie's face at the mention of her husband, Edwin. She moved her own mouth into a slight frown; a mirror of what Janie was doing, sans the slight lowering of the chin. Quivering was too much. Not needed.

"Don't be sad, Janie," Brenda said in a voice dripping with honey sweetness. "I know this is hard. But your life belongs to you and you have to live it as you were meant to do. No more dreaming. No more wondering, baby girl. We are on the verge of our moment. We have to take it together. We have no choice in the matter. You know what we are? You know what brought us together?"

Janie bit down on her lower lip.

"We're soul mates," she said. Brenda relaxed her frown. "Don't ever doubt that. Don't ever. I know that God or some higher power—whatever She is—has brought us together. That's right. The world will be all over us. You know that. They'll be watching and hunting and trying to stop us from doing what we must do."

"I guess so," Janie said, fear evident in her voice.

Brenda reached across the table and grabbed Janie by her shoulders.

"Get a grip," she said. "This moment will not only set us free but will define the future for so many people. The world will be watching and we'll need to tell them the reasons behind everything we're doing."

"To help them, right?"

It was more than a question, almost an affirmation.

Brenda gave her head a slight nod. "Yes," she said. "It isn't about just *us*. Just you and me. I wish both of us could have come from other circumstances. Come from backgrounds free of the torment that sent us here . . . me to be a zoo animal, you to be a zookeeper. But life isn't fair. I get that. Life is what we make it. We're the example of living with authenticity."

Brenda stopped talking to assess. She watched Janie as a cat watches the family goldfish as it twirls in the waters of its bowl.

*Like the betta fish.*

"And we'll help people, right?" Janie repeated.

Exasperation was in order. Maybe a little bit of the takeaway was called for just then.

"Are you even listening?" Brenda asked as she let out a sigh. It was the kind of nonverbal punctuation at which she was particularly skilled. She was good with words. Good with presenting her concepts, no matter how outlandish. Repulsive even. She could sell peed-on snow to an Eskimo.

"Really?" she asked, drawing away slightly as though she were disgusted by what Janie said. "Really? This isn't about *us*. This is about the world. That's why we need to get our act together and get out of here. I didn't do any of those things they pinned on me. None of them whatsoever."

Janie didn't say another word. Brenda was a lot of

things, but Janie was all but certain a liar was not among them.

"Are you with me, baby? Are you about to let go of the past and be what God wants us to be? She's calling for us. She wants us to be together, and yes, my love, She wants for us to help others."

*Brenda was all about empowerment.*

"She loves us, doesn't She?" Janie asked. Before Brenda, Janie never used the feminine personal pronoun for God. It felt funny when she did it, but also empowering.

"More like adores," Brenda said.

Janie felt her body relax a little.

It felt so good to be loved for who she was.

"I'll be ready tonight after work," Janie said. "I'll send for you."

### After everything happened

Kendall Stark didn't know it, but she wouldn't be in need of a second tuxedo mocha that morning as she arrived in her offices at the Kitsap County Sheriff's Department in Port Orchard. The email link that was about to be forwarded to her would provide enough of a jolt.

The new public and media relations specialist, Daphne Brown, cornered the detective and spoke with a kind of breathless excitement that tempered just about everything that came out of her mouth.

*East Port Orchard Elementary wants you to talk about stranger danger safety! Tonight!*

*We are out of creamer in the break room! Where do we keep it? I need some!*

*We have a serial killer on the loose!*
*Do you like my hair this way?*

Kendall said good morning and waited for whatever urgent missive only-one-speed Daphne had.

"We've already heard from all the morning shows," Daphne said. "I'm so excited. They want you on."

Kendall shook her head. "I'm not doing it," Kendall said.

Daphne pulled at one of her curls and it bounced back into position. "You don't even know what it's about," she said. "How can you even say that?"

"It's not a *what*, Daphne. It's a *who* and I know that who is Brenda Nevins."

The younger woman's eyes widened a bit, but before she could speak, Kendall preempted her from doing so.

"There's nothing you can do," Kendall said. "I'm not required to go on camera. *You* are. You can do it."

Daphne dialed down her pushy enthusiasm. She'd been to a conference in Seattle the week before and had learned new techniques to influence what she considered a "resistant personality type."

Daphne fiddled with her department-issued smartphone.

"You better watch the link I'm about to send you."

"What link?" Kendall asked.

Daphne glanced up, a satisfied look on her face.

"Watch it," she said. "Then call me so I can work my PR magic."

Kendall didn't acknowledge Daphne's boast. She had no plan whatsoever of encouraging Ms. Brown to do anything, let alone work any kind of self-professed public relations hocus-pocus. She was so sick of Brenda

Nevins that she couldn't imagine enduring one more minute of thinking about her. Brenda was on the front page. Brenda was the top-of-the-hour news. Brenda had even been featured on the cover of *USA Today*. She was a murderous prison escapee and that made her a problem for the special agents of the FBI, not the investigators from the local Kitsap County's Sheriff Department.

Brenda had moved off the front pages. Janie Thomas's husband, Edwin, had buried his wife in a family plot in the memorial park just off the highway in Gig Harbor. TV producer Juliana Robbins's parents had claimed their beloved daughter's remains and placed them in an urn on their mantel—vowing they'd never let her go again. Bar owner Chaz Masters, who had become a footnote to the story in the way the white and middle aged often do, was honored with a wake at the Grey Gull—an event that only brought out a handful of barflies, a blogger, and a local newspaper reporter who normally filled in for the sports editor.

None of those who loved the dead had really moved on, of course. Most never would. The fact that Brenda Nevins had smeared her kind of evil all over Kitsap County had not brought anything but misery to Kendall Stark, Birdy Waterman, or any of the others who'd wanted justice to prevail.

It wasn't that Brenda Nevins, whom federal investigators were all but certain had fled to Canada, wasn't an icepick-in-the-eye kind of torture to Kendall. It was simply that Kendall couldn't do a thing about her.

"She was our Hurricane Katrina," her husband Steven had said a few weeks after the murder spree began. "She came and destroyed as much as she could and in the morning it was over. Only the wreckage was left behind."

He was right. That's exactly what she was and what she did.

After extricating herself from Daphne, Kendall made her way to her office and, against her better judgment, powered up her laptop and went right to her message inbox.

There it was, an email from Daphne Brown. No message. Just a link to a YouTube clip. Kendall clicked on the link and waited until the advertisement for a trip to Greece on a luxury liner reached the ten-second mark so she could X it out.

The video was entitled: How My Story Began, Part One.

Kendall could feel her heart rate accelerate a little as the clip worked its way from start to finish. Feeling a little sweat collect at the nape of her neck, she pushed her chair away from her desk and dialed Birdy Waterman's number.

"Hi Kendall," Birdy said. "What's up?"

"Are you in your office?"

"Yes," Birdy said. "Gloves about to go on."

"Can you come over here?"

Birdy hesitated a beat. "I'm about to start an autopsy on a crash victim from yesterday."

Kendall pushed. "But you haven't started, have you?"

"No, but . . . what's this about, Kendall?"

Kendall looked at the YouTube video cued up on her screen.

"Put the corpse back in the chiller and get over here," she said. "Brenda Nevins has posted a video blog. You need to see it."

"Video blog. What is she, fourteen?" Birdy said.

"This is no joke," Kendall said. "Come over as soon as you can."

The image was in high definition—clear and leaving no room for doubt. Brenda Nevins had not ever been a person who could lay low. She took the microphone, looking at the camera.

"The light is on so I guess you can see me. Or you can see me when I post this. I'm not stupid enough to do this live. It pissed me off to lose the chance to be on TV to tell the world my true story. The morons in the legal system really screwed me over. I don't like to be screwed with. I'm the one who does the screwing. Right, Janie?"

She turned and tilted the camera to Janie Thomas, who was bound and gagged on a chair. Silver duct tape cocooned her forearms to the armrest. Her feet were out of view. The gag appeared to be black fabric, some clothing item.

"Looks like underwear," Birdy said. "Wonder whose?"

Kendall didn't reply. Her office was silent. Still. Her eyes were glued to her computer's screen. In particular, Janie's terrified eyes riveted the detective. Though farther back in the shot, there was no mistaking the pleading coming from them, an urgent message that was stronger than words.

*Help me.*

Brenda let the camera linger first on Janie, then on herself before she started talking again. She wore full makeup and a teardrop necklace that Edwin had reported Janie was wearing to work the day she went missing from the prison. The teardrop, an amethyst, nestled between Brenda's breasts.

*Brenda was nothing if not consistent. She was always one to make sure people's eyes landed right there,* Kendall thought.

Brenda started talking again. "Janie, you know your baby doesn't like it when you don't answer her. Makes me annoyed. When I get annoyed I need to do something to liven things up. You know, to break the tension."

For the first time, Birdy noticed a curl of smoke in the frame. She tapped her finger on the screen.

"She's going to burn her," Birdy said.

"It's one of her favorite things to do," Kendall said, sliding back into her chair. "She did it to her child."

"Who does that?" Birdy asked, a rhetorical question if ever there had been one.

The answer, of course, both women knew, was a sociopath like Brenda. Maybe no one had seen someone so profoundly evil in the annals of crime. Kendall had. She'd been in the cage with the predator when she interviewed her on the Darcy Moreau case. She'd seen the charm and pretense of being human, the sickening game of those who have no other purpose in life but to win others over and destroy them.

Brenda tugged at the chain around her neck, the amethyst rising and falling, swinging back and forth like a hypnotist's watch.

"I know I shouldn't smoke," she said. "It's a nasty habit that I picked up in county jail and carried over to prison. Not much else to do in that hellhole." She stopped and looked at Janie over her shoulder. "No offense."

Then back at the camera, those gorgeous, but life-less eyes. "Smoking really scares me. I do not want to be one of those women whose mouth is a sagging sphincter that wicks out lipstick and is an instant sign that she's getting old."

Brenda reached in the direction of the curling smoke. Her fingertips now held a cigarette. She took a deep drag and then examined the filter before exhaling.

"Plus I have to constantly reapply lipstick and in prison—not that that's a problem at the moment—decent cosmetics are hard to come by. I let a hideous creature from Preston fondle my breasts in the shower as payment for a tube of L'Oreal that came into the institution in someone's butt. Gag me. The things one has to do to look halfway decent."

Brenda let out a laugh.

Kendall shot a look at Birdy.

"She thinks she's a star," she said.

"A Kardashian, maybe," Birdy said, her eyes still on the video.

Kendall was caught off guard. Birdy was more into Kerouac than Kardashian. "You watch that crap?"

"No," Birdy answered. "But Elan's girlfriend Kelsey does. She's over a lot."

The exchange between the forensic pathologist and the detective was that kind of forced break in the tension that people engage in when watching a horror movie.

*The popcorn is stale.*

*Have to go to the bathroom.*

*I just remembered I left the water running.*

"Suddenly," Brenda said, getting up and walking over to a now squirming Janie, "I'm hungry. Do you like Indian food, Janie? I love curry. Don't get me started on tandoori chicken. Love. Love. Love tandoori. Surprisingly, there was a fantastic Indian place in the Tri Cities that I used to go to with my boyfriend. It had the best tandoori in the Northwest. Better than Seattle. Honestly. So, so good. Well, Janie, do you like Indian food?"

Tears rolled down the superintendent's face.

Brenda ignored them.

"When I was a girl," she continued, "we held dandelion blossoms to our chins and if it reflected gold on your skin it meant that you liked butter. Did you ever do that?"

Janie didn't answer. She couldn't if she had wanted to. The black panties used to keep her quiet were tied so tightly that the corners of her mouth dripped blood.

Brenda swiveled around to face the camera. Her eyes met the camera's lens with the precision of a newscaster.

"Did any of you?"

She held her stare for a beat and then turned back to Janie.

"I want to make sure you are seeing this, but it's hard to manage the camera, the shot, the script, *and* the talent. I have newfound respect for TV producers and camera crews. What they do is not as easy as it looks."

Brenda took one more drag on the cigarette, making sure the camera captured its cherry-red tip.

"Let's see if you like Indian food," she said, her tone completely flat and devoid of irony. As the cigarette's red-hot tip moved toward Janie's forehead, the terrified woman turned away, her cries muffled in the lingerie that had so successfully silenced her.

"Don't fight me," Brenda said, in words that were splinter-cold. "You know you can't win. You're weak. I'm stronger. You're smart. I'm smarter."

She grabbed Janie by the hair with her free hand and yanked so hard that it looked as though the captive woman's neck might snap.

"She's a monster," Kendall said.

Birdy didn't say anything. There wasn't anything to say.

"Let's see if you like Indian food!" Brenda said.

And then while tears streamed and Janie struggled, Brenda pressed the lighted tip of her cigarette into the center of Janie's forehead.

"Don't squirm, stupid bitch! Once I moved when the crappy stylist my mother took me to was cutting my hair. I ended up with bangs that made me look like a trailer park kid!"

Through the struggle, Janie's quiet scream was captured.

"A monster," Birdy said.

"Pull yourself together, Janie! You like Indian food! You do!" Brenda said, laughing as if she'd pulled off some practical joke.

Kendall knew it was a pretend laugh. All of Brenda's emotions were as bogus as her breasts. She was incapable of recognizing the pain of others because to her, others were only objects. Things to be used. Things to get her whatever it was that she wanted.

*To serve her needs.*

Brenda turned to the camera and whispered. The whisper was fake too. Loud enough for Janie to hear every word.

"Everyone who is watching this already knows that

Janie didn't get her Indian dinner out. You already know that she's dead."

She paused, looking down at the cigarette she'd ground into Janie's forehead. It was still smoldering, so Brenda took another puff, breathing in the burning tobacco and the incinerated flesh of the woman who'd helped her escape from prison. She made a face and quickly extinguished it.

"Did you find my mark on Janie, Dr. Waterman? Sorry about your little boy, Detective Stark. Kids love cookies. I was a cookie monster when I was a little girl."

Kendall looked at Birdy, gauging her reaction to being named. The reference to Cody and the incident at school was spine chilling. It made her skin crawl. If anything on the video was a shock to her, it was the fact that the two of them had been named.

Birdy stared at Kendall.

"She was too badly burned for me to observe the cigarette burn," she said.

They both watched until the clip found its way to its end.

"I hope this goes viral," Brenda said and the screen went black.

Another advertisement for a cruise popped up.

"She got her wish, Birdy," Kendall said, ignoring the ad and wondering why the advertising tool on You-Tube thought she was in her sixties. "More than five hundred thousand views and climbing." She refreshed her laptop screen. "Five thousand more since we started watching."

Birdy looked at her friend. Her expression was grim.

"This is going to encourage her, Kendall. She's a narcissist who lives for this kind of attention. She craves it like we crave our morning coffee."

Kendall reached for her lukewarm tuxedo mocha. "Right. She's going to do something big."

"Unless we stop her," Birdy said. "She has to be stopped."